Merry Christmas

Betty

Enjoy!

Sandy

Madame Cleo's Girls

Madame Cleo's Girls

A NOVEL
Lucianne Goldberg

POCKET BOOKS

New York   London   Toronto   Sydney   Tokyo   Singapore

POCKET BOOKS, a division of Simon & Schuster Inc.
1230 Avenue of the Americas, New York, NY 10020

POCKET and colophon are registered trademarks of
Simon & Schuster Inc.

Printed in the U.S.A.

For William R. Grose.
who took me to the dance.
Thank you. Bill.

Acknowledgments

A very special team made this work possible: my agent, Evan Marshall; my editor, Claire Zion; my copy editor, Eugenia Leftwich; and my men, Sidney, Joshua, and Jonah Goldberg—steadfast, all.

PROLOGUE

On a May morning in 1990 a low-slung silver Citroën eased its way into the broad plaza of the Place de la Concorde. The car, with its darkened windows and enigmatic license plate, the single letter C, was familiar to many as that of the infamous Madame Cleo.

Those who did not have firsthand knowledge of the women who worked for her knew from gossip made legend that a Madame Cleo girl was far more than a prostitute. Madame Cleo's girls were the world's most beautiful and accomplished women for hire, who, for a price, fulfilled the ultimate fantasies of the rich and powerful.

The young man at the wheel wore black livery, a chauffeur's cap, and leather driving gloves. In the back seat sat an elegant older woman, wearing a large black mink beret that fell in lush folds to the right shoulder of her black mink coat. Facing her was a young man with long, straight blond hair. The two chatted, oblivious to the morning rush-hour chaos that immobilized central Paris.

As the driver edged over into the far right lane, the woman abruptly stopped talking, distracted by something she saw over her companion's shoulder. She froze, her eyes widening in what looked like horror, and she started shouting at the driver, *"Mon Dieu! Armand! Attention!"*

The driver gripped the wheel, his head snapping to his left as he swore under his breath. An innocuous black Renault was forcing its way into the lane beside the Citroën. Nestled obscenely in the corner of the open back window was the muzzle of a gun aimed directly at the Citroën.

The first blast of gunfire to hit the side of the car sent the couple in the back seat crashing to the floor, their bodies covered with shattered glass. The second blast, at closer range, sprayed the length of the car.

The driver's cap flew into the back seat as the Citroën careened violently out of control, raced toward the curb, and came to a crashing halt against a lamppost.

Terrified pedestrians on the sidewalk stared as the driver of the black Renault seemed to lose control of the wheel. The shooter's car careened into the next lane, into the path of an oncoming van. The ear-splitting collision of the Renault and the van sent people scrambling in all directions.

The cool morning air was rent with screams, the deafening sound of screeching tires and crash of metal. Cars, vans, trucks, buses, and motorcycles tangled into a chaotic snarl. Those closest to the gunfire abandoned their vehicles and ran from the plaza.

From the front seat of the bullet-riddled Citroën came a low moan. The driver's door had flown open. He lay sprawled across the seat, clutching his left arm, through which a bullet had made a clean passage.

In the back seat, the man lay motionless on top of the woman. Neither dared to speak.

The street filled with running and shouting uniformed policemen holding weapons aloft. In the distance the undulating wail of an ambulance siren echoed in the air.

The first policemen to reach the Citroën lifted the wounded driver from the front seat and carried him to the sidewalk. Others helped the terrified couple out of the back seat. Their smart clothes were mussed and their hair sparkled with bits of broken glass.

The blond man watched, trembling, as two policemen gently escorted the woman to the curbside.

"*Je suis bien, merci,*" the woman said to the policemen with an eerie calm. "Please see to my friend."

"Oh my God, oh my God," the blond man kept repeating. "I knew this would happen. I just knew it. They want to kill us!"

The woman stepped toward him. "Martin, get hold of yourself," she snapped.

"I told you so, Madame, I told you so," he whimpered, pressing his knuckles against his chattering teeth.

She was an inch away from his face, speaking under her breath. "If you become hysterical, Martin, I'm going to slap you. Now stop it."

"Madame?" a voice said behind her. She turned to see a tall middle-aged policeman with a blaze of gold braid curling across the visor of his cap. He stepped toward her and flipped open a leather notebook. "May I have your name, please?"

The woman clutched the collar of her mink and blinked up at the policeman. "I beg your pardon," she said.

"May I see some form of identification?" He licked the stub of a pencil and held it over the pad.

"Identification?" the woman exclaimed in indignation. Over the policeman's shoulder she saw a familiar face approaching. "Ah! Captain Dusseau! Thank goodness you're here."

An officer of higher rank than her inquisitor stepped forward. "I'll handle this," he said brusquely to the younger officer. "This is Madame Cleo. She does not need to be interrogated. Go see to the gentleman there."

The policeman's face froze, his mouth going slack. Then he nodded and turned toward the still-shaking blond man.

The captain slipped his hand protectively under Madame Cleo's elbow. He guided her around the demolished car. "My dear Cleo," he said, lowering his voice respectfully, "it is wonderful to see you again, although I wish our reunion were under more happy circumstances. Please don't worry about your driver. He's going to be all right. It's a clean wound. I am concerned about you."

"I'm fine," she said with a weak smile. "A little shaken, perhaps. It was all so sudden."

"Do you have any idea who would do such a thing?"

Madame Cleo slowly shook her head. "Any one of thousands, my dear Captain. I have many enemies. Especially now."

"And many friends. Myself included." As he spoke he gently picked bits of glass from her hair and clothes. Another officer handed her the mink beret he had found on the floor of her car.

"*Merci*," she said with a little nod. "Who were those men? Did you catch them?" she asked, turning back to the captain.

"They ran into the crowd after their car crashed, Madame. But do not fear, we'll get them. Rest assured, there will be a thorough investigation. My men will go over every inch of the attackers' car."

Cleo glanced down the street at the shooter's smashed car. The van that struck it had been pushed up onto the curb and sidewalk. "What should I do, Captain? Am I free to go home?"

"Of course. I will take you myself," he said. "Give me a moment to speak to my men. The lieutenant there will escort you to my car."

"Thank you," she said, turning to her assistant, who had stopped whimpering, although he was still dazed. "Come, Martin. The Captain will take us home."

As they walked to the police car they passed the wreckage of her car. The hood was grotesquely folded back and the fender swung loose. An arc of bullet holes creased the roof. The tires were flat and a stream of gasoline coursed down the back fender.

Just before Madame Cleo and Martin climbed into the back seat of the police car, she looked back to see Captain Dusseau trotting toward them. He put his hand on Madame Cleo's arm to stop her. "My men just found this in the street," he said, dropping a clear plastic bag that held something made of metal into her hand. "Does this mean anything to you?"

She opened her hand and looked down. In the bag was a gold cigarette lighter upon which had been engraved an elaborate crest. She recognized it immediately. "I have one like this. There are only a few of these in existence. They're from Cartier, made for a friend of mine."

"How can you be sure this isn't yours?" the captain asked, lifting it carefully from her hand.

"I am absolutely positive," she said firmly. She reached into the pocket of her mink and extracted a lighter identical to the one the police captain now held suspended in the evidence bag.

"May I speak to you privately?" the captain asked, cutting his eyes at Martin. "One of my men can drive your companion wherever he wants to go."

"Of course," she said, turning to her aide. "Martin, I need to chat with this nice man for a bit. I'll see you back at the house."

Reluctantly, her assistant nodded, then got into the police car. When he was out of earshot, the captain put a protective arm around Madame Cleo's mink-clad shoulders and walked her slowly toward a grassy plot and away from any curious listeners.

"Who wants to kill you, Cleo?"

Cleo stopped walking and leaned against the iron guardrail. She shook her head slowly and stared at the ground.

"Don't you have any idea?" he asked.

"No, Alain. It's just that I don't even want to think it could be true."

"How much more proof do you need than being machine-gunned in broad daylight? I don't think this was a case of mistaken identity, my dear. Not in that car." He glanced toward her crumpled Citroën being hooked onto a police tow truck.

Cleo looked out across the broad plaza. "This is what happens when one sells one's soul."

"*Pardon?*"

"I have agreed to tell my life story for a book to be published in America."

"So I have heard. Tell me, my dear, why have you done such a thing?"

"Money, Alain, money. I owe millions in taxes."

A look of disbelief crossed the policeman's weathered face. "Why have you just not paid them? Cleo, a rich woman like you? Why should you sell your secrets? Sell a painting or some of your jewels."

"The government says my money is flesh money. They say everything I own comes from the backs of women. If I use it I'll be admitting to the crime of procuring and go to jail. And, of course, if I don't pay them, I will also go to jail."

Cleo smiled, a slow, unhappy smile. "So now you see why I must sell my secrets," she said.

"And others' as well."

"*Oui.*" Madame Cleo sighed and glanced at her watch. "I must go home, Alain. I am quite faint."

"Of course," he said, taking her arm as she began to walk back toward his car. "I understand."

Madame Cleo looked up at him and wordlessly brushed his cheek with the back of her hand. It was a gesture half of affection, half of apology for having lied to him. She knew exactly who owned the other Cartier lighters. But by the time her old friend learned she had deceived him, she would have accomplished what she had to do.

PART
I

PART
1

CHAPTER

∽ 1 ∽

Peter Shea, contributing editor of *Fifteen Minutes* magazine, closed a copy of the bound galleys of the new novel he had promised its author he would read. He glanced at the first page, realized he couldn't concentrate, and gave up.

He wedged the book into the seat pocket in front of him and closed his eyes. He was feeling cramped and irritable. The air in First Class was never any better than it was in tourist, and the plane had been sitting on the runway of the Montego Bay airport for nearly an hour without the air conditioner on.

He opened his eyes long enough to find one of the tiny, foul-smelling marshmallows the airlines called a pillow. As he punched it between his shoulder and cheek, something interesting caught his attention.

The couple reclining in the right-hand bulkhead seats of the First Class section seemed to be trying to swallow each other's heads. A long white silk raincoat covered both their bodies, and, from the movement under the fabric, a lot of hand and leg action was going on.

The woman, sleek and dark with a gold-bronze tan, had lifted her long, dark, red hair over the back of the seat, where it hung, moving slightly in the air from the overhead vent. She moaned softly from time to time and wiggled in her seat.

It would have been clear to even the most casual observer that the woman was being driven into a sexual frenzy by her companion.

The couple had been the cause of the plane's delay in departure, or so Peter had been told when he questioned the stewardess earlier. That they were waiting for a VIP piqued his curiosity. Peter Shea made his living being curious.

When the couple finally boarded and were ceremoniously shown to their seats, Peter had raised his head, and had widened his eyes with interest. He recognized them both. The man with his hand pressed protectively against the small of the woman's back was the New York financier and power broker John Wesley Ayler, referred to in print as "Black Jack" Ayler for reasons having to do, Peter seemed to recall, with his war record. The war, Peter estimated with finger arithmetic, would have to have been the Second World one.

Peter knew the woman wasn't Mrs. Ayler. He knew her only as Christine, and she had been the pivotal source for a profile Shea had written on a Hollywood drug scandal. Christine was a very glossy, very stylish, very high-priced call girl.

He knew enough about Jack Ayler to detest the man. Arrogant, hypocritical, and rich, Ayler's reputation was nearly spotless.

Peter removed a small spiral pad from his shirt pocket and made a note to speak to his editor about a profile on Black Jack Ayler. Traveling with a call girl was at total odds with the public image Ayler paid handsomely to have disseminated. Perhaps there were other aspects of the man's life that needed examining.

The little sighting pleased Peter and raised his spirits. He enjoyed firsthand evidence of human frailty. It was his job to pay attention to what he saw and heard. It was also his nature.

Shea had spent the weekend interviewing an American embezzler hiding in ill-gotten splendor in the hills above Kingston. The interview had taken a considerable amount of trouble to arrange and it had not gone well. Shea welcomed the distraction of the scene the amorous couple were now providing.

He screwed the cap off a miniature bottle of Johnnie Walker Red and poured it over the two ice cubes in the glass on the tray, took a sip, and began to mentally sketch out the lead of the article he would write about Ayler. He would open with a vivid description of the scene being played out in the seats in front of him. It was a perfect example of the irony he liked in a story: a man who sought and found acceptance and public praise, going about his private business in a public place. It more than spiced the story that his companion was a call girl. For Peter Shea there was a very personal element to such a story.

Revenge.

He took another sip of scotch and wondered if, after all the painful self-discovery, the eons with the shrink, the flagellation of public confession he had had to endure, if after all that there would ever be enough revenge. Had his former addiction to self-promotion and craving for respect among his peers been replaced by an obsession with evening the score? Perhaps so, he told himself as he scratched the label from the tiny plastic bottle with his thumb. Where is it written that a Black Jack Ayler could get away with the kind of behavior that had nearly destroyed Shea? Why could a man like Ayler, whose gleaming white head was now bending toward the woman as he pressed his tongue into her ear, flaunt his lust in public, when the briefest of encounters had taken Peter to the depths of despair and near total ruin?

It had been nearly three years now and he had learned to deal with it.

Or had he?

He signaled the stewardess for a refill and knew it would never be over. The anger would always be with him. Not the white-hot fury he once had felt. The rage that had nearly destroyed him had been tempered by insight, good luck, and time. Still, the sight in front of him triggered the old responses, and the demons he thought he had finally put to rest raged again.

Peter Daniel Shea was the last kid in South Boston to get polio. His mother still had the clipping from the *Globe* that said so. She kept it in her scrapbook with the pictures from the fund-raising events his father and the Police Boys Club had organized to pay for his physical therapy afterward.

The irony was that just about the time little Peter's fever spiked to the warning 103° point, some laboratory somewhere was putting the final touches on Dr. Jonas Salk's miracle.

The disease put him in bed for three years. When, finally, he could walk again, one leg was slightly shorter than the other. By high school, he had controlled what would have been a noticeable limp into a slightly rolling gait people took for the cocky swagger of a kid who had fought hard and won. Only Peter remembered the cruel remarks, the stinging words like "gimp" and "wobble ass" that had echoed through his grade school yard. Only Peter knew how close pain and a sense that he wasn't as good as other people lay to the surface of his being.

Fortunately for Shea, a guy in South Boston with a chip on his shoulder was considered a well-balanced Irishman. Out in the real world it was a different story. Shea learned early that to get ahead, one had to suppress one's anger. And Shea had a violent, raging temper that too often got the best of him. But he knew that collecting injustices kept one from being thought of as a team player. Wit and charm were the coins of success.

After college, he rose through the ranks of the newspaper business, first as a local reporter for *The Boston Globe*, then, inevitably upward, to the next rung on the ladder. By the eighties he had become the most dashing of career journalists, a foreign correspondent for WorldWide International News Service.

When WorldWide moved him to its Paris office, life opened up to him as never before. Paris revered anyone with access to the American media, and Peter had the best access in town.

Hostesses clamored for him. He entertained at the best restaurants on his liberal expense account. He heard and read himself quoted on world affairs. Few who were important turned down a request to be interviewed by Peter Shea of WorldWide International News.

By the time the second year of his Paris assignment rolled around, he had almost unwittingly begun to serve his own celebrity more than WorldWide. He wrote off his failed marriage and a few determined enemies as small prices to pay for the limitless perks of fame and power.

One summer evening in 1987, as he dressed for dinner in his apartment in a residential Paris hotel, the front desk rang to inform him there was a messenger on the way up.

Peter slipped into his dinner jacket as he made his way to the buzzing door. He opened it expecting to see one of the messengers from the office arriving late with one of the bundles of American magazines and books that were sent by overnight courier from New York. Instead, he found a man dressed in an immaculate black business suit, wearing an incongruous black visored cap.

"Mr. Peter Shea?"

"Yes," he said, his eyebrow cocked quizzically.

"Would you sign here, please?" The man slipped a small clipboard with a single blank sheet of paper under the chain on the open door.

"What is this?" he asked.

"A delivery for you," the man said.

"I assumed," Peter said. "But what?"

"An invitation, sir. If you'll just sign, please."

Peter shrugged, signed the receipt, and handed it back.

It was then that he noticed that the valise the man was carrying was handcuffed to his wrist. The messenger deftly unlocked the case and extracted a glossy black envelope. "Thank you, sir," he said, handing the envelope to Peter. He turned and walked back down the hall to the elevator.

With a slight flutter of interest, Peter strolled back into the living room and turned the envelope over.

On the flap was a blob of real sealing wax into which an elaborate crest had been pressed. Some press agent had outdone himself on this one, he thought, assuming the envelope contained an invitation from some commercial entity wanting publicity in the American press.

He slipped out the enclosure and stared at it in mild astonishment. He couldn't quite believe it. He was being invited to a weekend gathering at the country estate of one of Europe's wealthiest men, Baron Felix d'Anjou. The function was given each year, a notorious affair known as La Fantastique. One had to have arrived at a certain level of power and influence even to be considered as a guest. Neither the function nor those who attended ever received publicity. The guest list was as exclusive and secretive as the goings-on there. Peter had heard rumors, of course, of debauchery on a grand scale, of agreements made and deals consummated.

As the personal implications of such an invitation dawned on him, he began to wonder why he had been given one. La Fantastique received no publicity because to speak of it meant never to be invited again. Therefore, he deduced, the invitation was strictly social. He was being invited for the same reason world political leaders, captains of industry, and other men were asked: because each was powerful and important in his own right.

He turned the envelope over to make doubly sure there was no mistake. "I'll be damned," he said, aloud. "I'll be goddamn-doodley damned!" He read the invitation again, slowly shaking his head.

There it was in black and white. The presence of Peter Shea was "respectfully requested." A smaller card informed him that a car would call at his hotel at noon the Friday of the event to transport him to the baron's château in the Loire Valley.

At last, Peter Shea had arrived.

He liked the feeling. He liked it so much that, alone in his room, he blushed. All the work, all the politicking and elbowing, all the hustling to be the fastest and the first, had paid off. Suddenly, he leaped into the air and whooped, making the joyful noise of a gimpy little Irish kid from South Boston who had, at last, reached life's "fuck you" level. The invitation in his hand was absolute proof.

In such a state, he never would have believed the truth, if someone

13

had been willing to enlighten him. But, in fact, the men with whom he would mingle at the baron's were not, and never would be, his peers. Indeed, he had been invited *only* because of his position, and the possibility of his future usefulness to the other guests.

The baron might not want publicity for La Fantastique, but that didn't mean that he and his other guests didn't still desire a key media connection. To know the WorldWide correspondent was of importance to such men; Peter Shea himself was nothing.

Despite his obliviousness to this fact, Peter was still not without slight misgivings. For one thing, he would be forced to return to Paris on Saturday for an important appointment with an exclusive lead. Therefore he waited until the Thursday before he was to leave for La Fantastique to inform his editor in New York. He planned to keep it as casual as possible, "routine house party with some new sources, world-class schmoozing, power yakety-yak." He had the conversation all worked out in his head.

"Not a red-hot idea, Peter," Gordon Jimison, his editor, bellowed into the phone that Thursday.

Peter felt a little vein in the side of his head start to throb. "What did you say?"

"Of course, if you plan to write about it . . ."

"Don't be ridiculous, Gordo," he said in a voice that implied his editor's lack of sophistication could hardly be tolerated.

"Why wouldn't you?"

"Because . . . because . . ." Oh, how he hated having to explain. "It simply isn't done."

"Well, *excuuuuse* me. Do you still work for this company or have you let the froggies make you an honorary duke?"

"Come off it, Gordo. I don't have to write about every move I make over here."

"Correct. But if it gets around that you were there and didn't write about it, it's going to look pretty damn bad to several people in this office. Namely, the chairman. Bracknell is not unfamiliar with La Fantastique. There may be a lot of power-brokering but there's also booze and broads. He's not too smiley about the company being compromised."

"There's booze and broads right here in this hotel, and Bracknell is paying for it," Peter said.

"Pete," Gordon said, after some hesitation, "save yourself some grief. Don't do it."

The temptation was too great. The mere fact that he had been invited at all meant he didn't have to be told what to do by some sniveling, jealous editor who would probably turn to jelly if he found himself in the same room with any *one* of the guests at La Fantastique.

"Fuck you!" Peter snapped, just before he slammed down the phone. "Fuck you all and the horse you rode in on," he yelled to the walls of his hotel room. "In your hat!"

He was *Peter Shea*. A man whose words and insights were read by millions. A man who changed minds and lives with the stroke of his typewriter. Had he not been shot at and missed? Had he not walked with kings? He wasn't going to be told he couldn't take a weekend in the country by some candy-ass in New York who had to run home to watch the kids so his wife could make it to her second job.

He spent the rest of the evening drinking in the hotel bar, singing do-wop tunes around the piano bar with a *Paris Match* photographer he had first met in the Afghan mountains when he interviewed the leader of the *mujahedeen.*

Those in the bar that night eventually left completely familiar with where Peter Shea of WorldWide International News would be spending the weekend.

Not a few were impressed.

The crunch of gravel under the tires of the black Rolls alerted the servants. As the car moved slowly into the circular drive in front of the château, the baron's household staff moved single file out the front door. Uniformed footmen and maids in black silk dresses and lace aprons quickly formed a tidy semicircle at the head of the driveway.

After the car rolled to a halt, the head footman helped two women to alight. A slight breeze caught their dark silk dresses and wide straw hats, flipping fabric and hat streamers about in a festive swirl. To the unknowing eye, the women could have been the daughters of aristocrats arriving for a country weekend.

Dudley, the baron's very proper, very British majordomo for more than thirty years, watched their arrival from his outpost at the side of the towering entrance to the château. He made no effort to conceal the slight disapproving curl of his upper lip.

The baron had been sending to Paris for girls since the first La Fantastique in 1957. At first, the practice had not been a success. The girls provided were not the sort that Dudley found appropriate to such a gathering. There had been problems with alcohol and drugs. In one grim case, after the 1959 La Fantastique, there had been a case of venereal disease reported shortly afterward, which had threatened to become a scandal. Fortunately, the baron had been able to keep things quiet. Dudley had no way of knowing what it had cost his employer but he had overheard conversations over the years to the effect that a wing of a certain hospital in New York had been built and dedicated in the name of the guest who had found himself so inconvenienced.

All that changed when the baron retained the girls of Madame Cleo. As a matter of fact, Dudley reminded himself with no small satisfaction, it had been he who had first heard of the Paris madame who hired women who met extremely rigid tests of beauty, comportment, and intellect. His information came from some of the world's greatest intelligence sources, the drivers, valets, and butlers to the wealthy and powerful men of Europe.

The first Madame Cleo girls had come to La Fantastique the same year the shah and the presidents of three Latin American countries had been guests. Dudley later heard that the shah sent for a Madame Cleo girl on his deathbed.

Each year there would be one or two girls who were special. Girls who were meant for a specific guest the baron wanted to ingratiate himself with. For those girls the baron sent the black Rolls.

Dudley realized he was daydreaming and forced his attention to the task at hand. The special girls had to be attended to. The others would arrive later, but these two were Dudley's personal responsibility. The presence of any of the women at this particular event had always filled Dudley with a mixture of mild disapproval and reluctant voyeurism. Paid women were not in the best of taste to his way of thinking, but these women, exquisitely mannered and beautifully turned out, were entertaining to observe and, thank goodness, never ill behaved.

As the footmen scurried by him with the luggage, Dudley quickly recalled the descriptions given in the dossiers that Madame Cleo's aide had messengered down from her house in Paris. Squinting into the clear, bright light of the setting sun, he picked out the blonde first. She was the one the baron and Madame Cleo had chosen for Lord William Mosby. Dudley would put her in the room where he had earlier that afternoon installed certain required items for Lord Mosby's private pleasure. He would need only a few moments to give her instructions.

The other girl wore her dark hair slicked back into a chignon. Dudley studied her for a moment. She was lithe and slim and as carefully made up as a prima ballerina. He recognized her from the picture in her file. She would be Sandrine, whose mother was supposed to be a wealthy American designer. The mother, so the baron had playfully told him, had once had affairs with three of their eminent guests for the weekend: the Italian count who had arrived earlier in the day and was, at the moment, playing golf on the baron's private course beyond the vineyard; the head of a German automobile company who was still en route to the château; and a formidable Swiss banker of Lebanese descent who had attended every year that Dudley could remember.

He would put the girl with the experienced mother (and *all* that luggage, he noted with alarm) in the room that connected to that of the American journalist, Mr. Peter Shea, on the same floor as Lord Mosby. He turned and hurried into the house. The other women, the guests flying down in their own planes, the musicians and waiters recruited from the town would all arrive within the next hour. There were so many things to be seen to.

Peter Shea brushed an imaginary piece of lint from his immaculate dinner jacket and studied himself in the freestanding looking glass set before the leaded windows of the high-ceilinged room to which he had been assigned. It was a small smile. The kind of half turn of the lip that self-approval elicits, accompanied by a slight nod, a squaring of the shoulders, and a two-handed tug at his satin lapels.

His room was in the far wing of the château. The white-gloved footman who had shown him there an hour before had briskly pointed out the accommodations: how the ancient but adequate plumbing worked, where to find the telephone and television complete with VCR and a discreet library of X-rated tapes in French, German, Italian, and English. There were writing supplies in the desk by the fireplace. The footman informed him that anything he might require in the way of food or drink was available from the hall porter at any time, day or night. Peter had to remind himself that this was a private home, not a three-star country inn. He had refused the footman's offer to unpack and press his things, wondering if tipping a private servant was appropriate. He decided it wasn't.

Before the footman turned to leave he informed Peter that drinks would be served in the ground-floor conservatory at seven sharp. If Mr. Shea would be good enough to ring extension seven when he was ready to go down the footman would return and escort him, as he doubted that Peter would want to waste time trying to find his own way.

"I assume everyone is dressing," Peter said, feeling a bit awkward. He had packed his tux as insurance but it would have been disastrous not to ask.

"Yes, sir," the footman had answered. "Dinner jackets, sir, white or black."

Still attempting nonchalance, Peter asked, "This will be all men this evening, right?"

"For drinks and dinner, sir," the footman said with a nod. "After dinner the baron invites a few ladies for brandy in the library."

The man had bowed and backed out of the room leaving Peter feeling a bit sheepish. What had he expected? he chided himself. Girls leaping out of a cake, charging into the room cancan style with their petticoats lifted over their heads, squealing and kicking champagne glasses out of the hands of the rich and powerful? Hookers sent to the room like chicken sandwiches from room service? Perhaps if he walked into the bathroom one would materialize naked on the edge of the tub holding a jar of Emotion Lotion. *What a rube I am,* he thought, as he flipped open his bag and began to hang up his things. Half of the sex men talk about in life is wishful thinking and the other half is bullshit. If he really thought about it he had never actually talked to anyone who had attended one of these weekends, let alone got laid at one. Everything he knew about the baron and his talent as a host had been gleaned from hearsay. He pictured the women the baron would invite for brandy. In his mind they all looked like Margaret Thatcher.

Now, dressed and ready to go downstairs, he was glad that the evening would be strictly male. This was the inner loop of power and access. The baron knew how to do things right. Women would have changed the tone, altered the chemistry and texture of an extraordinary moment in his life. He was relieved.

At dinner, a seated affair for sixty in a hall hung with flags and dominated by one of the largest chandeliers Peter had ever seen, he made conversation with the Italian minister of finance on his right and attempted to converse with a Swedish Nobel Laureate in particle physics to his left. It was heavy sledding, and he ate and drank too much.

At the baron's signal, everyone rose and slowly made their way down a long corridor lined with seventeenth-century portraits to a library only slightly smaller than the dining hall, where a quartet of flute and strings was playing Mozart, or so Peter learned from a rather saturnine-looking bishop walking a few paces in front of him.

By eleven Peter had to press his lips together to keep from yawning. He had been standing in a circle of men who were discussing the Iranian hostage situation for almost an hour when over the shoulder of a French plastics manufacturer he saw them. Several women wearing high-fashion cocktail gowns, very elegant and subdued, simply materialized, like swans on the surface of a private lake. There had been no warning, nothing by way of introduction. They were just—there. There wasn't a Margaret Thatcher among them. They were tall, beautiful, exquisitely dressed in French or Italian couture. It was as though the baron had hired fashion models simply to decorate the room. Perhaps they were titled relatives of the baron's. But so many! Surely, he thought, these couldn't be the women he imagined lolling about in some hideaway in the château wearing crotch-high black stockings and Chanel No. 5, waiting to dally with these giants of commerce.

He was fascinated. Who were they? What were they? The Catholic boy buried deep in his South Boston soul was still working on the problem when a German arms dealer Peter had been talking to stopped in midsentence and said with a sigh, "Ah, the girls of Madame Cleo have arrived at last. A king's ransom for any one of them. You live in Paris, Shea. Have you ever known one?"

Peter turned to the German a bit too quickly. "Madame Cleo's girls? You mean they're prostitutes?" he blurted out just before he felt the heat rush up his neck and onto his cheeks. He slammed his mouth shut against the words, hating that he had said them.

The German fixed him with a cold gaze and said, "Not what they are usually called, Mr. Shea. If there is such a thing as perfection in the female form, it is a Cleo girl. I thought you journalists had more subtle imaginations."

Feeling sheepish, Peter moved away and began to circulate around the room. For the next hour his attention was torn between gleaning information from each conversation he found himself in and watching the women operate. They were indeed remarkable. They held themselves poised, shoulders back, heads high, moving smoothly from man to man after a few soft words of greeting. Each guest with whom they spoke received admiring, undivided attention.

He was finishing his third brandy when he felt a familiar twinge in the bad leg from standing so long. He made his way toward one of the deep, brocade-covered couches that flanked the fireplace. Before his brandy glass could come to rest on the polished surface of the low table in front of the couch, a linen coaster was whisked under it. He looked up to see a young woman standing above him, smiling. Her hair fell like a thick dark curtain about her perfect features.

"The baron likes to be careful of his things," she said pleasantly. "I'm told this table once belonged to the empress Eugénie."

Peter started to reply but couldn't. More from nervousness than desire, he quickly pulled a cigarette from the open pack inside his dinner jacket. It had not yet touched his lips when a flash of blue-gold flame rose under the tip. He inhaled and then smiled up at the girl as she snapped the top of a sleek gold lighter closed.

"Thank you," he said, impressed with the gesture. There was something extremely alluring about a woman anticipating a man's needs, and clearly this beautiful creature knew it. If she had been just sexy and slightly cheap he would have made some smartass and probably funny remark, but this was not a girl one cracked wise with.

"My name is Madeleine," she said, seeming to sense the impact she was having on him. She placed the lighter on the coffee table next to his drink, silently implying that he might find it useful later. "May I join you?"

Peter made an attempt to rise but she sat down beside him before he could get up.

"How do you do, Madeleine," he said, trying to drop his voice a register or two to cover his nervousness. "I'm Peter. Peter Shea. Do you have a last name?"

"I never use it," she said. "I don't use my real first name, either."

Peter laughed, grateful for the opportunity. "Seriously?"

"Seriously."

"Why is that?"

"Perhaps because I only exist in this moment. We know who we are and names don't matter."

"That's a very romantic notion."

"Ummm," she said, lowering her eyes.

"Then I shall call you Madeleine."

"Thank you," she said, extending her hand. Then she pushed herself out of the low couch. "Come, I'll show you the baron's wine cellar. It's quite a remarkable place. And we can be alone there."

Surprised and delighted, Peter rose. Spotting her lighter he picked it up, admiring its weight and sleek design. "Don't forget this," he said, slipping it into the palm of her hand.

He let himself be led across the room toward the high doors of the library. To have done otherwise would have taken strength he had never possessed. She was irresistible.

They crossed the terrace into the blue night and walked down the sloping lawn toward a long low building.

Inside, she lit the two fat candles that were placed in readiness on a ledge and handed one to Peter. Even these simple gestures seemed impossibly seductive. "No electric light is permitted in here," she said, her voice as soft as the candlelight. "The best of their wine has been asleep since just after the American Civil War."

She smiled slowly, and for a minute, her face very close to Peter's, he thought she would kiss him. Instead, she turned to lead him down the corridor, her lithe body slipping through the deep shadows.

As the remarkable wine tour continued Peter trotted behind her like some awed school kid afraid he might do something dumb in front of the beautiful new teacher.

"What do you do, Peter?" she asked as they reached the end of a line of enormous barrels.

"I'm a writer. A reporter, actually. For an international news service."

"Fascinating. So, you are only interested in things that are immediate and exciting."

"You could say that," he said, smiling. But by now he wasn't listening to her anymore. He was ready to grab her. He had to make some kind of move. He reached for her hand to help her up the two uneven steps that led out of the underground world. As they stepped out into the night she was still holding his hand. He turned and studied her face. "What are you interested in?" he asked, hoping to God he didn't sound like a jerk. Did one proposition a call girl? Did one have to be amusing, or audition? He was, for the first time in his adult life, at a complete conversational loss.

"Right now, I'm interested in the immediate and exciting," she said smoothly.

Peter felt his breath coming in shallow bursts.

"Your leg is bothering you, isn't it?"

"Ya . . . ya . . . yeah, a little, I guess," he stammered. "How did you know?"

"Because you favor it. It's slightly shorter than your other one. Polio, I suspect, even though you're a bit young for that. You must have been one of the last."

"Good Lord," he said, half in shock. "Are you a witch, too? No one has ever—"

Quickly she raised one finger and pressed it against his lips. "Shhhhh," she whispered. "Come with me. I know something that will make it feel a lot better."

"But . . ." He hesitated. Perhaps he should go back to the library and mingle. After all, that's why he had come. But he wanted this beautiful girl. Wasn't it what this kind of arrival in life was all about? Wasn't this the stuff of fantasies? She was seducing him. He could be no more intoxicated than if he had consumed the baron's entire wine cellar. Of all the many rich, powerful, and far better looking men in the library, he, Peter Shea, had ended up with this incredible girl. It made his mind reel.

From the great house he could hear the laughter and music of a party in the making. A band had arrived in their absence.

She sensed his hesitation. "Don't worry, Peter. No one will miss us," she half whispered. "We don't have to go to your room, you know. We can do whatever your heart desires."

Whatever my heart desires! What his heart desired at that moment was to sink his face into the soft, satiny space between her breasts and never come up for air. He reached out and took her hand again. Wordlessly, they crossed the lawn and stepped back through the open terrace door. As they passed the long bar, Madeleine leaned across and whispered something to the bartender.

When Peter opened the door to his room—to which, somehow, Madeleine had unerringly led him—he saw that a tray of glasses and a bottle of champagne had been set on a table near the fireplace.

Madeleine preceded him into the room. He closed the door and leaned against it, watching Madeleine expertly open the bottle and pour them each a glass. She lifted hers in a toast. "To you, Peter. I hope I'm everything you desire."

She walked toward him, carrying both glasses, then tilted her head and kissed him. It was a long, slow, almost open-mouth kiss that tasted like fresh peaches. He reached down and removed the glasses from her hands, setting them down on a small table next to the door. As he slipped his arms around her smooth, satin-covered body, he thought, *This is it, Shea, you lucky bastard. It doesn't get any better than this.*

It did get better.

It got better and better until he stopped counting the orgasms.

He was lying in a garden chaise at the edge of the baron's terrace dressed in linen slacks and a blue Lacoste shirt. Dark glasses covered his eyes against the bright morning sun and the threat of anyone trying to make conversation. A waiter had handed him the cup of coffee he cradled against his chest as he pretended to sleep. The only thing he wanted to do was relive the most remarkable night of his life.

He hadn't made love throughout the night for a long, long time. Earlier in life, he stopped because it was hard to do in the back seat of a car. Occasionally he would in college, when his damn roommate didn't insist on being let in by one in the morning. After college, when he began working as a grunt reporter on the lobster shift at the *Globe*, he was usually too soused, too tired, or too inadequately accompanied to do much that was memorable.

Then he met Sarah Jane Finney, who worked at the *Globe*.

They dated, made love during their lunch hour in his apartment on Boylston Street, and she got pregnant. As far as Sarah Jane was concerned, it was one of God's laws that the pregnant Irish married. Peter loved her enough so that, after the miscarriage, he didn't even consider calling the wedding off.

Sure, he had done his time whoring around. He had even been in love a couple of times after the divorce. But for the most part sex was something that happened after a press party, after a dinner everyone was too drunk to remember. If he couldn't remember dinner, he usually didn't remember the sex afterward except that it felt good and cleared his head. But what had happened to him with Madeleine, this woman who floated into his life once he had finally made it, was beyond mere sex. It was deliverance.

Without a word she slipped into one position after another as smoothly as an Olympic swimmer. When they had tried them all she asked, softly, against his bare shoulder, if there was anything he had never done. By then he was too sated, too dazed with erotic euphoria, to be embarrassed or coy.

"All I want is more," he had said.

With one fluid motion, she moved down his body and placed her mouth over his penis. When he was on the verge of bursting, she delicately straddled his face and almost weightlessly began to move her hips in a circular motion. When she had almost satisfied herself, she moved back down and slipped his still throbbing erection up between her legs again.

Awash in sensation, wallowing in lust, he swore he felt his mind leave his body.

Aware that his thoughts were about to cause an embarrassing physical reaction if he didn't quit, he pulled the top of his dark glasses down and scanned the sun-dappled terrace. There were only men sitting about in groups, chatting, reading, eating breakfast. The women had vanished as though they had never existed. Would they come back? Where were they? And where, he wondered, his heart expanding with longing, was Madeleine?

He accepted another cup of coffee and brushed an unbearable thought from his mind. There was every chance that he would never see her again. She had left at the edge of dawn. He sensed more than saw her go. When he was fully awake he realized he didn't know her real name. All he knew was that she worked for Madame Cleo in Paris and would, very likely, never respond to any attempt he might make to see her.

He glanced up to see a familiar figure approaching. Lord William Mosby, the media mogul who, not content with the magazines and newspapers he already owned, had once made an unsuccessful run at WorldWide. Peter didn't particularly want to talk to the man lumbering toward him, but he was torn. He wanted Mosby to see that he was a guest.

As Mosby moved closer, he punctuated each heavy footfall with a snap of a riding crop against his gleaming boots. Tight jodhpurs and a bright turtleneck did little to conceal his girth. Shea put down his coffee cup and struggled out of the chaise. "Lord Mosby," he said, extending his hand. "Peter Shea. WorldWide."

Like that of a giant turtle, Mosby's head retracted for an instant.

"We met last year at that NATO conference reception in Berlin," Peter volunteered, a bit too eagerly.

"Of course. Shea. Yes. Yes." Lord Mosby spoke in that marble-mouthed way upper-class Brits have. His lips barely moved.

"Will you join me for coffee?"

Lord Mosby nodded, then plunked down in the chair beside Peter's chaise.

"Shooting this afternoon?" Mosby asked.

"Sadly, no. I'm afraid I have a dinner appointment in Paris this evening," Peter replied. "I'll have to start back." He did have to return to Paris. He was setting up an interview. But he did not want to say "interview" to a man who employed hundreds of grunts who did interviews.

"Quite." Lord Mosby paused while a waiter served him coffee, then turned to address Peter directly for the first time. "Odd seeing *you* here, Shea. Hope you're not here in a professional capacity. Things, ah, things go on here that are not for dissemination. Strictly an off-the-record affair, don't you know."

"Absolutely, Lord Mosby. No, no. This is purely social."

Lord Mosby made a grumping sound and took a slurp of his coffee. "The baron puts together a remarkable party, eh?" he said, swallowing loudly.

"He certainly does, sir."

Peter's mind raced. He wanted to ask about the women. His attention was riveted when Mosby put down his coffee and said nonchalantly, "Where do you suppose the ladies get to during the daylight? I've been coming to this affair for years. The only thing the baron is stingy with is the women. We only see them after sundown."

Peter laughed nervously. "I'm curious myself," he said, leaning forward in his chair. "I met one last night that I wouldn't mind seeing again."

Lord Mosby's large face swiveled back toward Peter, his expression suddenly softening. "Ah, yes. Ah, so did I, Shea," he said, looking a bit sheepish. Then he smiled. "Remarkable. Simply remarkable."

"I don't suppose we have any hope of, ah, seeing the ladies again," Peter said tentatively.

"I wouldn't make inquiries if I were you, Shea. Bad form."

The reporter in Peter got the best of him. So what if he pressed Mosby? He may have owned half the world media but he didn't own WorldWide. The worst the man could do would be to grumble at his club about that pushy Peter Shea. In Peter's world, pushy wasn't exactly a bad personality trait. "I was told the girls work for a Madame Cleo. She's located in Paris, right?"

"What's your point, Shea?"

"I thought I'd give this Madame Cleo a call and describe the girl."

Mosby lowered his chin onto his chest as though examining his coffee for floating bugs. "WorldWide must be doing better than I thought."

"How's that?"

"That call would cost you upwards of six thousand pounds."

"For the girl?"

"My good man," Lord Mosby said, his tone as patronizing as the British can get. "For Madame Cleo's phone number."

Apparently having had enough conversation with the gauche American journalist, Mosby pushed himself up out of the chair and picked up the riding crop he had placed on the table. "You've not been to La Fantastique before?"

"No, sir. I haven't, and I must say it's a most . . ."

"Thought as much," Mosby said. He turned and walked across the terrace in the direction of the baron's stables.

Peter watched him go, liking him not one whit better than he had before he had spoken to the man. From his vantage point he could see a groom standing beside the weathered stable door holding the reins of two saddle horses, one dappled, the other a shining black.

Peter sat up straight in the chaise and pulled off his glasses. Seated on the black horse was a pretty little blonde.

"Up yours, Lord Lard Ass," he muttered under his breath.

He glanced at his watch. There would be time for a swim after the buffet lunch, then he would head back to Paris.

By three, he had showered and packed. All he needed to do was inform the hall porter that he was ready to leave and his car would be brought around.

He jiggled the phone. No sound. He dialed the number the footman had given him for service. Nothing.

Cursing, he looked out into the empty hall. There wasn't a soul in sight. He stepped back inside, lifted his bags, and resigned himself to finding his way out of the place.

He was halfway down the stuffy, dark hall when he heard the voices coming from the half-open door to his right. He could not resist glancing in. What he saw caused his jaw to drop.

Standing in the center of a room not dissimilar to the one he had just left was an enormously fat woman in incongruous red satin underwear and platform high heels. Another woman, a blonde, was standing behind her preparing to drop a dress over the woman's enormous teased hairdo. He could not have imagined a more incongruous sight. The large woman must have sensed his presence. She reached out with one high-heeled shoe and kicked the door closed with a resounding bang.

The bong of the seat-belt sign above his head snapped Peter out of his reverie. He reached down and fastened his seat belt, thinking how much he had changed in three short years. He had always believed people didn't change after forty. How wrong he had been. Back then, in Paris, when he was the old Peter Shea, his attitude was virtually always one of a defensive anger at others to mask his own sense of inadequacy. He had always had to guard against the gnawing feeling that, in reality, he was an imposter in a world filled with people better than he was, more elegant, more powerful, and often more worthy. If there had been a turning point in his life it had all started with the price he'd had to pay for that one night with that angel of a girl.

Driving toward Paris he had thought about little else than Madeleine and his chances of ever seeing her again.

When he arrived at his hotel in the late afternoon, the desk clerk handed Peter two messages. One informed him that his dinner date with his source, a Haitian exile who was arranging for Peter to interview deposed President-for-a-While "Baby Doc" Duvalier, would be delayed.

The other message was from New York. Gordon Jimison wanted

Peter to call him at home as soon as he got in. Odd, Peter thought, Jimison always played golf on Saturday, fire, flood, or invasion. He hoped he wasn't going to be jerked off the Duvalier assignment.

"Pack it in, Shea," Jimison said gruffly as soon as he picked up Peter's call.

"What's up?"

"You've done it now. The powers that be want you back here, pronto."

Peter sat down on the edge of the bed. "What the hell is this, Gordo?"

"The chairman just got a call. Seems you went to the baron's weekend after all."

"Right, I did. So what?"

"I told you not to go near that damn thing."

"Jesus H. Christ! I don't believe this!"

"Peter, I'm sorry. This isn't personal. I warned you the baron's little fuck-meet was a bad idea unless you announced yourself as a working reporter and covered it."

Peter felt his throat closing with rage. "Listen, you dumb son of a bitch—"

"No. You listen, Peter. We overlook a lot of crap because you're damn good at what you do, but things have been getting out of hand. Bracknell has blown his top a couple of times over your throwing your weight around over there. I've tried to cover your ass, but accepting the baron's invitation was the final straw. Particularly the broads."

"The broads?" Peter said, preparing to lie. "I don't know about any broads. Someone's bullshitting here and it ain't me."

"This was pretty high-level bullshit, then."

"Gordon," Peter said, trying to calm down. The reality of what Gordon was telling him was beginning to sink in. He sensed that Jimison knew something he didn't. "Where did this come from?"

"Peter, I'll level with you. Apparently your presence was unnerving to someone with enough clout to call the chairman and make a case out of it."

"So the bit about the so-called broads is just a smoke screen, I take it."

"I can't say that it isn't, Pete. I'm just following orders. But I can tell you, someone didn't like whatever you were up to down there. You better hightail it back and make your case on your own."

"What do you mean, make my case?" he said, outraged. "I have an interview all set with Baby Doc. I'm the only one he'll talk to. I'm due in London on Thursday to cover the Thatcher conference, and then I'm booked to Geneva. I don't have time for this Mickey Mouse shit. Make my case! Did it ever occur to anyone that I might have been set up?"

"You couldn't have been set up if you'd stayed away, like I told you to. That's not the point."

"Shit."

"Are you coming back?"

"No."

"If you don't, you're on your own, fella."

That did it. Being summoned home to explain himself was beyond humiliation. A fire storm, fueled by his own guilt, raged in his head. Spent and running low on vocabulary to express himself strongly enough, Peter ended the call with a stupid cliché. "You can tell that asshole he can't fire me. I quit!"

His anger was like another person, standing off to one side murdering himself. The same thing had happened when he and Sarah Jane finally split. In their last confrontation he had said things so hurtful, so unfair, so demeaning to them both, that he knew as he said them he was killing their marriage with his words. But he could no more have helped himself than breathe underwater, which was the way the rush of anger made him feel. He had never learned to ease up for a heartbeat or three to regain his rationality. His relentless fury pounded his brain into useless mush.

When he calmed down, denial, as always, took on its familiar happy face. The chairman would realize that whoever had ratted on him was wrong; Jimison would call him back all hail-fellow and apologies. In the meantime, the answer was booze.

He canceled his dinner with the Haitian go-between and repaired to the little bar in his hotel. He was early. The usual crowd had not yet arrived.

As he nursed his first drink, he said to Ronnie, the indulgent expatriate bartender, "Who knows? If I'm truly out at WorldWide it could be a blessing in disguise. I've still got a little flat in the Village. Now's the time to kick back and write the Great American Novel."

"Ummm."

"With my name it has to be a best-seller. Then there's the miniseries. Even a feature. I was getting tired of the rat race, anyway."

"Sure, Mr. Shea."

It was Ronnie who had to tell him later that evening, after Peter had sprung for the drinks of a half dozen new "friends" at the bar, that he couldn't sign for the drinks. His company account at the hotel had been canceled.

When what Ronnie was telling him made him realize the speed with which his privileged world was deteriorating, he did something he had not done since he was a child.

Peter Shea, former foreign correspondent for WorldWide International News Service and man of no small moment and esteem, vomited all over the mahogany bar in the chic little Left Bank hotel where Oscar Wilde had lived and, some said, Frank Sinatra had drunk champagne from Ava Gardner's high-heeled Italian pumps.

There were several people in the lobby. They all saw Peter Shea being carried to his room.

A collective moan rose from the other passengers as the pilot announced that their landing was being delayed. They would circle JFK for a "few short moments." Yeah, sure, Peter thought, and he shifted irritably in his seat.

He glanced forward, in the direction of the First Class john. Something was going on in front of the bathroom door. He leaned toward the open space between the seats to get a better look.

The stewardess was leaning her forehead against the door, speaking in a low but urgent voice to whoever was on the other side. Peter could catch only a word or two. She seemed to be alerting someone that the plane was about to land. The door remained closed and locked. Whatever reply the stewardess received sent her rushing down the aisle. As she went past Shea, she muttered and rolled her eyes.

"Great," he said sarcastically as she passed. Now they would circle the airport for an hour while the crew hauled out whoever was stuck in the john.

In seconds, another crew member stormed back up the aisle, followed by the young male flight attendant who had shown Shea to his seat. Bringing up the rear was the greatly agitated stewardess.

There were only half a dozen other passengers in First Class. The commotion in front of the john door had all their attention. Shea glanced across the aisle and noticed that Ayler and the girl were not in their seats. He leaned back in his seat and smiled, delighted with what was happening. There was only one place on the plane that the lovers could be.

Using some sort of metal instrument, the steward snapped open the flimsy bathroom door. Shea saw the stewardess's hand fly up and cover her mouth as the three of them stared into the open door. The crew member reached back and pulled a blanket from an overhead rack and handed it to the bathroom's occupants.

A moment later, a mortified Jack Ayler, fresh tan several shades paler, stepped into the aisle. He had a blue airline blanket tied,

Italian-waiter style, around his middle over a pink Polo shirt. He stepped to one side to make room for the steward to help Christine, who apparently had been on the bathroom floor.

As Christine hobbled into the aisle, her clothes askew, the stewardess tossed Ayler his pants, grabbed another blanket lying in an empty seat, and held it up as an impromptu curtain in front of the woman.

As the male flight attendant breezed back down the aisle trying to suppress a smile, Peter stopped him. "What was all that about?" he asked.

The young man paused, leaned down toward Peter, and whispered. "He had her up on the counter. She slipped to the floor and got her leg wedged against the door. They were bare-assed when we opened it."

As the attendant continued down the aisle, Peter pressed a fist hard against his teeth to restrain the laughter constricting his throat.

That did it! he thought, instantly revising the lead on the article he would do on Jack Ayler.

If his editor didn't want the story he'd find someone who did, two-year exclusive contract with *Fifteen Minutes* or not.

He nodded and closed his eyes. She would want it, though, he reassured himself. No way would Fedalia Null, the redoubtable editor who had made the magazine the smashing success it was, say no to him on this one. She always met him halfway. She had gone even farther than halfway to save his life.

CHAPTER
∽ 2 ∾

In the days when Peter Shea was riding high in Paris he would have sneered at the very idea of a publication like *Fifteen Minutes* magazine. Anyone who would have lowered himself to write for such a throwaway could never be taken seriously. "Amateurs," he would have snorted over the rim of his scotch glass. "Yuppie scum," he would have sniffed, ignoring a tiny pitch of warning in the back of his mind that times were changing, that something new and vital was happening in a world that he was out of step with. Back then, when he was drunk with his own self-importance and seemingly endless power, he would have told those who felt his opinion was the ultimate take on everything that *Fifteen Minutes* wasn't journalism, it was "infotainment," printed matter that pandered to the lowest fan mentality and wasn't worth the trees it took to print it.

Such a low opinion of the publication might have been justified had not a brash and improbable young woman stepped in to turn the magazine around.

When Mosby Media purchased what was to become *Fifteen Minutes* magazine, it had been a rag called *Star Watch,* a mixed bag of canned interviews from press agents and features based on rumors about soap stars. It was printed on newspaper stock in ink that rubbed off on your hands, and it advertised roach motels, mail-order "imperfect" L'eggs, and vinyl handbags with a lot of zippered pockets for $9.95 (two for $15). Owning it meant little except a mailing list of over seven million Americans who wanted a weekly fix of celebrity gossip.

British press lord Billy Mosby didn't actually know he had purchased it at the time. It was part of a package that included an antique-car magazine and a monthly on wrestling.

Somewhere south of Fourteenth Street, Lord Mosby's American headhunters found a brash young woman with a lot of ideas and a lumpy work history. When the headhunters found her, she was editing a small monthly catering to the downtown scene.

Her name was Fedalia Null.

Fedalia was not like the other sleek, chic women who ran the lucrative popular magazines of the eighties.

Fedalia Null was different.

She was given carte blanche, a three-million-dollar budget, and a year to turn the tired *Star Watch* around. Within a month she fired everyone on the masthead, moved the editorial offices to a Mosby-owned building on East 57th Street, and set about organizing the magazine around her master plan.

Fedalia broke everyone and everything down to the Warhol formulation of fifteen minutes of fame. Using that as her guide, she set about publishing a monthly magazine that celebrated those who had most recently met the test.

What exploded the magazine into the national consciousness was pure Fedalia. In 1987 she bought a home video, taken by a vacationing accountant, that showed Senator Gary Hart cavorting on the deck of the *Monkey Business*. She had her new art department freeze one of the more revealing shots of the senator and Donna Rice licking off each other's suntan lotion and ran it on the cover.

Midtown newsstands sold out before lunch and two stars were born: *Fifteen Minutes* magazine and Fedalia Null.

In the two-day scramble it took for the rest of the media to catch up with the sensational story, Fedalia found herself interviewed on as many talk shows as her freshly rented limousine could speed her to.

If the media establishment was sneering behind their hands, Fedalia didn't see or care. She was just following the first rule of a free economy: finding something people wanted and selling it to them.

She painted her executive offices orange. Not the Howard Johnson orange of the sixties but a pulsating burnt-sienna lacquer the color of exploding tiger lilies. Instead of chairs, she installed chaise longues covered in fake pony skin. Her desk was a ten-foot-wide slab of high-gloss slate in the shape of a boomerang. At it, she sat in a chair that was a replica of Pope Hadrian's throne, which she had flirted out of a Broadway set designer. The effect was decidedly Aztec-Vatican and fit her like the fishnet hose on her ample legs.

Like many heavy young women, she had a very pretty face, with wide-set clear blue eyes and a cupid's bow mouth. No one ever described her hair color with any consistency, as it changed depending on her mood. She credited a fondness for Häagen-Dazs and mayonnaise for her creamy, flawless skin, and knew, because she had once been thin, that underneath it all was a stunning body.

Fedalia could not leave herself alone or settle on a look. For more than a decade she had used every free gimmick, cosmetic, wig, and piece of fashion frippery laid on her by eager press agents and promoters desperate for a line of free publicity. Fedalia Null looked like a one-woman costume party. When she finally hit her stride and was profiled in *Spy* magazine, she was referred to as looking "overproduced."

Fedalia was born hungry and stayed that way even when Lord Mosby, in his glee and gratitude for the success she had made of his improbable property, raised her salary and perks to a generous six figures.

If Fedalia had come from slightly more in life she would have been ashamed to talk about herself. As it was, her background was so bleak it made for colorful conversation. She used it when she needed to enliven cocktail parties, often to the chagrin of those who wanted someone so successful to have a more predictable background.

Fedalia's mother had been a fifteen-year-old runaway who was "rescued" by a St. Paul supermarket manager who caught her shoplifting to feed her infant daughter. Her mother married the manager. In the years that followed, several other "rescues" and, possibly, marriages were effected. By the time Fedalia was fourteen she had given up on remembering her "stepfathers." She packed what little she had and hit the road, driven by her desire to be anyplace but where she was.

Her thumb provided the ride. After two years on the road she landed, like a tired Day-Glo Nerf ball, on the streets of New York's West Side in a six-block grid of midtown meanness. In the early seventies the police referred to the area as the "Minnesota Strip" because so many of the hookers strolling the pavement were, like Fedalia, fair, blue-eyed teenage runaways from the Midwest.

On the strip there was money to be made, drugs to be had, and pimps circling each new girl who arrived bewildered and underrepresented. Hungry and worn to skin and bone, on her very first night she found herself huddled in a reeking doorway on Eighth Avenue. She looked up to see a woman wearing jeans and a leather jacket smiling at her.

"You want tuna on white or peanut butter and jelly?" the woman asked, reaching into a canvas backpack on her shoulder.

Fedalia was about to say something smartass when the woman put out her hand. "I'm Sister Jo. I'm a nun, don't be frightened," she said with a sweet smile, reminding Fedalia that there were still people who had clean teeth. "You must be cold. If you don't feel like a sandwich, how about a hot shower and some soup?"

Fedalia looked down at her torn clothes. She couldn't remember how long it had been since she had changed, much less bathed. Hot tears she thought had long ago permanently dried up sprang to her eyes, then rolled slowly down her cheeks.

"Why are you crying?" Sister Jo asked softly.

" 'Cause it hurts too much to laugh," Fedalia had replied. "You mean it about a hot shower?"

Our Lady of the Bodily Ascension Mission occupied five spartan whitewashed floors of a brownstone on West Forty-sixth Street near the river. There, Fedalia found hot food, clean sheets, and a back room filed with stacks of old *Rolling Stone* magazines. At the mission, among the nuns and the other girls no more fortunate than she, Fedalia also discovered something else: unconditional love in the form of Jesus Christ.

Fedalia's perception of Jesus was somewhat skewed. For her, he was a combination of father figure, mystical true love, and Hunter Thompson. Each aspect provided her with something she had never experienced. All that seemed fine with the nuns. After what they had seen in their ministry, there were certainly worse things for a girl to hold on to than a Gonzo Christ. Fedalia had discovered unfailing rules to live by. The nuns, an unexplainable sense of humor, and a good brain whizzed her through a GED and early entrance to Fordham.

After graduation, she followed what she felt was her destiny and applied for a job at *Rolling Stone*. She was hired based on her encyclopedic familiarity with the publication since its inception.

Ten years and several jobs later, she was hired as the editor of Mosby Media's new magazine, never having lost the belief that her Gonzo Jesus loved her and that everybody deserves and gets a second chance.

One morning in October 1988, Fedalia looked up to see her secretary, a drop-dead black girl named Vickie, standing in her office door.

"The trash bag is here," Vickie singsonged. She was holding the corner of a large padded Jiffy bag with two fingers of one hand and her nose with the other. "You want to go through it now?"

The "trash bag" Vickie was referring to arrived once a week by messenger from an agent named Wendy Klarwine. The Klarwine

Agency was known for its representation of sensational nonauthors and their ghostwritten stories. Wendy Klarwine was forty-two, single, tiny, and almost beautiful—all hair and determination. In her twenty years in the business she had whipped those people in the publishing industry who paid writers for their work into thinking that if they didn't pay attention to the junk she peddled they wouldn't get a run at the good stuff. Begrudgingly, magazine editors toed the line, as they wanted to be able to buy and publish sensational excerpts from Wendy's hot books. Hence, the weekly "trash bag" from Wendy and the worthless articles by writers on her "Z" list.

Fedalia groaned as Vickie emptied the Jiffy bag onto the boomerang. "Just look at this crap," Fedalia said, flicking at the pile of paper with the eraser of her pencil as though she didn't want to actually touch it.

"You gotta at least look at it," Vickie said over her shoulder as she returned to her office. "Klarwine is auctioning Imelda Marcos's hairdresser's memoirs this week. You're gonna have to talk to her."

Fedalia made a face. She was about to push the entire mess to one side when something on the top of the pile caught her eye. She picked up a sheaf of stapled paper and read the first paragraph of an article entitled "The Girl with the Drowning-Pool Eyes."

The landing strip had been cut out of the lush forest that surrounded the baron's château. The larger, faster private jets belonging to heads of state and multinational corporations arrived first. Then came the smaller planes. By noon, the fields around the magnificent eighteenth-century stone mansion held what looked like a private air force.

La Fantastique, the most secretive gathering of the world's most powerful men, was about to begin. The beautiful girls of Madame Cleo would come later, appearing out of the night, elegant, exotic, and able to permanently alter one's perceptions of sex-for-hire.

Fedalia was intrigued, more with what the writer revealed about the highest priced prostitutes in the world than the fact that power brokers got together to debauch in secret. She finished the article, then flipped back to see who had written it. "Vickie!" she called. "Who was that reporter who went berserk at the White House correspondents dinner that time?"

Vickie hooked her heels into the carpeting and walked her typing chair to the side of the door. "Wasn't that something? The poor guy completely lost it. Taking over the microphone like that. They said Patrick Buchanan and the Secret Service had to pull him off the dais."

Fedalia closed her eyes and spoke very slowly. "What was his name, Vickie?"

"Oh, sorry. That was Peter Shea from WorldWide."

"WorldWide fired him, right?"

"I think he'd already been fired when he did that. I read they sent him to the ha-ha hotel."

"You are a font of information, Victoria," Fedalia said with a chuckle. "Now, call Wendy Klarwine and tell her I'd like this Peter Shea to stop by. I want him to write something for us."

"You found Peter Shea in the trash bag?" Vickie asked, raising her eyebrows. "How appropriate."

"Don't be unkind, Victoria. Great legs and a smart mouth do not guarantee you won't make an ass of yourself someday. Now get me Wendy."

A week after Peter Shea's agent told him the editor of *Fifteen Minutes* wanted to see him, he made his way uneasily down the long turquoise hallway leading to Fedalia Null's office.

The walls on either side were lined with framed photographs of people who had met the Warhol test: Meagan Marshak, the "researcher" with Nelson Rockefeller when he died in her apartment; the marshmallow salesman who had punched out Frank Sinatra; Henry Weinberg, the Liz Taylor boyfriend with the shortest shelf life; and many more too cleverly obscure for him to take the time to figure out. In a place of honor above the entrance to the office foyer was a photo of Valerie Solanis, the woman who shot Andy Warhol.

He scanned the pictures and smiled. The woman's taste may have been bizarre, but it was certainly consistent.

He had been reluctant to come. In the past year he had left his Village apartment only to buy groceries and to keep his weekly appointment with Dr. Benedict in the psychiatrist's high-rise office a block away.

After Wendy Klarwine called him about the magazine's interest in his article he had sat staring out the window for more than an hour. The piece on La Fantastique had been the first thing he had attempted to write since his breakdown. Now, ironically, it was that article that got him dressed in a suit and tie and onto the uptown train.

When Wendy first mentioned the magazine to him he had forced himself to look at it. To his surprise, he found it informative, intelligent, and refreshingly zany. Still, he had not wanted to have a face-to-face meeting with the editor. In the past year his only human contact had been with Dr. Benedict and Wendy Klarwine. It was Dr. Benedict who had gotten him finally to call half the agents in town. Wendy Klarwine was the only one who had agreed to represent him when he explained his fragile and agoraphobic state. Wendy, thankfully, not only came to him but kept her limousine waiting.

As he entered the editor's office, a gorgeous black woman looked up from her desk. "Hi," she said brightly. "You must be Mr. Shea. I'm Vickie."

"Good morning, Vickie," Peter said, squinting at the orange walls. They looked wet.

"You can go right in. Ms. Null just got off the phone." Vickie gestured toward the room beyond and went back to her word processor.

Fedalia Null was seated behind a desk that looked like a Delta wing jet. Her paper-white hair was a photo negative of Gloria Steinem's. It fell to her shoulders. Two-inch-wide black streaks like parentheses curled down either side of her pretty face. When she stood he could see an ample figure under what appeared to be a velvet tent. Interesting, he thought, at a time when most working women were so thin they were in danger of having vultures circling them, watching their every move, here was a woman built for comfort rather than speed.

"Peter," she said, beaming and extending her hand.

"Ms. Null," he said, shaking her hand.

"Please. Call me Fiddle."

"Fiddle it is," he said with a nod.

"Please sit down."

Peter looked around the room and, having no other choice, perched uncomfortably at the foot of a chaise covered in some kind of black-and-white fake fur.

"I loved your piece," Fiddle said, returning to her throne-sized wooden chair. It looked like something dragged off the altar at St. Patrick's.

"Thank you."

"Fascinating. Particularly the stuff about the women. I've always been intrigued by Madame Cleo girls. People say some of the fanciest society women in New York are former Cleo girls. This piece should raise some eyebrows. What made you decide to write it?"

"Nobody else has done it."

"Well, I loved it. I just wish we could use it."

Peter frowned. "Excuse me?"

"It's really not for us, Peter. If you're familiar with the magazine

37

you'll see our focus is personalities. Now if you had done an interview, say, with one of the girls and revealed that she had, oh, I don't know, been driven into prostitution by a tragic affair with Ed Koch, then we'd have something we could run with."

"I don't think I understand," Peter said, tightly. "I thought the article was why I'm here." Inwardly, he kept repeating Dr. Benedict's mantra, *calm down, calm down.*

He shouldn't have come. His skin was still too thin, his ego reflexes too raw and ready to react to even the slightest hint of rejection. If this bizarre woman and her sleazy magazine didn't want the only thing he had been able to get on paper in a solid year, she could shove it right up—

"There *is* something I would like you to write for us," she said, interrupting his inner diatribe against hope.

"I really don't do personality pieces."

"I know. You are a deep-thinking foreign correspondent. A powerful, famous guy," she said pleasantly.

"I *was* a deep-thinking foreign correspondent."

"Goody. Then you get my point," she said, not so pleasantly.

Peter glowered at her. What was this, some kind of jerk-around? What was this woman driving at? "No, I'm afraid I don't."

"You had a fascinating fifteen minutes of your own, Peter. Snapping out on national television is pretty spectacular stuff. The fact that you vanished only makes it more interesting. People want to know why it happened, and the best person to tell them is you."

Peter pushed himself up from the backbreaking chaise and jammed his hands in his pockets. "You remember that, huh?"

"Remember it? Have you forgotten, I'm the girl who collects people's Warhol formulations for a living. Sadly for you, after a lifetime of hard work, that was yours. What happened?"

"What happened was that some bastard got me fired for taking a gratuity in the form of the girl with the drowning-pool eyes," he said, jabbing his finger at the copy of the article that lay spread out on Fedalia's desk. "One day, when I get my act together, I'm going to devote a lot of time to finding out who stabbed me in the back."

"Too bad you didn't focus on that in this piece. I happen to think that's riveting, and so would my readers."

"I happen to think it's sick and sorry and best forgotten."

Fedalia shook her head with a swinging gesture that swept her hair over her eyes. "Wrong. Wrongo. Wrong-o-roonie, Mr. Shea. There's a whole lot more there. There always is. That's why this magazine is so

successful. We go find the years behind the fifteen minutes of fame."
She paused and took a long hard look at him. "What do I have to say to
make you change your mind?"

Peter took a long deep breath. "Nothing," he said softly. "I couldn't.
It would be excruciating."

"What? To write about a breakdown? There's no shame in going
bonkers, or haven't you caught most of the guests on Phil Donahue
lately? If they aren't recovered compulsive hand-washers or recovering
lesbian mothers of twins, they've done two tours at the Betty Ford
Clinic. And you know what? People telling about being down and
getting back up do a lot of good. How people find their way back from
cuckoo land is what's happening. Get with the program. Shame is
definitely out. Uplift is in. Triumph is the game."

"How can you be so relentlessly upbeat?" Peter said, frowning at
her. "I fucking well destroyed myself."

Fedalia lifted both palms in an elaborate shrug. "So?" she said. "Use
it. It's yours, you lived it. Maybe what happened to you will help
someone else."

Peter shook his head. "It's too soon. I'm not well."

"Sounds like you don't want to be."

He took several shallow breaths to damp down the anxiety he felt
welling up in his chest. "I already have a shrink, thanks," he snapped.
The minute he said it he was sorry. There was something sweet about
the woman for all the seeming hardness of her attitude.

"I know what you're thinking," she said softly. "You're thinking that
if you were ever going to tell the world what happened to you, you'd
do it in some slick publication like the *Times* magazine or *Vanity Fair*."

Peter looked at her and slowly nodded. "Maybe."

"Have they asked?"

"No, of course not. They don't know I'm alive."

"Maybe you aren't. You could be. I'll pay you ten grand to find out."
She picked up her pencil, scribbled on a notepad, tore off the sheet, and
handed it to him. "Stick this on your bathroom mirror. It's my IOU."

"Thanks, but no. A big, fat, not ungrateful no."

Fedalia pursed her lips and squinted out the window. She turned
back toward him and leveled her gaze. "When's your rent due?"

"I beg your pardon?"

"You don't need money. Tacky old stuff," she said, making a face.

"My apartment is rent-controlled. It's not a problem."

"Is that a new suit?"

Peter looked down at the shabby Brooks Brothers gray flannel.

"Everything I have is still in storage," he said. "I don't go anywhere, anyway."

"Not to a movie or a Broadway show? When's the last time you had a meal in a really fine restaurant? Like the ones I'm sure you ate at in Paris."

"Look, Ms. . . . . Null," he said. "I didn't drop by to take a beating. Wendy said you were interested in my doing a piece. You are, but it's not a piece I'm prepared to do."

"You'll change your mind," she said, smiling. "You had a bad patch there for a while. At least when you snapped it was pure theater. People talked about it for weeks. Come on, Peter, you didn't go on a three-state killing spree. Don't take yourself so seriously."

Peter smiled. Then he laughed. It was a wonderful feeling. He hadn't laughed for a very long time. "That's what my shrink tells me."

"Maybe I missed my calling," she said.

He put her note in his jacket pocket. "Let me think about it, Fiddle. Okay?"

"Okay. I hope you'll think fast."

"I'm sorry if I was rude," he said. "And thank you. Being asked to write anything at all is a ray of sunlight after a year in the dark."

Fedalia stood and extended her hand to him again. "Well then, pal, tan while you can."

For a month of sleepless nights after their meeting Peter could think of little else but Fiddle's offer to publish the story of his ordeal. He worried the idea as he would have bothered a sore tooth. He knew that each poke guaranteed another shot of pain and yet he was unable to resist. Her interest in him made him feel, for the first time since his breakdown, that he was still worth something to someone other than his shrink, his agent, and the owner of the Korean laundry across the street.

As he paced the tiny apartment, it occurred to him that nothing would happen if he tried to write this most personal confession. There weren't any ghosts looking over his shoulder. There was no one who would ever know he'd put the words down. If what he wrote was garbage he could tear it up and eat the pages like people in espionage movies chewed up secret codes.

On a Saturday night a month after meeting Fedalia Null, Peter sat down in front of his faithful old Remington portable. The nearly antique machine had seen the world with him. Whenever he saw one like it in a thrift shop or junk store he bought it and stashed it in the closet for spare parts.

With trembling hands, he rolled a piece of paper into the machine and placed his fingers on the keys.

He could not make them move.

The television was on behind him, its reflection shimmering in multiples in the small windowpanes in front of his desk. It reminded him of something—a way out of his paralysis. It was worth a try. He dove for the phone book under the couch and pawed through the pages to find the N's. There were only two listings for the name Null. One was a Franklin Null on East 94th Street, the other an F. Null on Gramercy Park. That had to be Fiddle. Everyone knew a first initial was a listing for a single female.

He glanced at his watch. It was just before ten. Great, he thought sourly. At ten on a Manhattan Saturday night, surely she would be out doing something glamorous. He would just have to leave a message on her machine.

"Ms. Null? Are you a human or a machine?" he asked when he heard her voice after the first ring.

"This sounds like a dirty phone call from Camus," she said, laughing. "Hi, Peter."

"Hey, you recognized my voice?"

"Of course."

"I'm flattered," he said, leaning back and resting the heels of his loafers on the battered coffee table with a clunk. "Forgive me for calling you at home at this hour."

"The only thing I won't forgive you for is calling me Ms. Null."

"Sorry, I guess I lived in Europe too long . . . Fedalia."

"Fiddle," she corrected. "Turn down your television. I can't hear you too well."

Peter reached over and turned down the sound. When he put the receiver back to his ear, she said, "Better. What video are you watching?"

"Video? Oh. I don't have one of those thingamajigs."

"Good Lord! Do you have a flush toilet yet?"

"They just delivered it," he answered, playing along. "Listen, what I'm calling about . . ."

"Umm?"

"That thing, you know, that computer thing I saw on your desk. How complicated are those to use? I mean, is it like operating a fighter jet or can any three-thumbed creature do it?"

"It's a piece of cake once you get the hang of it. Why?"

"I swore I'd never give up a typewriter, but something drastic has happened to my ability to write. Actually, it's more basic than that. I can't even type. I look at my old machine and I freeze. I thought if I got some of the new tools of the trade it might help."

"Oh, it will help all right. It will change your life," she said. Her voice had suddenly become animated. "But you don't want one of those big monsters that Vickie and I have. You need a laptop. You want one?"

"I don't know what I want. I just know I suddenly can't type another word on this thing I've used for twenty years. Too many memories, I guess. I have this feeling that anything I put into it will come out as hate mail."

"Tell you what," she said. "If you promise to write that article on it, the magazine will buy you one."

"Am I being seduced?"

"Absolutely. If you're free tomorrow afternoon I'll take you shopping. I'll buy the laptop. You buy a VCR. I can show you how to work 'em both."

"I can't let you do that," he said, meaning it. "But I'll take you up on your offer to help me buy myself one. Are you sure you know what you're getting into? I've just now figured out the push-button phone."

"Trust me, and welcome."

"Welcome? To what?"

"A brave new world, Peter."

Fiddle knew the manager of an electronics store in the Thirties. They spent Sunday afternoon sitting in his back office while Fiddle, with the patience of a physical therapist teaching a grown man how to walk again, showed Peter how to operate a remarkable machine. He approached it, initially, with the aloof distaste a hardened veteran displays for anything new. But within minutes he realized how simple it was. The soundless, friendly little machine snatched whatever he tapped into the keyboard and flashed his words, clear and crisp, upon the bright screen.

When Fiddle wisely left him alone with it to go and find a printer, he found his mind and hands flying. With the same sense of wonder he'd felt long ago when he'd sold his college rattletrap Ford and slipped behind the wheel of the sports car he'd bought with his first big-city paycheck, he fell irrevocably in love.

Dizzy with gratitude and revelation, he asked Fiddle to dinner. As they walked south in the failing late-afternoon light toward a new little restaurant that she suggested, he lovingly clutched his new five-pound companion under his arm. In his other hand he carried a portable printer. He was having the VCR delivered to his home Monday.

At the beginning of dinner Peter was vaguely aware that he was uneasy. This was the first time since his breakdown that he had dined with anyone, let alone a woman.

But Fiddle made it easy. She talked about the day's news, the weirdos and crazies that were part of her life as the editor of a magazine that attracted the offbeat and the cast-off. As the meal continued, she told him about the nuns who had rescued her from the garbage heap of her life. She told him what she had done to survive, without guile or apology, as though she were recounting someone else's story.

When she finished the horrendous tale she said she hoped she hadn't bored him. He had not been in the least bit bored and said so. "My God," he said. "I don't know where you got the strength."

"It's no big deal, Peter," she said lightly. "None of the bad stuff is, once you look the demons in the eye and forgive yourself."

They were both silent for a long minute. Then Fiddle said, "So, you're going home to do this article for me on that newfangled machine?"

All he could do was nod.

Again, she made it easy for him, providing a graceful excuse for his eagerness. "You're addicted to that little machine already, right?"

Again, he nodded, this time smiling warmly at her.

"Wait till you get your VCR. Then you'll need a cable hookup, then a fax. You'll probably need a modem to get on line with one of those research services. For fun you might want to get a Walkman, or how about a CD stereo?"

"Whoa, whoa!" he laughed. "I'm going to get the electronic bends. One thing that goes buzz at a time."

"Sorry, but this is such fun," she said. As she spoke she pushed aside the lock of hair that had fallen over her forehead.

For the first time he noticed she had done something different with her hair. It didn't look the way he remembered it. He studied her face for a moment and then looked away. He liked her, she was pleasant company and easy to be with, what he thought of as a "low-maintenance" woman. One did not have to make an extraordinary investment in entertaining her. She was the direct opposite of the long-legged, neurotic fashion models he had invariably homed in on in his wilder, other life.

He quickly pushed his thoughts away. If he was going to start up something with a woman now it would not be with Fedalia Null. She represented his final rehabilitation and reentry into real life. No way was he going to clog up the works by making their relationship anything but pleasant, slightly formal business.

He looked up and signaled the waiter. "I can't thank you enough for all your help today, Fiddle," he said a bit stiffly. "All this is very exciting."

"This is on the magazine, Peter," she said, handing a credit card to the waiter with a two-fingered flip. Clearly, she had had it palmed for some time. "Get used to it," she said when he opened his mouth to protest. She smiled and gathered up her bag. "We'll be doing this again."

He put her into a cab, then stood holding the new machinery that he hoped would justify her faith in him and watched as the cab moved out into the early evening traffic. He felt slightly guilty that this ebullient woman had no idea how truly fragile he was. Slowly, he turned and hurried toward home.

He closed the door of his apartment and tossed his raincoat on the couch. Gently, he lifted his new machine into place and switched it on. The soft green glow of the screen was the only illumination in the room.

He pulled his chair up to it, placed his hands on the keyboard, and began to type. Tentatively at first, then faster and faster, twice as fast as he had been able to move on his old Remington.

The words pouring onto the screen took on a life of their own. He wrote straight through the night. He paused briefly at dawn for a shower and coffee. Then he read the instructions for the printer. He printed out what he had written and returned to the living room to read it. By noon he had finished the longest article he had ever written. It was also the most honest.

He knew if he started to rewrite he would change his mind about making such a painful confession. He gathered the pages up, stuffed them into a manila envelope, and messengered them to Fiddle at the magazine.

Fiddle did not change a word of the article. She published it in the January 1989 issue of *Fifteen Minutes*, with a red strip running across the upper right-hand corner reading "Journey to the Edge and Over by Peter Shea."

It caused a sensation.

In the following months, Fiddle assigned him several more articles. Now, in the spring of 1990, Peter Shea was an established star. So much so that Fiddle and Peter's first eye-lock moment—that split second when two colleagues become aware that they utterly trust each other—came when Fiddle passed on a morning's conversation with Billy Mosby in which he referred to Peter as his "protégé."

Fiddle had considered adding, "There's no deodorant like success." Their eye-lock told her she didn't have to.

Fiddle was convinced that more people bought the magazine because of him than anything else. Peter's stories went behind the things people did that got them attention. They quickly became must-reads, and, in some cases, caused bigger scandals than they documented.

As each new article appeared, the rips and tears in his psyche began to heal. Slowly, tentatively, he regained the respect of his colleagues and his devastated self-esteem. The difference was that now he knew how quickly it could disappear. He no longer took fame for granted. He was only as good as his last article.

Fiddle's zeal for making Peter electronically sophisticated was, at first, self-serving. It gave her more excuses to be in touch with him. If they had no assignment to discuss she could always come up with a new gadget she thought he might be able to use. That first year, she taught him how to use innumerable electronic toys, up to and including a phone system for his apartment that did everything but iron his shirts. She saved her most exciting, challenging assignments for him, carefully showcasing his work while she waited, sometimes in emotional turmoil, for him to notice that she had fallen in love with him.

She took to inviting him to stop by the office in the late afternoon. Often they had dinner or drinks. Their evenings together were warm, casual but not romantic. When, in the spring of 1990, Peter told Fiddle she was his best friend, she became morbidly depressed. She had just given him the assignment to interview a Jamaican-based embezzler. After he left Vickie poked her head around the office door.

"You see his jacket?" Vickie asked, her eyes large with appreciation of the soft cashmere sport coat Peter had been wearing.

"Of course," Fiddle said gloomily from behind her desk. "I helped him pick it out. At least I showed him the ad and arranged for him to get it below wholesale."

"God, he's cute," Vickie said, walking to the sideboard to fix their end-of-the-day drinks. "When is that Harp going to get the message about you? I see the way you look at him."

Fiddle glanced at her watch and nodded. "That Harp, you of the racial slurs, is making this fucking magazine. Besides," she said defensively, "I'm his best friend."

"Great," Vickie said, rolling her eyes.

"I know, I know," Fiddle said, scribbling into a leather-bound date book, its elegance diminished by the logo of a soft-drink company on its cover.

Vickie poured them each a drink of straight vodka, plopped ice cubes into the glasses, and handed one to her boss. "Just what you always wanted, huh?" Vickie said softly, taking a seat at the end of the chaise.

Fiddle threw the Mark Cross pen she had been using across the room. It had been sent by Elizabeth Taylor's press agent as some kind of promotion for the movie star's perfume. The pen bounced against the far wall and dropped to the carpet.

"Hey, that's Liz Taylor's pen," Vickie said, looking over her shoulder.

"Wrong. It's my pen and I don't give a damn. My life is full of that crap. Pens, ship's decanters, silver crap engraved with the names of some of the finest hotels. Matched luggage that says Gucci that the store wouldn't take back because it wasn't theirs."

"I was the one who tried to return that junk," Vickie said with a grimace. "That was embarrassing. Who gave you that?"

"Oh, I don't know," Fiddle said with a disgruntled shrug. "Some airline. Who the fuck cares?"

"Wow, may I get you some nails to chew with your drink?" Vickie said as the depth of Fiddle's anger became evident.

Fiddle tried to speak but her voice broke. She dropped her head into her hands.

"Yikes. You aren't going to cry, are you?" Vickie said, then began to sing in a Frankie Valli falsetto. *"Big girls don't cry . . ."*

"Can it," Fedalia said with a snuffle, and reached for a tissue on her desk. She blew her nose loudly and pitched the hankie in the general direction of the wastebasket.

"Sorry," Vickie said.

"S'okay."

Vickie took a slug of her vodka. "Aw, I hate seeing you like this," she said sympathetically. "It's getting bad, huh?"

"Yup," Fiddle said as she wiped her eyes, leaving a great streak of black mascara over each cheekbone.

"Why don't you just come right out and tell him how you feel? The two of you are so great together."

Fiddle shook her head slowly. "I'd just scare him. He's too banged up to be in love with anything but his work."

"But you *are* his work."

Fiddle leaned forward. "Victoria, I know we couldn't be less alike.

46

You're a sleek, black, agnostic twelve-year-old and I'm an eighty-year-old mottled-pink Catholic manqué. But we're both women, right? And you gotta help me."

"Come on," Vickie said, laughing. "We're not so different. Anyway, for the purposes of this conversation, we're girls." She set her glass down on the rug and hugged her knees.

"And Brown University taught you the difference?"

"Not really. Life did, though. Being a woman is like, political. When someone we love doesn't love us back, we're all girls."

Fiddle leaned her forehead on one hand, stared down at the mess on her desk, and sighed. "What am I gonna do, Vicks? No matter what they say, this city is full of men. I could fill my life with a whole smorgasbord of men. I could get one who can dance, one who makes me laugh, one to have wild and crazy sex with. But no. I have to fall for one who doesn't even see me as a woman."

"Don't say that," Vickie protested. "Peter Shea would die for you."

"I don't want him to die for me. I want him to notice when I cross my legs. I want him to sit in front of my fireplace and let me feed him. Since the day he walked in here in that Tweedledum suit and white socks, he's fascinated me. He's so . . ." Fiddle stared up at the ceiling searching for the word. "Vulnerable," she said finally.

"Not an unattractive trait in a man," Vickie said, nodding.

Fiddle twisted her mouth in disgust and began stacking papers on her desk. Her drink was still untouched. "Damn! I should be over at *Cosmo* writing Mouseburger copy while I wait for my orthopedic shoes to be resoled."

"Maybe he's too banged up for anybody to get the dents out. Ever think of that?"

Fiddle shook her head and rearranged the black velvet headband holding back her hair. "I used to think that about myself, Vicks. I had this other life once. I was so far down I never thought I'd ever get up. Someone came along and saved me. I guess I'm trying to do the same thing for Peter."

"You wanna tell me about that other life?" Vickie asked.

"Absolutely not," Fiddle said. "What I want from you is some kind of foolproof scheme. The kind of thing that drop-dead beautiful women know about that those of us who aren't don't."

Vickie reached for her drink, took a sip. "Hmmm," she mused. "You could off-load about ten kilos of fat. Oh shit, there goes my job."

"This is fun," Fiddle said, making a face. "I'm so glad we're having this little chat."

"Sorry, chief, but you asked."

"Okay, okay," Fiddle said. "But you know what? I don't care. The fat's not who I am."

"What about your clothes, hair, nails, posture," Vickie said, picking up steam. "You are kind of . . . well, eccentric."

"I repeat, Vickie, that's who I am. I want Peter to fall in love with *me*—not someone I'm pretending to be."

"You're resisting my advice, *mon général.*"

"No, I'm not," Fiddle said with a short laugh. "I'm resisting an acting career. Go ahead, Sunshine."

"Well, frankly, Fiddle, I wonder if he's worth your heartache. The guy came in here with a black belt in Fuckup and you made him the hottest journalist in town. Maybe there's more wrong with him than right."

Fiddle finally lifted her drink. She had championed Peter Shea for almost a year and a half. She couldn't stop now. She began to tell Vickie about Peter's failed marriage, his drinking. Vickie already knew about his fall from grace at WorldWide but Fiddle told her again because she liked talking about Peter Shea.

When Fiddle finally wound down, Vickie stood up and gathered up the empty glasses. "Okay, commandant, I can see I'd never change your mind about him. I hereby declare this slumber party over."

Fiddle stood up and brushed imaginary crumbs off the front of her corduroy tent. "You're the best thing that's happened to me, Victoria," Fiddle said softly.

Vickie looked away, slightly embarrassed. "That's not true. The best thing that ever happened to you is you, oh fearless leader. Don't worry. We'll get his attention. You'll see."

CHAPTER
❧ 3 ❧

The black Super Puma helicopter hovered above the Mosby Media office tower that rose from the center of London, paused for a moment, then dropped through the bright May morning sky as the pilot eased the huge craft down toward the rooftop landing pad.

Four men in dark suits dropped from the open door as the pilot cut the engine. Their suit jackets, whipped by the prop wash, revealed the shoulder holsters strapped under their arms.

A few moments later, two more men stepped out and stood at attention on either side of the door. For a moment all was still, then Lord Mosby's pink head appeared in the open door, one hand held fast to the top of his head to prevent the wind from lifting the carefully arranged gray wisps of his comb-over. In his other hand he carried an overstuffed, tattered briefcase, which he handed to one of his waiting aides.

Mosby stepped clear of the helicopter with the unlikely little hop of a heavy man showing he can be light on his feet, then hitched the belt of his sagging trousers over his ample paunch.

A harried aide jogged across the roof toward him, one hand on the top of his head in a futile effort to preserve his own carefully arranged hair. In his other hand he clutched Lord Mosby's schedule for the day.

"Morning, Gerard," Lord Mosby called into the wind as his aide came abreast of him. "What's on the docket?"

"Good morning, sir. We've had a spot of trouble with your conference call with the Japanese, so we've shifted things around. I thought you'd want to see the Americans first. They're having coffee in the conference room."

Lord Mosby tucked his head down and plunged toward the open rooftop door. "Who's here, exactly?" he shouted.

"It's quite a delegation I'm afraid, sir. There's Miss Klarwine, of course. With her is Dawson Segura from your New York publishing house, and two lawyers, a Mr. Horwitz representing Mr. Segura and one from Paris, a Monsieur André Guibbaud."

"I know Guibbaud. Good man. What's he doing here?"

"I believe he's the lady's personal representative, sir."

"The lady?" Lord Mosby said, absentmindedly.

"Yes, sir. Madame Cleo. She's here as well."

They had just stepped inside the rooftop entrance. Lord Mosby abruptly stopped at the top of the stairs, causing a jam-up of aides in the small space between the door and the stairs. "You mean she's *here?*"

"Why, yes, sir. Is that a problem, sir?"

Lord Mosby shook his head a bit too forcefully. "No . . . no. That's quite all right. It will be interesting to meet the lady," he blustered. With that he turned and plunged down the carpeted staircase, pulling the others behind him like a gray whale leading a school of pilot fish.

The Mosby Media building was world headquarters for Lord Mosby's media empire. Mosby Media owned newspapers, magazines, film companies, and television properties in America and in Europe. The thirty-four-story building, a black-glass and cement monstrosity, was so architecturally inappropriate for its mid-London location, and so aesthetically annoying, that it had been publicly criticized by Prince Charles before it was even finished.

Lord Mosby's rooftop arrivals were cause for an all-hands-on-deck alert to the executive staff on the top floor. As Mosby and his men moved through the carpeted hall that led to the conference room, wide-eyed employees peeked from doorways, and those unfortunate enough to be caught in the hall scrambled for cover.

For all of his heft, Mosby moved faster than his younger, more fit traveling companions. When he reached the end of the hall he extended both arms and flat-handed the mahogany doors to the conference room. The heavy doors whipped back, striking the burnished walnut walls with a resounding *thwack* that caused those seated around the long conference table to jump in their chairs. Everyone, that is, except Ula Divers, Lord Mosby's secretary, who was so executive that she had two secretaries of her own. Ula was seated at the far end of the gleaming table next to Lord Mosby's empty chair. When everyone else jumped, Ula didn't even look up. She was long accustomed to Lord Mosby's entrances.

The people seated at the table drinking coffee from exquisite Royal Crown Derby cups regained their composure like a startled flock of birds resettling themselves on a perch. The men patted their expensive ties. The two women smiled politely and put down their cups.

Lord Mosby circled the table maintaining his familiar crouch. He shook hands and nodded as Ula introduced everyone, mumbling "'ello-'ello-'ow-ah-you-fine-fine" as he went.

He reached Madame Cleo last and extended his hand. "Madame," Lord Mosby said, lowering his pale jutting eyebrows. As he bent to brush his lips across the back of her hand she greeted him in heavily accented English. "How do you do, Lord Mosby." As he straightened she whispered, "*Bonjour*, Billy darling."

For a woman who would never see sixty again, she was lovely. Small and slender with perfect posture, she was dressed completely in gray cashmere. Her calf-length dress was covered by a long matching coat lined with pale pink silk. Around her neck looped ropes of pink pearls of such size and luster a single bead would have been worth a fortune. Her chin-length bone-colored hair was cut bluntly at the jaw and brushed back from her high forehead to emphasize her remarkable eyes, silver irises rimmed with black.

Wolf's eyes, Mosby thought, as he hesitated for an instant to stare at her. Knowing his back was to the others, he winked.

Mosby took his seat at the head of the long table, glancing briefly at the pile of memos Ula had slipped along the table for him to read. He pushed them aside and looked up at the eager faces around the table. "Shall we begin?" he asked briskly.

Wendy Klarwine cleared her throat. Lord Mosby had always wondered why she described herself on her letterhead as a "literary" agent. There was certainly nothing literary about the business he had done with her in the past.

Wendy Klarwine was short, sharp, and tough—a fuzzy ferret in a hard-edged business suit in the wrong shade of blue. Klarwine had a knack for representing the kinds of properties that made Mosby's publications headlines and money. She specialized in personalities, their stories and scandals. They were people who could not write themselves but were teamed with hacks Klarwine also represented, sometimes as pure ghostwriters, often with shared bylines. Finding a writer to grind out the sensational stories Klarwine sold Mosby Media at enormously inflated prices was never his problem. He was not interested in how the package was put together, simply the final result and how shocking the headline would be.

Often her clients' stories were big enough to warrant full-length books that Mosby published through Haddon Brooks, the American publishing arm of his empire, a once venerable company named after the two patrician old men from whom he had purchased it. Rumor had it that the change from fine works of literature (for which Haddon Brooks was deservedly famous) to the scandal-mongering volumes being published under the new Mosby management had sent the newly rich Mr. Haddon and Mr. Brooks to early graves.

Since the Mosby takeover, the Klarwine agency had sold Haddon Brooks the ghosted works of conspiracy buffs, whistle-blowers, defectors, and spies. Operators who found Grassy Knollists, UFO kidnap victims, or Elvis at a mall knew to call Wendy Klarwine first. In short order she would find a high-speed writer and a publisher with a fat checkbook and would arrange worldwide syndication of the tale to be told. It only had to be plausible. It helped if the subject owned a clean shirt and could sit upright long enough to speak on television but that wasn't a must. Wendy made millions for everyone—her clients, the publishers, and herself.

When Wendy had contacted Mosby the week before, saying she was representing Madame Cleo's memoirs, he had been taken aback. Mosby had known Madame Cleo for years. It was a highly personal relationship, one he simply did not discuss. Considering the lady's profession and contacts—by definition secretive and discreet—he found it hard to believe what Wendy was shouting over the transatlantic phone line about. He had taken the time to try to reach Madame Cleo at her home in Paris but without success. The only way to satisfy his curiosity had been to agree to the meeting about to take place.

It was shocking that Madame Cleo was actually present. It meant that she was prepared to do what Wendy swore was true, produce her memoirs. This was a most astonishing publishing coup for Wendy, and Mosby intended to buy the book at any price. But first he had to know why his old friend would do something so unthinkable.

Wendy opened a large black crocodile briefcase and placed a hand-sized tape recorder on the table. "It goes without saying that everything we say here is in the strictest confidence."

"That won't be necessary, Wendy," Mosby said, nodding toward the machine.

Wendy looked undone for an instant and glanced across the table at the two lawyers.

"You can have a copy of my tape," Mosby said with a grin. "This room is wired."

With an embarrassed chuckle, Wendy slipped her machine back into the briefcase and cleared her throat, again. "Lord Mosby," she said, lifting her chin, "we are here, as you know, to discuss the memoirs of Madame Cleo. We are offering world rights to the book for an advance of four million U.S. dollars. We can work out the royalties later. Our main purpose this morning is to reach an agreement on the price."

"That's a lot of money," Mosby said.

"That's world rights, Lord Mosby. That would include the book for your American publisher"—she gestured toward Dawson Segura to her left—"serialization in any or all of your magazines and newspapers, and translation rights in all non-English-speaking countries. I think it's a fair price. What Madame will reveal will be of international interest. As you know, her career has spanned five decades, she has known the most powerful, the most influential . . . ."

Lord Mosby held up his hand. "Don't oversell, Miss Klarwine. I'm well aware of who your client is and the possibilities of what she may have to say. There are, however, some questions I'd like to ask Madame Cleo."

"Of course," Wendy said, too eagerly.

"In private."

Wendy's happy expression faded. She looked back to the lawyers. Both were frowning. Dawson Segura dropped his eyes to avoid involvement in the awkward turn of events.

"Well, I, ah . . ." Wendy began, clearly flustered.

Mosby knew he had presented her with an agent's nightmare: permitting an uncoached client time alone with a potential buyer. There was an uncomfortable silence around the table until André Guibbaud, Madame Cleo's Paris lawyer, spoke up. Unlike Segura and the American lawyer, Guibbaud was not in the employ of Mosby Media. Guibbaud turned to Madame Cleo and asked her in French, "Is that all right with you, Madame?"

Madame Cleo, who had been sitting quietly staring at a copy of Monet's *Houses of Parliament* on the far wall, smiled sweetly and lowered her eyes. "Of course," she said.

Mosby stood. "Miss Divers," he said, addressing his secretary, "would you see to fresh coffee for everyone. Perhaps a glass of preluncheon sherry would be in order. Excuse us, please."

As Mosby and Madame Cleo moved toward the double door, an aide who had been standing to one side stepped forward. Waving him off, Mosby swooped out of the room.

He steered Madame Cleo down the long hall and into the privacy of his vast office, where he closed the door.

"Do sit down, my dear," he said, pointing toward a leather chair in front of his desk. He took a seat behind the desk, removed his glasses, and rubbed his hand around his face as though to wash it of fatigue. Then he scowled at her. "All right," he demanded, "where have you been? I've been trying to reach you ever since Wendy Klarwine called. I can't believe you're going through with this madness."

"Darling, don't scold," Madame Cleo said, her pale eyes pleading.

"I had Ula ring the house in Paris, then the country house. Really, darling. Why for pity's sake didn't you come to me directly if you needed help?" His voice softened a bit even though he was still upset with her.

A single tear trailed down her cheek. "You couldn't reach me, Billy darling, because I was in jail." Trembling, she reached for her handbag and extracted a handkerchief bordered with heavy Belgian lace. "Can you believe it? In jail!"

"That's preposterous!" Mosby shouted.

"They threw me in a cell with the most disgusting women. There was blood all over the floor. You wouldn't believe how they treated me. They came to the house like brigands. There I was in a beautiful Dior gown being hauled off like a common criminal! At first they wouldn't let me use the phone. And to think of the money I have paid the police all these years! Finally, Martin and my darling lawyer got me out after paying a preposterous bail."

"I am appalled," Mosby said, shaking his head. "How did it come to this?"

"Oh, Billy, I've pursued every possible avenue of escape. My friends in the government can keep them from closing my business, but no one can stop the tax man. And his money, he says, must be clean. I've run out of time and options."

"Good Lord, what a spot."

"Now you see why I must sell my memoirs. That is the only way I can raise the money. You know, it's the money they want, not me. As long as they know I've made this sale, and the money will be coming in, they won't be coming to arrest me in the night like Nazis." She offered Mosby a black cigarillo from a jeweled case.

He shook his head and reached across the desk to light hers for her. "You, of all people," he said sadly. "A lifetime of discretion and trust spread out like so much cold meat on a buffet."

"It won't be cold meat, darling," she said more calmly. "It will be a boiling stew. Possibly poisoned," she added, exhaling a long stream of gray smoke.

"Just to follow the analogy, my dear, I would hope there would be some ingredients left out."

She pushed back a lock of pale hair and anchored it behind her ear. "You know I would never betray you, Billy."

"It's not me I'm concerned about. I couldn't bear to have Lady Mosby hurt."

"Ah"—Madame Cleo's expression softened—"our darling SueBee. How is she? And the baby?"

"Beautiful," Mosby said, beaming. "To my utter joy. Both of them. I don't want to see them hurt, ever."

"This would be your book, too, Billy. You understand."

Lord Mosby stared into the middle distance for a long moment considering his decision. There was no question in his mind as to the sensational nature of the memoirs or the financial rewards. But once the project got under way, would he be able to control it? He knew all about Cleo's ego. If he pressed her to make changes she didn't like, there would be other publishers waiting in the wings. And who would write it for her? Could he control the writer, as well?

Finally, he said, "What about your wealthy friends?"

"I couldn't ask you, or any of my friends, to give me such a sum."

"Someone could lend it to you."

"I wouldn't ask any of the people who have been so good to me over the years to launder money for me," she said, suddenly all business. "I have come with the most valuable thing I own: my life. I am offering it to you to buy my freedom." She fixed him with her wolf's eyes. "I would never betray you, Billy. Never. If you don't believe that, our business is finished this moment."

"Four million dollars, sixteen million francs, two million pounds. That's an interesting figure. How much do you actually owe the government?"

"Three million."

"And the extra million?"

"Wendy says that's what I'll need to pay a good writer."

"So much?"

"For the right one. Besides, dear Billy, I certainly can't do it without one."

Lord Mosby rubbed his chin for a long moment, staring into the space between himself and his old friend. "All right, Cleo. I'll do it. But on one condition."

Madame Cleo cocked her head and eyed him suspiciously.

"I must have the last say. Anything I don't approve of in the finished manuscript is out."

"I, too, have a condition," she said. "I don't want a word of this made public until the book is finished."

"Then we have a deal," he said. He stood, walked across the Persian rug, and pulled her to her feet. He reached down and gently brushed her cheek. It felt cool and smooth. "You are going to upset a lot of people, my dear."

Madame Cleo looked up at him and smiled. "Is that not the part of this that excites us both?"

For many years he had been married to Selena Ortund-Wick, the pleasant daughter of the sixth duke of Relling. They had produced two sons, now grown. His marriage, brilliant in appearance, was in reality a sorry, dull arrangement. His wife satisfied many of his professional and social needs, but none of his personal ones. The Ortund-Wicks, in their turn, always felt Mosby was somewhat of a bullying vulgarian. Because he could not bear to compound their opinion of him with even a hint of his unusual private desires, he had turned to the discreet services of the infamous Madame Cleo in order to satisfy them.

He had been using Cleo's girls, among others, since his days at Oxford. Only through prostitutes and their paid, nonjudgmental participation in his fantasy life was he able to find release.

Early in his marraige, he had rented rooms in another part of the city under a fictitious name. He planned for the apartment to provide his sanctuary, a hideaway where he could satisfy the demons that had obsessed him since boyhood.

One bedroom of the three-room apartment was set aside for gowns. Racks of accessories, wigs, high-heeled pumps, and opera-length gloves. There was an armoire tall enough to accommodate the full-length gowns, capes, and feather boas. Each splendid outfit had been custom-made by a seamstress of Madame Cleo's acquaintance in size forty-eight long.

Mosby retained a decorator, letting him believe that he was setting up a mistress. The bedroom was a shrine worthy of a movie queen, a sea of white satin, white fur rugs, and lace-covered pillows, drenched in the pink light cast by low, silk-shaded lamps.

When it was finished, Mosby dismissed the decorator, having saved the last essential touch to do himself. His fantasy theater now needed its most important element: an audience.

Cleo dispatched an exquisite redhead. The girl had either been instructed carefully or was a born, imaginative actress. Mosby did not have to do a thing. She immediately fell into the routine, calling him Daphne, helping him to the Art Deco dressing table in the all-white bedroom. She proceeded to make him up more beautifully than he had ever been able to do himself. She worked with the sable brushes she had brought with her, applying different subtle shades of foundation and blusher. Painstakingly, she pasted on long black lashes, one lash at a time, expertly layering on three muted tones of eye shadow.

While she worked she gaily chatted about the spring showings in Paris, what the couture designers were up to that season. She dropped tidbits of gossip about celebrities and stars, information that his own newspapers had yet to print. She was, he knew, talking to him as though he were her closest girlfriend. Under his gown, which she had carefully covered with a protective cloth, his excitement began to build.

She finished the face, then she expertly combed and teased a spectacularly lifelike long dark wig and led him to the oval looking glass beside the armoire.

He gasped in ecstasy, afraid he would reach orgasm too soon. She had found the woman he had dreamed was inside him.

He commanded himself to show restraint. He didn't want the evening to end.

Throughout that memorable night they were always two girls together, drinking wine, listening to Vivaldi, speaking of the things only women can discuss, their feelings, their dreams.

Then, without warning, she made a suggestion so startling, so unthinkable, that Lord Billy Mosby began to shake uncontrollably.

"I can't, I can't," he had said in a trembling voice.

"Of course you can, Daphne, darling," she had cooed. She walked to the armoire, selected a cape, and laid it over his bare shoulders. "This is going to be very exciting."

"Please don't," he said. He was beginning to hyperventilate.

She ignored his condition. "Just around the park tonight. Then perhaps, if you're good, next time we can stop in the pub at the corner. We'll sit way in the back where it's dark. Come on now. You'll see."

He tore the cape from his shoulders. "Stop it!" he shouted. His voice was no longer the falsetto he affected during their games. "Don't ever suggest such a thing again. Now you've ruined everything."

He had hurt her feelings. She didn't understand. His fear and distress came not from the possibility of discovery but from his overwhelming and erotic longing to do exactly the thing she was so casually suggesting. To appear in public as a woman had been one of the most urgent suppressed desires of his life. In the apartment he could control the fantasy. If ever he ventured into the real world outside, he feared he would never be in control of his obsession again.

The expression on the girl's face made him realize how rude he had been. They had been having such a delightful time and she had been so sweet. "Oh, my dear," he had said, taking her hand. "Please, forgive me. You don't understand."

Michelle slipped to the floor and rested her head against his knee. "Of course, I do, Daphne. I spoke too soon," she said softly. "Perhaps it would help if I made a little suggestion. Something for you to try. It will be our secret."

From that night forward, Lord Billy Mosby had been wearing women's underthings beneath his business clothes. As his obsession continued, so, too, did his guilt.

If he were ever to chronicle his own life, as Madame Cleo was planning to do hers, he would mark 1987 as the time of his rebirth, the beginning of a life free of the demons of that guilt. It had happened on a starlit night in the Loire Valley at the château of a wealthy French baron. He had taken his after-dinner brandy out onto the terrace to avoid speaking to people he didn't want or need to know. He was just raising his glass to his lips when he heard a soft voice behind him asking if he wanted company. He turned to see a very pretty blonde with large, expressive blue eyes. He recognized her as one of the ladies the baron had imported for his guests' amusement—a Madame Cleo girl.

Later, alone in his room, she watched as he undressed. He waited for a faint twinge of distaste or even surprise when she saw what he was wearing under his dinner clothes. It did not come. As he revealed the scarlet brassiere he was wearing, she walked toward him. "Here, let me do that," she said, gently helping him remove his silk shirt.

By the next morning all of the girls had disappeared, but to his amazement she agreed to ride with him later in the day. Afterward, they returned to his room in the château and spent an afternoon in an erotic haze, acting out his fantasies to the fullest. No one had ever brought him such joy and release. For the first time in his life, he had fallen in love. He offered her anything she wanted to stay on with him but she refused, saying only that she wanted nothing more than to be with him as long as he wanted her.

The subsequent week they spent together in Paris in a suite at the Crillon was the most exhilarating time he had ever known. By day they made love and slept. By night, they walked the streets of the Left Bank, dining in out-of-the-way cafés and dancing together in the darkened clubs of the demimonde where two women, at least two people who appeared to be women, could dance together until dawn. On their last day together she told him her real name and only then because he asked her to leave Madame Cleo and live with him until he could get his divorce.

Susanna Beatrice Slyde. His darling SueBee. The person to whom he had ceded total control of his life. A life that without her would be unlivable. The least he owed her was the obliteration of her past. And what better way to accomplish that than by controlling anything Madame Cleo might reveal about it?

CHAPTER
4

Peter was a few minutes late to meet Fedalia for lunch. Expecting a happy face, he was surprised to find Fiddle staring morosely into her wine as he slid onto the red leather power banquette in the front of the Russian Tea Room.

He tilted his head and tried to see the expression on her half-hidden face. "You okay, pal?" he asked, mildly concerned.

"No," she said, without looking up.

"What's the matter?" he asked, looking around for the waiter as he snapped his napkin open and spread it across his knees. "I'm supposed to be your crisis center. How come you didn't call me?"

Slowly, she looked up at him. "This is a very fresh crisis."

"I like the monocle. New?"

Fedalia touched the monocle she was wearing in her right eye. A black silk cord dangled against her cheek. "Came in the mail. Part of a promotional thing for a documentary on PBS. I'm feeling decidedly Weimar Republic today so I wore it."

The waiter poured Peter some wine from the bottle already on the table and disappeared. "It gives you a nice Prussian flair. I think you should wear it all the time."

Fedalia looked around as if to be sure her words would not be overheard. "Peter, you keep secrets, right?"

"You know I do, Fiddle."

"Okay. I'm bursting to tell you something. The only thing you have to promise is not to tell where you heard it."

"Promise," Peter said casually, holding up an open palm.

"Wendy Klarwine called me this morning. She's got a project that is so exciting I wish it were done this minute. It's a big fat secret. The only reason she told me is that part of the deal is that we'll publish excerpts."

"Maybe you shouldn't tell me, Fiddle," Peter said, then grinned. "But I hope you do. Just hold on a minute." Peter signaled the waiter again, then turned to Fedalia. "You want your blinis, right?"

"Right."

He ordered for Fiddle, and a chicken salad for himself. Fedalia tucked her napkin into the throat of her blouse, nursing-home style, in anticipation of her lunch. After a year and a half of working with her, she still surprised him. At first, he thought her strange habits were affectations. In time, he realized that Fedalia Null was completely herself, unique.

Since they'd ordered their usuals, it was only a few minutes before the waiter placed their food on the table.

"Okay, Fiddle, shoot."

She leaned toward him as far as her ample chest would permit. "Madame Cleo is going to do her memoirs," she whispered.

Peter let the information sink in for a moment. "Holy cow," he said slowly. "How did that happen?"

"A combination of forces, I'm told," she said, fixing her eyes on Peter. "But that's not the important part."

"Oh?" he said, his fork in midair.

"She will pay a writer one cool million to write it in her voice with all those juicy secrets she's been collecting for years." Fedalia jabbed her fork into her soft blini for emphasis.

"Some job!" Peter said appreciatively.

Fedalia nodded.

"Who's the publisher?"

"Haddon Brooks, of course."

"Do they have to approve the writer?"

Fedalia nodded. Her mouth was full. She swallowed and said, "Madame Cleo has to approve and then Dawson Segura. He's such a blue-ribbon prick. I love it that he has to handle a book like this. He'll probably use tongs on every page, he's so damn fancy. Like publishing *The Insects of Walden Pond* pays his six-figure salary?"

"Well! That's all very exciting," Peter said, keeping his tone nonchalant. He knew what Fiddle was building up to but he wanted to hear her say it.

"Peter, are you being deliberately thick, or what?"

"Sorry?"

Fedalia put down her fork and sighed. "This one's for you, babe. If ever there was a perfect subject and the perfect writer it's Madame Cleo and Peter Shea. All you have to do is call Wendy and tell her you're available. She'll flip. She gets to double-dip on the commission, she gets one of the best writers in America and . . . well, forget what you get. I'm drooling already."

"But, Fiddle, I've written about Cleo—or, at least, the girl with the drowning-pool eyes—before."

"Oh, Peter, who cares? You're the best she can get. And you'll be working for her."

Peter spied a salt stick in the breadbasket and automatically handed it to Fiddle. "Here, your favorite."

Fiddle took it, saying, "Don't be evasive. What do you think about the book?"

Peter shrugged. "How long do you think it would take? I mean, to do the book?"

Fedalia's fork paused in midair. "So you do want it," she said, smiling.

Peter took a long sip of wine and wondered if he had come far enough, grown easy enough with himself, to admit he wanted something even when it was being handed to him. In the old days, before he had gone quite mad, it had killed him to be direct. If he wanted something, he made the right phone calls, squeezed the favors owed, dropped pointed hints to those who could make things happen for him. Anything but straightforward honesty. To let someone know you wanted something made you vulnerable. It telegraphed your need. He was nothing, in the old days, but needy.

His need to avenge his firing had driven him to wangle an invitation to the White House correspondents dinner. The night of the dinner he had boarded the shuttle wearing his tux so that anyone, stranger or peer, who saw him would know where he was going, would know that he wasn't a failure. That he, Peter Shea, was still invited to important events.

Drunk and high on pills his doctor had told him not to take if he drank, he had marched to the dais in the grand ballroom of a Washington hotel and grabbed the microphone away from the bewildered dean of the White House press corps. There, in front of congressmen and senators, cabinet members and the world press, he had turned to the president of the United States and told of the injustices he had suffered. In his crazed ranting, he began to describe an exotic sexual encounter at a French château in language so explicit that not a soul in the huge ballroom dared move. People seemed to realize, all at the same time, what they were witnessing, and the vast room exploded in shocked fury. Through the haze of his rage he heard a shout. He felt rough hands upon his shoulders and voices in his ears. He was pulled, still ranting, from the stage. The last thing he remembered was lying on the dusty floor behind a curtain. He was surrounded by Secret Service men talking urgently into their lapels. He felt the sharp sting of a needle being plunged through his tuxedo trousers. Then nothing.

He never read the coverage of his professional suicide in the national press nor did he see it on the evening news provided by the network cameramen who had been in the ballroom to cover the president's remarks. Nor did he read the speculation the next day that an attempt on the president's life had been feared.

Later, his doctor at Silver Hill told him as much as he wanted to know, as much as he could stand at the time, cautioning him that to dwell upon it would only slow his recovery. He had so much to learn about starting to live again. The road back seemed so complicated, so overwhelming, that he despaired of ever sorting it out. His moral compass was irrevocably smashed. Each day seemed another black hole on the road, another sheer drop to an angry, roiling sea around every hairpin turn.

They permitted him to go home to his Village apartment more because his medical coverage had run out than because he was well enough to live alone. The healing had taken a year.

It had taken him a week to respond to Fiddle's invitation to set up an appointment. It had taken a month for him to agree to do the piece about his downfall for her magazine.

The article had not won the Pulitzer Prize, but it had earned him a life in the real world. His phone rang for days after publication. Wendy arranged a speaking tour and the "Today" show booker called. Publishers wanted to know if he thought there was a book in his story. He turned the "Today" show and the publishers down. All he had to say was in the article. Done was done and tomorrow was the bigger deal. He was free.

"Well?" Fiddle said. She had been waiting patiently for him to come to a decision.

"If I call Wendy, she'll know you're a fink and can't keep a secret."

"It's for a good cause, Peter. I'll take the heat if there is any. My feeling is that she'll be so thrilled she'll forget she told me not to tell."

"Why don't you order dessert, Fiddle. I'll call her now," he said, jiggling his pocket for a quarter.

"Five-five-five seven-two-nine-eight. Her phone's in her purse," she said with a knowing smile. "She's having lunch at Aurora."

"Got it," Peter said with a grin as he headed for the pay phone by the bar.

Wendy Klarwine liked getting calls at her table at Aurora. She excused herself and lifted a portable phone from her gigantic combination handbag–briefcase–overnight bag and hummed a seductive hello. Her warm mood was short-lived.

"I want to do the Madame Cleo book," Peter said without preamble.

"Jesus H. Christ!" Wendy shrieked. "How the fuck did you find out about that? Damn it! There are no secrets!"

"Not from people like us, Wendy love."

"Who told you, Peter? I demand to know."

"It's a secret," he said, enjoying her discomfort.

"Fedalia Null told you, didn't she, that cow."

"Look, Wendy"—Peter said, wincing at the insult to his friend—"I know. Okay? And I want a shot at it." He could tell Wendy was about to shift gears. He knew a lot of her response was for the benefit of her luncheon companion.

"Come by the office around three," she cooed. "We'll talk. This could be a very exciting arrangement."

He promised to do so and listened to her gush for another minute before hanging up. Of course this could be an exciting project. Fifteen percent of Madame Cleo's advance and fifteen percent of his would excite any agent.

He didn't care. Not about the commission. Not about the advance, and, frankly, not a whole lot about an old flesh peddler with tales to tell. It was the tales themselves that intrigued him like nothing had in a long time. In those tales lay the secret of who had gotten him fired and the whereabouts of the girl with the drowning-pool eyes.

Peter knew the tiny twinge of guilt he felt as he rejoined Fiddle in the booth could be quickly dispelled with an immediate confession. He began to speak as he eased himself into his seat.

"She knows you told me," he said.

"What did she say?"

"She said there're no secrets."

"No, I mean about the deal. Is she going to put you in the picture?"

"Apparently so. We have a meeting at three."

"You'll get it," Fiddle said, reaching across the table and giving his hand a reassuring squeeze.

"You really think so?"

"Absolutely," Fiddle said with an emphatic nod. "Just one thing, Peter."

"What?"

"Don't trust anyone."

"Huh?"

"This is a big, big splashy deal. Everyone involved is going to want a piece of the glory. Don't trust Wendy. Don't trust Madame Cleo not to pull something herself down the line. I don't care if everyone signs contracts and affidavits and confidentiality agreements in their own bodily fluids. No one, and I mean no one, can resist a publicity vehicle like this book is going to be."

Peter laughed despite the discomfort of having Fiddle rain on his parade. He wanted this book very badly and was willing to ignore any vague negatives. "You're such a cynic, Fiddle, me girl. Why do you say that?"

"Because Wendy is right," she said. "There are no secrets."

Wendy Klarwine prided herself on being a "closer." A deal was just hot air until it closed. The part of being an agent she loathed was the sitting-around part. The endless hours in meetings and on the phone where 90 percent of what was said was gasbagging and ego-tripping.

After her meeting with Peter that afternoon, she knew she was at that part of the Cleo deal that she relished: making it work.

The Cleo deal had to work. It wasn't just the enormous commission; she enjoyed a healthy income. What she craved more than the money was the rush that came from all the attention garnered by being the moving force behind a glamorous project.

Over time, she could make the same kind of money selling the definitive history of the insurance industry, but there was no psychic income in such projects, no personal applause, and certainly not a chance of hearing and seeing her name in electronic and print media.

For the rest of the week after her meeting with Peter, Wendy was seldom off the phone. Neither the phone console on her desk nor the one next to her bed at night stopped the continuous blinking of waiting calls from the lawyers of all the parties concerned.

She knew she had to move fast. It wasn't difficult to discern that Madame Cleo was the reluctant party; her lawyers had been dragging their feet since they all agreed to the deal in London. Besides, she knew Peter Shea was lying awake at night spending the money in his head, and after all, she reminded herself, he was her client, too. If good things happened to him, good things happened to her.

Finally, her ability as a "closer" paid off and she was able to make the most satisfying call of all.

"Congratulations, Peter. I hope I didn't wake you."

"You mean it's a done deal?" Peter said in disbelief.

"Signed and sealed. The contracts just oozed out of my fax machine with all the right signatures at the bottom."

"You're amazing, Wendy."

"Just doing my job, sweetie," she said. Then, unable to leave a compliment alone, she asked, "But why do you say that?"

"Well, you've sold me without the woman even meeting me. What if she doesn't like me?"

"She will. You'll see soon enough. I've booked you on an Air France flight on Monday. Is that okay?"

"Well, yeah, it's great," Peter said.

"Peter, is there something wrong?"

"No, no," he said. "It's just that it's all come together so smoothly. I can't believe it's actually going to happen."

"Believe it, doll," Wendy said. "We did it. It'll be the biggest book of the decade. Congratulations!"

And it would be, too, Wendy thought to herself as Peter thanked her again and she hung up the phone. Indeed, it was the deal of a lifetime. In fact, it was just too good to keep to herself. There was one more call she would have to make.

"I knew it!" Fiddle shrieked as she opened the *Times*, reading the headline of a boxed story at the top of the page.

She jumped up from the kitchen table, tightening the sash of her terry-cloth robe as she stepped to the coffee machine and poured a second cup. She finished reading the article and carried her coffee cup to the phone. Her hand trembled with anger as she punched in Peter's number.

He answered on the first ring, sounding far too wide awake. "Shea here," he said brightly.

"You see the paper?" Fiddle said.

"Morning, Fiddle. And, no, not yet. Wait, let me go get it."

"No, don't bother. I'm so mad I want to read it to you."

"Oh, Christ, what now?"

"Your darling, wonderful, miraculous bitch agent just couldn't keep her trap shut. I warned you, Peter. Remember what I told you that day at lunch? Don't trust anybody."

"Whoa, hold on, kid. What the hell is going on?"

Fiddle clenched her teeth and read the headline to him with a slow growl. "'American Publisher Signs Seven-Figure Deal for Madam's Memoirs.'"

"Oh, shit, no," Peter said under his breath. "But why are you blaming Wendy?"

"Just listen, then you can tell me," Fiddle said, cradling the phone on her shoulder and snapping the paper under the counter light. "'Haddon Brooks, the American book publisher owned by Mosby Media International, confirmed late yesterday that it has signed the notorious French madam known as "Madame Cleo" to write her life story. Haddon Brooks publisher Dawson T. Segura called the agreement "precedent setting."' Isn't that cute?" Fiddle asked, interrupting herself. "This deal is so secret Dawson Segura wouldn't even talk to me about it, but let the *Times* call and he's a regular Zsa Zsa Gabor."

"Go on, Fiddle," Peter said.

"'Madame Cleo has long been a mysterious figure among the international jet set. She is said to have controlled a prostitution network of the most beautiful and sophisticated women in the business, netting millions in fees.'" Fiddle took a deep breath. "Okay, here's the part. Ready?"

"Sure," Peter responded.

Fiddle raised her voice. "'According to New York literary agent Wendy Klarwine, who negotiated the complicated agreements, Madame Cleo will cowrite the book with *Fifteen Minutes* magazine correspondent Peter Shea.

"'Miss Klarwine, who also represents Madame Cleo, told the *Times*, "She is one of the most fascinating and colorful women of our time. Her life story will be the publishing event of the new decade. Her collaborator, Peter Shea, is one of America's most distinguished journalists. We couldn't have dreamed of a more exciting combination of experience and skill."'" Fiddle stopped reading and leaned her head against the wall. "Peter, I'm going to barf."

"Keep going," Peter said sharply.

"'Sir William Mosby, who, as the owner of Mosby Media, purchased the rights to the memoir, could not be reached for confirmation of the price paid for the unusual acquisition.'"

"That's it?" Peter asked as Fiddle fell silent.

"It? It?" Fiddle shouted into the phone. "I don't believe you, Peter. What I just read can, very likely, queer this deal. I can't imagine Madame Cleo's fancy Paris lawyers will be thrilled. They may pull out altogether."

"Wendy says everyone's signed everything. How can they pull out?"

"They can claim breach of confidentiality. Peter, Madame Cleo has insisted on this all being hush-hush from the beginning," Fiddle said, feeling her anger at Wendy spilling over to include Peter. "I'll bet her phone is jumping off the hook with clients who are scared crapless with this news, not to mention some of her former girls. I can't tell you how angry I am. Aren't you angry, Peter?"

"Only if this truly cancels the deal."

"And other than that?" Fiddle knew she was pushing for him to join her in blaming Wendy, but she didn't care.

"No," Peter said quietly. "You know why?"

Fiddle took a deep, exasperated breath, "No, Peter, why?"

"Because it feels good."

"What?" Fiddle shouted. "Being mentioned in the paper?"

"Yup."

Fiddle felt like screaming. "Peter Shea!" she exploded. "You're no better than Wendy Klarwine. You two are the party animals of ego. I can't stand it. I'll talk to you later. Maybe in this lifetime, maybe not."

When Fiddle slammed down the phone, Peter shrugged. He knew she wouldn't stay mad at him. Maybe if her name had been mentioned she wouldn't have been so angry. Dear Fiddle, he thought. So street smart, so bright, always ahead of the curve and on target about life. Didn't she know he had spent his life watching perfectly normal, self-effacing people turn into whores at the sound of a journalist's voice asking questions that would lead to the correct spelling of their names for all the world to see over morning coffee?

No, he decided, the piece in the morning paper wouldn't queer the deal. He would be on the plane to Paris Monday, off on his new adventure.

Or so he believed, until first thing Monday morning, when the phone rang.

"Don't get on the plane," Wendy barked.

Peter felt his heart sink. "Why not?" he asked, afraid to hear the answer.

"Madame Cleo's gone to London. She says something urgent's come up, something about the business. She says she'll see you later in the week."

"What's she doing in London?" he asked, trying hard to sound casual.

"Peter, I don't know," Wendy whined a whine Peter hated. It was an insulting sound, a whine that held a "stupid schmuck" implication that drove him nuts.

"You don't suppose she went to see Mosby about the article, do you?" Peter asked, giving in to his paranoia.

"Peter, the entire world is not wired to your butt. Maybe she went to shop. Maybe she's having a face-lift. Who cares?" Wendy shouted. "I'll call you when I know something. In the meantime, cool it. Things will work out."

The next few days were the worst of Peter's life since he left the ha-ha hotel in Connecticut. He had no assignments to work on. His apartment was packed up and ready to hibernate while he was away. His editor and best friend was pissed at him, his agent was pissed at him. The deal of a lifetime was probably coming apart at the seams and there wasn't a damn thing he could do about it. He couldn't think, he couldn't sleep, booze only made him angry, and he couldn't have gotten laid if he wanted to. Why pay a call girl if you can't get it up?"

He was watching a panel of complaining lesbian bikers on Geraldo when the phone rang for the first time since Wendy had hung up on him.

"Grab your socks, big guy," Wendy now said exuberantly. "You're on your way."

"It's on?" Peter asked biting his lip.

"It's on, we're on, she's on," Wendy trilled. "She'll see you tomorrow."

"She isn't pissed off?"

"Not at all. Her lawyer said she can't wait to get started. So move it, fella."

Peter hung up and jumped straight into the air with a shout of enormous relief.

Later, sitting in the First Class section of the Air France night flight to Paris, he sipped a double scotch and leaned back. If the last grim days had done anything, they had reminded him once again how awful his life had been when others controlled it. Maybe the whole world wasn't wired to his butt, but if he couldn't control whether it got kicked or not, nothing else mattered.

He closed his eyes and let the exquisite face of Madeleine swim into view.

To reach the Ile de la Cité, one of the two little residential islands in the Seine, one has only to cross a small wrought-iron footbridge. To actually own one of the elegant old mansions along the tree-shaded quays bespeaks a longer journey.

Madame Cleo would never have been permitted to purchase her

house at No. 4 Quai aux Fleurs in her own notorious name and therefore she had relied on the kindness of a wealthy client to make the arrangements. Her money and his influence with the authorities brought her the house that had once been the home of Baudelaire's mistress.

She sat alone, contemplating what life would be like without the comfort and protection the beautiful old house provided. Peter Shea, the man everyone, including Billy Mosby, said was the right one to do her book, was on his way to see her to talk about how they would go about revealing the secrets she had guarded for so long.

Her extraordinary effort to save herself was about to begin in earnest.

She nervously twisted the bracelet of her multi-faceted watch to find the dial showing Paris time. Martin had promised to call when the arrangements were complete.

She pulled a worn leather-bound ledger from the top drawer and opened it to yesterday's date. Twenty girls were somewhere in Paris or London or New York. Three for sure were in Rome. Two had headed out on airplanes toward assignments lasting longer than a night. She did some quick mental arithmetic. Her fees for the last twenty-four hours would be considerable, but they would do nothing to save her. Not a hundred girls and a hundred nights would make a difference.

If she had to go to prison she would have Martin get as many pills as it would take. She would never go through that again.

She reached toward the footed silver tray on the table behind her desk. It held a crystal decanter of pear brandy and two cordial glasses. Pouring herself a glass, she took a long sip and looked up at the sound of the office door opening. Her maid peeped tentatively into the room.

"*Oui,* Nanti?" she said.

"Martin is on your private line, Madame," the tiny old Indian woman said. "He's on his way over. Do you want to speak to him before he leaves?"

"*Ah, oui,*" Madame answered eagerly, quickly reaching for the phone. "Martin? Any problems?" she asked, speaking first.

"Everything is set. If you look outside there should be a few people there already."

Madame Cleo leaned back and pulled one heavy drape aside. A white van with the call letters of a national television network was maneuvering into the space directly in front of the iron gate at the bottom of the front steps. She smiled, released the drape, and returned her attention to the phone.

"A television truck just pulled up," she said.

"Great. There's more where that came from. They should all be in place by the time Shea arrives," Martin said, speaking quickly so that his clipped English accent sounded even more pronounced.

"Does everyone know about my being shot at this morning?"

"Yes, I've phoned them all."

"Martin, you're marvelous. This is all going to work out perfectly."

The full impact of being back in Paris again didn't hit Peter until he walked through the high doors of the Ritz early on Friday morning and swung his eyes around the cool, elegant lobby. He stood for a moment, letting the bellman carrying his bags walk past him toward the desk. He felt his knees go weak as the memories flooded back. What a life he had had here once!

The three-star garden restaurant held memories of exquisite meals and the finest wines, paid for by his abused expense account, memories of violin music and moonlight and a life that could not get any better.

He pinched the bridge of his nose to clear away the thoughts and walked to the registration desk. The clerk greeted him effusively, for a Frenchman, and handed him a phone slip reporting that a Mr. Bourke-Lyon had phoned to say Madame Cleo would expect him at three that afternoon.

Refreshed from a quick nap and shower in his too-large room, Peter asked the doorman to hail him a cab. His spirits lifted when he thought he saw the doorman's eyebrows rise ever so slightly when he gave him Madame Cleo's address.

As he slipped into the back seat of the taxi he heard Wendy Klarwine's nasal admonition—"the whole world isn't wired to your butt"—and dismissed the thought.

As the cab made its way down the sloping Quai aux Fleurs, Peter noticed that the street ahead was choked with haphazardly parked cars. A television van was parked directly in front of No. 4.

"Oh, Jesus," he breathed when he saw people milling around on the sidewalk next to the van.

"*Comment?*" grumbled the driver.

"Is there a back entrance to these houses?" he asked the driver in French.

"No, Monsieur, they go right through the block to the next street. The service entrance is below the front stoop."

Peter cursed under his breath and threw a handful of francs over the back of the driver's seat. "Okay, I'll get out here."

He hadn't even slammed the cab door before he was recognized.

71

"Yo! Peter! Peter Shea!"

Peter froze. He turned to see an old competitor, Terry Duggan from United Press, standing on the sidewalk a few feet away and grinning at him.

"You old son of a bitch!" Duggan called gleefully. "Congratulations!"

Feeling slightly embarrassed, Peter moved forward and took Terry's outstretched hand. "How ya doin', Terry," he said.

"Welcome back! I read about you in the paper, man. You bit the big one, huh? Monday's *Herald Trib* said the lady here is paying you a million bucks! I'm impressed."

"Yeah . . . well . . . ." Peter said feebly. Over Terry's shoulder he recognized more familiar faces. He saw Juan Ruiz-Marti from the Paris office of *El Diario* standing a few feet down the sidewalk idly chatting with Dan Forte, the guy who had replaced Peter at WorldWide. He waved weakly as Ruiz-Marti spotted him, then turned back to Terry. "Say, what the hell is going on here, anyway?" he asked.

The wire-service reporter jerked his thumb toward the house. "Seems someone fired an Uzi at your partner in there," he said.

"What?" Peter asked, astounded. "Where? When?"

"Don't forget 'who?', 'what?', and 'why?'" Terry said with a grin.

"All of the above."

"As far as I can piece it together, this morning someone drove up alongside her car and filled it full of holes. She's fine, but we heard the car looked like a sieve."

Peter gestured to the milling crowd. "Is that why everyone's here?"

"She called a press conference."

"To talk about getting shot at?" Peter asked, incredulous.

"Who cares, man? It's like Garbo speaks. None of us has ever seen this woman in the flesh. Our photo file's got nothing on her. Nobody else does either. And here she calls a press conference in front of her house like she's Madonna or something."

Before Peter could respond, he noticed a tall man with long taxi-yellow hair waving frantically from behind one of the beveled glass windows that flanked the front door. "Excuse me, would you, Terry? Nice to see you." He turned and hurried up the stairs. As he reached the top step the front door sprang open.

As Peter stepped through the door the young man grabbed his elbow. "Where have you been? She's been waiting for you," he said, in a florid English accent.

"I don't think I've had the pleasure."

"Forgive me, Mr. Shea. I'm Madame's aide, Martin Bourke-Lyon. You *are* Peter Shea, right? You look so American."

Peter inadvertently looked down at himself. "I do?"

"Brooks Brothers blazer, khaki slacks, penny loafers," he said lightly. "If you'll just come with me. Madame is in her study."

Bourke-Lyon turned and signaled to a wizened old woman wearing a bright sari. "Nanti will show you the way."

Peter dutifully followed the Indian woman down a darkened hall to the back of the mansion.

The atmosphere in the overdecorated little room was stifling. An exotic aroma seemed to hang in the air, a mixture of whatever perfume its occupant was wearing and, oddly, cigar smoke. The heavy drapes obscured a high window, but his sense of direction told him it must face the river. As his eyes grew accustomed to the light he perceived rather than actually saw a fragile figure seated at an elaborately carved writing desk of museum quality. The figure's head was shrouded in a low, blue-tinged ring of smoke.

Peter heard the heavy door clunk shut behind him. Then, silence.

Lacking an introduction, he had to assume that the woman bending over the desk was the woman who wanted to pay him a cool million to write down her life story. He could tell by the fit of the shoulders of the beige suit she was wearing that it was expensive. Her pale hair was partially hidden by an oversize pale fur beret as she made notes from the leather-bound ledger spread out on her desk.

She held up one finger to indicate she'd be but a moment, then put down her pen and looked up at him with a dazzling smile.

"Mr. Shea," she said in a smoky voice. "You are much younger than I had imagined." She lowered her head for an instant, looking up at him through thick black lashes. "And more handsome, if I may be so personal. Please, do sit down." She gestured to the tufted couch that ran parallel to her desk.

She had not offered her hand, so Peter simply smiled and took a seat.

Madame Cleo reached for a manila envelope on her desk and held it up. "Miss Klarwine sent along some of your magazine pieces. You are a remarkable writer, Mr. Shea."

"Thank you, thank you very much," he said, utterly charmed.

"May I offer you some Poire Williams?" she asked, reaching for the decanter behind her desk.

Peter held up his hand defensively, "Thank you, no," he said smiling.

"Coffee or tea then? I'll have Nanti bring a tray."

Before Peter could protest, Madame pushed a button on her desk. She then reached for a long black cigarillo and lit it with a distinctive heavy gold lighter.

Peter needed only the split second it took her to inhale to take control of the conversation. "I was disturbed to hear about your, ah, accident," he said.

"*Oui*," she sighed through a cloud of smoke. "However, I cannot say it came as a complete surprise."

Peter's eyebrows shot up. "Truly? You mean you expected someone to try and harm you?"

"Yes," she said, tenting her fingers. "As soon as the news about the book came out I felt something bad would happen." She raised her hands and pantomimed the sweep of an automatic weapon. "My driver, I, Martin, we could all have been killed!"

"Shocking," Peter said sincerely, slowly shaking his head.

Madame blew out her cheeks in a typically French gesture of resignation. "I'm sure it does not surprise you, Mr. Shea, to hear that I have lived the kind of life that guarantees an accumulation of enemies."

Peter nodded and smiled. "And an interesting life, Madame. That's why I'm here."

He wasn't sure what he had expected, a crafty old crone perhaps, lying and slithering around about herself, making it impossible to do any kind of a halfway realistic "autobiography." He couldn't believe his luck in finding this dignified, graceful charmer instead.

"I'm a very lucky woman, Mr. Shea," she said sincerely.

"Let me ask you, Madame," he began, feeling confident enough about her reaction to ask his first pointed question, to risk it right off the bat. "Do you have any idea who might have wanted to do this to you?"

She shook her head slowly, as though thinking it over. She lifted a heavy gold lighter from the desk. "The police found only one clue at the scene," she said, handing the lighter across the desk. "A gold lighter identical to this one. They found it near the attackers' car."

Peter took the lighter, feeling its weight for a moment. "This is a handsome piece. Cartier."

"Yes," Cleo nodded. "Turn it over."

On the other side Peter saw some sort of engraved seal or crest. "What does this mean?" he asked.

"That is the family crest of a longtime client of mine. Baron Felix d'Anjou."

Peter was suddenly aware of the beating of his heart and a tightness in his throat. "La Fantastique," he croaked.

A look of surprise lit her face. "*Mon Dieu*, Mr. Shea! You know of La Fantastique?"

"I should say I do," Peter said. Now his arms felt numb and the lighter felt almost unbearably heavy. He handed it back to Madame Cleo. "I was there once. At the baron's château. The summer of nineteen eighty-seven," he said, leveling his gaze at her.

Madame Cleo's hands flew to her cheeks, and her mouth opened to emit a tiny gasp. "My," she said after she gained control. "How terribly small our world is!"

"Indeed, Madame."

"Then you met some of my girls. I always send girls. I have sent them for years. The girls who are chosen to go are given souvenirs. That's where the lighters come from. That year, it was the lighters."

"Then you must suspect one of your girls."

Madame Cleo leaned across her desk and looked directly into his face with her pale gray eyes. "Possibly," she said tentatively. "Or possibly one of the men they have known and been close to. And you, by an incredible twist of fate, Mr. Shea, have possibly met the person who tried to kill me."

Peter moved forward on the couch. He hoped his excitement didn't show, but he was riveted by the implications. "Do you have any idea which one it might have been?"

As Madame Cleo started to answer, the door opened.

"Yes, Martin?" she asked briskly, frowning at the interruption.

"The press, Madame," he said, his voice bordering on hysteria. "They're getting tired of standing around. I'm afraid if we keep them any longer they'll get hostile."

Madame Cleo jumped from her seat. "Oh dear, oh dear," she cried. "Mr. Shea had me so fascinated I completely forgot the time."

Peter stood up a split second after she did, waiting for her next move. It was *he* who was fascinated—by the woman herself, by the surroundings, and by the fateful coincidence that made La Fantastique that July in 1987 so crucial to Madame Cleo as well.

Cleo moved around from behind the desk and lightly slipped her hand under his elbow. As he looked down at her his head swam a bit from lack of sleep and too much scotch consumed crossing the Atlantic.

"Come," she said, smiling up at him. "We will go out and meet the press together."

"Together?" he asked. The smell of her perfume wasn't helping him think. "Why me?"

"But why do you think I called a press conference, Mr. Shea?" she said, lowering her eyes. "Certainly not to talk about this morning's unpleasantness."

As they passed Martin on the way to the front door, Madame reached out and squeezed the Englishman's arm as if to calm him. "Everything is going to be fine, Martin," she said. "Just fine."

As Peter stepped out into the bright Paris sunlight with the infamous Madame Cleo on his arm, it didn't matter that most of the faces looking up at them were familiar, that most of the people waiting to hear her speak were old chums and adversaries from another, darker life. He was about to quaff the heady wine of retribution, redemption, and revenge. He had returned—the million-dollar man—to receive his former peers.

CHAPTER
✑ 5 ✑

Wendy Klarwine sat at her usual table at Aurora still on a high from the morning news from Paris.

She hadn't touched her grilled salmon and had only picked at her arugula salad amid giddy conversations with people who stopped by her table. Between phone calls and the constant stream of well-wishers who had seen the morning news, her ignored luncheon companion—a client whose gothic novel had been rejected by the fifth publishing house just that morning—was growing restive.

Wendy had received a tip that Madame Cleo was holding a press conference to be broadcast, due to the time difference, on all the major network morning-news shows. She had had her VCR ready and waiting.

Not since a client who was the wife of an NFL linebacker had walked cameras into the team locker room to announce she was writing a book about his women, drugs, and payoffs had Wendy had such client coverage.

What made the morning news a double whammy was the sight of her adorable Peter Shea, so cute, so funny, so fucked up—well, fucked up until she got him back on track and made him the hottest writer in town—standing next to Madame Cleo, beaming. And well he should, she thought.

She knew a lot of people had been upset about the premature announcement of the book, but she didn't care. She always followed her instincts, and leaking the story had worked. That's when all hell broke loose. She had worried for a few days over whether the leak would be traced to her, but now that someone had tried to kill Madame Cleo, she was off the hook. Who had time to nose around her with a much bigger story to go after?

She picked a damp leaf off her salad plate and stared up at the television miniseries producer putting the moves on her for a shot at the rights. She wasn't listening. What was to hear? She was thinking how projects like this one made up for the annoyances of her work. This was such fun, so delicious. Having a client shot at! Go figure.

She heard herself saying to the TV producer, "Have your girl call my girl, we'll do lunch," which everyone knew was code for "Get out of my face, you dork."

She turned to her sulking luncheon companion. "Are you mad at me?" Wendy asked, puffing out her lower lip. "Don't be mad, lovey. I'm not going to speak to another soul. I want to talk about you."

The novelist seemed to relax and took a sip of wine.

"Now," Wendy said, batting her eyes, "let me tell you why I think they're turning down your book all over town."

About eleven o'clock Friday morning Fedalia Null wet her finger and went in search of the last golden crumbs of her breakfast chocolate croissant, which had fallen on the proofs of Marla Maples, July's cover girl. The night before she had dreamed she was floating in a raft filled with butter and gravy on a sea of mashed potatoes made with heavy cream and Parmesan cheese. What had awakened her was the sight of an oncoming wave of melted cheddar cheese rising above the raft.

She had kicked off the covers and lain very still in her dark bedroom until the panic and shallow breathing subsided. She was sublimating her desire for Peter into dreams of food. She just couldn't deal with the frustration anymore, so she dreamed not of walking in the rain with him, but of running hand-in-hand through showers of milk chocolate, puffs of marshmallows falling like rose petals. The sun-drenched deck of the sailboat where she and Peter lay entwined, tanned and nude, became a rare filet bobbing in a béarnaise ocean.

Vickie knocked and came in just as Fiddle finished her coffee.

"I taped the morning news for you. It's by your lamp," Vickie told her after a brief good morning. "Better look at it. It's you-know-who in Paris."

Fiddle grabbed the tape from the desk and shoved it into the VCR on top of the TV. Within seconds, Peter Shea's face popped onto the screen.

As she watched it she realized how happy he looked standing in front of all the microphones. She hoped the publicity wouldn't throw Peter into some regressed state. She wished that, like a Roman charioteer, he had a slave standing behind him, muttering, "Remember, thou art only a man."

Suddenly she realized they were speaking about an attempt on Madame Cleo's life that had taken place earlier in the day. In panic she screamed at Vickie, "Find Peter in Paris! Now!"

When Vickie called out, "It's him on line one," Fiddle spun around and grabbed the phone. "Peter? I was just watching a tape of you on the news," she said. "What the hell is this about a shooting?"

"Someone took a shot at our girl."

"I know, but when? Why? Surely not because of the book."

Peter filled her in on the shooting as Fiddle sat in stunned silence. "This is scary. I knew Wendy's meddling would make trouble, but not this much."

"Don't be scared, Fiddle. Everything is under control. I have to say, I like the woman. She's tough and charming at the same time. Anything she decides to tell me will be fascinating."

"When do you start?" Fiddle asked.

"I'm meeting her here at the hotel for dinner at eight. We're going to set up the interview schedule. Don't worry, she seems to like me, too, so everything is fine."

Fiddle waited a heartbeat, then two. Perhaps he would say something about how much he missed her. Something personal, something she could hold on to.

He said nothing. The air between New York and Paris carried a faint hiss, nothing more.

"Well, ah, well, okay then, Peter," she said, no longer able to bear the silence. "Call me, okay?"

"You got it," he said.

After she hung up she pushed the play button again on the VCR. When Peter's face came on the screen, she hit the freeze-frame. She would leave the screen just like that all day. Having him in the room, even on grainy film, made her miss him a little less.

"How terribly awkward," Lady Susanna Mosby had responded when she learned that her presence in London was urgently required.

Within the hour she was headed to the city at the wheel of the little Testarossa Lord Mosby had given her for her twenty-fifth birthday. She leaned forward and turned on the radio to catch the news.

Until then her thoughts had only been of her husband's condition and why the doctor had been so cryptic on the phone.

The BBC report was startling.

She knew if she didn't get off the road instantly she would have a panic attack. She smashed her sandaled foot down on the power brakes of her racy Testarossa so hard her knee joint made a painful crunching sound. The little car, known for its ability to stop on a dime, did. It rested on the slant of the shoulder of the highway without having laid an inch of rubber on the road.

Susanna Beatrice Slyde Mosby, called SueBee since babyhood, leaned back against the headrest and tried to collect her thoughts. What she had just heard made her heart sink. "Lordy, lordy, lordy, why'd she want to go open that can a worms."

The voice ringing in her ears belonged to her other self and the life she had left behind to marry Lord Mosby. It held the drawl she had worked so diligently to lose. Over the years she had succeeded, in part thanks to the woman on whom she now vented her fury. Only when deeply provoked did SueBee revert to the thick Texas twang of her childhood. Only then could one hear the flattened a, the high-pitched nasality and common vocabulary of her buried past.

She felt hot tears filling the big blue eyes that were one of her greatest assets. SueBee's time with Madame Cleo was a secret she and Billy shared, unknown to his aristocratic family. She had taken all the silly London tabloid headlines when he divorced to marry her, because no matter what they speculated about her, they never got at the truth. Billy's power had seen to that. Now, a publishing company her husband owned had purchased Madame Cleo's story! It made no sense, unless Billy had some scheme to keep their names out of it.

She checked her makeup in the rearview mirror and reached for her bag to repair the damage. Whatever Billy's doctor in London wanted to see her about had to be received with the ladylike composure expected of her. She couldn't afford raw, red eyes or the jagged pink maps of Brazil that invariably blotched her fair skin when she was upset.

She calmed herself with the knowledge that Madame Cleo couldn't write a book in a day and that, in time, Billy would tell her what this was all about. She could deal with this after she sorted out whatever it was that had happened to Billy.

That morning, when she had returned from her usual ride, the butler had informed her that there was an emergency call from Billy's doctor saying there had been a "bit of an accident." She had hurried down the long corridor that led to her husband's study and the nearest tele-phone.

"This is Lady Mosby," she had said into the phone, expecting to be speaking to a nurse or receptionist.

"Good morning, my dear," said the deep voice of Dr. Jasper Wells, Billy's regular physician. "Not to trouble you, Susanna. But do you think you could pop up to London right away? I'd like to speak with you privately."

"Oh, dear. What now, Jasper?"

The doctor explained that her husband, Lord William Mosby, had been bumped by a lorry while leaving his club. He was all right, however, and resting comfortably in a private room at St. John's.

"Well, if he's all right, Jasper," she said, "what on earth is he doing in hospital?"

"For observation," he had assured her. "Don't want to take any chances, don't j'know. He'll be just fine."

"I don't see why I need to come up, really," she had protested. "I mean—"

The doctor had interrupted her to restate his case for the need for a chat. Reluctantly she had agreed.

SueBee knew that a "bit of an accident" was meant to keep her from being alarmed. It was so British to downplay something nasty. Had they found a lump? A growth or a shadow on a routine X ray?

"You're sure he's all right, Jasper?" she asked with the rising inflection with which the upper classes asked questions.

"Quite," he assured her. "I'll be in my office anytime after twelve."

After the call, SueBee had stood tapping her riding crop on the edge of the long map table beside the fireplace. She ran down a mental checklist of her husband's possible ailments. This would be his liver, probably. A lifetime of pâté and champagne, smoked meats, fine red wines, and old whiskey were bound to exact their price. If not his liver, years of raspberry fool and clotted cream, all the nursery food he loved, had undoubtedly paved every artery, especially the big ones leading to his heart. Then there were the cigars, a dozen a day. More, when he had important meetings. And yet he never seemed short of breath. Whether bounding from his helicopter across the rooftops of his printing plants or making boisterous, athletic love, Billy Mosby never seemed to tire. His energy was as boundless and unflagging as his appetites, for he loved her in the same way he led his life— totally.

Now, with one thirty-second item on the BBC, she saw how fragile everything good in her life was: Billy; the verdant estate in the rolling countryside of the Gloucestershire Cotswolds where her very own valley had its very own winding river; the apartment in London, two dozen rooms done to the last breath by Princess Fergie's decorator. There was the new villa in Sardinia, all pure white and deep blue. And

Billy's salmon-fishing lodge on an island off the coast of Scotland. They had given up the two-million-dollar apartment in Manhattan's Trump Tower only because they'd used it a total of ten days in the year since they bought it. And, of course, there was little Hildy.

SueBee had promised Billy no babies. He had been so emphatic about keeping her all to himself. It was amazing what forgetting to take just one tiny pink pill for a couple of days could do to one's life.

At first he had not been amused. But once Hildy arrived and he saw that SueBee wasn't going to breast-feed or stay home nights, he stopped mooning about it. He had never been child-oriented, even with the two grown boys he'd had by Selena. She shuddered at the name. Selena had told the *Mirror* that SueBee was "an aging man's fling" and that he would come to his senses. Ha! She had showed her! SueBee soothed her conscience about Selena with the fact that the marriage was already dead to dying when Madame Cleo sent her to the baron with special instructions to find Lord Mosby and see that he had a pleasant weekend. Little had she realized she had only to crook her finger at Lord Billy Mosby and all his money and power would be hers.

Press lord Billy Mosby, large and imposing, with skin so fair it looked as though he never had to shave, was the most important-looking man SueBee had ever seen. She hadn't known what to expect that weekend at the baron's château, nor had she really cared. What she found in Billy Mosby was the first man in her life who actually wanted to talk to her. To listen to what she had to say. His sexual proclivities were of no importance once she realized he respected her for who she was. Not in her wildest dreams could she have imagined— as she made her way toward him that night in the library after dinner—that from that moment forward she would never leave his side.

That morning, after the doctor's call, SueBee had gone to the nursery wing to tell Hildy's nanny that the picnic they'd planned would have to be postponed. The sitting room off the first-floor nursery wing, all white and rose, smelled of fresh-cut flowers from the nursery garden. Shelves filled with Steiff stuffed animals, games, dolls from every country Billy did business in, beautifully illustrated and autographed children's books, and wooden animal figures stood between the windows. The floor was covered with an immaculate, fluffy white rug. The child-scale Chippendale-style upholstered chairs and love seats had been custom-made in the woodworking shop on the estate and covered with white Fortuny fabric.

Mrs. MacIntosh, the nanny, had been reading to Hildy when Susanna came in. The little girl, a one-year-old miniature version of SueBee, let slip an excited squeal when she saw her mother entering in her riding clothes.

"Mummy! Mummy!" she sang with delight, tumbling across the thick rug, her arms raised. The blue satin streamers in her fine blond hair flew behind her. Mrs. MacIntosh frowned slightly at such an unladylike display. "Mummy, Mummy!"

SueBee bent one knee to the floor and picked up her little girl for a big hug. "I'm sorry, darling," she said softly. "I came to tell you we can't have our picnic today. Mummy has to go to town to see Daddy's doctor." SueBee kissed the plump rise on the back of Hildy's hand. "We'll have our picnic tomorrow. I promise." Unspoken was that regardless of SueBee's love for Hildy, Billy came first. Shaking off memories of the morning, she turned the key in the Testarossa and listened to the powerful hum of the engine, then glanced over her shoulder to make sure the road was clear and roared back onto the highway.

She had to talk to Billy about the Madame Cleo business. If the book even mentioned her, chances were the Wayleen police would hear about it and find her. She couldn't explain the problem to Billy, because there were some things in her past even he couldn't forgive.

But she knew Billy also wouldn't want her mentioned in the book. The last thing he needed was for his family to know he had married a call girl.

She had to talk to Billy. First she would get him out of that dreary hospital and back to their beautiful apartment at Albany where he was happy and comfortable. She downshifted for more power and streaked into the passing lane.

Billy Mosby smelled an aroma he knew only too well, the smell of sun-drenched peaches and jasmine bath powder.

He opened his eyes. SueBee was leaning over him, pressing her lips to his forehead. She lifted her head and looked down at him, all dimples and comfort. Whatever sedative was oozing through his veins was making him dizzy and disoriented.

He looked up at his wife and smiled. "Darling," he said. He wanted to pull her close and hold her, smother himself in her softness. The morning's events had been so mortifying. All he wanted now was Susanna, his own nurse-mother-angel-lover. He wanted to wrap his arms around her waist and hold her forever.

The stonefaced male nurse in the corner scowled at them from the corner of the private room.

"Would you excuse us, please," SueBee said, her voice sweet but unmistakably in charge.

The nurse pushed himself up out of the plastic-and-chrome chair. He made a small disapproving sound at the back of his throat and sauntered, miffed, from the room.

SueBee edged onto the corner of the hospital bed. One foot remained on the floor. "Darling?" she said softly. "I've just come from Jasper's office."

"He told you?"

"Yes. He thought I didn't know and would be shocked," she said in a giggling whisper, then raised her voice to a schoolmarm's tone. "You're very, very naughty. You know that. After all your promises."

Lord Mosby stared down at his hands. Her reproach excited him. Their game was for him to look as though he was ashamed at having to be punished. "What did he show you?" he said sheepishly.

"The red strapless Lily of France."

He said nothing, letting waves of delicious humiliation wash over him.

"The red lace bikini panties!"

"Ummmm," he nodded. He still wouldn't meet her eye.

"You took them from my dressing cupboard, didn't you?"

"Are you angry with me?"

"You were going to wear them at your morning meeting, weren't you?"

Lord Mosby nodded slowly, picking at the thin hospital blanket.

"And that's what you were thinking about when the lorry hit you."

"Yes," he said, looking up at her. Biting his lip did not successfully hide the smile that was forcing its way through his dour expression.

"There could have been a photographer there, you know that."

Lord Mosby gasped in mock horror.

"Your picture could be eight columns wide across the top of the *Times* tomorrow morning. Wouldn't that be nice?"

Lord Mosby pulled himself upright, wincing at the pain in his back. He folded back the thin blanket and sheet. "Get in," he whispered.

SueBee slipped off her sandals and swung up onto the high bed.

Lord Mosby wrapped his arms around her and pulled her close. "Describe what the picture in the paper would look like," he said, pressing his erection against the small of her back. "Start with the caption."

SueBee reached around and slipped her hand between his legs. "All right, but quickly, darling. Then I'm going to get you out of this tiresome place and home where you belong."

The big south-facing bedroom at Albany was SueBee's favorite room in all of the vast apartment. It seemed an explosion of flowered chintz, love seats, a chaise, a high four-poster bed that had been in Billy's family for generations. She couldn't remember ever being unhappy in the room, except tonight.

"But why, darling?" she asked for the third time.

"Because I can't stop it from happening. How many ways do I need to explain it to you? If I don't publish the damn thing, she'll go to someone else with it. This way I have control," Lord Mosby said, shaking the pink pages of the *Financial Times* in irritation. He was propped up in the high bed against a stack of pillows. The bed tray the maid had brought sat untouched at the foot. Their arguing had killed his appetite, for once.

"How can you be so sure?" SueBee asked. She was kneeling on the little mahogany steps pushed against the side of the bed.

Lord Mosby rolled his eyes. "For the tenth time, darling, it is part of the deal," he said.

"But deals go wrong. People promise stuff and don't come through. I'm scared for all of us," she cried.

Lord Mosby put down his paper and looked over the top of his reading glasses. "You are being hysterical, SueBee. Trust me."

She pushed herself away from the side of the bed and stood up. "What about my friends? They don't deserve it either."

"Who in particular?"

"Sandrine and Angel."

He picked up his paper again. "Such friends. When is the last time you heard from either of them?"

SueBee studied the pattern in the needlepoint rug. "I hear from Sandrine," she said defensively. "Sometimes. It's hard for her. She travels all the time. And you know how Jourdan Garn is. He's so . . . private."

"I wouldn't worry about her, darling."

"And Angel . . ." SueBee said, not listening. "I don't know where she is right now. Lost somewhere, I think. Still . . . she got such a raw deal from Madame Cleo, she doesn't deserve another."

Mosby reached out and took her hand. "SueBee, my love, you can't be the world's nursemaid. I don't care about protecting those women. I can only protect you, and you have my promise. There will be no mention of your relationship to Madame Cleo in anything she publishes. Now, stop worrying about nothing and come to bed."

SueBee did as she was told. She undressed and crawled under the linen sheets next to the man who had never broken a promise to her. Still, sleep would not come. Long after she heard her husband's heavy regular breathing she lay awake worrying about the others and what this would mean to them and their new lives. Why *couldn't* Billy protect them? Why did Madame Cleo have to do this awful book in the first place? There must be a way to stop her. SueBee would do anything to keep Cleo from writing this book. Anything.

At each of Sandrine Garn's spectacular homes she had a favorite place to be. In New York it was the glassed-in atrium of the apartment at the Sherry Netherland. In the Paris and London houses she preferred her bedroom. Here, at their summer house, outside of Zurich, she gravitated to the terrace overlooking the lake.

On the morning she heard the dark news the terrace was drenched with sunlight. To any observer it would have been a scene of peace and serenity. The slender young wife of an enormously wealthy man, seated under an umbrella-covered table, reading the morning paper without a care in the world.

She pulled at the knotted sleeves of the peach cashmere sweater looped around her peach silk blouse. The bite from the breeze off the lake below gently ruffled the fringe of the umbrella. Gazing at the scene, one would never have guessed that behind the impenetrably dark sunglasses her eyes were bloodshot from drink. The glass of fruit juice on the table beside her contained enough vodka to still the shaking hands that held the paper in which she read the threat against her seemingly flawless life.

The house behind her had once been a summer palace for foreign royalty and was the latest acquisition in her husband's impressive assemblage of stately dwellings that spanned the world. Its old stone walls were covered with a moss that seemed to be the same shade and texture as the surface of the lake below the terrace.

Sandrine Garn finished the rest of her drink and pulled off her dark glasses. Beyond the terrace railing she could see two tiny sailboats skittering across the dark green water on the far side of the lake. She watched lazily as a lone bird glided toward her, turned, and circled the crenellated tower of the old castle, disappearing in the direction of the mountains behind it.

It would be years before she would complete the renovation of the house. Her husband, Jourdan Garn, had given her complete freedom to restore the exquisite rooms and fill them with the art collection that he had acquired so greedily over the last decade that most of it was still in storage in New York and London.

When Sandrine had marked Jourdan as the man she intended to marry she had hidden the fact that she was a call girl. She soon learned she need not have bothered. Jourdan Garn was one of those men who constantly needed to bolster their sexual self-esteem, and he was excited by the idea of marrying a woman other men paid money to be with. Sandrine knew he wouldn't have felt that way if she had been a garden-variety call girl. That she was a Cleo girl and, therefore, by definition, had been with some of the most important men in the world, seemed to make all the difference to him. Since they all had wealth and power, Jourdan deduced that it must be his sexual prowess that could get and keep such a woman. Of course, if any of his peers, those very men of wealth and power, were to learn the truth of his wife's background, Jourdan would have died—or killed Sandrine. He had always been obsessed with his reputation, which he seemed to consider as important to his amassment of power as the wealth he accumulated. When he'd married Sandrine, he'd gone to great expense to erase her professional past.

The marriage had permitted Sandrine to disdain the trust fund her famous mother had withheld from her. She, in turn, provided Jourdan with a trophy wife, thin, beautiful, and totally supportive in public. In private she was constantly battling Jourdan's unreasonable jealousy. As their marriage progressed, it seemed to have become more difficult for Jourdan to believe he could snare such a goddess, much less keep her happy. His sexual insecurity tormented him, and he began to believe that Sandrine's past was filled with men who would try to steal her away. Now, in restaurants he seated her with her face to the wall. If she spoke to a tradesman or waiter for more than a few seconds he would rudely interrupt. He monitored her phone calls and had the people on their various staffs spy on her.

Her life was a prison. But as flawed as their marriage was, she had grown used to the unspeakable luxury he provided. She could not imagine returning to a life without limitless money.

She folded the morning *Tribune* and stuffed it deep into the straw bag that held her hidden vodka. Madame Cleo and her damn book, she fumed, could ruin everything.

Suddenly the fog of her morning vodkas lifted. She had to talk to SueBee. SueBee would know what was going on. There had to be some rational explanation as to why SueBee's husband was publishing the book. Surely he would protect his own wife. Well, she thought angrily, I want the same damn protection. If SueBee wavered, Sandrine could fall back on Angel, wherever she was. Sandrine and Angel had known each other the longest, and they could team up against SueBee if she showed any reluctance to protect them. Besides, Angel had a first-class mind. She'd come up with something to stop this dangerous nonsense.

She leaned out from under the shadow of the striped umbrella and called to Jourdan's English butler, who was standing a few yards away snipping cuttings from the herb garden.

"Yes, Madam?" he answered, setting down the basket he carried over one arm.

"Would you bring me the phone, please, Woodward?"

The butler stood sheepishly at the edge of the terrace, making no move to go to the house.

"Well?" Sandrine asked sharply.

"Madam, about the phone . . ."

"For pity's sake, Woodward, don't tell me Mr. Garn has locked the damn thing up again."

"I'm afraid so, ma'am."

"Well, unlock it, damn it! He only does that to keep me from calling to the village for liquor."

"I know, ma'am," Woodward said, staring at the ground. He was no stranger to his master's efforts to keep his wife from drinking, but he and Sandrine liked each other. "I'm afraid he has the key with him, ma'am. And his instructions when he left for Paris this morning were that—"

She could see that he was embarrassed so she cut him off. "You have one in your cottage, Woodward," she said sweetly.

Woodward's face brightened, "Why, yes, ma'am, as a matter of fact, I do. Shall I bring it out?"

"Would you, Woodward? That's very sweet."

The instant the butler placed the phone on the table, Sandrine snatched up the receiver and dialed the operator in the village. "This is Mrs. Garn, Ghislaine. Would you call London information, please, dear. I want the number for the London *Daily News* and the extension of a Mr. Wallace." Nigel Wallace, the gossip columnist for the *Daily News*, knew everything, and had treated Sandrine nicely in the past. Within minutes she had not only SueBee's private numbers in the city and the country but the information that Lady Susanna Mosby was in residence at the Mosby flat at Albany and that an hour earlier Lady Mosby had canceled the couple's announced attendance at a charity event scheduled for that evening. The columnist's efforts to find out why she had changed their plans **had** been interrupted by Sandrine's call.

She hung up thinking how helpful having friends in the press could be. It was like having one's own private CIA.

"Sandrine?" SueBee's sweet, familiar voice called out over the miles between Zurich and London when she picked up the phone.

"Hi, sweetness, how are you?"

"I'm fine, dear. Where are you?"

"Switzerland," Sandrine said. "Bored and scared stiff."

"Scared? What's the matter?"

"About Madame selling her memoirs, and to your husband, no less!" Sandrine said sharply.

"I'm not happy about it either, hon, but Billy assures me everything is going to be okay."

"Did you see who's going to write it for her? Peter Shea, that guy I was with at La Fantastique."

"And you think he'll write about you?"

"Well, it makes sense that he would."

"You used some other name, didn't you?" SueBee asked.

SueBee's calmness in the face of what Sandrine perceived as a very real threat was annoying. "Yes, but even so, SueBee. The man is an investigative reporter."

"I'll speak to Billy again, hon."

"Oh, SueBee. I can see Billy protecting you, but he doesn't owe me anything. Besides, he's hated Jourdan since the start of the Litchfield lawsuit. He won't do me any favors. Not even for you."

"Let me try, Sandy. That's the best I can do."

Sandrine looked around to see if any of the staff besides the butler were hovering. "SueBee, I've been thinking," she said, her hand cupping the mouthpiece. "I think we should try to find Angel."

"I wouldn't know where to start looking for her."

"I'll bet that gangster lawyer of hers knows where she is. We might even be able to use him." It occurred to Sandrine that a call to New York on the butler's phone might cause trouble. "SueBee, would you call Barry Rizzo for me? I'd just as soon Jourdan not know anything about this."

"All right, if you want me to."

"Just call me back when you get Angel's number. I'll call her from the pay box in the village."

"Then what?"

"Then I think we all need to meet someplace."

"Can you come here?" SueBee asked. "Billy's going to be laid up with a bad leg for a few days. This apartment is so big he won't even know anyone's here."

Sandrine thought for a moment. She could tell Jourdan there was an important auction in London and that SueBee had invited her to come. SueBee was the one person from her past he never seemed to mind, probably because of her marriage to Mosby, whom Jourdan had been courting to help him with the Litchfield suit. There might be bad blood between the two men at the moment, but Jourdan seemed to think Sandrine's friendship with SueBee could only help his position. And, anyway, buying stuff at an exclusive auction was the one thing he thought Sandrine was good at. If he would let her take the Learjet, she could leave at a moment's notice. "As soon as we find Angel, darling, I'm on my way."

Sandrine gave SueBee the number on the butler's phone, hung up, and waited. Within minutes SueBee called back and said Angel was at the Seraglio Hotel in Las Vegas.

"Just ask them to page Princess Fatima," SueBee said with a giggle.

"Dear God," Sandrine gasped. "Don't tell me she's still in the life?"

"Sure sounds that way, doesn't it?" SueBee said. She wasn't laughing any longer.

The lobby of Las Vegas's gaudiest new hotel was swarming with people. It was fight night, and it would be a long one for the girls who were working the casino floor.

The nasal voice of the hotel paging operator grated on Angel's nerves. "Princess Fatima. Princess Fatima. Please pick up the house phone." A "Princess Fatima" call meant Angel had a job.

She slugged back the dregs of her Bloody Mary, gathered her cigarettes and sequined handbag from the bar, and slid off the barstool with a weary sigh.

Compared to the younger, fresher-looking girls who worked the casinos, Angel did better in dimly lit surroundings. Her years as a madam were beginning to show. She was still handsome, in a large-boned way, with a thick mass of dark red hair, high cheekbones, and wide-set eyes. And though the hips had begun to spread a bit, her bust line seemed so far to have successfully resisted gravity's inevitable pull.

Still, she had the look of someone who had stayed too long at the fair.

In 1987, when Madame Cleo fired her, Angel had no choice but to take the only job she could get. Cleo had put out the word on Angel, reducing the places she could work. There wasn't a top madam on the Continent or in the States who would touch her, and she was too broke to start up again as a madam herself. She could only work where there was gambling, as the power that controlled such playgrounds was far more structured and aggressive than Cleo's.

As she ambled to the bank of house phones on the far wall of the casino, the two moth-eaten camels that were led around the tented lobby on the half hour wandered toward her. As they passed, the one nearest her spit.

She pushed through the crowd only to have her way blocked by a man wearing the nastiest set of chains outside the South Bronx. He was staring down her cleavage.

She reached up and flicked the peacock feather on his white Borsalino and said, "Later, 'gator," in the up-late, out-of-patience voice she saved for dweebs she knew had spent it all on the dollar slots.

"Whatcha got for me, sugar?" he growled.

"A full-body condom, Spice," she said, pushing by him with lowered lids. Angel did not take walk-in business. If a client wasn't known and didn't come in through the switchboard, he was dead meat.

She hated fight night and the inevitable high rollers with their gold jewelry, coke, booze, and bad attitudes. Every girl in Vegas doubled her price on fight night. It was not a deterrent.

She leaned against the gold-flecked wall and picked up the house phone. "Fatima," she said, yawning.

"Angel, it's me, Maxine," drawled the operator. Maxine was one of the old-timers. Angel was particularly fond of her. She made it a point to keep track of where in the vast hotel Angel was working and to check up on her if she lingered. It was Maxine who had called the cops the time that creep in the penthouse tied Angel up.

"Whatcha got?" Angel said.

"This ain't a job, honey. I got a long-distance call for you from someplace in Switzerland, no less."

Angel was puzzled. Maybe one of her regulars was on a business trip, couldn't score, and wanted phone sex. "You got a name, Maxie?"

"Sure, I got a name. It's a lady, very fancy sounding. She says it's an emergency. Wait a sec. I got it right here. Ahh . . . Sandrine Garn."

Hearing Sandrine's name made Angel jump. Her days with Madame Cleo came flooding back. She'd once believed working for Cleo was going to be her big chance. She could quietly study how the old woman did it, get to know some of the best girls, and persuade them to come with her when she started her new business. But the old woman had been too clever by half. Now she was on the stroll in Las Vegas with only her memories to keep her company.

"You still there?" Maxie asked.

"Yeah, yeah. I'm here."

"Five-oh-one just checked out. Why don't you go on up there and relax? Vinnie's on fifth-floor security. I'll tell him to let you in."

"Thanks. Thanks a lot, Maxie. You're a doll." Her mind was racing. *Sandrine, Sandrine. How in God's name did she find me? And what in the world can she want?*

"You punching out for the night?"

Angel hadn't thought about it, but why not? "Yeah, I think I will. There's too much trash around tonight anyway."

"Tell me about it," Maxine said, laughing. "You wouldn't believe the calls I'm getting. I could have turned a couple of tricks myself tonight."

"You can take my calls if you like," Angel teased.

"Funny, not one of those guys who called mentioned they were into swollen ankles and spider veins."

Angel laughed. "Oh, stop it, Maxie. You're pretty darn cute."

"My grandchildren think so," she said, laughing. "Listen, let me know when you get to the room and I'll put your call through."

Maxine's husband, Vinnie, let Angel into 501, warning her it would be rented out soon and not to linger.

Angel called Maxine and told her she could put the call through. She slipped off her shoes, stretched out on the king-size bed, and stared at the plaster medallion displaying an oversized Aladdin's lamp affixed to the ceiling. If Sandrine had gone to all the trouble of finding her, maybe this was good news. Sandrine was rich now.

The ringing phone next to the bed brought her back to reality. When she heard Sandrine's voice on the line she felt a tightness in her chest. "God, it's good to hear your voice," Angel said. "How are you?"

"Angel! I don't believe I actually found you. What in the world are you doing in Las Vegas?"

"What do you think?"

"Oh, dear. I had hoped to hear you'd settled down."

"Well, I might be down but I wouldn't say I'm settled," Angel said, leaning toward the night table and pawing through her bag for a cigarette. "How in God's name did you find me?"

"Through Barry Rizzo."

"Barry," Angel snorted. "That goddamn goomba gangster son of a bitch. He's the one who sent me here in the first place. Some hellhole this is. No castle in Switzerland, I can assure you."

"I was surprised when SueBee told me where you were, Angel. When you left Madame Cleo we all thought you were going to start your own business. What happened?"

"A lack of cash." Angel said.

"She did take care of us, didn't she," Sandrine said, sounding nostalgic.

"After this dump, I'd go back to her in a second."

"Actually, Angel, she's why I'm calling."

"Madame?" Angel asked, feeling an old excitement. She had left Paris and Madame's patronage under some stress. All she cared to remember now were the good times.

"Madame Cleo is going to write her memoirs."

"I don't believe it!"

"It's true, Angel, and I'm nervous as hell."

"How about SueBee? Isn't she married to some fancy-ass Brit? She can't be thrilled."

"She's not, but at least her husband is the publisher of the book."

"Oh, great," Angel said sarcastically. "Still, if I were SueBee, I'd be nervous." Angel swung her legs over the side of the bed, now fully awake. "I don't care what the old lady says about me. Might even do me some good at this point, but you two . . . sheesh! You've got it all."

"Angel, can I ask you something without your getting mad at me?"

"Sure, babe."

"Would you let me buy you a ticket to London?"

Angel laughed. "You bet," she said. "Why?"

"Neither of us is thinking straight," Sandrine said. "We thought, well, you always had the best head of all of us. Maybe you could come up with something brilliant to stop this madness. Besides, we'd both like to see you again."

"You'll change your mind when you see me. I don't look so hot."

"I don't believe that, Angel. You were always smashing."

"Thanks," she said, meaning it. She hadn't had a compliment from a friend in a long while. In fact, she hadn't had a friend in a long while. A trip to London, seeing her old pals again, was just what her tired soul needed. "When do you want me there?"

"Right away. I'm going to leave here in the morning."

"Let me check on the flights out of L.A. I'll try to get there by Tuesday, too."

Angel hung up and took a minute to remember her days with Madame Cleo. Studying the medallion in the ceiling again, she thought she hadn't appreciated what an elegant life it had been until she left it. Her time with Madame Cleo was the only time in her life that money hadn't been a problem. She had been a fool to leave. It was her own fault.

Before leaving, she decided to call Maxine and tell her no more "dates" for a few days. She would be out of town. Maybe, just maybe, if she could really do a favor for her two rich friends, they would see to it that she never had to come back.

PART
II

PART

II

CHAPTER
∂ 6 ∂

Peter's Journal Entry—Paris, June 1, 1990

It became imperative that I get out of the Ritz. A room-service glass of orange juice and a boiled egg was thirty-two bucks American and only the Aga Kahn could have afforded the minibar.

Thanks to Madame, I am now ensconced in rooms on the top floor of a charming old building on the rue St.-Denis. It was once a hotel, now converted to small apartments. The cab driver who brought me here told me it had been a Nazi whorehouse during the war, which I think is in keeping with my whole mission. The floors rake at enough of an angle to let a dropped pencil roll slowly toward the wall. I've placed my writing table and laptop next to the open window where I can hear (and smell) the street life. If I lean out a bit I can see the river. There's an ancient concierge on the ground floor named Madame Solange who only speaks through the crack in the door. I'm about as far from my former Paris way of life as Saturn is from Smith & Wollensky.

It's only a fifteen-minute walk to Madame's house, which gives me a chance to get my mental notes together before our daily interviews. She has set aside the mornings for us to chat. This afternoon she let me sit in her office and watch her work. She has less high-tech equipment than a Manhattan bike messenger. With only three phone lines she and Martin deploy her powder-puff army to clients in any country on the map. No yellow-pages flesh peddler this lady. She seemed to delight in informing me when someone called whose name I would recognize, which I found charming. It's as though she wants to impress me with the scope of her contacts. I hope that means she trusts me.

Despite all the activity, she says she is in semiretirement and that what I overhear is dull compared to her salad days in the sixties and seventies. When I asked her how long she has been in the business she said, "Since the war," and didn't elaborate. I pressed for more of her background but she demurred, saying that, for the time being, she wanted me to help her figure out who tried to kill her in such a violent and public way. That's where I want to start, too.

She seems fascinated by the fact that I was actually at La Fantastique in 1987 and seems to want to talk about it more. I wonder if she suspects just how keenly interested I am in that weekend? I'll have to be careful to keep my feelings about Madeleine, and whoever it was who got me fired, to myself.

Separate from our sessions together I plan to do a bit of sleuthing on my own. I want to call Fiddle and see if she can line up someone who may have known Madame in the old days so I can ask her questions I already know the answers to.

My mail (I'm convinced because of Madame's contacts with the Paris postal authorities) is delivered to my door each afternoon—alors!—by a lady "postman" who isn't half bad—double alors!

There's a flower stall just at my corner. Perhaps I'll take Madame an armload. Puttering around a shop on St. Germain yesterday I discovered a perfume-testing counter. The smell in her office is patchouli! Perhaps the flowers will cut it a bit, as it makes my eyes sting.

Tomorrow's session is going to be about SueBee. The girl who eventually married "our" publisher.

SueBee Slyde was born in 1965 in the town of Wayleen, Texas, a long, dull, three-hour drive south of Dallas.

Just west of Wayleen, crouched low on the parched land under a wide, white sky was Fort Harris, a sprawling army complex of low, mostly windowless buildings made of corrugated steel. The military facility spread for mile after square mile across the cracked red land dotted with scrub-pine clusters.

Fort Harris for decades had been the training ground for the Army Tank Corps. Married noncoms lived in treeless developments that surrounded the base. Two-bedroom boxes, identical save for an occasional Cyclone fence or small plastic above-ground pool. Beyond these developments lay trailer parks where mobile homes, with their tires removed sat on tiny, well-tended plots divided by gravel walkways.

In the sixties a mobile home could be had for less than five thousand dollars down. For a career army man, no down payment was required. The bank knew where to find him.

At the Sunset Trailer Park, the last mobile home to the right just off Strawberry Walk belonged to Infantry Sergeant Darryl T. Slyde, a short, powerful fire hydrant of a "lifer." An enlisted man since the age of seventeen, Darryl Slyde spent his working days in an M60A1 armored vehicle, a hulking eyeless monster of steel armed with a fifteen-foot 105-mm weapon and two machine guns. Without the education and training required to become an officer, Sergeant Slyde knew he would spend the rest of his life in the army as an enlisted man. Even so, he was proud to be a tanker. Tankers saw themselves as a special breed of men. Hard as steel, mean as hell, and able to outdrink, outfight, and outfuck any man in the U.S. of A.

Darryl's favorite word was "sumbitch." His favorite drink was Seagram's Seven and 7UP, or "seven and seven," a mixture that intensified his nearly congenital anger at the world for dealing him what he thought was a marked deck. His life was frozen solid. There was no chance for advancement, no hope of change, no room or ability to grow. So stifling a life might have motivated a man with an imagination and a dream to change his circumstances. Lacking either, Darryl assumed the posture of silent rage, which he vented in an assortment of ways. His idea of humor was to moon someone helpless, like a barmaid, a roadhouse waitress, or a fuzz-faced gas-station attendant. His idea of justice was to split someone's lip with his scarred, cracked knuckles.

Despite the occasional discipline problem, the army preferred tank men like Darryl Slyde, short of stature and hard as nails. It made sense, when four men had to fit face to butt in a space not much larger than an average coffin.

Darryl was happiest in his tank. He found a comfort in the deafening noise and mind-numbing heat of the long hours spent inside a rolling steel furnace. If there was a soft place anywhere in his makeup, it was the patch of adoration reserved for his tiny snowflake of a daughter, Susanna Beatrice, who arrived at the base hospital in the spring of 1965. She had been named after her mother, a sweet country teenager Darryl had married when they were both seventeen. His wife died of what the locals called "milk fever" two weeks after giving birth. Actually, she had succumbed to a nasty virus aggravated by delayed and inadequate medical care.

Darryl Slyde was left with the responsibility of raising a baby so fragile, so pale and delicate, that for weeks after her mother died he was afraid even to pick her up. When he did, at the urging of the woman he had hired to stay with her when he was in the field, he never wanted to put her down again. He would lie with her sleeping on his chest on the sagging pullout in the trailer's living area for hours when he got off duty. He may have been incapable of dreaming dreams for himself, but his dreams for his baby daughter were boundless.

While ignorant of life's grace notes, Darryl knew from his own experience that an education was the path to a better life. His dream was for SueBee to get a college education no matter what it took. No way was his little girl going to be a hairdresser or sling beer to drunken tankers until she married. Indeed, just the thought of her marrying made him clench his fist and work his jaw.

SueBee was almost ten when she began to take notice of the men who came to the trailer to drink and play cards on Saturday nights. She was permitted to sit next to her father while he played. She loved the games, and all week she looked forward to Saturday nights. It wasn't long before she could play a better mental game than her father or his friends could. Cards were easy. They had numbers on them that she could memorize. They weren't like the letters SueBee found so difficult to read. Her failure to comprehend the words in books and magazines was the only thing that made her cry. But the first time she threw down a schoolbook in frustration and buried her face in her hands, the look of bewilderment on her father's face upset her even more than her inability to read.

One Saturday night after the cardplaying she discovered a way to deal with her problem. Her father was standing at the tiny sink of the motor home scraping the remains of a macaroni-and-cheese dinner into a paper sack when the idea came to her. She was lying on her stomach on the bright orange shag rug, half-watching a rerun of Ben Casey and Dr. Zorba removing a brain tumor. The rest of her mind was preoccupied with the fact that her history assignment was due on Monday and required her to read an entire chapter on the Second World War.

"Daddy," she called.

"Yes, babe," he answered from behind the refrigerator door.

"My assignment for history is about the war. I'd like it a lot if you'd read it to me." She waited, squeezing her eyes tight against a negative answer.

"Sure, honey. Just let me get this stuff put away and I'll be right over."

That night he read to her for the first time. She snuggled against his shoulder and listened as she had never listened to anything before. It was easy to tell where he was on the page because he ran his finger under each word. The slow speed with which he read permitted her to commit the information to memory.

When he finished she stayed very still against his shoulder for a long time.

Finally he closed the book. "How was that, honey?"

"Just wonderful, Daddy," she said softly. "That was the wonderfullest thing. Promise me you'll do that every night."

Darryl reached up and tweaked her tiny nose. "I can't promise every night," he said with a chuckle. "But if you like it so much we'll do it again real soon."

That night, nestled on the pullout couch behind the chenille bedspread her father had hung as a privacy curtain, she silently began to recite what he had read to her. She realized she remembered almost every word.

The following week there was a test on World War II. SueBee got an A.

Her father continued to read to her. When he did she always did well. But it wasn't enough. There were more times than not when she couldn't use him as a crutch, and her world became more and more a place of isolation and fear. There was a maddening conflict between what the world told her about herself and what she knew in her soul. In school she always chose a desk in the very back of the classroom, not because she wasn't interested but because there she wouldn't be noticed. Up front the jumble of letters on the blackboard was close enough to drown her. When Darryl helped her she got excellent grades, but when he didn't her work was hopeless. Her teachers noticed the marked contrast and, not knowing about her father's help, assumed she was lazy. They did not hesitate to point it out to her and, worse, to the other students. By the time she got to high school she had internalized the constant humiliations, and in defense drew further and further into herself.

By then, like a blind person who comes to depend on and thereby sharpen his other senses, she had learned to fake it.

Her shyness and preoccupation with her struggle to learn set her apart from the other kids. The boys teased her because she was delicate and pretty. They soon learned, however, that to pay too much attention to SueBee Slyde meant having Sergeant Slyde banging on your parents' door—armed. It wasn't worth the hassle. As for the girls, when they went off to each other's homes to play after school, SueBee was seldom, if ever, asked. She was too quiet, too proper, and not fun. At least not the kind of fun adolescent girls sought. She didn't seem to care about boys, makeup, rock music, or clothes. What else was there to life? For SueBee, although no one seemed to know it but her, all there was to life was her struggle.

As SueBee grew she retained the pale corn-silk hair she had been born with. At twelve her trim little body began to blossom. By the time she reached her last year at Wayleen Senior High she was a true beauty, crippled by a secret disability that made her an outsider.

The final hurdle she had to clear was her Scholastic Aptitude Test. There was no way to prepare in advance. It was the ultimate examination of a student's cumulative knowledge and, for SueBee, an insurmountable task.

Hilda Weissman looked at her appointment book and saw a nine-thirty meeting that had migraine potential. She had been dreading it all week. A request from a parent asking to see her usually meant a confrontation, something Hilda hated. But as principal of Wayleen Senior High School there was no avoiding it.

She had received a letter from one Sergeant Darryl Slyde, the father of a senior student, requesting a meeting in her office. She had been surprised. She had dealt with her share of concerned parents and knew which students had them. In the four years she had been principal she had never once heard from this particular parent. She had to think hard to picture exactly who Susanna Slyde was. Then she remembered. The girl had briefly been in the glee club Hilda had organized. Hilda remembered her as a beautiful child who was pathetically shy.

After receiving Sergeant Slyde's letter she had the girl's file pulled. It contained an essay she had written. One look at the reversed letters, erasures, and cross-outs told Hilda what the problem was. The girl was dyslexic. That the condition had gone undetected for so long infuriated her.

Before her transfer to Texas, Hilda had taught English at a posh New York private school where learning disabilities were spotted by the first grade. Susanna Slyde was just one more reminder that she was a long way from home.

Her move to Texas had been a reluctant one. Her father-in-law, who had been in general practice in Wayleen all his life, had died suddenly, and Hilda's husband, Alfred, insisted on returning home to take over his father's practice. The only pleasant thing about the move was an offer to administrate a high school rather than just teach.

Texas could have been the moon compared to their life back East. At first she hated the heat, the red dust, and missed her network of like-minded women friends. She missed New York and all it had to offer. She did not hold the county school system in particularly high esteem, and when something like the Slyde girl's case turned up, it deeply offended her as an educator.

The girl had been permitted to slide through grade school and most of high school with reading levels well below average. The fact that she had gotten this far was a miracle of will and determination that Hilda wanted to examine further. Perhaps talking to her father would shed some light on how the girl had managed. If he knew about her problem she found it passing strange that he had waited so long to talk to her.

When she heard a tap on her office door, she smoothed back a few stray strands of her salt-and-pepper hair and pressed her fingertips against her temples. "Come in," she called.

Standing in the doorway was a stocky red-faced man wearing a sergeant's uniform. His lips parted in what must have been intended as a smile. She knew from his missing two front teeth that he was a tanker from Fort Harris. Most of those men were missing teeth. It came from slamming around inside those tanks like eggs in a can.

He had taken great care with his appearance. His shirt had been custom-tapered. A sharp crease ran from his collar points to his belt along each side of his barrel chest. He removed his overseas cap and stood at attention as though waiting for further orders.

Hilda Weissman smiled. "Ah, Sergeant Slyde. Please come in," she said. She stood and gestured toward the hard-backed chair in front of her desk.

He nodded once and marched, ramrod straight, toward the chair, where he sat down. The hands holding his cap rested stiffly in his lap. His face was weathered and lined, although the man could not yet be forty. She saw nothing in his face or coloring that could possibly relate to the fair-haired, porcelain-skinned girl who concerned them both.

Sergeant Slyde stared straight ahead, his eyes fixed somewhere on a wall calendar in back of Hilda's head. "I came to talk about my daughter," he said, getting right to the point.

"How can I be of help, Sergeant?"

"I want to know where to send her to college and how much it will cost."

Hilda blinked in surprise. "College?" she said.

"Yes, ma'am."

Hilda thought for a minute. Better go slow on this one, she told herself. This sort of man is quick to take offense. "Have you and Susanna discussed college?" It was a stalling tactic but she needed to get a better fix on him before she disabused him of his plans. No way was Susanna Slyde college material.

"SueBee," he corrected.

"Pardon?" she said, leaning her head to one side.

"She's called SueBee," he said. "That was her mother's name."

"Oh, I see, I see," Hilda said a bit too eagerly. "Well, yes. Ah . . . SueBee."

"Her mother's dead."

"Yes. I'm sorry. I saw that in her records."

"I raised her by myself," he said, his eyes meeting Hilda's for the first time. His expression was almost defiant. "She's all I've got. Just her and the army. I had my twenty in this year. I could'a retired but my pension wouldn'ta paid for college."

Hilda pressed her temples again. Oh Lord, she thought, this isn't going to be easy. She opened the folder on the desk in front of her. "Sergeant Slyde, I'm afraid what I'm going to say will disappoint you."

"How's that?" he said, his eyes narrowing.

"I don't know how to put this any other way, sir. Susanna's . . . sorry, SueBee's reading and writing, her abilities are simply not college entry level. She's going to be very lucky to graduate with her class in June." There it was, she had said it. Now she had only to sit back and wait for his reaction.

The flesh on Sergeant Slyde's forehead dropped into a drapery of overlapping folds that seemed to almost obscure his small black eyes. His mouth tightened to a slit. "What are you tellin' me, ma'am?"

"Here are her tests," Hilda said, pushing the folder across her desk knowing full well the man could never decipher the SAT score chart on the top of the pile.

He leaned forward, scowling at the file, pretending to read what must have looked like Japanese. When he straightened up his concerned expression had been replaced by one of rage. It was as though she had insulted him personally.

"I don't git it," he said. "She don't run around. She don't go with boys the way some of these trampy girls do. I don't permit it. She does her homework. I know, because I work with her. Why, she's the best little cardplayer you ever seen. Better'un me. You gotta read to play cards, right?" His voice was getting louder with each word. "I don't believe what you're tellin' me here. The girl got herself to her last year in high school. How'd she do that if she's so dumb?"

Hilda deliberately softened her voice. "I'm not criticizing her, Sergeant. Nor you. You've done an amazing job raising her all alone. She's a remarkable girl. Against the odds she has compensated for her problem. She did it, she got herself through. She's to be greatly admired for that."

"Sounds like you're still sayin' she's dumb. Right?" He rose from the chair and began to twist his overseas cap into a narrow tube of fabric. "So dumb no college will have her."

"Please, Sergeant Slyde. That's not at all what I'm saying. I'm just saying that she doesn't have the grades to meet college entrance requirements. I'm saying for SueBee's sake you should change your plans for her. She would be miserable in college, even if she could get in. She has a problem. The problem has a name. It's a very real problem, but there are things that can be done about it."

Slyde's face was beet purple. Hilda felt sure that had she been a man he would have punched her. He clearly wasn't accustomed to a female authority figure, particularly one who was telling him something he didn't want to hear.

The girl had been clever. She had fooled everyone, most heartbreakingly of all this well-intentioned man.

She reached for the folder and rifled through the papers. "Let me try to explain. Think of a giant switchboard. When you plug into it, a connection is made. When we read, the eye sees a word or a sentence and sends a signal to the brain's switchboard. In your daughter's case, the eye sends a signal but the switchboard either disconnects or gets the message wrong. Look here," she said, pulling a page from the folder. "Here's an essay SueBee wrote. See all these crossed-out words? See how the paper is torn where she bore down so hard trying to get the signal to connect? It has absolutely nothing to do with how smart or how dumb a person is, any more than the color of his or her hair does."

Sergeant Slyde took the paper and studied it.

"When SueBee's eye sees the word 'd-o-g,' for instance, her brain translates it as 'g-o-d.' When she sees 'put,' she reads a meaningless 'tup.' She has to have known for years that something wasn't working so she trained her mind to memorize things, like taking a picture, in a way. The name for such a condition, and it is more common than most people realize, is dyslexia."

Sergeant Slyde looked up at her, his angry expression somewhat muted by confusion. "Why didn't someone tell me about this dis . . . dis . . ."

"Dyslexia," Hilda said. She paused to assess his mood, then plunged ahead. "I can only speculate, Sergeant. I think it was a combination of no one paying attention and your daughter's very clever ability to compensate."

In the anguish of his disappointment he had folded SueBee's test paper in half and was running his thumbnail along the crease. "Ain't good enough," he mumbled.

"Excuse me?"

"Ain't good enough," he repeated more forcefully. "Your reason ain't good enough. Your reason stinks. All these years . . ." He stopped speaking and turned to face the window. "Now she ain't gonna go to college." He turned back to face her with reddened eyes. The man seemed so defeated, so helpless. He stared down at his hands for a long time. Finally he looked up at her. "Mrs. Weissman, what am I gonna do?" His anger had turned to despair.

She could feel the throb of a big blood vessel in her right temple and knew that within minutes she would have a full-blown migraine. It would travel to her stomach and ruin the rest of her already ruined day. She had to do something for the man, even if it was a stopgap move. "Sergeant Slyde, may I talk to SueBee?"

"Yeah . . . sure," he said with a sigh. He pushed himself up out of the chair. "You gonna tell her or should I?"

"That we know she has a problem?"

"No. I meant about, you know, not going to college."

"Why don't we wait until I see what SueBee wants to do with her life? Maybe she has some plan she hasn't shared with you."

He untwisted his hat and put it on, holding it front to back and carefully setting it at an angle. Since coming to Wayleen, she had seen a lot of military men make that gesture, as though a correctly placed hat gave them a measure of control.

"Thank you, Mrs. Weissman," he said simply, and then he turned and walked out of the office. But his ramrod posture had been replaced with a stoop.

Hilda Weissman put her head down on the desk and waited for the migraine to descend. "Oh, dear," she sighed, "what have I gotten myself into?"

A student aide found SueBee as she was dressing for gym class and told her the principal wanted to see her.

"Why?" she asked, studying the note with the principal's initials on the bottom.

"Don't ask me, Slyde," the girl smirked. "You been screwin' around in the parking lot?"

The words stung. All sexual remarks did. SueBee knew kids only said dirty things to her to see her blush. Everyone knew she wasn't permitted to date. She also knew she hadn't done anything wrong, ever. The note from the principal could only have to do with her test results. She folded the slip carefully and put it between the pages of her ring binder. Then she went to see the principal.

Hilda Weissman looked up from her desk at the sound of SueBee clearing her throat.

"Hello, Mrs. Weissman. I'm SueBee Slyde. You wanted to see me?" she said softly, her books held tightly to the front of her white cotton T-shirt.

Mrs. Weissman's face brightened. "Of course, SueBee. Thank you for coming."

Seeing her made SueBee feel guilty all over again that she had quit the glee club. It happened the day they handed out the songbooks and she felt the familiar panic attack coming. She never told Mrs. Weissman why she hadn't come back. She hoped she didn't think it was because SueBee didn't like her.

SueBee walked tentatively toward the desk. It smelled of cleaning fluid and Mrs. Weissman's perfume. "I got your note," she said, then realized how stupid that must sound. Of course she had gotten the note. That's why she was here. Please, she thought, I know what she's going to say, please let me get this over with. She took the chair in front of the desk and sat on the very edge, balancing her books on her knees. She could see a file in front of the principal and wondered if it had her SAT results in it.

Mrs. Weissman leaned back in her chair and pinched the bridge of her nose as though she had a bad headache. "Susanna?" she began, "Have you given any thought to what you want to do next year?"

SueBee had thought of little else for three and a half years of high school, but it seemed so impossible she had kept it to herself. In her heart she knew someday someone would find out about her and she'd have to give it up. Her dream, she figured, had about five more minutes to live. "Well," she said, "my father always wanted me to go to college, but I know that's not possible."

"But what about you? What do you want?"

SueBee turned and looked out the window. The office was on the first floor and looked out toward the football field. It was deserted, and in the distance she could see the wind picking up balls of brush and tumbling them along the dusty ground. "I kinda, well, once . . . I thought I'd like to be a nurse."

"That would require college, Susanna. You know that."

SueBee took a deep breath and exhaled. "Look, Mrs. Weissman, if this is about my SATs . . . please. I know I messed up. I always have on tests, particularly when I don't have any advance warning of what's going to be asked."

Mrs. Weissman picked up a yellow pencil and wove it between her fingers. "Why does that make a difference?" SueBee could tell she knew the answer. She just wanted to hear SueBee say it.

She stared down at the tops of her blue-and-white running shoes. "Because I can memorize things," she said.

"SueBee," Mrs. Weissman said. "I can call you that, right? That's what your daddy calls you."

SueBee's head snapped up. "How did you know that?" she asked with alarm. A feeling of betrayal welled up in her.

"He asked to see me. I spoke to him this morning."

"He was here?"

"Yes."

"Oh God! You didn't tell him, did you?" Quickly, she pinched her lips together. *Why had she said that?*

"Tell him what, dear?" Mrs. Weissman said gently.

"You know," SueBee said, dropping her eyes again.

"SueBee, you have nothing to be ashamed of. A great many people have this difficulty."

There, SueBee thought, someone finally knows. But even now, after all this time, all the hiding, all the lying, even now they hadn't got it right. "It's not just a difficulty, Mrs. Weissman," she said too loudly for the room. "I can't read! Everything is a jumble. Some things I recognize, others just look like hen scratching. I try but I just can't make myself understand. I'm dumb! I'm just dumb." She was shouting. She could feel the tears in her throat and wanted desperately to swallow them away. "I always will be."

"Susanna, you don't really believe that," Mrs. Weissman said harshly. "You think that's what I want to hear? You are not dumb. Far from it."

The tears won and SueBee buried her face in her hands. "Everybody always said so. Everybody except my father."

"Well, everyone except your father is wrong," Mrs. Weissman said.

SueBee felt an arm slide around her shoulders and heard Mrs. Weissman's voice just above her head. "You have a problem called dyslexia. It is a condition where the eyes send the brain the wrong signal. What breaks my heart is that had you been in a different school, a different place, someone would have diagnosed it years ago and saved you a great deal of pain."

SueBee didn't know whether to believe what she was hearing or not. How could the anguish of her entire life be sorted out so simply? And even if what Mrs. Weissman was saying was true, what could anyone do about it now?

"Don't cry, dear," Mrs. Weissman said, her arm still around SueBee's shoulders as she knelt next to the chair. SueBee couldn't stop. It was like a dam had burst inside her head. She didn't know whether she would drown of shame or relief. *At least now someone knew.*

Mrs. Weissman stood up and went back behind her desk. "Listen, SueBee, would your daddy let you come over for dinner sometime? I'd like you to meet my husband. I think I have an idea."

SueBee found a tissue and blew her nose. She couldn't deal with social plans at the moment. She had a much bigger worry on her mind. "Mrs. Weissman?" she asked once she was under control.

"Yes, dear."

"I'm not going to graduate, am I?"

There was a long pause before she answered. SueBee held her breath. "I think something can be arranged, SueBee. Let me see what I can do."

"Thank you," SueBee said softly.

"Now, how about coming for dinner?"

"Okay," SueBee answered weakly, "I'll ask my daddy. I usually cook for him during the week, though."

"Then let's make it on Saturday."

"Okay, Mrs. Weissman. I think that will be all right." SueBee bent to gather her things and walked toward the door, then turned. "Thank you, ma'am," she said with a sweet smile. "For everything."

"You're very welcome, dear." Mrs. Weissman returned the smile.

SueBee thought she had died and gone to heaven. Dr. and Mrs. Weissman lived in a real house with a driveway and a big lawn all around it. There was an upstairs, and real flat carpeting that was pale blue. It was nothing like the bright orange shag in the trailer, which always caught the heels of her loafers and gave up little fuzz balls that stuck to everything. There was a huge kitchen with a freezer all by itself, not part of the refrigerator, and two bathrooms. The one downstairs had just a sink and a toilet. It was only for guests and had silver-and-white striped wallpaper, and towels and a rug to match the walls. On the sink was a dish shaped like a shell, with little balls of soap in it that no one had ever used. How could a bathroom be so beautiful? She was afraid to use the soap or the little towels next to the sink, so she just rinsed her hands and dried them on toilet paper, which she flushed away so it would look like nothing had been touched.

The dinner was delicious. Dr. Weissman cooked it on a big grill in their backyard, where they ate. It was all bricked in and had thick wooden chairs with pillows on them. SueBee figured they must be very rich, him being a doctor and all.

They had barbecued chicken and corn on the cob, and Dr. Weissman, who was tall and thin and had very curly, very red hair and wore half-glasses, even asked her if she wanted some wine. She said no, she had never tasted wine, and God help her if her daddy found out.

They talked about everything that interested SueBee—television, the movies, and their lives before they came to Texas. After dinner, Dr. Weissman brought out a big tray with bowls of nuts and jimmies and sprinkles to put on ice cream. SueBee, who usually ate ice cream out of the container, had never seen anything so grand.

She sat contentedly eating the hot fudge sundae she had fashioned. The light from the kitchen fell across the picnic table. Out in the dark yard, little specks of fireflies lit and faded in the warm night air. She was feeling so contented she had almost stopped wondering why they had asked her to come.

Dr. Weissman helped himself to more coffee and sat down next to SueBee. "SueBee, my wife tells me you're interested in nursing."

She dropped her eyes, embarrassed yet flattered that they had been talking about her. "Yes, sir, I was."

"Not anymore?"

SueBee looked over at Mrs. Weissman. The panic she was feeling was somewhat dispelled by the pleasant expression she saw. "Well, sir. I have a problem . . ." She stopped. She couldn't bring herself to say it out loud.

"My husband knows all about it, SueBee," Mrs. Weissman interrupted. "What we were wondering is, would you like to come and work in his office part time. If you like it you could work full time after graduation."

SueBee looked first at Dr. Weissman, then at his wife, then back again. Dr. Weissman was nodding.

"I don't understand," SueBee said. "Doing what?"

"I need someone to answer the phone," Dr. Weissman said, scooping up some more pistachio ice cream. "I have a nurse, but she spends most of her time with me in the back or in the lab. I should have someone out front to make my patients feel more comfortable. It's routine stuff but it's important to me."

SueBee had to ask, even though she was afraid the words would stick to the roof of her mouth. "Would I have to read?" She felt her face coloring.

"Oh, a little," he said lightly. "The appointment book mostly."

SueBee felt her heart skip. "I can do that! I can read a line or a name. It's just when it's a whole block of words that I get so frustrated."

"I take it from your tone that you'll come help me out," Dr. Weissman said, smiling.

"Lordy, lordy, lordy," SueBee said slowly, shaking her head in disbelief. "I never in my life thought something like this would happen to me. Of course I will, Dr. Weissman. First, I'll have to ask my daddy."

A slight frown crossed Mrs. Weissman's face. "Do you think it will be all right with him?" she asked.

"I'm sure he'd like me working for a doctor," SueBee said, hoping to heaven that she was right.

"Done, then," Dr. Weissman said, slapping his open palms on the knees of his chinos. "Hildy, would you see about getting a proper white uniform for SueBee in the morning?"

SueBee's jaw dropped. A uniform! She looked over at Mrs. Weissman. "You mean I'll wear a nurse's uniform!"

"I think it would look better for the patients, don't you?" she asked.

"Why, yes . . . yes, I think it would." SueBee was trying hard to control her utter joy. Her daddy always said it wasn't right to show your feelings. It was difficult. She wanted to leap into the air and shout her excitement. "Thank you," she said quietly. "Thank you both very, very much."

Later, after she was home safe behind the chenille-bedspread curtains, she sat at the head of the bed and hugged her knees. She should have said more. She should have hugged and kissed the Weissmans. All she had said was "Thank you," which was all her heart would let her say. What she meant was, *Thank you for wanting me. Thank you for showing me that two intelligent people think I'm smart and worthwhile.* Maybe, just maybe, it was possible that someone besides her father could need her.

"Now, Colonel, relax, relax. Move your knees just a little farther up and your elbows forward. That's it. That's better." SueBee's voice was like a purr. As she spoke she lightly stroked the muscled forearm of the anguished man on his elbows and knees atop the examining table. His rear was the highest part of his body. Most of his considerable weight was on his elbows. SueBee continued to stroke until gradually he stopped weeping.

Dr. Weissman sat on a wheeled stool at the foot of the table with an examining light strapped to his forehead. He was inserting a four-foot steel tube into the colonel's rectum. Despite a hefty shot of Valium before the procedure, the humiliated officer was in despair.

SueBee had been assisting Dr. Weissman in the examining room ever since his nurse, Mrs. Nichols, quit to have her baby. Dr. Weissman taught her as they went along. Since graduation she'd been in the office full-time doing everything from taking blood pressures to doing simple lab work. It was really very easy, and she wondered why anyone would need to take chemistry to figure out whether a piece of litmus paper had turned pink or blue.

Among the many things she had learned in the last few months was that a lot of the military personnel came to Dr. Weissman with problems they didn't want noted on the base hospital records. She had seen several cases of advanced syphilis and homosexual soldiers with bad rectal tears. There had been men who had everything from canker sores to abscessed bites picked up in the whorehouses around town, and an officer's wife with infected cigarette burns in her vagina. In Texas it was against the law for a doctor to do a gynecological examination without a female in the room. Because of that, SueBee received what had to be the world's most thorough crash course in female medical treatment. It dawned on her very quickly that the basis for most illnesses suffered by women was sex.

Every time they got a new and unusual case, SueBee looked it up in the wonderful book Dr. Weissman had given her, which had pictures of everything and anything that could happen to the human body in living four-color full-page glory.

At first Dr. Weissman was concerned that SueBee might be squeamish about such a sudden introduction to the vivid underside of humanity. He was pleasantly stunned at her unquestioning and cheerful acceptance of even the most repellent sights, smells, and conditions. The little girl who couldn't read, never had a date, and, he was positive, had never seen a penis, let alone the condition a private first class could get his into on a whoring weekend, took to her newfound duties with an eager glee and efficiency that left him all but speechless.

"Forget that she should be a nurse, Hildy," Alfred Weissman said to his wife during one of their daily lunch-hour phone calls. "This girl should be a doctor! Remember I told you I showed her how to lance a boil? Well, this morning we got a doozy. An infection the size of your fist on this big buck of a warrant officer's butt. She lanced it with one stroke. It shot pus halfway across the office. Her uniform was covered, it was in her hair, on her face. She didn't even take the time to wipe it away, just kept working away on him while he moaned and screamed like a stuck pig."

"Feh!" Hilda said with a combination of disgust and fascination at her protégée's progress.

"And she's so good-natured about it. When she finished this fella asks how long the thing will take to drain. SueBee tells him it will take a while. The guy was kind of nasty because it hurt. 'What's "a while,"' the guy asks, imitating that cracker accent of hers. She looks at him and says, 'A whale is a big mammal that swims in the ocean.' Even this big guy with his screaming butt had to laugh." He glanced at the button on his desk that signaled that SueBee had a patient in the outer office. "Gotta run, sweetheart. See you tonight," he said, hanging up quickly and picking up the intercom. "Yes, nurse," he said in his official doctor's voice.

"Can I come in a minute?"

"Sure, SueBee, I'm off the phone."

A second later SueBee stepped through the door and closed it behind her. Hilda had done a good job rounding up some nicely fitting uniforms. The girl must wash in bleach, because he never saw her looking anything but immaculate. He pulled his eyes away from her rounded breasts and tiny waist.

"What's up?"

"There's a lady out here who's in bad pain. All she would tell me is that she has a big lump inside her thigh that's so painful she can hardly walk."

"Hmmm. Where's she from?"

"I don't know for sure, but I've seen her down at that Best Western where all the soldiers go, just hangin' around the cars. She's wearing hot pants and a purple off-the-shoulder blouse."

Dr. Weissman chuckled. "You don't miss anything, do you?"

"I try not to," she said, smiling sweetly. "Now, Doctor, I couldn't say for sure, but from the questions I asked, I think she might have an infected Bartholin's gland. From the way she held herself with both hands when she said 'inside my thigh' I just knew she's talkin' about her vagina. Now, my book shows those gland abscesses getting really huge. And if she's doing sex . . . having sex? Anyway, if she's doing it with all those soldiers she probably—"

Dr. Weissman held up his hand and tried to suppress a smile. "Hold on, hold on," he said. "I'm the doctor here."

"Oh, right." She smiled.

"Why don't you send the lady in?"

"Got it," she said, and disappeared.

Dr. Weissman was able to release his smile, shaking his head slowly. He knew she was probably right.

The September afternoon heat had reached 115° by noon. The baked crust of the earth shimmered as far as an eye could squint. Out on the practice range south of the base sat the steel oven Darryl Slyde called his office. Inside sat the usual crew of four men: the driver, the gunner, Slyde the loader, and the tank commander. The therometer inside the tank read 125°.

Theirs was more than a routine maneuver. Their commander had recently received a flurry of correspondence from the Pentagon and had accordingly stepped up battle maneuvers at Fort Harris.

On his metal seat behind the gunner, Darryl wiped the running sweat from his brow and prepared to load another live shell into the forward 105-mm gun. Suddenly something happened. Before a word was spoken the shell exploded.

Sergeant Joe McGraw, the driver of the tank maneuvering directly behind Darryl Slyde's, was one of his cardplaying buddies on Saturday night and the first to see the hatch of Darryl's tank blow off. Momentarily blinded by the flash of flame that shot into the air, McGraw threw his arm over his eyes and screamed. Any tanker knew that the force of an internal explosion was so tightly contained it literally fried the men inside.

As McGraw lowered his arm, he squinted through the observation slit in front of him. Darryl's tank had stopped rolling and stood shuddering. Joe McGraw knew what he would find when the tank was cool enough to climb aboard. He also knew it would make him lose his breakfast.

SueBee Slyde slipped her medical picture book under the reception desk when the phone rang. Dr. Weissman didn't like her to read it on the job. It didn't look right. If he should walk out of his office while she was on the phone he'd say something about it.

"Doctor's office," she answered in a pleasant voice.

"This is Colonel Rice at the base hospital. May I speak to Dr. Weissman right away, please."

"I'm sorry, sir. He's with a patient," SueBee said. She didn't know the officer calling but someone of his rank demanded instant respect.

"Put him on, damn it!" he snapped. "We have an emergency here!"

"Yes, sir!" she said instantly. She noticed that her hand was shaking as she reached for the intercom. She felt a chill run down between her shoulder blades. Something really bad must have happened at the base for the hospital to be calling an outside doctor. Their own medics usually handled any emergency.

Within seconds of taking the colonel's call Dr. Weissman streaked past her desk toward the outer door. "I'm over at the base hospital," he shouted, and slammed the door.

SueBee sat quietly at her desk thinking about her dad. She wondered if she could reach him at the barracks and see if he knew what was going on. She remembered he was on maneuvers and went back to studying her book. The assignment she had given herself for the day was to memorize the pictures on cardiac resuscitation.

Sergeant Slyde's company commander's call was the next she received. It was he who told her that her father had had an accident. He was sending a car for her right away to take her home. Someone from the base would stay with her.

She was still trembling as she leaned back in the khaki-colored army field sedan. The driver said nothing as they pulled away from the curb and headed east toward the trailer park. He didn't have to. In her bones she knew her father was dead.

The pretty lieutenant with the army-nurse insignia on her uniform was waiting for SueBee on the front step. As SueBee got out of the car she shook her head to stop the lieutenant from saying anything. She could tell by the look in the woman's eyes what it was going to be and she didn't want to hear it. She had seen that look all her life when people knew she didn't have a mother, and she hated it. It made her feel different, not normal like everyone else. She had learned to refuse the helping hand, ignore the pitying word. If people did it to make you feel better, it didn't work.

Throughout the long night people came and went in the little motor home. Sometimes there were so many they stood out in the fenced-in yard. Her father's battalion commander was there with his wife. Neighbors came with so many covered dishes and plates of cake there was no place to put them. Her father's poker buddies milled about, their hands shoved in the pockets of their bright polyester slacks.

Throughout the vigil SueBee sat in the corner of the maple couch picking at the nubbly fabric, her eyes downcast.

No one would actually tell her what was going on. She knew her father had been severely burned but there was no one to explain what they were doing to or for him. She tried asking at first but no one knew. She didn't know what to do, so she fell into a numb silence that hid her inner screaming.

At one point, as she stared into space, she was aware of someone kneeling in front of her with a plate of brownies. The frosting on top had begun to melt into a black brown puddle around the edge of the plate in the warmth of the night air. The smell reached her consciousness, it was so sickening. She recognized the face of Mrs. Carter, who lived in the big RV at the end of their walk. In Mrs. Carter's eyes was that look, the look that said, "You poor little helpless thing."

Suddenly, she heard a familiar voice screaming "Stop it! Stop it! Stop it!" To her astonishment, the voice was hers. Her hand shot forward and hit the underside of the plate. Brownies flew straight up past Mrs. Carter's shocked face. "Someone tell me *something!*" she screamed. "Is he cooked? Is all his skin gone? Do the bones show through? What is happening to my daddy? For God's sake someone tell me something!" She clutched a Dallas Cowboys throw pillow to her chest and rocked back and forth.

"She's hysterical," someone beside her whispered.

"Well, can you blame her, poor darlin'," said Mrs. Carter, who had managed to pull herself up from the floor and was trying to retrieve the spilled brownies from the orange shag rug.

SueBee was aware of people huddling around staring. Just staring. No one would tell her what she desperately needed to know. Was she alone in the world? Was her father going to die?

"He's dead, honey," said a voice from the open screen door. She looked up to see a large man in the uniform of a full colonel with chaplain's crosses on his lapel stepping into the crowded room. "He died about an hour ago. His last thoughts were of you."

She recognized him as the colonel Dr. Weissman had done the proctoscopy on. The one who had been crying until she rubbed his arm.

SueBee remained silent, hugging the pillow and rocking. Inside she was raging. *She was in his thoughts. Thoughts?* You couldn't hear thoughts! How did he know what thoughts her father was thinking? She didn't care about his last thoughts anyway. She cared about what had been done for him to ease his pain. She could never remember seeing her father even wince in pain. She had seen him hammer his thumbnail flat and take no never-mind. Once his motorcycle slipped sideways on the gravel walk, pitching him several yards and landing him on the side of his face. The next day his whole right side was covered with bloody raw open wounds. "Road rash," he had said laughing. "It's just road rash, honey bunch."

One couldn't possibly burn to death without feeling pain. It must have humiliated him to be seen like that. He had died all alone. Why wasn't she taken to him? Why wasn't she told something? Did they think she wasn't strong enough? Did they figure she was just a girl?

Well, she wasn't a girl anymore, she thought, as she sat staring long into the night after everyone had left, after all the food had been eaten or put away and all the pitying words had been said. Mrs. Carter offered to stay, but she said no, she was alone now and might as well get used to it. If she needed help, thank you very much, there were at least two dozen people only a whisper away in the crowded trailer park.

As she sat and rocked, an almost physical thing happened deep inside her. It was as though a huge wound was closing with scar tissue—a scar made of her own resolve. Her father's love and his protection, as strict as it had been, were the only things she'd had until she met the Weissmans. Now her work as Dr. Weissman's nurse was all there was to live for.

But she had to live in a wider world, too. One in which she could test the confidence she found when she put on a white polyester uniform. Even without the proper insignia or the cap that would have proved that she had graduated from a certified nursing school, she was treated as if she were a nurse. She had passed her own test; now she had to take her newly found self-respect to a larger place. Her problem was how. How to do it without the Weissmans? Among the three of them they had conjured up a clever conspiracy. There had to be a way to expand it. But how?

After the full-dress funeral with honors at the base chapel and the attendant paperwork at the company clerk's office, she was driven back to the motor home. She had just turned eighteen, the age of majority in Texas, which made the legal matters less bothersome. She would need no guardian. She would collect her father's insurance money in due time, and the motor home and its furnishings, such as they were, along with his motorcycle and Chevy van, were all hers.

She walked to the kitchen area and looked for something to drink. A half-empty bottle of her daddy's Seagram's sat forlornly on the counter. Why not, she thought. She might as well see what it tasted like. There was no one to say no. She poured the same amount she had seen her father pour, added half a bottle of 7UP from the fridge, and sat down on the couch. She took one sip and suddenly felt relaxed and warm. She hated the taste but she liked the feeling. It made her feel brave and in control.

It was time to plan. Mentally, she dumped everything she possessed on the coffee table and began to take stock. She had no money problems. That went on the plus side. She wasn't bad-looking. Another plus. She had a serious reading disability that she had no idea how to fix, so she would continue to make do. That was a big negative. And there was one other thing on the negative side of the table. Something she began to notice about herself when she listened to the Weissmans. It was the way she spoke. That marked her more than her inability to sort out the written word. The people on television didn't sound like she did except maybe on the Grand Ole Opry. The Weissmans never said "ain't" or "gonna git." There had to be a way to change.

She reached across the coffee table and turned on the television in search of a model. After several clicks around the dial she found what she was looking for. Katharine Hepburn was drinking champagne at a Christmas party in an office and speaking to a group of women. Excited, SueBee didn't bother to check the name of the movie in *TV Guide*. She ran to the kitchen and rummaged through the junk drawer where her father kept duct tape, screwdrivers, and drill bits. There at the back was the tape recorder he used to play his hillbilly tapes when he worked on his motorcycle. She found the proper batteries and an old Johnny Paycheck tape among the junk, popped them in, and raced back to the TV. She would record everything Katharine Hepburn said right over Johnny Paycheck. Then she would memorize how she said it.

It was a beginning.

SueBee punched the Off button of her latest Hepburn tape and put the machine on the floor next to the bed. Since her father died she had moved into the larger space at the back of the motor home. It had a double bed and three windows. She also felt closer to her father, sleeping where he had slept all of her life.

She missed him—missed having him to talk to, to cook for, to wait for at the end of the day. Most of all she missed his protection. Gradually, since he died, his poker-playing buddies had started to come around, rapping on the screen door of the trailer, wanting to come in.

They treated her differently now that there wasn't a man around, sweet-talking her, asking her to go out with them, go for a drive or to the movies or for something to eat. But she knew what they wanted. They wanted to have sex with her. They wanted to touch her breasts and put their tongues in her mouth. They wanted to get naked and lie down with her in her father's bed and put their penises in her.

Well, she had certainly seen what that got you! It got you sick. It got you sores. It got you pregnant. Sometimes, she supposed, it got you a husband.

She wanted a husband like she wanted a long, furry tail. She had cooked and cleaned enough to have been married fifty times and she was only eighteen.

The men who came around got ugly with her when she said no. But who needed them? They were clogging up her works, slowing her down on her master plan. Particularly Elroy Tilley.

Everybody called him Big Boy. He was the same shape and only a little bit smaller than the aluminum Air Stream trailer just behind hers, where he lived with his two even bigger brothers. Everyone knew the Tilley boys were semi-retards and steered clear of them.

Big Boy had taken to coming around just after dark. He nearly drove her crazy with his picky habit of coming scratching on the screen door. He didn't even have the manners to say hello properly; instead he'd stand outside and scratch with his dirty fingernails, staring at her as she stood at the sink doing the supper dishes. He had squinty red-rimmed eyes and a big belly that he pressed up against the screen.

Every time he showed up she would tell him to go away. Finally, one night she couldn't stand him out there in the dark, scratching, scratching away. Without warning she walked over and slammed the inside door on him. She didn't care if it made him mad.

Each night for the next week she lay awake listening for his dumb scratching. When Saturday night rolled around and he hadn't returned she began to relax. Relieved that Big Boy had finally gotten the message, she punched the pillow to get just the right indentation and snuggled her head into it. "Terribly awkward," she said in her best Hepburn voice. "It's all terribly awkward, darling." She smiled to herself, wondering if she would ever, ever have the occasion to say such a thing to another person. She drifted off to sleep and in her dream she thought something was pulling on the hem of her nightie, trying to push it away from her legs. Sleepily, she reached toward her ankles and felt a hand.

She sat bolt upright. There, silhouetted against the window, she recognized the massive bulk of Big Boy. The room smelled like beer and sweat. She yanked herself free, tearing her nightie, and snapped on the bedside lamp. Big Boy made a grunt of surprise and momentarily covered his eyes with his hairy arm. In his other hand he held his enormous erection. It was protruding from the fly of his dirty jeans.

"Get out of here, Big Boy!" SueBee screamed. "You filthy thing. Get out!"

"I'm gonna fuck you," he mumbled. His lips were wet and great rings of sweat darkened the underarms of his T-shirt. He made no move to come closer, just stood over the end of the bed with his thing hanging out.

She felt her breath closing off. There was such a huge fear lump in her throat she knew she wouldn't be able to scream again if she tried. For an instant she thought of throwing the lamp at him, but it was too small to do much.

She scrambled off the bed and backed into the corner before she realized she was trapped. She couldn't run by him or around the bed before he could grab her. Suddenly, her eyes fixed on the shelf over the bed where her father kept his war-relic collection. A dusty jumble of old helmets and belt cartridges lay under a mounted machete.

She began to tremble and realized her helplessness was only inflaming Big Boy. At any instant he would be on her and there would be no escape. Without thinking, she reached for the machete, yanked it from its rusty mountings, and swung wildly.

Big Boy didn't scream. Not right away. Not until a great arc of blood sprayed into the air. Then he let loose the loudest, most pitiful sound she had ever heard. It was the sharp wail of an animal, a night-shattering sound. Then he pitched face forward onto the bed, quivered for a moment, and lay still, whether unconscious or dead SueBee didn't know.

She didn't know until she rolled him over exactly what she had done. As he fell over the side of the bed she saw his penis was still in his hand. A piece of it, anyway. The rest was just a bloody stump.

In shock, she stepped over Big Boy, closed the bedroom door, and walked to the bathroom. She felt a weird sort of numb calm as she stood under the hot shower, watching the blood swirl down the drain.

Like a robot, she pulled down the clean white uniform that she had hung to drip-dry on the shower rod and put it on. She walked to the tiny kitchen and began going about her usual morning routine although it was still the middle of the night. As she poured juice and boiled the water for coffee, she carefully avoided looking at the closed bedroom door. She was afraid if she looked at the door she might hear a sound, or worse, see it open. Maybe Big Boy had already bled to death. Maybe not. She didn't want to think about it. In her state of shock, she felt that doing nothing would mean nothing had happened.

The ring of the Princess phone on the kitchen counter cut through her fogged mind. She moved toward it like a sleepwalker.

She knocked the poorly weighted phone off the counter, retrieved it, and said, "Ummm," into the receiver.

"SueBee? That you?" It was Dr. Weissman. He sounded sort of out of breath. "Sorry to wake you. Get your clothes on. I'll pick you up in five minutes."

"What?" she said, shaking her head in an attempt to clear it.

"I'll be in the Emergency Service ambulance. We'll meet you at the end of your walkway. Okay?"

"What's going on, Dr. Weissman? What's happened?"

"There's been a big accident out on the interstate. Near the Wayleen exit. Big semi jackknifed and hit a whole bunch of cars. The state police say there are bodies all over the highway."

"Oh, my goodness," SueBee cried, now fully conscious.

"And wear your uniform, kid," he cautioned. "I want to be able to get you through the police line with me."

She hung up and stared down at herself. Dr. Weissman would have thought she was crazy if she had told him she already had her uniform on.

The desk clerks on the evening shift at the Fairmont Hotel in Dallas hadn't seen such security precautions since the Johnson days, when a presidential visit meant having the Secret Service swarming all over the place. The meeting had been going on all week. In attendance were the top executives from the four companies that constituted the Aramco partnership, including not only Henry Kissinger but Sheikh Omar Zahidi Zaki, who traveled with his armed entourage of white-robed men in menacing wraparound Ray-Bans.

The meeting in the presidential suite had been scheduled to complete its business by late afternoon. It was nearly 11 P.M. and they were still at it. The block-long line of limousines outside the main entrance had been waiting for hours, and the drivers were getting bored and testy.

Danny Roebuck, the driver of the lead car for the Arab delegation, desperately wanted a drink but knew it was worth his job with the Regency Limousine Service to attempt finding one. He had a long drive ahead. He had been driving the "towel heads," as he derisively called his current employers out of earshot, for a week now. He couldn't wait to get on the road to Austin where he would get rid of them once and for all. But a belt of bourbon with a beer chaser sure would make the boring wait easier to take.

He flicked his last butt into the gutter, crumpled the empty pack, and hissed "shit" just as every glass door of the hotel entrance exploded open. Armed men, some in those crazy Arab nightgowns they wore and some in dark suits with wires running from their ears to their buttonholes, held the doors open. Behind them people poured through the lobby and out onto the street. Danny spotted the head sheikh he was driving in the center of a circle of men moving slowly toward him. He raced around the big car and yanked open the back door. The sheikh and three of his men swept into the waiting car. Danny trotted back to the driver's side, relieved to finally get going.

The drive to Austin was a long and boring one. They wouldn't be there until dawn, but what the hell, he was on platinum time now and there was a mortgage payment overdue.

He expertly wheeled the big stretch limo into the deserted street and headed out to where he could pick up the interstate. The three other limos that were part of the sheikh's official party slipped into line behind him.

Danny glanced in the rearview mirror to check his charges. Three of them were sitting side by side behind the glass partition, the head sheikh in the middle, staring straight ahead behind their shades. A security man in a suit rode shotgun on the jump seat. Earlier that week Danny had asked one of the other drivers what was the big deal with the Arabs and those shades. The other driver didn't know but figured they had bad eyes from staring at so much sand.

Funny people, he thought. They all spoke English, he had overheard them. They all talked like Sean Connery so they must have gone to fancy schools. He read in the *Dallas Morning News* just yesterday that the head guy, Sheikh Omar something, was from Saudi Arabia. He was an envoy of the king and had gone to Harvard and Oxford. The paper said the towel heads had come to Texas with Kissinger acting as kind of a messenger boy. They were meeting with the big oil people to try and pressure the U.S. government to abandon its support of Israel. Strange stuff, what with Kissinger being a Jew and all, but, hey, what did he care? Jews, Arabs, dagos, niggers . . . it was all the same to him. All he cared about was that they had the bread to be driven around day and night and were good for a big tip when he got them to Austin.

He wished to hell he had a cigarette. Half the night on the fucking road! He consoled himself with the fact that even these guys had to take a leak sometime. He'd pick up a couple of packs then. Maybe even sneak a roadhouse drink.

It wasn't long before his passengers lived up to Danny's expectations. Just as his headlights hit the overhanging sign reading WAYLEEN REST STOP, a disembodied voice in the back seat asked him to try and make the exit ramp.

He glanced over his shoulder to see if he could maneuver safely into the right lane. The towering grille of the eighteen wheeler barreling up the center lane was the last thing he ever saw.

Once a huge propane explosion up near Amarillo had been shown on TV. Cars and debris and twisted metal and gallons of blood were strewn as far as the camera could see. And bodies, too, under white sheets. That was exactly the scene that greeted the Wayleen Emergency Rescue squad as they piled out of the back of the ambulance near the exit of I-40. Police searchlights stabbed the pitch-black night. A state police helicopter hovered so close to the ground it was nearly impossible to hear anything else. As Dr. Weissman heaved open the back door of the ambulance a chill night wind swept his hair back flat. He reached for the navy blue nurse's cape hanging on the hook by the door and tossed it back to SueBee, who was standing right behind him. Once her feet hit the ground the helicopter cut its engine and she could hear screaming. She couldn't tell if the sound came from the police or from victims calling into the night.

SueBee and Dr. Weissman, his black leather bag in hand, started to run, stumbling through the rocky grass on the shoulder of the highway. Behind them came the driver lugging folded stretchers and a paramedic carrying a heavy aluminum box filled with medical supplies.

The air smelled of things burning: rubber, gasoline, and something sweet she recognized from the office as the cloying stench of burned human flesh. Suddenly her nostrils were assaulted by another familiar smell, the pungent mixture of sweat and cold, raw meat that she knew was blood. To her astonishment she realized she was running through it; it was all over her white shoes like spilled, splattered paint. As SueBee and Dr. Weissman moved closer, policemen with huge flashlights waved them on toward a cluster of swirling, blinking lights. More men stood in the middle of the six-lane highway next to an enormous overturned tractor trailer, lying on its side like a huge wounded beast. The high steel cab was twisted back like a head on a broken neck. Under the body of the truck lay a long black limousine, its front end jutting grotesquely into the air, wheels off the ground.

"Jesus Christ!" Dr. Weissman gasped, stopping dead in his tracks.

SueBee nearly bumped into him. She stopped and stared at the sight.

"Are you Dr. Weissman?" asked an enormous state trooper standing to their right.

"Yes, Officer," Dr. Weissman answered. "What's the situation here?"

"Well, the limo was sideswiped. When the truck flipped, it spun around and fell on the limo. You see there," he pointed to the rear of the truck. "That there big piece of metal housing sheared off and—"

"Officer," Dr. Weissman interrupted, "what I need to know is how many were in the car and if they're still in there."

"Can't tell. We torched open the driver's door. He's dead. We can see three others in the back but with the collapsed roof and all . . ."

Dr. Weissman walked around to the other side of the truck as the others followed. "I see the limo door on this side is open. Could anyone have been thrown free? Maybe someone's down the embankment there."

"No way, Doc. We already searched. It's just them three in the back."

"What about the other cars?"

"The Temple emergency squad is handling them. We better concentrate on these folks."

SueBee stood clutching the front of the cape Dr. Weissman had thrown over her. Between the wind and the rapid speed with which everyone was speaking it was hard to hear.

"Come on, SueBee," Dr. Weissman yelled. "If these people are alive they'll be in shock. I'll need adrenaline syringes, glucose IVs, the whole shock kit." He waved at the aluminum case of supplies. The paramedic was already on his knees on the ground snapping open the metal latches. Dr. Weissman turned back to the trooper. "How fast can your men get that mangled door off? I have to get to these people now or not at all."

In less than two minutes the men had burned open the door. As they pulled it free SueBee stared into the back seat. All she could see was what looked like a mound of crumpled laundry, a great pile of cloth soaked with blood. "What in the world *is* that?" she shouted, pulling at Dr. Weissman's sleeve.

"They're wearing robes of some kind," he said. "One, two . . ." he counted. "Wait, there's another man underneath."

"We better start peelin' 'em out, guys," the trooper said to the two cops who had handled the door. "This looks pretty bad."

The ambulance driver started handing SueBee lightweight hollow rods, which fit together to fashion the mobile intravenous rack that could be clipped to the side of a stretcher. She grabbed each piece as quickly as he handed them to her, shoved it into the next, screwed in the top bracket, and hastily hung the plastic bag with its long tubing.

The crew labored feverishly until all the bodies had been pulled free of the twisted steel. She heard the doctor say that whoever had been on the jump seat was crushed and it looked like the two other men were dead as well.

A policeman near the cab of the truck called out, "Anybody ID these people, yet?"

"We just ran a check on the plates," said another trooper with a mobile phone to his ear. "The car is from a Dallas livery company. It was leased to Aramco. Looks like we've got some Arab VIPs. A U.S. Army chopper is on its way from the Saudi consulate in Austin right now."

The three bodies from the car were lined up on stretchers on the edge of the highway. Dr. Weissman moved silently from one to the other, pulling a white sheet over each of the pulverized heads.

"That's it, SueBee," he said. His voice had a weary, hollow sound to it. "We can't help these poor devils now. I'll need that folder of forms in the glove compartment."

"I'll get it," she said eagerly.

The shortest route was around the back of the truck, where a big metal panel leaned precariously. She gingerly stepped around its jagged edges in the dark. As she did her leg brushed against something ticklish. Startled, and afraid she would lose her balance, she looked down for an instant to see a hand, fingers frozen in cramped arcs of agony. She squinted and bent down, wishing there was more light. As she did so the hand moved and closed around her ankle. In the dim light the immaculate white cuff on the wrist of the hand seemed to glow. She leaned closer and saw a heavy gold watch encircling the wrist under the cuff.

"My God, it's alive," she whispered into the darkness. "Hello?" she called. She reached down and walked both hands, one over the other, up the length of the arm under the metal. "Are you okay?" she called.

"Don't leave me . . . please," a man's voice croaked. "I'm . . ."

His next words were drowned out. Another helicopter seesawed toward a landing on the highway in front of her. Through the open doors she could see two men in dark suits, with neatly trimmed beards and sunglasses. No amount of screaming for help could possibly be heard in the chaos. She dared not leave.

"Hold on!" she called into the space between the arm and the metal. "I'm going to try and get you out." She knelt and placed both hands under the jagged edge of the metal sheet. With every bit of strength she could find she lifted. She could feel the veins in her neck and forehead popping out. Nothing. It didn't move a centimeter. In desperation she crawled between the truck and the leaning steel plate. She placed her shoulder against it and heaved with her last bit of strength.

It moved! She took short, panting breaths to still the panic rising in her chest. She might be crushing the poor man underneath doing it this way. She gave one more lunge and the plate rose into the air and flipped over.

The helicopter lights bathed the body of a man. He was wearing a long white coatlike garment and a white scarf over his head. Somehow the black-and-white cord holding it was still in place.

SueBee threw herself down beside him. His eyes were closed and a trickle of blood and mucus ran from both corners of his mouth, clotting his dark mustache and short beard. Quickly, she reached for the large vein in the man's neck. She felt nothing, only cold, damp skin and prickly hairs under his beard. She pressed her cheek against his nose. He was not breathing. She moved down his chest and pressed her ear against it, listening more for a rhythmic vibration than a sound. Stillness again. If he was dead it had just happened. He had moaned only a moment or two before.

She squeezed her eyes shut and tried to call up the pictures in the book Dr. Weissman had given her. Up came the first frame of the cardiac-arrest sequence. The picture was a simple line drawing of a man putting his finger in an unconscious person's mouth. She ran her forefinger around the inside of his mouth, clearing away blood and mucus. The next picture showed the victim's head being tilted back. She pulled off the headdress he was wearing and pressed on his forehead. With her free hand she lifted up on the back of his neck. Now the pictures were clicking into place like a slide show at school. Click: she placed the heel of her hand on his forehead and with her forefinger and thumb pinched his nose shut. Click: She placed her mouth over his. Click: She blew into his mouth, one, two, three, four quick puffs. She took another deep breath and started to chant quietly. "Blow." She blew. "Stop and say chrysanthemum as you listen for breathing. That's about a second." She blew and said chrysanthemum again and again, until her lungs were burning and she had to stop.

Frantic that he was still not breathing, she swung one leg over his ample chest. The cape tangled in her legs. She ripped it free. She reached down and tore the fabric of his tunic open, buttons flying in all directions. Rhythmically, one hand cupping the other, she began rocking back and forth, applying pressure to the bare, hairy cavity of his chest, releasing it and applying it again. Nothing happened.

She had run out of pictures from the book. She held both arms over her head. This wasn't in the book. She had seen Ben Casey do it. She wove her fingers together into a single fist and, with a force she didn't know she possessed, slammed down onto his chest right above the heart. Once. Twice. A third hammering blow produced a gurgling sound deep in the man's throat. Blood oozed from his mouth. She opened her eyes and looked down. His eyes were open. He was breathing!

"SueBee! SueBee! Where the hell are . . ." Dr. Weissman's voice filtered through to her conscious mind as though through a giant ball of cotton. "What the fuck!"

Suddenly Dr. Weissman was by her side. "Jesus, girl, what's happening here?" he said.

Still astride the man, SueBee looked up at Dr. Weissman. "I found him here," she said, trying to catch her breath. "He wasn't breathing."

Dr. Weissman stared at her. "How in God's name did you know—" He cut himself short and started to yell, "Stretcher! Stretcher! Over here!"

Suddenly she was surrounded by feet and legs and voices all talking at once. Someone was dragging her off the prostrate man and lifting him onto a stretcher.

"This is the guy they're looking for," said the paramedic at the head of the stretcher as he began to slip on the uneven ground.

"Easy, easy, take it easy," said the one at the foot.

"Who is this sucker, man? Some fuckin' king or somethin'?" asked the paramedic as he regained his footing.

"You got me, man. The place is crawlin' with blue suits lookin' for him. They're droppin' out of the fuckin' sky."

SueBee followed as they struggled toward the highway. Dr. Weissman walked along at the other side trying to do an examination as they moved.

"He's from A-rab-ya," said the paramedic at the head of the stretcher. "Some kinda royalty or somethin'. We're supposed to git him on that chopper over yonder."

"You shittin' me, man? You mean we got some fuckin' nigger king here? Woooweee!"

SueBee stumbled along wondering what men would do if the world took the word "fuck" away from them. Would they even be able to talk?

"No!"

SueBee looked down. The man was looking directly at her. "No!" he croaked again.

"Wait!" she shouted to the paramedics, but they kept moving. "Please!" she said, running to keep up. "He's trying to say something."

The head paramedic rolled his eyes and stopped.

The man on the stretcher reached out and closed his hand around

SueBee's wrist. "Don't leave me," he said. His eyes were black and wide. "Please don't leave me."

"I won't leave you, sir. I promise. They're taking you to the helicopter. I'll be right here," SueBee said softly. "You're hurt. They're going to help you."

"No! I want you to help me."

"It's all right. It's all right. I'm here," she said.

SueBee shot a look at Dr. Weissman that said, What in the world am I supposed to do?

"We gotta move it, kid. This guy's in bad shape," he said quickly. "Walk as far as the chopper. He'll calm down."

As they approached the big helicopter the two men in suits she had seen landing in the chopper jogged toward them. They looked alike, their faces grim, their eyes blocked by their big sunglasses. One thrust a clipboard with some papers on it at Dr. Weissman as the other one leaned over the man on the stretcher.

"We'll need you to write a brief report, Doctor," said the one with the clipboard.

"A report?" he said incredulously. "Here? There's no time for that. Who are you anyway?"

"I'm with the Saudi consulate, Doctor. This man is Sheikh Omar Zaki, a representative of the king. We will need your report for the doctors."

"Where are you taking him?" Dr. Weissman asked. SueBee could see he was not the least bit pleased. "This man has just experienced cardiac arrest!"

"Yes, sir. We'll take care of him."

"Now, look, I'm the attending physician here and I can be held responsible. I want to know where you're taking him."

The man from the consulate took a deep, exasperated breath. "His plane is in Austin. From there we will take him to the New York University Medical Center, where the Saudi royal family's doctors will attend to him. We will have doctors aboard his jet. There is no reason for concern. Now, will you please write us a short report simply stating what happened."

Dr. Weissman scratched the back of his head. "I'm afraid I can't, sir. I don't know what happened."

"But didn't you find him?"

"No, sir," Dr. Weissman said, lifting his chin defiantly. "I did not. My nurse here, Miss Slyde, found him. Not only that, she saved his life."

The man snatched the clipboard out of Dr. Weissman's hand. "Then she can write the report," he said angrily, handing it to her.

She took it reflexively. She could feel the cold sweat of panic around her hairline. She looked at Dr. Weissman silently screaming *Help me! help me! You know I can't write well enough!*

Dr. Weissman stared at her. She could tell his mind was racing to find a way to get her out of the situation.

In shame, she looked away. She handed the clipboard back to the Saudi official and gathered her stained and crumbled cape around her. "You won't need a written report, sir," she said firmly. "I promised this poor injured man that I wouldn't leave him. I'm going with you."

She reached over and put her hand on Sheikh Zaki's shoulder. He reached up and covered it with his own, looking at her as no one had ever looked at her before.

SueBee and Dr. Weissman walked on either side of the stretcher toward the helicopter.

Seeing the helpless man lying at her side, SueBee remembered Big Boy. In all the shock and confusion of the night her mind had blocked out everything but what was happening around her. She looked across at Dr. Weissman. She could never explain what had happened. There was only one thing to do.

As the stretcher was lifted onto the helicopter, SueBee climbed aboard and took a seat next to it.

Dr. Weissman poked his head through the open door. "SueBee, are you sure you know what you're doing?" he shouted up at her, his face tight with concern.

"I do," she said firmly. "But I want you to do something for me."

"Sure," Dr. Weissman said, stepping to one side so the crewman could begin to close the big middle door. "What is it?"

"Run by my trailer. I think someone's hurt there."

A look of total bewilderment crossed Dr. Weissman's face. He opened his mouth to speak as the big door slid closed, blocking him from view. Outside she could hear his voice calling. "SueBee! No! Don't!"

Then she couldn't hear him anymore. The big propeller above her head started to whine. As they rose straight up into the blackness she looked down. He was waving frantically, but getting smaller and smaller every second. She leaned her forehead against the vibrating coolness of the window.

She felt the bottom of her stomach drop as the helicopter rose higher, dipped forward, and then roared out into the night. Below her the lights of Wayleen flickered. On television, when they showed Los Angeles or New York from the sky, the lights spread out for miles like a great sequined carpet. The lights of Wayleen huddled in a cluster like a little twinkling handkerchief thrown down in the middle of nowhere. Until now she hadn't realized what a tiny speck of earth it occupied.

"Bye-bye, Weissmans," she whispered to the window. Her breath made a little mouth-shaped cloud on the glass. "Thank you for everything. Bye-bye, Big Boy. I hope you didn't bleed to death. Bye-bye, Daddy. I love you."

The man on the stretcher beside her made a low, wet sound deep in his throat.

It was getting light as Dr. Weissman pulled his car to a halt on the gravel drive in front of SueBee's walkway. He jogged the few yards it took to reach her trailer, pushed open the door, and looked around. Everything seemed to be in order in the cramped little front room. As he crossed the bright orange rug he stopped, bent down, and put his finger into one of the coin-sized splotches that extended from the front door to the back bedroom area.

Blood, he thought, *and fresh, too.* He stepped into the bedroom and winced. It looked as though someone had been killing chickens in the room. The bed, the rug, even the wall on the right side of the bed were all smeared with bright streaks of blood. Whoever had been injured in the room must have had help leaving; he wouldn't have been strong enough to walk.

When he got back to the office, he learned that Homer Tilley had called his answering service saying he was taking his brother to the county hospital and for Dr. Weissman to "Come quick, my brother got his prick cut off."

Dr. Weissman was well aware that he should call the police.

He didn't.

CHAPTER
❦ 7 ❦

Peter's Journal Entry—Paris, June 13, 1990

Madame's tale of the most intimate details of SueBee's beginnings took us a week. She spins a fascinatingly detailed story. Clearly, she knew SueBee extremely well. When I asked her about that she said, "I knew all my girls very well."

I asked if SueBee ever found out what happened to Big Boy. Madame said no, she hadn't, and she knew SueBee privately feared she had killed him and hoped that no one from Wayleen—like the police—would ever find out what had become of her.

I was riveted by what she told me about Omar Zaki. When he was at the UN in the mid-eighties I interviewed him in his suite at the Waldorf. The paper called him "the Gaudy Saudi," and after I saw how he lived, I believed it. Madame told me he had been a client of hers for thirty years, that he ordered as many as two dozen girls a week from her for his friends and associates. She had a great line. She said: "Zaki handed out women like cigars. You could flick one off a balcony when you finished with her for all he cared. Of course, no one did. Not my girls!"

Zaki had close ties to the Saudi royal family and made his money from arms deals. Every terrorist and outlaw group in the world did business with Zaki. Of course, they had to find him first. He had houses all over the world.

With great pride, Madame showed me a watch Zaki had given her. I had noticed her wearing it before because it had several faces. Each dial was set to a different time zone so she could tell what time it was in the country Zaki was in before she called him.

As I was leaving I asked where Sheikh Zaki took SueBee and Cleo said, "To the Waldorf Towers." I found myself catching my breath. She's not my Madeleine, then. She must have been the pretty blonde in the nurse's uniform who opened the door of the suite the day I came to interview Zaki? Why couldn't Zaki, with all his international wheeling and dealing, have wanted Madame not to write about him, as she inevitably would? Could he have been Madame's assassin? But, no, he hadn't been at La Fantastique. He couldn't have been the owner of the lighter Madame showed me. But maybe he got it as a gift from SueBee? Then again, maybe SueBee herself had reasons for going after Cleo. Maybe the now terribly grand lady didn't want the world to know about her humble, dyslexic, dick-whacking days in Texas. Maybe Mosby himself didn't know about his wife's criminal past. And maybe the former SueBee Slyde wanted to keep it that way.

When I got back to my rooms the concierge had had someone put up some drapes, which was very nice of her but unnecessary. I've tied them in a real tenement dweller's knot. It gets hotter by the day here. This afternoon there are gulls arguing for space in the eaves just below the roof. They make a hell of a racket.

My post person, Giselle, brought fresh bread when she delivered me Wendy's care package of magazines.

Next week I'm having a fax put in so I can send my notes back to Wendy. I'm paranoid about having my only copy in this firetrap.

There are roaches. Big red French ones that fly. I mentioned the bugs in passing to Madame today during a break in our session and she was appalled. She got on the phone and spoke to Madame Solange. Clearly, the two women are close. When she hung up I asked why such an old lady was running the building and she said, "I set her up there many years ago when she retired. Mme. Solange was a madam herself." Interesting.

The police phoned while I was at the house today to say they had run a check on the plates on the shooter's car. It was rented with a stolen credit card belonging to an employee of an Italian firm. I had a chum at Corriere della Sera in Rome run a check on the company. Seems it went out of business two years ago.

Tomorrow, Madame wants to tell me about a girl named Sandrine and how she snagged Jourdan Garn. As much as I know we should start talking about her own past, I want to hear this one. I know who Garn is, of course, who doesn't? He's one of our ten richest men, and from those who know, a blue-ribbon first class SOB. I'd love to know how this girl got him. When I asked Madame she said, "With the oldest, quickest trick in the book."

As I sit here looking out into the pale Paris sky I wonder: Are we men all fools, patsies, and sex addicts? Has some enormous con game been perpetrated upon us to make us think we control the world? The more time I spend listening to Madame Cleo, the more I realize that we don't control it and never have.

Sandrine grew up as the shy only child of designer Tita Mandraki. Her mother wasn't famous when Sandrine was born, but she desperately wanted to be and spent a great deal of time and energy finding a man to marry and divorce quickly. The first one she zeroed in on, Otto Mandraki, was old and rich. He was the perfect person for her, a man who had made a fortune importing Oriental rugs. Shortly after they met, Tita found herself pregnant, a fact that made them both delirious with joy. Otto was thrilled because he had never had a child. Tita was delighted because a child meant that her financial security was assured.

When Sandrine was four, her father pitched forward into a plate of mussels in white wine at the Lotus Club and died before the New York City EMS could get his stretcher out of the freight elevator. He left more than enough money for his widow to get her artistic career off the ground and a substantial trust fund for his adored baby daughter. The interest on the trust would go to Tita until her daughter reached twenty-five, by which time he felt she would be married, and he wanted her to have independent money. Then the principal would pass to Sandrine.

Tita wasted no time in moving to a loft in SoHo with her little girl and Martha Dyer, the woman who had been Sandrine's nanny since she was born.

The loft became a hectic salon for types who liked to hang out around rich artists. Tita was not without talent, and through her new circle of friends, she began to win some attention.

By the time Sandrine was six years old her mother had married and divorced three other men, each younger than the last. By the time Sandrine was eight her mother's line of dramatic clothes had made her famous. Soon afterward, another marriage ended and they moved to an enormous penthouse on Park Avenue. Sandrine, at last, had a room with four walls, and Martha had the privacy of her own little suite in back of the kitchen.

Sandrine's childhood was a lonely one. While she never lacked for material comforts, she reached her teenage years feeling as though she lived on quicksand, a victim of her mother's moods and whims and relentless zeal. The one pleasure she'd had in her childhood were the classical ballet lessons Tita had considered part of her "training." But when she reached adolescence, and her beauty became evident, Tita began to compete with her daughter directly. The ballet lessons were cancelled. Sandrine retreated into her books and schoolwork and depended on Martha Dyer to interpret the constantly changing value system by which her mother lived.

She was twenty-one years old before anyone, other than her nanny-housekeeper, Martha, told her she was loved. It was the most profound experience of her life.

Sandrine looked out at the passing landscape and tried to calm her nerves. Sleeping peacefully in the train seat next to her was the most beautiful boy she had ever known. She had met Jamey Grainger during the first week of her senior year at Hammelburg College. From that moment on they were seldom out of each other's sight. They ate together, studied together, and, to Sandrine's great joy, slept together when they could. And while she was hardly a virgin, Sandrine had never before been with someone who made her feel wanted, worthwhile, and loved.

She'd had a hard time reaching her mother to tell her she would be bringing Jamey home for Christmas vacation. Tita was always out somewhere. Finally, after a week, she succeeded. Her mother seemed vaguely surprised—Sandrine had never brought a boy home before—but pleased. She rang off saying she had a luncheon appointment with someone Sandrine knew she was supposed to know and be impressed with. She wasn't impressed. None of the things her mother thought were important—parties, people, names, exotic houses in fancy places, and society gossip—meant anything to her. It all seemed so empty. For Sandrine, the only thing in her life that meant a thing was Jamey. She was fairly bursting with pride and apprehension at bringing him home. Just the thought of introducing Jamey to her mother made her palms grow damp.

She wanted everything to be perfect and knew it probably wouldn't be. Since September her mother had been living with an Italian she had brought home from Rome. He was tall and shiny. He had shiny, darkish skin, and shiny black eyes and hair. He wore shiny silk jackets without putting his arms in the sleeves and held his cigarette palm up, between two middle fingers with shiny nails. Sandrine had hated him on sight. She hadn't told Jamey about Vito, the shiny Italian, hoping against hope that he would be gone by the holidays.

As the train moved through the New England winter landscape she pictured herself and Jamey framed by the bare-branched trees of the campus walk, as they had been that morning. In her mind, their chilled words floated before them in little clouds.

"I love you, Sandrine," he had said, gathering her in his arms. Replaying those words sustained her as she hoped there would be no surprises waiting on Park Avenue, that her mother would be pleased with Jamey, that Jamey would be pleased, and that she would have to deal with as little anxiety as possible and could enjoy the most wonderful thing that had ever happened to her.

It had taken a while for him to agree to come home with her for part of the holidays. He had wanted to use the quiet time in the empty dorm to finish a huge sports mural he was working on. Finally she convinced him with promises of trips to the artists' hangouts of SoHo. He had agreed to take the first week of the vacation with her in New York before going home to his own family in Boston.

She glanced across at him, asleep in the seat next to her, and smiled. Jamey's arms were folded across the front of the green L. L. Bean sweater she had ordered for him for Christmas. Behind his closed eyelids fringed with black lashes were eyes that matched exactly the deep green of the sweater. His presence made her feel as though she had accomplished something amazing, like capturing a unicorn. Looking at him made her fingertips tingle. She wanted to sink her hands in the thick dark hair and bury her face in the warm, cinnamon-scented space between his neck and shoulder. "Jamey," she whispered, and brushed his cheek, giving in to the irresistible urge to touch him. He shifted in the seat and leaned toward her as he slid his arm around her waist.

For the first month they were together, she had not discussed her mother. Jamey had asked about her, of course, but Sandrine would cut him off by saying that talking about her mother was boring. She didn't like it when people acted silly about her mother's celebrity, and she didn't want to risk seeing Jamey act like all the rest. When she realized his only interest was her mother's involvement in the art world, she began to open up and talk about their tense relationship.

Sandrine was silent during the cab ride from Grand Central Station. All she could think about was the way the apartment had looked when she left for school. The day before, some bizarre nude statuary her mother had purchased in Rome had arrived. It lay about the foyer waiting to be assembled by the Italian, a copper torso *pène complemento* here, a steel rear end there. She had ordered tall onyx vases full of gold-sprayed swamp grass to complete the effect, which, as far as

Sandrine was concerned, was vulgar. The one thing she could count on, however, which lifted her hopes, was that her mother's artistic whims were as changeable as her moods. If there was a God, both the Italian and the decor would be long gone by now.

The day doorman at her building tipped his hat as she and Jamey stepped out of the cab from the station.

"And welcome home to you, Miss Sandrine," he said in a thick Irish accent.

"Thank you, Jimmy," she said, smiling.

"Here, let me get those." He bent to lift Jamey's backpack and her small bag from the open trunk.

"Is my mother home?" she asked as they followed Jimmy through the lobby to the elevator.

"Don't know, miss. I've been on my break. But Miss Martha's up there. I just sent up another load of groceries."

Sandrine said hello to the uniformed elevator man as they stepped inside.

"Wow, this is impressive," Jamey said, looking around the mahogany-paneled elevator as they ascended to the top floor.

"This is a wonderful old building. Our apartment used to belong to the Roebling family, the people who built the Brooklyn Bridge," she said proudly. "It's really too big for us but my mother likes space."

"How long have you lived here?" he asked, his arm around her waist.

"We moved here after my father died," she lied. "A long time ago." Actually, her mother had won the apartment in a nasty, well-publicized divorce from one of her husbands, something that was never discussed. At least she wouldn't have to worry about her mother correcting the lie. She lied about it herself.

Sandrine held her breath as she opened the door to the penthouse. Until she heard Jamey gasp, she dared not look.

"Gee!" he said. "This is beautiful."

For an instant Sandrine thought she was in the wrong apartment. The huge foyer had been completely redone as if it were a stage set. Gone were her mother's bizarre sculptures and vases of swamp grass. Standing around the walls of the entrance foyer were dozens of silver wicker baskets of Christmas ferns and holly. In the center of the oval room stood a Christmas tree so enormous that it must have been lowered from the roof. The tree was covered with hundreds of white porcelain angels and antique wooden ornaments. The decorations seemed suspended in a fog bank of angel hair and skeins of tiny lights the size and brilliance of one-carat diamonds.

The balcony railings that ran along three sides of the foyer were draped with thick garlands of evergreens tied at intervals with gigantic white moiré bows. The air was filled with the sound of a symphony orchestra softly playing Christmas carols. Sandrine couldn't believe her eyes and ears.

"Come on," Sandrine said, trying to act as though everything was as expected. "I smell something wonderful. Let's go see what Martha is up to in the kitchen."

Sandrine's heart was bursting with relief as she led the way down the long pantry hall that separated the kitchen from the rest of the rooms on the first floor. What wondrous thing had happened? The apartment looked like an English Christmas card, the movie Christmas she had dreamed about and never had. Tita had never bothered much about the holidays and they never, ever had a tree. When she was little, Christmas was always spent in Italy or Spain or Nassau, wherever the man in Tita's life at the moment had wanted to be. Her best Christmases, when she was older, were spent alone with Martha. They would walk all the way down Fifth Avenue to midnight Mass at St. Patrick's. Sandrine wasn't a Catholic; she wasn't anything. But Martha was a daily communicant and always had tickets for High Mass at Christmas. After Mass they would sit dressed in their nightclothes before the fire in the library and have hot chocolate and little crustless chicken sandwiches. Until he died, Martha's older brother George would join them. Then, sitting in front of the fire with a man and a woman who loved and respected each other, Sandrine would pretend she had a family. Those were the only times she ever felt that way and the memories were very dear.

She pushed open the swinging double doors to the kitchen to see Martha standing by the big black stove, red-faced and somewhat frazzled. At the far end of the butcher-block island, three white-clad men in chef's caps were laboring over the slicing and arranging of several huge smoked salmons on silver trays.

When Martha saw Sandrine in the passageway she threw up her hands in delight. "Dreenie!" she called, breaking into a wide grin. "You're home!"

Sandrine rushed toward the stout, sweet-faced woman and threw her arms around her.

"Dreenie?" Jamey inquired with a chuckle.

"That's my baby name, only Martha calls me that," she said, over her shoulder. She turned back to Martha and said proudly, "Martha, I'd like you to meet my friend James Grainger."

Martha dried her hands on her apron and offered one to Jamey. "How do you do, Mr. Grainger," she said properly.

"Hello, Martha," Jamey said, grinning and shaking her hand enthusiastically. "It sure smells good in here."

Martha brushed a sandy strand of hair away from her sharp blue eyes. "These ovens have been going all day," she said, sounding exhausted. "Four turkeys, four hams. I've got a half-dozen pies cooked already and still more stuff to go."

"Good Lord, Martha!" Sandrine said, laughing. "We're only going to be here a few days. How much food did you think we could eat?"

Martha stared at her quizzically for an instant, then said, "Well, we've got a hundred coming for the buffet. Another fifty or so are coming in for dancing after. I *hope* this will be enough."

Sandrine felt her face beginning to burn. "Oh . . . of course," she said weakly. "I guess I forgot." She straightened her shoulders and forced a smile. "Where's Mother?"

"Having her hair done, of course," Martha said. "She promised she'd be back before six."

"Look, we'll get out of your way, okay?" Sandrine bent forward and brushed Martha's soft warm cheek, smelling the faint scent of talcum powder.

"Okay, honey. Welcome home."

"Right," Sandrine said tentatively.

She led Jamey into the library off the foyer. Had she seen the room earlier there wouldn't have been any doubt that Tita was planning a party. How dumb of her to think any of this had anything to do with her homecoming. There was an open bar set up beside the fireplace, and a band platform had been laid out between the windows that faced Park Avenue. She was beginning to wonder if her mother even remembered she was coming home.

She left Jamey with a beer and the five o'clock news and slipped back through the pantry. Martha was standing by the butcher-block island going down a long list with a man in a tuxedo. "Excuse me, Martha, could I see you for a sec?" she asked softly from the door.

"Sure, hon," Martha answered without looking up. She excused herself and joined Sandrine in the pantry.

"That's a mighty handsome young man you've got with you. I wonder where we should put him. The two extra bedrooms are full of the things they moved from the ground floor. There's the guest room, I guess, but I'll need some help getting your mother's treadmill out of there.

Sandrine frowned. "How come there isn't a room ready?"

"But, sweetheart, we didn't know you were bringing someone home. If we'd known . . ."

"I told Mother," Sandrine said sharply. "I told her weeks ago!" She could hear her voice rising uncontrollably.

"You did?" Martha said with a shrug. "Well, she never said a word to me."

"Marthy, is that Italian still around?"

Martha began arranging a pile of silver forks on the pantry counter into an even and totally unnecessary line.

"Marthy?"

"He's gone," she said flatly, not looking at Sandrine. Then she muttered, "Thank the Lord."

"When?"

"About a month ago."

"Was it . . . you know . . . bad?"

All the forks were lined up evenly. Martha looked around for something else distracting to do. Sandrine could see tears forming in her eyes. "Oh, Dreenie," she said finally, biting her lower lip. "I almost left. After all these years. Can you imagine?"

"What happened?"

"Terrible fights. Yelling in the middle of the night. Doors slamming. You know me, Dreenie. I never listen in, it's none of my business, but with my room right down the hall there I couldn't help it. The man was nothing but a lounge lizard. He borrowed money from your mother, used her charge accounts and her name to get free stuff around town. He took some young women to Le Club and charged it to your mother's account. When she saw the bill . . . well . . ."

"I don't want to hear about it," Sandrine said, interrupting Martha's report. "It all sounds so sickeningly familiar."

"I like your young man," Martha said, eager to change the subject for both their sakes.

Sandrine's spirits lifted. "Isn't he wonderful?"

"He is that," Martha said, nodding. "Are you in love?"

"I think so," Sandrine said, smiling. "I really think so."

"The two of you look grand together."

"Thank you, Martha," Sandrine said softly. "I'm really, really happy."

"High time," she said, smiling a conspiratorial smile. She reached up and gently looped one side of Sandrine's shoulder-length hair behind her right ear. "I was wondering if you would ever bring a young man home."

"You make me blush."

"You're nervous about introducing him to your mother, aren't you, love?"

Sandrine studied the pattern in the pantry-floor tiles, nodding slowly. "You know how she gets. She won't like him."

"Now, honey, why do you say a thing like that?"

"I just know. You know how she gets."

"Dreenie, if you're brave enough to bring him home, you're brave enough to ignore her opinion."

"I'm not brave, Martha. I'm in love."

"That's a kind of bravery right there, Sandrine. Now, you go take care of your fella and let me get back to work. Your mother will be home any minute and I haven't even *started* on the salad greens."

Tita was already home.

By the time Sandrine returned to the library her mother was seated on the opposite end of the sofa deep in conversation with Jamey. They were talking about art.

That evening would be the last time Sandrine spent more than a few minutes with Jamey for the rest of the holidays.

That spring was supposed to be the most exciting time of Sandrine's life. In a little more than a month she would be graduating. The whole world was supposed to lie before her—with Jamey. Instead, her world had collapsed.

In the bruise-purple light of a damp April morning Sandrine sat on the grimy windowsill of her dorm, numb with humiliation. As she watched what was going on below her window she wished with all her heart that she could disappear.

No, she thought, disappearing wasn't good enough. She wanted to die.

Below, at the curb, she could see the glistening roof of her mother's limousine reflecting the movement of the low-hanging clouds. Tita Mandraki was moving back and forth on the sidewalk beside the car giving orders to the two men who were carrying Jamey Grainger's belongings to the trunk of the limousine.

Tita Mandraki didn't so much run as dart—short bursts of quick, forceful movement that unnerved an observer. Sandrine's earliest memories were of her mother darting across her studio to streak an arc of red onto a canvas that brushed the ceiling, darting swiftly across the sun room in the penthouse to drape a chiffon scarf around a sewing dummy. Darting, flying, moving with an energy that was completely controlling in its ability to distract. She was as mesmerizing and oddly annoying as a hummingbird.

The flowing crimson cape she was wearing was trimmed with foot-long red foxtails. Occasionally, she would stop and readjust the drape of the fabric, flinging foxtails into the air. Her hair was a glistening magenta. At Christmas, when her mother stole Jamey, her hair had been the color of an eggplant.

With a stab of pain, Sandrine remembered the way the back of her mother's head had looked as she sat on the low couch hypnotizing Jamey. The eggplant, pontificating about art. It was the beginning of a nightmare the culmination of which she was witnessing below her window.

Sandrine had watched it happen before her eyes, mute, powerless, disbelieving. She had swallowed her anger as her mother murdered her very soul.

Tita laughed, she giggled, she trilled, she told Jamey she could tell he was a wonderful artist by the shape of his hands, then held them.

"More champagne, Jamey?" she had asked, her great dark eyes with the silver lids looking up into his. "Dance with me, Jamey," she had demanded, lifting a long, thin white arm toward the front of his J. Press tweed jacket, a finger crooked, beckoning, ensnaring. That first night, the night of the party, Sandrine had finally raced to her room and locked the door, weeping, while downstairs the music pulsated and Tita Mandraki, artist, designer, socialite, and thief swept the only man her daughter had ever loved away from her. Sandrine thought it would just last the length of the party, that her mother was simply trying to impress him. But the slow killing continued for seven horrible days. And then it went on and on. Jamey stayed on. To compound her agony he acted as though nothing at all had happened. He treated her just the same, kissed her good night and good morning as always.

After the first few days of torture Sandrine raced to Martha's room weeping, hysterical, begging for her to do something to make her mother stop. At least Martha had confirmed she wasn't imagining what was going on. But there was nothing either of them could do.

The only sound in the dorm came from Sherry Dolman's stereo next door playing Roy Orbison's "Only the Lonely." The haunting lyrics tore at Sandrine's heart. She dropped her head to her knees and heard again her mother's voice relentlessly, cunningly taking Jamey away from her.

"Today I want you to see my studio, Jamey. Sandrine can go shopping. She's so bored with my old studio.

"Jamey, do you ride? Let's go for a ride in the park. Sandrine hates horses.

"Jamey, I'm lunching with Andy Warhol today. Would you like to meet him?

I'll book Côte Basque for the four of us for twelve-thirty. Oh, dear, I forgot. I made a dentist's appointment for Sandrine . . . at one o'clock."

Of course Jamey wanted to see her studio. Of course he wanted to ride in the park. And what aspiring artist in his right mind wouldn't want to meet Andy Warhol?

Sandrine went to the dentist and when she got back to the apartment there was no one there but Martha. Her mother and Jamey didn't return until well after midnight that night. In the morning he was gone and so was her mother. Sandrine went back to bed after breakfast and by ten o'clock she had a temperature of 104°. Martha took care of her through the rest of the holidays and, when her temperature finally broke, she told her. Jamey and her mother were in Antigua.

Now Sandrine raised her head to see Tita's huge Mark Cross trunk being carried out of the dorm. It had to have been filled with Jamey's things. Following them, the dorm handyman and the limousine driver eased down the steps with the sports mural Jamey had started before the Christmas holidays. Since then, it hadn't been touched. She knew Jamey would come out next and she couldn't bear it.

She walked to her rumpled bed. On the night table was a bottle of Valium she had taken from her mother's bathroom at Christmas. At least she wouldn't have to read about this in the scandal sheets and gossip columns. She wouldn't have to face her classmates or the inevitable reporters who showed up whenever her mother did something outrageous. She wouldn't even write a note. Martha was the only one who cared, and she would know why she'd done it.

The Grossman Institute in Pawling, New York, kept around-the-clock security outside the grounds not so much to keep the patients in as to keep photographers for the *National Enquirer, People* magazine, and the *Star* out.

It had taken Tita Mandraki almost two days and many, many phone calls to her rich and famous friends to get her daughter committed. If Sandrine hadn't been in a near coma, Tita could not have accomplished such an impossible task. As it was, all it required was a doctor, a private ambulance, and two attendants to transport the girl from the college infirmary to the private psychiatric hospital.

During her first week at the institute, Sandrine did nothing but sleep. Her sessions with Dr. Herbert Epstein began during the second week of her stay. Before seeing the Mandraki girl he had asked to see her mother.

On the late-spring morning the hum of the air conditioner was the only sound to be heard in the library–sitting room where Dr. Epstein sat slumped on the chintz-covered couch, his face knotted in concentration as he read over the scribbled notes he had made after his meeting with the famous designer.

Tita Mandraki was a stunning, skittish woman of inordinate charm. She told him the girl's crisis had interrupted the start of her honeymoon but assured him her most recent marriage could not possibly have been the cause. She said she had no idea why the girl would want to kill herself, her grades were excellent, and she was popular with her peers, although slow in making any permanent relationship with a young man. Although somewhat withdrawn and shy, she had never had any behavior problems or abused alcohol or drugs.

The mother had an annoying inability to sit still; during their meeting she paced his small office, her arms folded across what looked to be a very expensive suit. She insisted that their relationship was loving and warm. Her daughter, Sandrine, was, according to her testimony, the very model of the perfect child.

Aside from the part about the good grades, Dr. Epstein didn't believe a word the woman had said.

He diverted his reach for the can of pipe tobacco in the end-table drawer to answer the low buzz of the phone beside him.

"Darling? Am I interrupting?" his wife asked.

"Of course not, Sheila. I'm just waiting for my next patient. That designer's daughter you were so excited about."

"Tita Mandraki! That's exactly why I'm calling," Sheila said excitedly. "Do you have the latest *Time* magazine there?"

"Hold on," Epstein said. He leaned forward and pawed through the slippery pile of magazines on the coffee table. Extracting a copy of *Time*, he checked the date. "Yup," he said.

"Look at the 'People' section. Page sixty-seven. There's a picture of Tita Mandraki getting married in Aspen."

"Oh yeah?" he said with mild interest, flipping to the page. "So? I knew she just got married."

"Take a look at the groom."

Epstein folded the magazine and held it under the lamp to his left. There was a small color photo at the top of the page of celebrity chatter. Tita Mandraki, wearing a long, unadorned tube of cream-colored silk, a wisp of a veil tied around her cap of glistening dark hair, was looking up into the eyes of a tall good-looking young man. A *very* young man, he noted. "Interesting," he mused.

"Herb! Look at him, he's younger than Daniel, for heaven's sake!" his wife exclaimed. Their son Daniel, a medical student at Cornell, had just turned twenty-five.

"How do you know that?" Epstein said, being deliberately argumentative. His wife had a way of jumping to conclusions about people and things. The fact that she was usually right only served to heighten his impish need to make her explain herself.

"I read the paragraph below the picture," she answered with a patiently smug tone. "He's twenty-two. She, my dear, is forty-five."

"Mmm," he hummed.

"And how old is her daughter?"

Epstein flipped a page of his notes and read the entry at the top of the page. "Let's see, twenty-two herself." He picked up the magazine again and read the caption aloud. "Jamey . . . Jamey Grainger. Art student. Hammelburg College. Secret ceremony."

"Get my drift?" his wife asked.

"Thank you, my dear. This is very, very helpful."

"You're welcome, I'm sure," his wife said with a laugh. "Don't forget the Dickersons. Eight o'clock. The Red Coach Inn. It's our treat. Helene and Ted's anniversary."

"Mmm," he murmured again, his eyes still on the picture. "Right."

He finished filling his pipe, dipped the flame of his lighter into the bowl, and inhaled deeply. Perhaps now, he thought, he had something to go on.

The library coffee table was set with a full tea service that had been laid out by his secretary. China cups, a silver teapot, sugar bowl and creamer, and a porcelain dish of butter cookies. Seeing patients in such a setting had always seemed less than professional to him, but the board at the institute insisted on relaxed informality. The private sanatorium justified its exorbitant fees by assuring their "clients" a homelike atmosphere, where "patients," their brochures assured one, "were considered guests."

He stood when his nurse showed Sandrine into the library. She was dressed simply in tailored jeans, boots, and a turtleneck. She had thick dark hair, and a pretty, oval face not unlike her mother's. Her face was free of makeup, and expressionless, except for the dark eyes, behind which lay an almost palpable anger.

"Good morning, Sandrine," he said, extending his hand. "I'm Herb Epstein." He waited until he realized she wasn't going to shake his hand and withdrew it. "Please, sit down."

She took the chair opposite him in silence, her eyes riveted on his. He sat down, crossed his legs, and picked up his pipe. Her eyes followed his moves as a wounded animal's might follow its tormentor.

"Sandrine," he began, "I don't blame you for not wanting to talk to

144

me. I can't imagine you appreciate being here. I know you would like to go home. Home has to be more pleasant than this place."

He thought he saw a flicker in the eyes. Perhaps it was just the light, or wishful thinking, but he was encouraged enough to proceed. "If you will trust me, talk to me about anything at all, we can make a good start at getting you home soon. I understand you are an excellent student so I know you are intelligent. I've met with your mother and she tells me—"

"My mother was here?" Sandrine said, breaking her silence.

"Yes, of course," he answered, incredulous. "You didn't see her?"

"No."

"That surprises me a bit, Sandrine. I would have thought . . ." Dr. Epstein paused. His thoughts were not important, hers were. "Why do you think your mother didn't ask to see you?"

She straightened her shoulders and, her eyes on his, she said, "Guess."

With that one word, the doctor and his patient began a psychological standoff that lasted for the rest of Sandrine's twenty-eight-day stay at the Grossman Institute. Dr. Epstein refused to play a guessing game with her, and she refused to volunteer any information. Clearly, her anger at her mother was so strong that nothing would dislodge it. At the end of the month, Sandrine quietly packed her bags and slipped into the waiting taxi. From the window of the library, Dr. Grossman watched her go, knowing her stay there had been an utter failure on everyone's part. Most particularly Sandrine's.

Sandrine lay in the deep, soft folds of the eiderdown comforter of her four-poster bed and traced the outline of the flowers on the drapes. The apartment was still except for the hushed sound of the late-afternoon traffic far below on Park Avenue.

Today, just like every day since the long summer of her return from the Grossman Institute, she had awakened well after three in the afternoon.

There was no reason to get out of bed. She wasn't going anywhere—not back to school, not to a job. Nowhere except deeper into her sense of loss and rejection.

Jamey and her mother had taken a studio in Paris, apparently planning to stay indefinitely. There was no way for either Sandrine or Martha to know for sure. Tita never wrote or called. Her lawyer paid the bills from New York. It was as though Sandrine's "crime" of attempting suicide had been so hideous that she had been deemed invisible—a nonperson—permitted to use a bedroom of a fancy Park Avenue apartment rent-free. She felt as though she had been thrown away like trash but no one had bothered to place her on the curb.

She rolled onto her stomach and checked the clock again, wishing it was later than mid-afternoon. She longed for the night that had become her life. In the night, she had discovered, there was no pain.

Her new, secret life had begun quite innocently not long after she returned from the institute. One of her college friends had called to ask if she wanted to join a group for the evening that ended up in a downtown club. Overnight, a whole new world opened to Sandrine, one where she was completely free. The night world gave her both anonymity and attention, for when she danced under the flashing lights of an otherwise pitch-dark club all eyes were upon her. It was a world she could enter alone, where she felt beautiful and wanted. It was the most liberating experience of her life and she couldn't get enough of it.

She threw back the bedcovers and padded down the long hall to her mother's empty suite. Standing in front of the long mirrored closet she tried to picture how she wanted to look that night. Slowly, she pushed open the door and took inventory.

The first section of the closet held evening clothes by Galanos, de la Renta, Yves Saint Laurent, and Scaasi. The next section held row upon row of slacks and silk blouses all color-coded with matching shoes and boots underneath. Next to that was riding gear.

Sandrine returned her gaze to the evening clothes and selected a strapless dress, short and beaded. It looked black until she turned it in the light. Then it shimmered a gunmetal gray. Perfect, she thought, smiling, as she laid it on the king-size bed. She yanked a full-length silver fox throw from the section for Tita's furs. She found a pair of silver strap sandals in the shoe compartment. She gathered everything she wanted to wear and headed for the door. As she passed her mother's high Sheraton jewelry chest by the door, she paused to pull open the top drawer. There, shimmering on black velvet, was the fabulous diamond bib her mother wore only to really big events. She stared at it for a long moment, pondering whether she dared take it. She shrugged, thinking what the hell, and lifted it from the drawer.

As she did every night, she waited until she knew Martha was sound asleep before she dressed and slipped from the apartment.

She knew Martha was vaguely aware of her nocturnal activities, but she didn't want to flaunt her behavior and worry her one friend in the world.

As she waited for the doorman to get her a cab, she scanned the slate-colored sky. In the darkness, surrounded by the lights and the beat of the city, she felt her heart pounding. She was free to be whoever she wanted to be, whoever she said she was. No one ever checked, nor was anyone permitted to take her home. They had to take her at her word. One night she was a Broadway actress, the next an attorney. She had spent several evenings with a group she hooked up with at an after-hours club, speaking with an English accent after telling them she was the daughter of a duke. Another night she had pretended only to understand French. She never liked to speak much anyway; by not speaking she always learned something new, something she could apply to her next impersonation and encounter. Occasionally, if she was in the mood, she had sex with someone she met in the night, at his hotel or apartment. Each time it was different, depending on who she was that night. Each time she would leave him silently, while he slept or smoked or looked the other way, slipping out into the safety of the night, leaving him to wonder who she was and why she had not, like the other girls he met in the night, asked for money or more love another time.

She never gave her real name or number. She never believed anything anyone said, for she assumed they were lying about themselves as well. She never met anyone she cared to see again. There were always more where they came from.

Most intoxicating of all, disguised in the sensuous anonymity of night, she was, at last, in control.

Sandrine usually arrived at Wings, her favorite club, which was in a seedy warehouse on West 18th Street, before midnight. The huge room didn't even start to jump until two, but she liked to come early and sit quietly at the bar, sizing up the scene before the crowds poured in. As usual, she settled onto a stool at the corner of the bar where she had an unobstructed view of the dance floor. At the moment it was filled with people from a private party. Whenever she sat alone at any bar she raised her chin, presenting her profile. Particularly in clothes that revealed her back and shoulders, she sat ramrod straight. The effect was spectacular.

Gary, the regular Wednesday night bartender, looked up from the steel sink where he was washing glasses to see Sandrine smiling at him from the corner of the bar. He smiled back, picked up a clean bar rag, and walked toward her.

"Hey, gorgeous! Lookin' good," he said, widening his eyes to show his approval of her dazzling dress, and spectacular diamonds.

"Hi, Gar," she said sweetly, flipping her long dark hair out of her eyes. "You, too."

Gary shook out the bar towel and carefully wiped the two square feet of wood in front of her, his eyes resting on her cleavage. The girl was a cool one. She had become a regular at the club, always arriving alone. That, in itself, wasn't unusual; a lot of women cruised the club. They were invariably hookers and the management had a pretty stiff policy about getting rid of them fast. Generally, they never got past the door.

Sandrine was different. Whatever her game was, she was no hooker. He had heard that she was Tita Mandraki's daughter, but he didn't believe it. He'd once asked her about it and she'd laughed, telling him she'd heard Tita Mandraki was really a man. But she certainly had the style to be a celebrity's daughter, the way she dressed and spoke, *when* she spoke, which wasn't often. From what he could tell, the only reason she came in was to drink, dance, and give the men who drooled over her a hard time. Occasionally she left with one, or with a group. On his nights off, he often ran into her near dawn, in the raunchier clubs downtown, still dancing.

He pushed a napkin toward her and emptied the ashtray in one swift pass. "The same?" he asked, knowing she seldom ordered anything but straight vodka on ice.

"Tonight, I think, champagne, Gary."

"I'd advise against that, love," he said out of the corner of his mouth. "You don't want the by-the-glass swill, and I'll have to charge you if I open a fresh bottle."

She shifted her weight, crossed her long legs, and smiled a closed-mouth smile as she lowered her lashes. The implied rich-lady put-down of her body language sent him scurrying to the cooler under the counter on the double.

He popped the cork on a bottle of Moët & Chandon and poured a flute to the rim. She held the flute aloft, letting the light from the pin spot over her head catch the ascending bubbles. "Happy birthday to me," she said in a low voice before taking a long pull at her champagne.

Gary cocked his head to one side. "You're kidding?" he said.

"Nope."

"And you're celebrating it by yourself?"

"I'm not by myself," she said pleasantly. "You're here. And pretty soon, the whole room will be full of people."

Gary looked away. Somehow, it was such an incredibly sad thing for her to say. This beautiful girl had to *want* to be alone if this was the way she chose to spend her birthday.

"Where's your family, Sandrine?" he asked softly, hoping he wouldn't hurt her feelings.

Sandrine looked up at the ceiling. "My parents are dead."

He waited for her to go on but she didn't. "I'm sorry," he said. It was a weak response, but her answer had slightly stunned him. "So, ah, you live alone?"

"Sorta kinda," she said lightly.

Gary waited but she seemed to have said all she was going to say. At least she had told him something about herself. A real breakthrough after so long. He decided not to press. "Well," he said, raising the empty glass he had started to polish. "Happy birthday, kid."

"Thank you, Gary," she said, smiling at him.

Suddenly he felt very protective of her. He wished he had the night off so he could take her someplace. Buy her dinner, a balloon, a carriage ride through the park, something to let her know someone gave a damn that it was her birthday.

With a drum roll and a crash, the band at the other end of the room exploded to life and rolled into the pounding rhythm of the new Prince single. Within seconds the dance floor swarmed with gyrating bodies that materialized out of the darkness.

"American Petroleum Association convention," he said, making a face.

"I think I'm going to dance," she said, sliding off the bar stool. "How about a treat for the birthday girl before I go?"

Gary looked over his shoulder and moved closer. "I've got black beauties," he whispered, "if that's the way you want to go. Otherwise I've got some Twoeys and a couple 'ludes. I was saving them for when I get off."

"I think a beauty is called for," she said.

He dug into the pocket of his black cotton jeans, palmed an amphetamine spansule, and placed his hand over her open palm. She slipped it into her mouth and washed it down with her champagne.

He knew it would only be minutes before she was flying. She lingered for a while, finishing her champagne, and then gathered up her bag, turned, and glided toward the floor. As she walked away Gary noticed she was snapping the fingers of her right hand in time to the music. The pill was beginning to work already.

From time to time as the night wore on he would glance out onto the floor. He had seen Sandrine dancing many times and it never ceased to amaze him. Once she hit the swirling lights and began to move to the music it was like a scene from *Saturday Night Fever*. As other dancers began to notice her they always moved toward the edge of the floor to watch. Even the few who lingered to compete with her soon gave up and joined the onlookers. She always danced by herself, turning her back on anyone foolish enough to try and join her. She moved as one with the music, head high and slightly back as though in a trance. The dress she had chosen showed the long, fluid lines of her body even more than usual.

Gary didn't dig girls, never had, but watching Sandrine dance always gave him a hard-on. She had the sexiest moves he had ever seen in the night world where parading one's sexuality was merely the entrance fee.

The chemicals in the pill she had taken reached Sandrine's brain the instant the tip of her high-heeled shoe stepped onto the hard wood of the dance floor. She could feel her mind, muscle tissue, skin, and bloodstream smooth into a continuous ribbon and melt into the music. But the real electricity she was feeling against her skin came from the hundreds of eyes upon her, watching—envious, lusting eyes that lifted her higher and higher until she could no longer feel the floor beneath her feet. With each beat of the music a small explosion went off in her head and reverberated down her body, fueling the new energy, the euphoria, and feeling of potency she craved. She owned the room, the world, the universe. No one could touch her. Nothing but exhaustion could stop her. The feeling of control was total, more exhilarating than drugs or drink, and far more powerful than sex so far had proved to be. She had reached the place she sought in the night, the place where there was no pain. Once there she re-created her favorite fantasy: in the distance, at the back of the room, alone and ignored, her mother watching her, unable to compete with Sandrine's beauty and the attention being showered upon her.

After an eternity, when the continuous music swirled into a slower, more fluid rhythm, she left the floor, glassy-eyed and breathing hard, to find the barstool Gary was saving for her despite the scowls from the three-deep crush now along the bar. The crowd parted as she approached through the scattered applause. She ignored the flattering remarks and invitations from the men. She didn't want to be chosen. She wanted to do the choosing, in her own time. If she was in the mood.

Gary poured her another glass of champagne without asking. The conventioneers swarming the bar made him wish he had another arm. He didn't speak to Sandrine in the frenzy. But later, around two o'clock, early for her, she said good night and tipped him generously when she left with a guy with slicked back black hair, wearing a sharkskin suit.

Sandrine slipped her arm through the man's curved elbow. She had chosen him because he had been staring at her intently from the edge of the dance floor for almost two solid hours. As they left through the cavernous lobby, she noticed that they were the same height. When he turned to smile a crooked, knowing smile, their eyes met.

"Where to, dollface?" he asked.

"I want to go downtown and dance," she said, tossing back her head and gulping the night wind as they stepped out onto the street.

"Come on, beautiful," he crooned. "Haven't you had enough?" They always called her things like "beautiful" and "baby" because she would not give her name. He put his arm around her waist and pulled her toward his face. "Why don't we go get a nightcap someplace quiet?"

She was still buzzing from Gary's pill, and suddenly a drink, and soon, sounded good. Then they would go dancing. She didn't care where they ended up. She didn't care about him, either. He was all-right-looking. He had good teeth and nails and nice after-shave. Other than that he was just shoulders and shoes that could dance.

She told him her name was Desirée, the *nom de fuck* for the night.

The man raised his arm and a cab speeding down West 18th swerved to the curb.

As she slid across the back seat dragging her fur, her companion leaned through the opening in the scratched Lucite partition and said, "The Waldorf, please, my man."

Sandrine sat up straight and stared at him angrily as he closed the door and settled back. "The Waldorf Hotel? You said a nightcap."

"A nightcap at the Waldorf," he said pleasantly. "I told some business friends I'd catch up with them at the Bull and Bear. No sweat."

"Okay," she breathed. "But just one." The idea of the Waldorf was leaden. Quiet, stuffy, a businessman's hangout and about as far from the music and dappled light of another disco as one could get. But at least a drink one-on-one would give her a chance to practice her current persona, which she was eager to do.

She relaxed into the seat and let the man hold her hand. Let me see, she thought, who is Desirée? On a whim and in keeping with the way her body was feeling, she decided Desirée was hot. Desirée would show this man, whoever he was, that as much as he wanted her, she wanted him more. She leaned over, delicately flicked her tongue against his earlobe, and felt a shudder of desire run down his body.

The Bull & Bear, a vast, dark restaurant on the ground floor of the Waldorf, was nearly empty at such a late hour. The captain's frown said that the kitchen was closed in case they were foolish enough to expect food.

"We're meeting a group," her companion said, stepping up to the captain's station and smoothing his slicked-back hair.

"There's only one group here, sir," the captain told him. "They're at a back table. What is your party's name?"

The man craned his neck around a standing fern. "Ah, I see them," he said. "Come on, Desirée. They're over there by the window."

As she walked around the tall fern it took one look to see that this was not her idea of a fun evening. At a long table against the window sat six or seven men. One had on a business suit; the others wore Arabian *thobes* and what looked like dish towels over their heads secured with circles of black cord. All but one or two were wearing dark glasses. At the head of the table seated in a wheelchair was an older Arab with what looked like a five-pound gold Rolex jutting from the sleeve of his robe. As they approached the table he turned and said something to a pretty blond nurse seated alone at a table immediately behind him. The nurse stood, stepped to the back of his chair, and turned it so he was facing out into the room to receive the approaching guests.

Sandrine cringed. *Oh no, don't tell me I have to sit around and make conversation with this bunch. I'll die!* She could see she would have to abandon her Desirée fantasy to get her drink. In her imagination Desirée was wild and abandoned. Desirée would jump up on the table and pull her dress over her head in front of all the towel heads. Suddenly, she didn't have the energy for all that. Once she had decided who she was going to be for the night, it was annoying to have to give it up.

She noticed that the man with her now seemed very jittery and agitated, as though the scene was not what he had expected either. He pulled her toward him and pressed his mouth against her ear. "The man in the wheelchair is Sheikh Omar Zaki. I didn't know he was going to be here," he said. He was speaking so rapidly she had a hard time understanding him.

"So?" she said, feigning boredom with the presence of one of the wealthiest men in the world.

"See the nurse?"

"Yes."

"Go sit with her," he whispered.

"Are you crazy? No way," she said angrily. How dare he? she thought. She pulled away from him. "I'm going dancing. This setup is all yours."

The man grabbed her forearm and squeezed it very hard. "Look, don't make a scene. These fellows aren't crazy about having women around when they're doing business. Just go sit down and I'll be right with you. We'll have a nice quiet drink together."

The temptation to storm out of the room was irresistible until Sandrine glanced over at the nurse. Something in the way the blonde was looking at her made her hesitate. Her eyes seemed to plead with Sandrine to join her. Inadvertently, she smiled at the nurse, remembering how much she'd wanted that drink. "Five minutes," she warned. "Five minutes and I'm out of here."

Disgusted at having gotten herself into the situation, Sandrine flounced over to the nurse's table, tossed her fur and bag over the back of an empty chair, and plopped down opposite the sweet-faced girl. "Hi," she said nonchalantly. "You mind?"

"No, not at all, please," the nurse said eagerly. "I was hoping you'd come over here. I'd love some company. I've been here for hours. Would you like a drink?"

"Yeah, I sure would," Sandrine said, looking around for the waiter, who was right behind her. "Bring me a vodka on the rocks," she said. "Make it a double." She looked back to the nurse. "Won't you join me?"

"Another hot tea with lemon, please," she said sweetly to the waiter in a pronounced southern accent. The waiter took their order with a nod and disappeared. The nurse looked back at Sandrine. "My name is SueBee," she said, "SueBee Slyde. I'm from Texas, and the only people I know in this whole city are sitting right over there."

"Well!" Sandrine said with surprise. She thought for a moment. She wasn't hot Desirée anymore. She had decidedly cooled off, and sitting with an Arab's nurse in the Bull & Bear was definitely not sexy. She shot a glance at the men at the next table. "My name is Sandrine," she whispered. "But don't say anything. I told the guy I came with something else."

"Whatever for?" SueBee asked innocently.

"I don't know," Sandrine shrugged. "I don't particularly like him."

"I thank you, then," SueBee said, smiling some more.

"For what?"

"For tellin' me your real name."

"You're welcome," Sandrine said. The girl was nice. A little naive maybe, but nice. "Have you been sitting here all evening without a drink?" she asked.

SueBee leaned closer to Sandrine and said in a half whisper, "I don't drink. Even if I did, I couldn't do it here. None of these people drink in public. It's against their religion."

"But they do in private," Sandrine said, laughing.

"You bet!" SueBee was still whispering. "Johnnie Walker Red is their big thing. Maybe because they can't get it at home. You should see them pack it away up in the suite."

"The suite? You mean all of you are staying here?"

SueBee nodded enthusiastically. "Uh-huh, in the Towers. Everyone but the man in the suit talking to your friend. He's Sheikh Zaki's lawyer. One of them anyway."

"Who are all the others?"

"Bodyguards. Except for the little one on the end there, with the pointy little beard. He drives and carries the watches."

Sandrine was now alert and fascinated at the odd gathering she had stumbled into. "Watches?" she asked, frowning with curiosity.

"Sheikh Zaki likes to give out gold watches as he moves around. You know, like tips."

"Are they real?"

"Of course they're real," SueBee said defensively. "See for yourself." SueBee extended a starched white sleeve. Below her cuff she wore a slim gold Piaget with a diamond-studded band.

"He gave you that? It's beautiful."

"He gives me lots of things."

"I'll bet," Sandrine said, not quite sure she wasn't being put on. From the corner of her eye she could see Mr. Sharkskin perched on the edge of a chair at the far corner in deep conversation with the man wearing a suit.

"So that fella is not your boyfriend?" SueBee asked.

"Far from it," Sandrine said. "He's just some guy I picked up at Wings. He said he'd take me someplace for a drink. I didn't know we were going to a United Nations meeting."

"What's a Wings?"

Jesus, Sandrine thought, where does this one come from, Pluto? "Have you been in town long?" she asked.

"Nearly three months," the girl said, not realizing that Sandrine was being sarcastic.

"You've been in a Waldorf suite for three months?" Sandrine asked, incredulous.

"Ummm. I'm so bored I could scream. It's a twenty-four-hour-a-day job. I haven't spoken to anyone except his staff since I got here."

Finally, the waiter returned and plunked a glass of vodka and a cup of tea down on the tablecloth. "Will that be all?" he asked glumly.

Sandrine looked up at him and fluttered her eyes. "Would you bring me a pack of More's, please."

"Lobby drugstore's closed," he grunted. "I'll see if we have them in the machine." He made no move to go.

"Oh, ah . . . see the man in the gray suit at the end of the table over there? Ask him for the money." She lifted her glass and filled her mouth with vodka as the waiter trudged over to the other table, got a couple of dollar bills, and disappeared.

"He better not be so grumpy. He won't get a watch," SueBee said, watching him.

SueBee's open innocence suddenly struck Sandrine as wonderfully funny. She threw back her head and laughed loudly enough to make several of the men at the next table stop talking and stare.

"What's so funny?" SueBee asked, starting to giggle herself.

"Oh, I don't know," Sandrine said, calming down. "How in the world did you get mixed up with this crew? You couldn't work for an agency here, they'd never let you stay cooped up in a hotel suite for three months. That's like slavery."

"Not really," SueBee said, smiling. "The suite is really nice. Sheikh Zaki owns it. There are four or five bedrooms, a fireplace, even a white piano just like in the movies. He's even got a full-time chef, too."

"And you just stay up there and keep the sheikh company?" Sandrine was impressed at the tediousness of such a chore.

"Oh, no. I feed him, give him his heart medicine. I bathe and dress him. We watch TV a lot. He's crazy about the soaps and quiz shows."

"You do anything else for him?" Sandrine asked meaningfully. "If I'm not being rude."

"Yes, actually. The medication he takes gives him terrible constipation. It can be very painful, so I sit with him in the bathroom, sometimes for hours. We play cards."

Sandrine swallowed hard. She didn't know whether to be shocked or amused. "The two of you play cards while he sits on the john? What does a job like that pay, if I may ask?"

"I don't know. I don't need any money, really. If I do, one of his men gives me some. He keeps saying when he's well enough to go home he'll take care of me. That I shouldn't worry."

"I'd worry," Sandrine said flatly, and took another swallow of her vodka. This girl was either retarded or a complete innocent. Still, she liked her. She was the first honest person other than Martha that she had talked to in ages.

"You think I should be worried?" SueBee asked with alarm.

The expression on SueBee's face stopped Sandrine from giving her a stern answer. She sensed someone standing behind her chair. Before she could turn and see who it was, SueBee stood up and walked around the table. Sandrine turned slowly and saw the little man with the pointy beard talking to SueBee behind his hand. SueBee nodded and returned to the table smiling.

"He wants to meet you," SueBee said, breathlessly.

"Me?" Sandrine said with surprise. "Who?"

"Sheikh Zaki. Do you mind? He's really very sweet. He told Mr. Nebeh, there, to come and get you." She nodded toward the sheikh's watch carrier. "He said you have the face of an angel. He wants to give you a gift."

Sandrine glanced over at the sheikh. He was staring at her, waiting for her to trot right over. She raised her chin, flipping her long hair away from her face as she pushed back her chair. "SueBee," she said, standing up and gathering her bag and fur. "The best part of the evening has been meeting you. Call me sometime when it gets to be too much." She took out a card some guy had foisted on her during the evening and scribbled her number and address on it.

"You're leaving?" SueBee cried in disbelief. "But what about Sheikh Zaki?"

Sandrine threw her fur over one shoulder and smiled. "You tell your boss I already have a watch."

She turned and walked back through the empty restaurant aware that all the eyes in the room that were riveted on her back belonged to men who had never met a woman who would refuse an introduction to the billionaire Saudi, let alone a gold watch.

As she pushed through the revolving door onto Park Avenue she saw Mr. Sharkskin running at a tumble down the short flight of stairs from the lobby toward her. "Wait!" he shouted, waving frantically. "Desirée, wait!"

Sandrine had reached the only cab parked at the stand at such a late hour and was yanking open the door as he reached her. There were beads of sweat along his high hairline. "What are you doing?" he demanded.

"Removing myself from an unpleasant situation," she said, with one leg already inside the cab.

"But Sheikh Zaki wanted to meet you! Don't you know who he is?"

"Of course I know who he is. But who are you, his pimp?"

"Desirée," he said in a shocked, how-could-you voice. "Please don't go."

"Consider me gone." She slid into the back seat only to have him push in right behind her.

"Where are you going?" he asked, slamming the door.

"Dancing. That was the deal."

"I'm going with you."

"Suit yourself," Sandrine said with a shrug. "Driver, do you know where the Palladium is?"

"You got it," the driver said. Without turning around, he peeled away from the curb.

As they rode wordlessly downtown all Sandrine could think about was regaining the high she had felt out on the dance floor at Wings. If this guy wanted to tag along, fine. She didn't have to make up her mind about him yet.

Red, blue, green, yellow, and violet, a rainbow of pills was available in every outstretched hand at the series of dark and smoky clubs Sandrine visited that night. But she was unable to re-create the euphoria she had achieved earlier in the evening.

When she finally collapsed into Mr. Sharkskin's bed in a tiny, musty room at the Summit Hotel, it was with the vague hope that perhaps there she would find what she was looking for. But her body, in another universe and beyond the reach of her senses, was numb. The man was on top of her for a while. Not for long—at least not long enough to wake her up.

Martha moved hurriedly up the stairs, bending to clean up Sandrine's familiar mess. There was one high-heeled sandal on the stairs. One of her mother's designer gowns had been carelessly tossed over the railing at the top of the stairs. A discarded black garter belt, a half-slip, and one torn black stocking lay in a trail that led to Sandrine's closed door.

If Mrs. Mandraki and Mr. James woke up before the mess was cleaned up there would be hell to pay. Fortunately, they had arrived from Paris in the wee hours of the morning and probably wouldn't surface until noon.

Martha had no idea what time the girl had finally gotten home, but she knew from experience that it would have been getting light out, far too late to tell her to be quiet, that her mother was home and sleeping.

Now that Mrs. Mandraki was back perhaps something could be done about Dreenie's shenanigans.

It was really getting out of hand. Whatever in the world she was up to, out all night every night, couldn't be good, but Martha knew it wasn't her place to say anything. The girl wouldn't listen to her anyway.

Several times she had almost called Mrs. Mandraki in Paris but thought better of it. The girl deserved to live her own life, she had earned it, Lord knows. But the way she was doing it wasn't right. Martha hadn't said anything either about the girl using her mother's things. It seemed a pity, closets full of expensive, beautiful clothes going to waste up there in the master bedroom. She had always carefully cleaned and pressed the things Sandrine used and put them back exactly where they belonged. When she discovered a pile of lapis lazuli bracelets that belonged to Sandrine's mother lying in a puddle on Sandrine's bathroom sink, she started checking the jewelry case. Just last night she had noticed that the big diamond necklace that was always in the top drawer of Mrs. Mandraki's jewelry cabinet was missing. She'd have a look around Sandrine's room and try to get it back in place before anyone was the wiser.

She pushed Sandrine's door open just far enough to see the shape of her body under a linen sheet. Her dark hair fanned out over the pillows like fallen ribbons. She tiptoed into the room and placed the clothes she had collected on the dressing-table bench. Silently, she crept around the room pushing aside magazines and record album covers, looking for the necklace. She checked the bedside table, the floor under the bed, and then every place she could think of in the bathroom. It wasn't in Sandrine's pockets or in her handbag. It was when she was sifting through the jumble of cosmetics strewn about the surface of the dressing table that she heard the sound clear down the hall from the other end of the apartment: Mrs. Mandraki was screaming at the top of her lungs.

Martha turned and rushed to the door. She ran the length of the long carpeted hall as fast as her bedroom scuffs would let her. As she stepped through the master bedroom door Mrs. Mandraki was standing in front of her jewelry case; she had one hand to her mouth and was still screaming. Mr. James, in his undershorts, was standing just behind her.

Martha stood frozen in the door as Mrs. Mandraki turned around and screamed again at Mr. James, "Call the police, Jamey! Call nine-one-one. My Bulgari necklace is gone! I've been robbed!"

Martha knew neither of them had seen her. Quickly, she turned and moved back down the hall toward Sandrine's room. She would have to wake her up now and tell her that her mother was home.

CHAPTER
❧ 8 ❧

Peter's Journal Entry—Paris, June 23, 1990

It's Saturday morning—my working man's weekend off—and my rooms are sweltering. So I've taken a cab and my laptop to the Tuileries to get some air. The contrast between the sun and shade here in the park is so vivid I can hardly see in the sun, and it's almost too dark to see in the shade. I've settled for a bench near a Henry Moore sculpture of a nude woman whose wide thighs are throwing just enough shade to make it tolerable. I shall have to move with the sun.

We've spent this week on Sandrine Mandraki. By week's end I took her out of the Madeleine sweepstakes. There was an innocence to Madeleine I could not discern in Sandrine. But I do think she is a better candidate for Madame's assassin than SueBee. Sandrine's awfully slick. Slick and capable of murder. Problem with her mother's approval, low self-esteem, obviously not a type who would want it known that she was a call girl now that she's made it. Furthermore, I can imagine the social-climbing Garn's displeasure. If Sandrine didn't do it, he probably did.

Madame shrugged and pushed out her lower lip when I said I suspected both of them. But she didn't deny that they'd been to La Fantastique.

I've made a note to do some more checking on Garn. From a purely gossip standpoint I was interested to learn about the mother. Tita Mandraki was one of the singularly most unpleasant women that I ever met in New York. I was once at a Broadway opening where she nearly knocked eighty-year-old Dame Vivian Roundtree to the ground to get her purple hair in front of a television camera. Having seen Tita several times at dinners around town, and read many profiles of her, I've only learned now that she had a child! I thought the only "child" she had was that pretty boy-toy husband.

There was quite a fuss when her diamond necklace was stolen. The paper ran it on the front page for two days as a Park Avenue heist. She must have collected a ton from the insurance company. How interesting that her daughter was responsible.

I had put my tape recorder away and was putting on my coat when Madame blithely said that Tita Mandraki had worked for her in the late fifties and had married one of her best clients, Otto Mandraki. When Sandrine came to work for her Cleo recognized the name, and the resemblance between daughter and mother. Cleo said nothing about her special knowledge, which I'm finding she is exceptionally good at.

Maybe, somehow, the batty mother did it? Nah, forget it, Shea. You're going to drive yourself mad.

Our sessions have now moved to Cleo's back garden. The little unair-conditioned room had become unbearable. Between the drapes, the velvet walls, the Oriental rugs over the carpeting, and the silk-draped lamps, I thought I was going to smother.

The garden is quite pleasant, with many shade trees and a fountain next to our comfortable wicker chairs.

Martin, Cleo's assistant, dropped by to listen and stayed to add his two cents about Sandrine. He doesn't think she could have ever dreamed of killing Madame. He seemed to base this on nothing more substantial than the fact that he liked her a lot.

Martin is an odd duck. Terribly proper and upper crust. I wonder how he got mixed up with Madame Cleo in the first place.

So . . . Monday she wants to tell me how Sandrine and SueBee ran into each other again and how it changed their lives.

The Henry Moore nude's thighs are no longer any protection. I'm going to have to move.

The day after SueBee met Sandrine at the Bull & Bear she couldn't get her out of her mind. Their brief conversation had been the first time SueBee had spoken to anyone close to her own age since she left Texas. There was something so sophisticated about the girl, and she wore such beautiful clothes. SueBee even liked the casual way she treated the man who brought her to the restaurant. It was as though Sandrine called the shots in her own life and didn't have to depend on anyone, particularly not a man.

As she sat on the edge of Zaki's bed, going through their morning routine, she began to think about her own dependence on him for the first time.

The headboard of Zaki's bed had been made to order. It was a giant crest washed with fourteen-karat gold. High blackamoor lamps stood as sentries on either side. At the foot of the bed lay a king-size sable throw, neatly folded to form a triangle. Once Zaki had told her proudly that the bed had had to be hoisted up the side of the Waldorf and through a hole specially made by removing two windows of the bedroom.

SueBee repositioned herself on the bed. In one hand she held a bottle of glycerin and rosewater. The other hand moved in a circular motion across Sheikh Zaki's chest, making little moisture trails in the black hair.

"Are we going any lower today, SueBee?" Zaki said. His mouth was slightly open and his eyes hooded.

"We'll see," she said sweetly, without looking up.

"Mr. Python misses you," he said coyly.

"Ummm," said SueBee.

"Mr. Python wants to come out and play."

It was their game. Every time she gave him a rub he started up about Mr. Python. "Roll over," she commanded.

Sheikh Zaki made a pout. "But I'll have to roll over on Mr. Python and he's trying to get out."

"Never mind about Mr. Python," she scolded. "I need to do your back or you'll get those terrible sores. Now roll over."

Grudgingly, Zaki rolled over in the enormous bed.

SueBee eased the pillows out from under his head so he was lying flat. She poured more glycerin and rosewater into her palm and started at his shoulders.

As she worked, her thoughts returned to Sandrine. She wondered if maybe she had told her too much about Zaki. At least she hadn't told her about playing the Mr. Python game.

He had started playing the game as soon as he came back from the hospital and they all settled into the suite. She didn't mind, really. It was just an extension of a back rub. She considered it no big deal, and it seemed to make him very happy. And keeping Zaki happy was her only insurance.

It had upset her when Sandrine said SueBee should be worried about getting paid. What in the world would she do if Zaki and his men just flew off to Arabia or wherever they came from?

She needed to work. She couldn't get a job as a nurse. She wasn't one. She would be in some kind of pickle without a job or a place to live. He must be paying those men who hung around in the living room of the suite cleaning their nails with those little carved knives and staring at her through those dark glasses. They only talked that bugga-bugga talk she couldn't understand so there was no asking them.

Zaki's chef, a great big man with no hair and a big black mustache, did speak English. Once, when they first got there, she went into the kitchen to pick up Zaki's dinner tray. The chef turned his mean eyes on her and told her she should go back to Texas if she "knew what was good for her." Well, she knew what was good for her all right, and going back to Texas definitely was not.

While thinking about her situation she had worked her way down to the elastic waistband of Zaki's silk pajamas. She rubbed across his lower back and up to his shoulders in long, sweeping strokes.

His eyes were closed and he moaned, "Mr. Python is sooooo lonely." He made it sound like "wone-wee." He always talked a kind of baby talk when he was getting impatient to play the game.

"Roll over," she said, giving him a playful tap at the base of his spine.

"Huh?" Zaki said, raising his head. His eyes were wide and hopeful.

"I said, roll over. I want to ask you something."

"Okay," he said eagerly.

"And after we have our talk I'll see how I feel about visiting with Mr. Python."

"Really?"

"Well, it depends," she said primly.

From that time on, every Friday night during SueBee's tenure as Sheikh Zaki's nurse-companion, Zaki's secretary, Mr. Hakim, a spider-thin little man with protruding teeth that looked like praying hands, handed SueBee three one-hundred-dollar bills. He took it from the briefcase that never left his side, the one containing what Zaki called his whip-out money.

With her first "paycheck" she bought four crisp new uniforms, demure until SueBee raised the hem to just over the knee and tapered the top to a tight, body-skimming fit. She punched holes in the belt to accommodate the cinch that emphasized her nineteen-inch waist, and shortened the long sleeves into girlish puffs.

She completed her outfit with a pair of four-inch white patent leather pumps she found on sale at Alexander's.

SueBee's new look was an instant hit with the sheikh, and, even though the more religious members of his entourage covered their eyes when she entered the room, she would catch them peeking through the spaces in their ring-bedecked fingers.

Zaki's health had improved and he now traveled, holding meetings in various cities and abroad. But he always returned to the Waldorf suite and SueBee. He would say he wasn't feeling well and wanted a massage, an Epsom salts bath, whatever he could dream up as an excuse to go to bed for a few days and get her undivided attention.

On the two occasions when she confronted him with her boring existence and her need to move on in life, he caused such a scene the doctor had to be called. The first time he became furious and red-faced, pacing the floor and promising her he would die if she left. On another occasion he clasped his chest, pitched forward, and pretended to be having a heart attack. Trapped and helpless to change her circumstances, she resigned herself to staying indefinitely.

The spring 1985 session of the United Nations opened with Sheikh Omar Zaki as a member of the Saudi mission. He announced to the staff that he would be using the suite as both home and office. SueBee was relieved. At least now there would be more people in the enormous rooms and something to do besides watch TV and take long walks in the park.

The suite became a hub of activity, with constant meetings, dinners, and parties that lasted long into the night.

During the day the place was awash with sweets. The stuffed dates, sugary nut pastes, and honey-soaked cakes, all grainy on the tongue, were so sweet that they made SueBee's throat close with the first bite. Official visitors were served fruited nonalcoholic drinks, sugary things that did little to quench the thirst.

Nighttime was a different story.

Most evenings SueBee watched from the kitchen as the living room filled with men in dark suits and long *thobes*. They flirted and talked with the most beautiful women SueBee had ever seen. They wore clothes like those she saw on "Dynasty" and "Dallas" and the kind of jewelry she saw in shop windows during her walks on Fifth Avenue. At night there was liquor—lots and lots of it, served from a bar that was hidden during the day by Zaki's houseman.

Late one night, SueBee lay in bed in her room behind the kitchen watching Johnny Carson and mentally counting the money she had put away in a shoe box under the bed. She had tried to sleep but the music coming from the huge new stereo in the living room was deafening.

At the moment it was blasting the Bee Gees so loud she was afraid her ears were going to bleed. Whenever a tape played out she could hear the squeals and laughter of the women Zaki had brought home from some nightclub.

Lately he had taken to spending the hours before midnight at places like Regine's or the Plaza's Oak Room, and at evening's end brought whoever was still around back for more drinking. Women seemed to just happen to Zaki. Several times she had been in the living room watching a movie on the VCR when the door had burst open, sending her scurrying down the hall. Invariably, Zaki would have women stuck to him like stray hairs on a piece of Scotch tape. He would stumble into the room, one arm around a girl, the other hand throwing around whip-out money from the briefcase.

She was dying of thirst. Perhaps, with all the fun they were having no one would notice if she slipped down to the kitchen and grabbed a Pepsi.

As she padded down the back hall in her bare feet she could see into the living room. The men were all sitting together on the long couch drinking from open bottles of Johnnie Walker and watching X-rated videotapes without the sound. The girls were draped around on the furniture like dressed-up porch dogs. They drooped over couches and chairs, smoking under hooded eyes and looking terrific and bored.

Retrieving a Pepsi from the fridge, SueBee slipped back to her room and stuffed a rolled-up bath towel under the door to muffle the sound. She turned off the TV, plugged her ears with Kleenex, and crawled into bed. With a pillow over her head and a blanket over the pillow, she just might be able to get to sleep.

When she awoke it was nearly noon. She quickly showered and put on her uniform. Zaki usually awoke by noon and wanted his breakfast tray.

She found it neatly laid out on the kitchen counter. All that needed to be done was to heat his tea water, squeeze his juice, and get the half-and-half from the fridge for his instant oatmeal.

While she waited for the water to heat she arranged Zaki's pills on a dish: the pink one for his blood pressure, the little white one for his gout, his blue water pill, and his usual envelope of powdered laxative. When all was ready she checked the tray. She realized he would want his morning cigar. The doctor forbade it, but SueBee figured one wouldn't kill him, and it made him so happy. Besides, how could a cigar harm a man who could stay up all night drinking Johnnie Walker and giggling with girls?

The canister in the butler's pantry was empty. She would have to get one from the big Dunhill humidor in the living room.

The instant she opened the kitchen door to the corridor she was accosted by a smell that made her eyes sting. It was the now-familiar metallic morning-after aroma of old smoke, spilled liquor, perfume, and human sweat.

"Lordy," she muttered in disgust. "Doesn't anyone know how to open a window?"

She crossed the dining room and went through the arched entrance to the vast living room.

"Jesus H. Christ!" she said, surveying the devastation she found there.

In the center of the enormous, boomerang-shaped coffee table sat the high glass contraption the men brought out during their parties. It was some kind of gigantic pipe arrangement that permitted smoke to swill around inside and filter through water. Whenever they used it they got really silly, which probably accounted for all the giggling the night before.

Scattered around the glass coffee table were dirty glasses, overflowing ashtrays, and, looped over a bronze statue of a horse, a pair of bikini panties and a black garter belt. She could see one sling-back pump under the couch and a black fur coat piled in a heap over several loose pillows at the far end of the couch near the window.

Someone had broken something. Bits of glass glinted in the deep white pile of the carpeting. In front of the monster stereo, dozens of tapes were scattered about. A pile of X-rated videos was stacked precariously on top of the huge TV console. The VCR had been left on after the last movie ran out, and it stared at her with its blind blue eye.

SueBee surveyed the scene and slowly shook her head. "Criminy!" she said. "Wait till the hotel maids see this."

As she spoke, SueBee heard a moan from the couch. The fur coat moved, and SueBee realized that it wasn't covering loose pillows. There was somebody sleeping there.

"Hello?" SueBee said to the coat to see if it would move some more. How tacky, she thought. It's one thing to leave all this mess around, but bodies, too?

"Sorry," she said. She would just as soon not get involved. All she wanted to do was get Zaki's cigar and get out.

From the humidor on the bookcase she selected one of the slender cigars he liked with his morning tea and slipped it into her uniform pocket. As she passed the coat to leave the room it moved again. "'Scuse me," she said to the coat. "Didn't mean to wake you."

"S'okay," slurred the voice. Out of the fur rose a head of dark tangled hair. A girl pushed the hair away to reveal a rumpled face.

Her makeup was smeared into dark circles under her eyes. She looked tired and dreadfully hung over.

The girl stared at SueBee and pulled the fur up under her chin. "Where the hell am I, anyway?"

"You don't know?"

The girl struggled to push back the coat and sit up. She looked up at SueBee, focusing on her uniform. "Oh, shit," she said, going limp. "I'm in the hospital."

SueBee giggled. She pushed a cluster of dirty glasses to one side and sat down on the edge of the coffee table. "No. You're not. You're at the Waldorf Towers," she said, smiling. She saw the girl was about her own age, and that was enough reason to sit down and chat. "This is Sheikh Zaki's suite. I'm his nurse. Well, kinda. I *was* his nurse. Now I just look after him."

"Ohhhh," the girl groaned, and lay back flat on the couch, staring up at the ceiling. "Don't tell me I came home with one of them."

"Could I get you something?" SueBee asked. She felt sorry for the girl. She didn't look well. "Some juice or some coffee?"

The girl slowly turned her head and studied SueBee with a puzzled expression. "Christ, I know you."

"You do?"

"You're that little nurse from Texas."

"Well, I'm from Texas, but I don't think we . . ."

"The Bull and Bear," she said. "Jesus, you're still here?" She groaned again and covered her face with the sleeve of the coat. "How can you stand it? One night with those Arabs is too long."

"They're Saudis," SueBee corrected sweetly.

"Same thing," Sandrine said, her voice muffled under the fur. "Oh, God . . . Now I remember. We met them at some club that had swings on the ceiling and came back here to smoke that damn hubble-bubble thing and drink scotch. What a bunch of deadbeats."

"If you didn't like them, why did you go out with them?" SueBee asked protectively.

The girl rolled her eyes and said, "Get real."

SueBee pushed up from the coffee table and smoothed her skirt. "Excuse me. I have work to do."

Sandrine sat up. She was wearing a very tight black sequin-covered top with a small tear at the side seam. "Don't go," she said. "I don't want to be alone. I think I'm going to be sick."

Now that she was sitting up, SueBee remembered her. Sure, she thought, the girl who walked out when Zaki wanted to meet her. "Sandrine, right?" she said excitedly.

"You got it," Sandrine said, pulling up the strap of her top.

"Well . . . gee . . . ah. Gee. How have you been?" SueBee asked weakly, not knowing what else to say.

Sandrine ignored the question and looked around the littered room. "You mean those bitches ran off and left me here?" she said angrily. "I don't believe it."

"I take it you came with a group?" SueBee asked stiffly. In her heart she disapproved of such carryings-on, but she felt sorry for Sandrine. SueBee knew what she needed. A good hot steam in the tub, some caraway tea, and sleep.

"Yeah . . . a group. Four of 'em. We all work for . . ." She stopped speaking as though she had remembered something important. Frantically, she started pawing at the coat. She jammed her hand into one pocket, flipped it over, and searched the other. "Goddamn it!" she snarled. "It's gone. I knew it. I knew it!"

Sandrine stood up and began to throw the cushions on the couch around, knocking over glasses. She pulled a long back pillow out and flung it to one side. SueBee caught the huge lamp on the end table before it could crash to the floor.

"What's the matter?" SueBee said, alarmed. "Look, don't throw things around. You're going to wake the sheikh."

"I hope to hell I do," Sandrine shouted. "That son of a bitch!" She picked up a big metal ashtray with the seal of the Saudi royal family in the center and hurled it at the television set. It bounced against the edge and dropped to the carpet, knocking off a piece of the cabinet's veneer. "Your sheikh is a blue-ribbon shit. He gave us each a thousand dollars to come back here with him, then he goes off to bed. I'll bet one of those greaseball camel drivers stole my money!"

"I don't believe they drive camels," SueBee said evenly. "Sheikh Zaki has a new stretch Mercedes that Mr. Nebeh drives." It was dawning on SueBee that Sandrine was still drunk. She didn't want to leave her alone, and yet, if Zaki didn't get his breakfast, he would start buzzing the intercom and wake everybody up. "Look, Sandrine," she said as calmly as she could, "if you'd like to, you know, freshen up, I'll take you to my room. I'm sure I can find something for you to wear. You don't want to leave in broad daylight looking like that."

Sandrine looked down and saw the rip in her dress. "Damn it, damn it, damn it," she said, and started to cry.

SueBee gathered up Sandrine's coat and took her arm. "Come on," she said. "Let's get you cleaned up." She pulled the shoe out from under the couch and held it up. "Is this yours?"

Sandrine nodded sheepishly, took the shoe, and slipped it on.

"I'll come back and look for the other one later," SueBee said, leading Sandrine hobbling on one shoe toward the hall. "Just let me take the sheikh's breakfast in to him. You jump into the shower."

Sandrine meekly let SueBee lead her to the bedroom. "You'll probably want this," SueBee said, holding open the bathroom door.

Sandrine sat down on the closed toilet seat and buried her face in her hands.

"Why are you crying?" SueBee asked. "Is it the money?"

Sandrine nodded, removing her hands and reaching for a tissue on the back of the toilet.

"Well," SueBee said with a toss of her head. "Let me see what I can do."

As she walked down the hall to retrieve Zaki's tray she could hear the water running in her shower.

Zaki was sitting up in bed reading the *Financial Times*, his reading glasses parallel to his thin mustache.

"Good morning!" SueBee chirped, closing the door with her heel. She set the tray on top of the sable throw folded at the foot of the bed and began to arrange his pillows.

"Good morning, my dear," he said, smiling. "Did you sleep well?"

"Thank you, yes," SueBee said, looking at him with mild rebuke. "From time to time."

"Did our little party disturb you?" Zaki asked, folding his paper and setting it aside.

"You have some leftovers."

"Leftovers?" he said, studying the tray she placed on his lap. "This looks fresh to me."

"I don't mean your breakfast. I mean the girl under the fur coat in the living room."

Zaki frowned up at her. "Truly?"

"Ummm." SueBee snapped open the napkin and tucked it into the top of his black silk pajamas.

"I'll tell the staff to tidy up in the future," he said, chuckling. "I hope you sent her on her way."

SueBee folded her arms and leaned against the post at the foot of the bed. "I will. She's taking a shower at the moment. She seems a bit upset."

Zaki's spoon of oatmeal paused in midair. "Upset? What's she got to be upset about?"

"Money. She says you gave her a thousand dollars and now she doesn't have it. She thinks one of the men took it while she was asleep. That's a lot of money to give someone."

Zaki's spoon resumed its journey. He chewed carefully and swallowed before he answered. "I didn't give it; I paid it. That's what those girls charge."

"Charge? What do you mean charge?"

"Those were call girls, my dear. They charge for their company. Hakim gets them from an escort service."

"Sheikh Zaki! I don't believe you! She's a very nice girl."

"Of course," Zaki said nonchalantly. He took a sip of his tea and tried to slide the envelope of Metamucil under the linen place mat.

SueBee pretended not to notice. "I met her once with you. In the restaurant downstairs. I know her name and everything," she said, persisting. All along she was thinking the thousand dollars was some kind of present from Zaki, given in an expansive mood. She didn't want to think that Sandrine was a prostitute. "She lives on Park Avenue even."

Zaki threw back his head and laughed. "Some of the best hookers in the world live on Park Avenue."

"Well, I think you should be ashamed of yourself," SueBee said hotly. She realized she was feeling a bit jealous. It wasn't that she had the remotest romantic feelings about Zaki. But she felt responsible for him. He was her charge, her patient; it was her job to see that he was well. She didn't know which annoyed her more, the realization that Sandrine was a prostitute or the idea of Zaki paying women to do things to him that she was perfectly capable of doing herself.

She moved to the head of the bed and began to hand Zaki his pills one by one to wash down with his tea.

When he had swallowed the last he pushed his tray away. "Don't be angry with me, SueBee," he said, looking up at her with big sad black eyes. "I didn't do anything with those girls."

"It's none of my business," she said with a sniff. She pulled the envelope of laxative out from under the place mat. She tore it open with a yank and poured the contents into his juice.

"SueBee, call girls serve a very important function in life. They make social affairs uncomplicated. They are one of life's niceties, like a good meal or a new car or, for that matter"—Zaki reached over and plucked at the pocket of SueBee's skirt—"a good cigar."

SueBee took one step backwards, putting her pocket just out of reach. "Drink that!" she commanded, nodding toward his juice. "You know I see you hide it every time."

Zaki made a face. "It's like mucus," he pouted.

"Drink it," she repeated. "And when you're finished you can call Hakim to bring in your whip-out money. I'm going to need a thousand dollars for the lady in my shower."

"I'll need more juice to take this awful stuff," Zaki said, ignoring her.

SueBee lifted the phone. "I'll call Hakim. He can bring the juice *and* the money."

"You are a woman of great heart, SueBee, my girl," Zaki said, smiling and taking her hand. "I'll miss you."

SueBee put down the phone. "Where are you going?" she said, bewildered.

"Home, my dear. The king . . . well, I've been away far too long."

"But . . . who will take care of you?" she said, trying to control her alarm.

Zaki chuckled, patting the back of her hand. "I'll manage, my dear. Besides," he said, grinning up at her, "you have taken such good care of me I won't need anyone."

"You're very bad at taking your pills yourself," she said. She knew she was grasping at straws. All of this was so sudden. How could she have been so stupid as to think this arrangement would go on forever? "Couldn't I go with you?" she said. Instantly, she was sorry she said it. It sounded needy and pushy, two things she prided herself on not being.

Zaki plucked at the lace edge of the top sheet. He looked sadder than she had ever seen him, almost as though he were going to cry. "SueBee, you must understand, my country is not a place for Western ladies. Women must stay behind walls, cover themselves, they have no life of their own. A pretty unmarried blond American girl, well, I'm afraid . . ." His voice trailed off. He looked away and sighed deeply. SueBee felt faint.

"I'm stunned," she said, looking away to hide her tears.

Zaki pushed himself up in the bed and pointed to the phone. "Call Hakim now," he said brusquely. "Tell him to bring the document case from the top drawer of my desk. I have a little parting present for you. Don't open it in front of Hakim, though. You know how peevish he can be."

SueBee and Sandrine sat opposite each other in the booth of a Greek coffee shop on Lexington Avenue.

"That's a nice color on you," SueBee said, nodding at the red turtleneck she had lent Sandrine to go with the blue jeans and sneakers she'd also lent her. Sandrine's sequined dress and one shoe were tucked into an Alexander's bag on the seat next to her. "I just wish we could have found your other shoe."

Sandrine stared into her coffee. "You've done more than enough, SueBee. I don't know how to thank you."

"You don't have to thank me, Sandrine. Zaki felt bad that someone might have taken your money."

"Whatever," Sandrine said, with a smile. "I'm just grateful to you for sticking up for me. I can use it to pay my rent. I'm broke."

SueBee nodded at the waitress hovering with a fresh pot of coffee. She waited until she had moved on to speak. "How come if you're so broke you live on Park Avenue?" she asked.

"Because I don't. Not anymore. My mother threw me out a long time ago."

"Oh dear," SueBee said, shocked. "How could she do that?"

"I borrowed some of her jewelry and lost it. She got pissed off, although she told the cops and the insurance company she was robbed because it was the only way she could collect. Then one night we had one of our big fights about her husband and I threatened to tell about the necklace," Sandrine said, with a shrug. "That's when she threw me out."

"Why were you fighting about her husband?"

"He used to be my boyfriend. I brought him home from college and she ran off with him. It was all a big mess."

"Your mother married your boyfriend?" SueBee said, incredulous. "Brother, and I thought I had it rough."

"Not so rough," Sandrine said with a weak smile. "Kind of gives new meaning to Mother's Day."

Sandrine's flip manner didn't fool SueBee. This was one unhappy girl. "Do you ever see her?"

"Only in the newspapers. Her life's blood is getting her picture taken," Sandrine said, making a sour face. "Someday I'll have to see her in person, though. She controls a trust fund my father set up for me that kicks in pretty soon."

"Will that be hard for you to do?"

"The hardest," Sandrine said, for the first time the expression on her face showing how deeply hurt she was.

"Is that why you're working as a . . ." SueBee hesitated.

"As a call girl?"

"Uh-huh."

"Kind of. I also do it because I like it."

"You like sleeping with men you don't know?"

172

Sandrine leaned forward. "I'd be sleeping with them anyway. Why not get paid?" she said, pronouncing each word distinctly as though SueBee might be hard of hearing.

"I guess," SueBee said, unconvinced by Sandrine's argument. There seemed to be some logic missing but she couldn't think what it would be. She looked down at the tuna melt the waitress was sliding in front of her. She looked up at the waitress and asked, "Could I have a pickle, please?"

"You got," she said, and walked away.

SueBee poked around on the plate and found a limp pickle under a piece of lettuce.

"Here's the deal, SueBee," Sandrine continued. "I can work when I want. I make good money. I go to the best clubs and restaurants. Sometimes I even go on trips—Aspen, the Caribbean islands. The service I work for is a class operation. I actually meet some important people. Believe me, some of the names you'd recognize.

"You see, guys treat you differently when they're paying you. It's kinda perverse. They act like they're some kind of hot stuff because they're with an expensive, beautiful woman. Like it's some kind of feather in their cap. They're big time in other men's eyes because they're doing something naughty and fast-lane. It never occurs to them that the only reason you're with them is their wallet and has nothing to do with who they are or what they've got—least of all their dicks."

SueBee winced at Sandrine's directness but pretended she was reacting to the waitress who had returned with Sandrine's ham-and-egg sandwich, which she served with a noisy thud. Her hands free, she tore the check from her pad and let it float onto the table from two feet up. It seesawed in the air and landed in a puddle of water on the tabletop.

"What's the matter with her?" SueBee asked after the waitress had slouched away.

"The waitresses in here are like that," Sandrine said. "A lot of us come in here for breakfast after a night on the town. These women feel they're making an honest living and we're all a bunch of street scum. It makes them feel better to put us down."

"That doesn't bother you?" SueBee asked.

Sandrine let out a sharp short laugh. "No. Having to be a waitress in a greasy spoon is what would bother me."

"How did you start, anyway?" SueBee asked, truly interested.

"You mean what's-a-nice-girl-like-you . . . that bit?"

SueBee smiled. "Sorry," she said, "but I'm curious."

"It's okay, everybody is. I was hanging out in the clubs anyway, you know, dancing—I love to dance—fooling around, picking up guys. One night I had a bad scare when one of them went psycho on me. The next night I was in this club with a black eye and I met a really nice woman who said I was going to get killed and that I needed protection. She gave me the phone number of a girl who runs an escort service. Her name is Angel. I kind of liked the idea of someone watching out for me, you know, keeping the creeps out of my life. So I signed up with Angel. She screens my dates. I can take 'em or leave 'em. The pay is good and it's not nearly as sleazy as people think. I was sleeping with guys anyway. This way I get protected and paid."

"Then why are you so broke?" SueBee asked. She had finished her tuna melt and was still hungry.

"I dunno. I just spend my money. Clothes, jewelry, stuff. I can drop ten grand in Saks in one afternoon. Maybe it comes from knowing that pretty soon I'll be getting my inheritance. And if I don't I have a fallback position."

"Oh? What's that, Sandrine?" SueBee asked.

"Simple. A very, very rich man. I want to live even better than my mother lives. I want it all, and the only way I'm going to get it is to marry someone so spit-rich I'll never have to worry again."

"Wow," SueBee said softly. It was all she could think of to say. It seemed like an odd thing for someone to want, but the look in Sandrine's eyes made SueBee believe her. "You going to eat that?" she asked, pointing to Sandrine's untouched ham-and-egg sandwich.

"I don't know why I ordered it. I can't eat. After we smoked that Arab pipe last night I got the munchies and ate a whole plate of the nastiest sweet stuff I've ever tasted," she said, pushing the sandwich toward SueBee.

"That's Arab candy. They all love that stuff. Zaki gets it air express from home. I hate it, too, but I don't tell him."

"What do you do for Zaki anyway?"

"Not a whole bunch. Give him his breakfast, his pills. Fix his pillows the way he likes them. Keep him company. Little stuff."

"Yeah. I remember now. You told me you sat with him in the john. I thought about that for a while."

"Sometimes I give him hand jobs so he can sleep," SueBee said, taking a big bite of Sandrine's rejected sandwich.

Sandrine had just taken a sip of coffee. She was so startled she exhaled across the cup, sending a spray of coffee into the air. "Ah-ha! I thought so!" she crowed. "You were acting pretty snooty when you found me this morning for someone who's been giving Ali Baba hand jobs!"

"I did it with my mouth once or twice," SueBee said easily. "Only because he fussed so much. I didn't like it. It tasted like Clorox."

Sandrine fell forward onto the table and pounded it with an open palm. When she lifted her head her lips were pressed together to keep from laughing. "Oh God, you are a piece of work, SueBee girl. Did you tell him that?"

"Unh-unh, I didn't want to hurt his feelings," SueBee said with her mouth full. "I don't like to tell people things they're better off not knowing. None of that matters anymore anyway."

"Why not?" Sandrine said, with her hand over her broad smile.

"Why don't you finish up laughing, Sandrine," she said evenly. "Then I'll tell you."

Sandrine pushed a curtain of hair out of her face and sat back against the leather booth. "I'm sorry, hon. I wasn't laughing at you. I was laughing at how casually you put things. I mean, here you are diddling around with one of the richest men in the world like you're flipping burgers at McDonald's. The girls I know would be killing themselves to be in your position."

"I'm not in the position anymore," SueBee said sadly. "Zaki told me this morning that he's going back home. I've got to find a job."

"But you're a nurse, for heaven's sake," Sandrine said with a frown. "This city needs nurses like crazy. You'd get another job in a minute."

SueBee stopped chewing, swallowed hard, and put down the sandwich. "Sandrine, I'm not a nurse," she said quietly.

"You're not? But . . ."

SueBee shook her head. "It's all a fake. I was working as a receptionist for a doctor back home. Sheikh Zaki got in a car wreck near where I worked and the doctor took me to help out. It just happens I was wearing a white dress and a nurse's cape. Things just happened. Zaki hired me and I've been with him ever since. It's the only job I've ever had except for that one back home."

"What about going back home?"

"Unh-unh," SueBee said, vigorously shaking her head. "Can't. I cut a guy's weenie off just before I left. The Wayleen police might want to give me a hard time about it."

"You did what?" Sandrine hooted.

"Well, he was sticking it in my face and saying rude things. You know, a girl has to do something."

Sandrine doubled over, convulsed with laughter. When she finally composed herself, she brushed her eyes dry and said, "Oh God. SueBee, you make me feel good."

"Do I? Thank you," she said, smiling at her new friend.

"So what are you going to do?"

"I don't know. This all happened so suddenly I haven't had a chance to think about it."

Sandrine sat staring out the window for several minutes. She turned back to SueBee with a suggestion. "You want to move in with me until you get organized? We could split the rent. That is, if you have any money. If you don't that's okay, too."

"Oh, I have money," SueBee said brightly. "I have nearly every penny Zaki paid me hidden away." Suddenly, SueBee remembered the envelope Zaki had given her in the bedroom that morning. In the confusion of getting Sandrine properly dressed and out of the Towers, she had forgotten all about it. She figured it would at least be a couple of weeks' pay. "Hold on a sec," she said, reaching for her handbag. "Maybe I have more than I think." She pulled a narrow manila envelope out, unwound the string clasp on the flap, and reached inside.

To her chagrin, instead of the several large bills she had anticipated, there was only a single sheet of heavy paper with something typed on it. "You read it," she said sheepishly, and handed it to Sandrine. "I'm too nervous."

Sandrine studied the document and started to smile. "SueBee! This is a scream!" she said. "Do you know what he's given you as a good-bye present?"

"What?" SueBee said, leaning forward in anticipation.

"Two Arabian horses."

SueBee slumped in her seat. "Don't tease."

"I'm not! It says so right here. Two Arabian horses. They're at that stable on the West Side. Their feed and board are all paid for," Sandrine said. "What a neat gift!"

SueBee sat staring into space in stunned disbelief. "What on God's green earth am I gonna do with two Arabian horses. I've never ridden a horse in my life!"

"Maybe Zaki figured anyone from Texas needs a horse. Too many cowboy movies, I suspect," Sandrine said, laughing.

"Damn," SueBee said. "Horses! I don't know which end of a horse eats. What ever am I going to do with them?" She turned the piece of paper around and pretended to be studying it. She could make out a few words but none of it really made any sense. "Maybe I could sell them? What do you think?"

"No! Don't do that. I just had a brainstorm," Sandrine said, excited. She was practically bouncing on her seat. "This is gonna be great!"

"What's so great about it, Sandrine?" SueBee said, groaning.

Sandrine leaned across the table, her eyes sparkling as she spoke. "Think about it, hon. The clothes! Those great little black velvet hats, the tight jodhpurs. High polished boots, riding crops. Yeeow! We'll drive 'em crazy!" she shouted loudly enough for heads to turn in the other booths.

SueBee stared at her, not comprehending. "You'll have to help me, Sandrine. I just don't get it. Who are we going to drive crazy?"

"Men, silly! It's a great way to meet men! Rich men!"

SueBee's shoulders rounded in resignation. "I don't know, Sandrine. I think I've had the richest man I'm ever going to find."

CHAPTER
9

Peter's Journal Entry—June 29, 1990

I don't know. Maybe it's being back in Paris again with no other distractions but this project. Maybe I'm getting too involved with Madame. She's an oddly mesmerizing woman. I've never known anyone quite like her. At the start of each of our sessions I fully intend to take control of the day's subject, but as anxious as I'm getting to get her on to talking about herself I am helpless to get her to change course. It's not that I don't want to hear what she is telling me. I'm still curious about Madeleine and my old job, but I'm beginning to realize how difficult it may be to get Madame to talk about herself. This is supposed to be her autobiography. We'll have to start concentrating on that pretty soon.

Yesterday I asked a kid in the Herald Tribune *bureau here to run down the clip files on her. If Cleo knew I'd done that I'm sure she would have thrown a fit. Besides her tax troubles, the only thing the Trib kid turned up was an arrest for procuring in the early fifties that was quickly dismissed, and a mention in the sixties when she moved to the mansion on the Ile de la Cité. Other than that, it's as though the woman never existed. There aren't even any fingerprints on file for her, something required when anyone buys property in the city of Paris. I suspect her friends in high places have been instrumental in keeping her as anonymous as she is.*

This afternoon, postperson Giselle brought black raspberries the size of pin cushions. I think she'd like to put the moves on me. If I weren't so preoccupied I'd do it. I've been here a month. Ordinarily, I'd have looked up one of my old girlfriends. The flesh is willing, but the spirit is weak.

Celebrity notes from all over: Giselle has an aunt in Lyons who knows a guy whose daughter may or may not have worked for Madame Cleo in the fifties. I once met a guy who said he had a neighbor who used to walk Merv Griffin's tailor's dog. It's like that.

Cleo wants to go to the Ritz for lunch Monday for a change of pace. I'm grateful. The back garden is now as hot as the house.

The apartment that Sandrine was kind enough to invite SueBee to share was not a suite at the Waldorf. Far from it. The one bedroom sublet on East 55th Street needed a paint job, and the grime-encrusted windows looked out on the adjoining building eight feet away across an alley full of Ripple and Night Train bottles. The furniture might have looked okay in the Salvation Army thrift shop. Close up in a small apartment it was pretty sorry stuff. As far as SueBee was concerned she had moved into Graceland.

Sandrine closed the ledger in which she kept a meticulous account of their expenses. Without the records provided by a checking account or charge cards it was a must. Sandrine, like many of the girls who worked for the escort service, lived an all-cash life. As far as the IRS and the Social Security Commission were concerned, she did not exist.

To pay her bills she used a messenger service. Once a month her runner, Pepé, a nice Hispanic boy who also dealt a little pot, stopped by the apartment and took individual envelopes of cash marked for those to whom she owed money.

She slipped the ledger into the top drawer of the desk in the living room and neatly stacked the pile of white number-ten envelopes on the table by the door.

"SueBee?" she called out in the direction of the bedroom. "Are you awake?"

"I'm in the kitchen," SueBee singsonged just as the birdcall teakettle began to tweet. "I didn't want to disturb you. You want some tea?"

"Sure, thanks," Sandrine called back.

Sandrine was settled on the couch reading a magazine when SueBee scuffed into the room in her nightgown and slippers. She placed a pink mug of tea on the coffee table and joined Sandrine on the couch.

"I've been thinking," Sandrine said. "You need a base. A front porch, so to speak."

SueBee took a sip of tea, made a face to indicate that it was too hot, and put it down. "What in the world are you talking about?" she asked. "What front porch?"

"We need to let the world see you. The only people who know you exist are that old groom at the Claremont stables and the checkout clerks at Gristede's. And since my big scheme with the horses hasn't panned out yet, I think you need to position yourself on a different sort of stage."

"I'm game," SueBee said.

"How much money do you have in the bank?" Sandrine asked, warming to a plan she had given considerable thought to every time she came home from a date to find SueBee asleep in front of a test pattern.

"A lot, why?"

"Do you have a thousand?"

"Of course. But what for?"

"Get dressed."

"Dressed? Now?"

"First, we're going to stop by your bank," Sandrine said, putting down her tea. "Then we're going to Twenty-one for lunch. You can wear my red Yves Saint Laurent."

"Lunch at Twenty-one costs a thousand dollars?" SueBee said, her eyes wide with disbelief. "Lordy, I don't think so, Sandrine."

"No, sweetheart," Sandrine said slowly. "We are going to take your thousand dollars and give it to a man named Charles."

"Sandrine, why would I give that kind of money to someone I don't know?"

"Because Charles is the maître d' at Twenty-one and a thousand dollars is about the right kind of tip for someone who is going to be your new best friend."

It took only three lunches at SueBee's banquette in the corner of the main dining room at '21' to get the results Sandrine had been hoping for.

Sandrine herself was well known to the staff, having been in the company of some very impressive guests on many occasions. Securing a prominently placed table had taken merely a mention that her blond friend from Texas, Miss Slyde of the Dallas Slydes, would be in New York for an extended visit and wanted to dine at her daddy's favorite restaurant exclusively.

"Charles, would you be so kind as to look after her," Sandrine had said from behind the little black Chanel veil that caught fetchingly in her eyelashes as she folded SueBee's ten one-hundred-dollar bills and slipped them into the breast pocket of his precisely cut black maître d's jacket. The sheer bulk of so much folded money caused him to hurriedly place his hand over his pocket, giving the appearance of swearing on his heart to care for Miss Slyde of the Dallas Slydes, the Slydes of the diamond drill bits, heavy machinery, oil-rig equipment, and four supertankers. He memorized the details in case, just in case, someone should ask. Charles had seen this game played before and knew the rules. There was no doubt in his mind that it would be only a matter of a few lunches before the pretty blonde with Sandrine would be noticed.

Once a week John Wesley "Black Jack" Ayler preferred to lunch alone at his usual table against the wall at '21.' He liked to observe the goings-on in the big dining room. He liked an hour or so of being fussed over without having to make conversation.

He debated having a second brandy, knowing he shouldn't. He had a meeting with the environmental people at four and a drinks appointment with the Chase Manhattan man at the Yale Club at six.

Dinner was still up in the air. Perhaps he'd call the escort service later. Since his last divorce he tended to rely on the company of professionals when he didn't have the time or inclination for the chase. After lunch he'd call his houseman, tell him dinner for two, and call the service. A few drinks with an attractive lady, a light supper, and a leisurely lay would get him to sleep by midnight. He needed his wits about him in the morning. The secret EPA report his operatives in Washington had been able to get him proved his engineers had been right. Only his people knew that the huge tower of the Bank Center was laced with asbestos. His team could get the stuff out if they moved fast enough, but with the report he had the jump on them all. His spirits were badly in need of a lift.

He pressed his closed fist against his solar plexus to ease the tightness and cursed himself for having eaten a rare steak for lunch. He was no youngster.

Until the waiter arrived with the check he hadn't realized how distracted he had been. He had been staring at a young blond woman seated at the premier banquette directly in his line of sight on the facing wall. Jack had been coming to '21' for nearly three decades and he knew that table was held for celebrities to "dress" the room. It was there that he had been introduced to the Duke of Windsor, to Katharine Hepburn, and to John F. Kennedy. The two women at the table had to be somebodies. He noted as well that Charles was inordinately attentive to table one, taking over for the waiter and serving the women himself. The girls were either starlets or Mafia mistresses.

Something about the blonde's angelic face and utterly feminine manner fascinated him. He let the check sit next to the salt and pepper and signaled for another brandy, pointing to his empty glass and making a circular motion.

He watched as Charles handed the two women menus. The blonde was probably nearsighted because she held hers very close to her face, as though she couldn't see it. Finally, he noticed, she had the same salad her friend did but not the wine.

He felt the old conquest juices stir and tried to catch her eye. As the room emptied out he was able to catch bits and pieces of their conversation. The dark one did most of the talking. He dismissed her. She was a bit too sleek, too calculatedly groomed and cool.

The angel's face, on the other hand, had a look as soft as a puffed chaise. He found her absolutely adorable.

When his waiter passed within earshot he asked him to send Charles over. "When he can find the time," Jack said with grinning sarcasm, raising his dark eyebrows in the direction of table one.

Within seconds Charles was at his table. "Yes, Mr. Ayler," he said with concern. "Your car is downstairs, sir," he said, bending to move the table away. "Shall I tell the driver you're on your way?"

Jack raised his hand. "Not yet, Charles," he said in a low voice. "That's not why I called you over. I wanted to ask you something."

"Sir?" Charles said, imitating his tone and leaning closer.

"Who's Honeysuckle Rose you're breaking your butt for over there at table one?"

"The ladies are personal friends of the management, Mr. Ayler," Charles said enigmatically.

"That's not what I asked you, Charles," Jack said evenly. "Who's the blond one?"

Before his eyes, Charles, whom he'd known for years, gotten drunk with a couple of times after hours in the grill, loaned money to when his kid got into an expensive college, and laid a collector-class shotgun on last Christmas, turned into Christ on the cross. "I'm so sorry, sir," he said, like some damn poufter English butler, "I'm not at liberty to say."

"Well, where is she from?"

Charles thought for a moment, apparently taking into consideration their long and, to him, profitable relationship. "All I can tell you, Mr.

Ayler, is Texas," he said, as though he were betraying a vital confidence by allowing that much information to cross his lips.

Jack Ayler did not suffer rebuke lightly. He felt his face redden and fought to control his annoyance. He hated to be denied. It was like feeling horns retract in battle, the shrinking erection of the near invisible dick. He had exposed himself and had to retrieve his pride. "Well," he said with a little chuckle, fishing inside his breast pocket on the odd chance that he would have a business card. He didn't, of course; Jack Ayler's face was his card. The gesture was involuntary and only added to his frustration. "In that case, please send the ladies a brandy for me," he said, trying to make light of the situation.

"I wouldn't advise that, Mr. Ayler. They've asked not to be disturbed."

The roar of *buuullllshiiit!* surged up in his throat as he struggled to suppress an outburst that would only compound the situation. He was beginning to feel his brandy. It was a contest now. He had to persist. "I see I can't win with you, my man," he said with what he hoped was a hearty, it's-really-not-important bravado.

"Yes, sir," Charles said. "Another brandy, sir?"

"No, no thanks," Jack said. He plunged his hand into his hip pocket, withdrew his wallet, and extracted a hundred-dollar bill. It was crisp enough to make a little snap between his fingers as he handed it to Charles. "Hold this table for me tomorrow."

"Tomorrow, Mr. Ayler?" Charles said.

Jack hadn't replied, but as his four o'clock meeting droned on he daydreamed, picturing the blond girl at table one, remembering how the corners of her upper lip curled when she spoke. Over scotch at the Yale Club he stood at the bar swirling the melting ice in his drink with a swizzle stick and gazing into space until the Chase Manhattan VP asked him if he was feeling all right.

When his butler let him into the house on Sutton Place, he went directly to the phone and called the Countess de Marco escort service. They were the best in town, efficient, discreet, and fast. The girls were consistently charming, and Angel, the woman who ran the service, treated him as though he were her only client, picking girls she felt he would like, even phoning him when a new one signed on. He liked that. There was something fulfilling about having reached a point in life where your taste in women was catered to.

"A southern blonde?" Angel had responded with surprise at his request. "Jack, darling! I always send you redheads."

"Not tonight, Angel," he had said. "Tonight I feel like a southern blonde. And pretty. I'd like her to be very pretty."

He answered the door himself. The girl on the step was a thin bottle blonde with a twangy Mississippi accent. He canceled dinner and took her directly to the master bedroom.

During their rapid, mirthless coupling she actually called him "honey chile." He paid and thanked her, then walked her to the door, quietly so as not to disturb his butler, who was watching TV in the kitchen. He helped himself to a nightcap from the dining-room sideboard and climbed the stairs to his bedroom.

In the middle of the night he awoke in a sweat and realized he had been dreaming he was making love to the blond girl at '21.'

When the girls arrived at '21' the following day Charles, of course, passed on his conversation with Black Jack Ayler.

"Good work, Charles," Sandrine had said, smiling up at him as he eased the table over their knees.

"If you look across the room you'll see he's back again today," Charles said, trying not to move his lips.

Sandrine made an elaborate show of holding her menu in front of her face and peeping over the top. "Is that him straight across by the window?" she asked.

"That's him."

"He's staring at me," SueBee said to her lap.

Sandrine cleared her throat. "I want him," she muttered, putting her menu down.

"Well, *have* him, Sandrine," SueBee said generously. "For heaven's sake, this was all your idea."

"It was my idea for you!" Sandrine said, sounding hurt.

"I'm not ungrateful, Sandrine," SueBee said, carefully unfolding her napkin and smoothing it onto her lap. "I just meant if you're interested in him, be my guest. It's the least I can do." Despite her earlier doubts, SueBee was having a good time. She was impressed by the people who stopped by the table. Sandrine seemed to know everyone, not just men.

As Charles wrote down their order, a woman paused at Sandrine's side of the table and smiled hello. She was a dazzling redhead with translucent teeth and a triple strand of emeralds under an emerald-green satin suit. From the brief conversation she had with Sandrine, SueBee could tell the redhead worked for the escort service too. She was with a network anchorman SueBee recognized right away.

As the two of them chatted, SueBee glanced across the room. The man was still staring. His hair, backlit by the filtered light, looked blue-white. His handsome, high-cheekboned face was younger than his hair. SueBee liked his full, sexy mouth framed by dimples that deepened when he smiled or laughed.

He was still looking at her. She lowered her eyes, feeling a flush pass across her cheeks and down her neck.

"You were looking at him," Sandrine said out of the corner of her mouth as the redhead moved on to another table.

"I can't help it," SueBee said, lowering her head as she spoke.

"Tomorrow," Sandrine said. "Tomorrow Charles is going to earn his money."

Black Jack Ayler moved quickly. He had a ten o'clock board of directors meeting and was late.

As he reached the front door of his town house, his houseman was waiting with his briefcase and fur-trimmed vicuña coat. "Good morning, sir," he said. "There's a message for you. It just arrived."

"Oh?" Ayler said, frowning.

"Charles from Twenty-one just phoned to say to be at the entrance to the Bethesda Fountain plaza on the transverse in Central Park between nine-thirty and ten. He said you would understand."

"Thank you, thank you very much," Ayler said, grinning as he walked to his car. His meeting was forgotten.

Copies of the *Wall Street Journal, Financial Times,* and *New York Times* lay neatly arranged on the back seat. Jack ignored them and stared out the window.

The mercury-colored sky over the East River was lifting, along with his mood.

As the chauffeur turned off Sutton Place and headed to the southbound FDR for the Wall Street office, Jack pushed the button that lowered the glass partition between them. "Drive around the park for a bit, Jerry. I want to kill some time."

The driver looked over his uniformed shoulder and nodded.

Just as they entered Central Park at East 59th, a flood of sunlight washed through the back window, warming Jack's shoulders. His spirit soared, as it always did when he was on the hunt.

As the car moved at a leisurely speed through the park he told the driver to pull to the curb at the top of the stairs that led to the Bethesda Fountain plaza and wait.

In a matter of minutes, two stunning young women astride equally beautiful Arabian mares cantered across the street just ahead of the car. Jack leaned forward in his seat. His heart beat against his rib cage. The girl riding the paler horse seemed to be having trouble. The horse had shied and was sidestepping, disregarding whatever she was trying inexpertly to do with the reins. The horse and rider were no more than six feet away from the hood of the limousine.

It was her! The blonde at table one! He pushed forward on the plush seat, grasping the rim of the partition.

"Follow that horse!" he commanded, laughing at the corny command. "Where do those riders come out of the park?"

Jerry glanced into the rearview mirror before he answered. "Well, sir," he said patiently. "They can only ride on the bridle path. If they're going back to the stable, the path lets out at Ninety-third."

"Then go to the stables and wait."

The driver nodded. "Right away, Mr. Ayler."

A short time later Jack saw the two women stroll out of the dilapidated uptown stable. They turned right and headed toward Columbus Avenue.

His Texas angel was wearing skintight beige jodhpurs, high, polished black boots, and a tight-fitting black velvet jacket. Her gleaming blond hair was caught at the back of her neck with a black velvet bow. As she walked next to the dark-haired woman she lunched with she casually flicked a riding crop against her leather-encased calf.

Jack leaned back against the seat. He owed himself this one. He had earned some sweetness.

And this girl couldn't have traveled far. He wanted that soft, golden cloud of a girl looking up at him in awe. He wanted to make love to her that second. "Don't lose 'em," he said urgently to his driver as the dark one raised her hand for a cab.

Jack's limousine followed the cab back across town until it pulled to the curb in front of an apartment building the color of old chewing gum on East 55th.

Jack didn't have to write down the address; it was seared into his brain. As the blonde pushed through the glass doors to the lobby and smiled at the doorman, he leaned back against the seat again and inhaled a deep, rejuvenating breath. He had found her. He would have her whatever the effort and price. The start-up cost would be minimal. A quick hundred backhanded to the doorman should do it.

"Who do you think would have a limo in this crummy building?" SueBee asked as she peered out the living-room window facing East 55th Street. She had noticed the big gray limousine double-parked in front of the building on several occasions throughout the week.

The bathroom door was open and she could see Sandrine soaking in the tub. She was wearing the plastic eye mask she kept in the freezer and was leaning the back of her neck against a waterproof pillow. Soap bubbles billowed over the edge of the tub and oozed slowly down the side every time she moved. "Gee, I don't know, Sue," she said innocently. "Maybe some mobster has a girl stashed in here. Lucky thing."

"Do mobsters have vanity plates?" SueBee asked. "From here I can see B . . . J . . . A on the plate. Not hard to remember. You know what, Sandrine? I saw that car outside the stable last Friday."

"You sure?"

"Absolutely. I first saw it at Bethesda Fountain. I remember because I thought it had spooked the horses. Then I saw it parked on West Eighty-ninth Street when we walked to Columbus. Now it's been hanging around all week. It gives me the creeps, Sandrine. You think it's one of your . . . you know."

"No, but I have other suspicions. Let's wait and see."

SueBee let the drape fall back into place and walked back to the couch. "Are you teasing me now?"

"Let's just be patient," Sandrine said. She stood up in the tub. There were puffs of soapsuds on the dark tuft of her pubic hair and white caps of foam on each nipple.

"*Frosty the snowman,*" SueBee sang, laughing.

Sandrine pulled a terry-cloth robe around her and slipped into her scuffs. "God, it's good to stay home for once," she said as she walked into the living room. Just then, they both jumped in response to the lobby buzzer.

She walked to the kitchen, pushed the button that released the downstairs door, and took two Tabs from the fridge.

"If they forgot the extra cheese, send it back!" Sandrine called from the living room.

When they opened the first huge box of long-stemmed yellow roses the girls just stared. By the time the delivery boy staggered into the apartment with the twelfth they were laughing hysterically.

"There's a nut out there, SueBee," Sandrine said as she pawed through a cloud of green tissue paper searching for a card. She found one attached to a stem in the last box. " 'For the Yellow Rose of Texas. I can't wait any longer. Dine with me. Call 555-9289 and say yes,' " she read aloud. "SueBee, my girl, these are for you. From a florist on Sutton Place. I've got to bow to the gentleman's taste. Honey, your ship just came in!"

SueBee reached for the card and studied it in disbelief. "This is kind of scary," SueBee said. "What should I do?"

"Make the call, SueBee," Sandrine said in a knowing voice. "Your investment at Twenty-one is about to pay off."

It had been a gloomy fall, and December had brought not snow but icy rain that pelted the dirty windows of the apartment on East 55th Street. Sandrine sat alone on the couch bundled in a king-size terry-cloth bathrobe she'd liberated from a client's hotel suite. There had been no messages on her machine when she got home. Not even from the escort service. All she had to look forward to that night was a dull dinner with a regular who never liked to do the clubs. She was beginning to feel as though the whole world was out dancing—except her. For a week the gossip column and TV news had been full of items about her mother's divorce from Jamey. She was suing him for theft. He was suing her for fraud. It was all too depressing and there was no one to talk to about it.

Every night when she returned from seeing a client, the apartment was dark and empty. She would be fast asleep by the time SueBee tiptoed in from a night on the town with Jack. Some nights, SueBee didn't come home at all. In the beginning she would call and say she was spending the night at Jack's town house on Sutton Place so Sandrine wouldn't worry. Lately, she didn't even bother to call.

Sandrine was lonely. She was also jealous. Not because SueBee was having a good time—but because SueBee was having a real love affair. Compounding that was the fact that Jack Ayler had taken her friend away. But even if he hadn't disrupted Sandrine's life, she would have hated him. Oh, at first she'd wanted him for herself. But that was before she'd recognized the specific species of male animal they were dealing with in Black Jack Ayler.

The Jack Aylers of the world were what kept madams and call girls in business. They were the kind of men who used call girls regularly when they weren't running some innocent like SueBee to ground. They were fun at first, full of boisterous energy and radioactive with the self-confidence that comes from control. They were take-charge men, fast with the big tips and surprises. Like all men who hate their mothers, they were charming, controlling, and utterly vain.

The Jack Aylers had usually been married more than once. They didn't marry sweet, accommodating women like SueBee but women who abused them, squandered their money, and made them miserable. She worried about SueBee and how she would handle it when this particular Jack Ayler dumped her.

The last week had been the worst. SueBee had been in Paris with Jack on a business trip. Two of Sandrine's regulars were also out of town. She had accepted a date with a well-known rock musician at the Chelsea Hotel. He was too stoned for any kind of conversation, let alone sex. The rocker paid her anyway but it was a wasted, demeaning evening. She immediately complained about it to the service and received a promise that it wouldn't happen again.

She heard the soft plop of the newspaper outside the apartment door and smiled. She knew that had to be David from down the hall. He was a dancer and forever broke. He had been stealing the morning paper since she took the apartment. He would read it, carefully refold it, and return it. Once, he even ironed it. She didn't care. She was never awake for a morning paper. Still smiling, she padded across the living room and opened the door.

As her eyes dropped to the hallway floor she stopped smiling. Her heart skipped half a beat. The big black headline on the *Daily News* screamed up at her, CALL GIRL COUNTESS CAUGHT.

"Oh no," she whispered. She retrieved the paper and closed the door with her foot.

Under the headline was a huge picture of Angel, the woman who ran the service. "Countess? Since when?" she asked the empty apartment. Angel Weinstein was from Brooklyn. She was no more a countess than Sandrine was. Countess de Marco was just the name of the service. It personalized the business and made a classy ad in the yellow pages. The press was amazing. Sandrine could not remember ever reading a story in which a madam or a call girl was described as ugly and dull. Now here was large, loud Angel. A countess?

She returned to the couch fighting mounting panic. Police raids usually meant seized records. What if Angel had something in her office with Sandrine's name on it?

A slick East Side call-girl service run by a statuesque Italian countess was raided by police last night. Midtown North vice-squad cops staked out the posh brownstone apartment of a woman calling herself Countess de Marco for several weeks. A police source told the *News* that they had received a tip that a million-dollar-a-month pay-for-play operation catering to an elite clientele was being run there. The countess, a stunning redhead, was arrested. Her office featured black satin walls, white fur rugs, and state-of-the art computer equipment.

"I run a legitimate computer dating service," a calm and collected Countess de Marco told this reporter as she left the Midtown North station house with her attorney, Barry Rizzo.

Sandrine was glad that Angel was represented by Barry Rizzo. He was one of the most powerful attorneys in the city. Angel's fate was in good hands. But what about her own? Her zeal for total independence since leaving her mother's home did nothing to provide someone to lean on. While her steady clients were important men in their own worlds, she had been relentless in seeing to it that she controlled her own. Most of them didn't even know her real name, didn't know where she lived, or that she even existed except in the fantasy world she provided when she was with them for pay.

She reached for the phone and punched in Angel's number. It had been disconnected. She sat for a long time on the edge of the couch trying to think of who to call. Perhaps one of the other girls knew something. She had to talk to someone.

As she walked to the bedroom to get her Filofax she heard the front door open and SueBee's voice.

"Sandy? You here?" she called.

Faint with relief, Sandrine whirled around and saw SueBee struggling through the door in an ankle-length dark fur she had never seen before. Over her shoulder hung a new Chanel bag on a long strap. On her other arm was a duty-free shopping bag.

Sandrine resisted the urge to run to her and throw her arms around her. Seeing SueBee renewed her feelings of rejection at being left alone. She leaned against the side of the bedroom door. "Well, hello, stranger. How did it go?" she asked calmly.

SueBee dropped her bags, ran toward Sandrine, and hugged her. "I'm so glad you're home, Sandy," she said. "I saw the paper. Are you okay?"

Sandrine returned the hug. "I'm fine. Don't worry," she said. She pushed SueBee away and studied the coat. "Wow, you did all right for yourself."

SueBee stepped back and twirled around, the coat undulating around her legs as she pressed the collar to her flushed cheeks.

"Isn't this something? Jack bought me this in Paris as a surprise. I don't even know what it is. All I did was shiver a little in my cloth coat in front of a window on that street where all the high-fashion shops are. He marched me right into the store."

"It's sable, SueBee," Sandrine said, laughing in spite of herself. "Fur doesn't get any better."

"Really?" SueBee asked, looking down and smoothing the lustrous thick fur with both hands. "I better be nice to it then," she said, smiling. SueBee walked to the coat closet by the door and gently hung up the coat.

"You want some coffee?" Sandrine asked, going toward the kitchen.

"My, yes," SueBee said, dropping heavily onto the couch. "I'm exhausted."

Sandrine put the coffee water on and leaned against the counter pass-through. "So? How was it?" she asked as SueBee plumped up the couch pillows and lay down.

"Oh, Sandy," SueBee said, sounding giddy, "I loved Paris! It was like living in a movie. London was cold and wet. I hardly saw Jack. He had meetings the whole time."

"So what did you do with yourself?"

"Oh . . . stayed in the hotel. Watched TV, you know. It wasn't so bad. The last weekend we went to an enormous country house with servants and horses and everything. That was awful," SueBee said, dejected. "I felt like socks on a rooster."

"What do you mean?"

"Those people were so snooty to me. I don't know. Things were so . . . fancy. The man who owned the house was some duke or sir or something. His wife talked as though she had marbles in her mouth and they did all these special things like tramping around in the wet shooting birds and cutting their grapes with scissors shaped like a stork. Most of them were blind-drunk by lunch. At dinner there were skatey-eight forks beside my plate. I had to watch the lady across from me to know what to do. Then . . ." SueBee turned to face Sandrine, leaning on one elbow. She started to giggle. "You're going to die, Sandy. Each guest had, like, their own butler, a waiter-type guy behind their chair. . . ."

"Footmen," Sandrine corrected. "My mother used to hire them for dinner parties."

"Right, thanks," SueBee said. "Well, when mine put this, like, glass bowl down after dinner, I thought it was clear soup with a cinnamon stick in it. I picked up one of the spoons I had left, 'cause my silver and my food didn't come out even, when I saw everybody dipping their fingers into it. It was a finger bowl! I almost ate it!"

"Oh SueBee, how dreadful! Did anyone see you?" Sandrine asked, placing a steaming mug on the coffee table. She pushed SueBee's feet clear to make room to sit down.

"I don't think so, but I can tell you I could feel the sweat running down between my shoulder blades. Every time I think about it I start humming to myself to block out the thought waves."

"I don't know, SueBee," Sandrine said lightheartedly. "It probably would have done the old poops good."

"Then someone asked me what my hometown was and I said

'Texas.' They all laughed so I pretended I meant to say it. This trip showed me I have a lot to learn about how rich people do things."

"What about Jack? Did you two get along?"

"Oh sure," SueBee said lightly.

Sandrine could hear something behind her answer that seemed less than confident. "SueBee? she said.

"Sandy," SueBee asked tentatively, "should I care that Jack mentioned Zaki a lot?"

"How do you mean?"

"Like, when he introduced me to people. He would say something like, 'SueBee is a good friend of Sheikh Omar Zaki.' And once, I was in the powder room with one of the women and she came right out and said, 'I hear you used to live with Sheikh Zaki.' I said I was his nurse and she looked at me like, 'Yeah, sure.'"

"How did Jack know about you and Zaki?"

"Oh, I told him," SueBee said lightly.

"I don't think you should have done that."

"Well, it doesn't matter because I've been saving my real news till last."

"Oh?" Sandrine said, raising her eyebrows.

"I'm pretty sure Jack is going to ask me to marry him. I mean, I said something about when we get married on the plane and he just smiled."

"SueBee! Honey . . ." Sandrine said, making no attempt to hide the warning tone in her voice.

"What? You don't think he will?"

Sandrine sighed deeply. She felt like a cheat not telling SueBee that men like Jack Ayler don't marry girls like SueBee. That he was using her and her connection with Zaki. It was horrid and cheap and not unexpected. "I'm sure he adores you, hon," she said, instead of what she meant. "Tell me more about your trip."

"Well, the French minister of finance sent his car to meet our plane when we landed in Paris. We had half a floor in the Plaza Athenée with our own staff. I had my own maid to unpack and press my things! The suite we had at the Dorchester in London was bigger than Zaki's was. The last night we were in Paris, the night he gave me the coat, he broke an appointment so we could have dinner alone in the suite. We had baby lamb chops and made love on the floor."

Sandrine pictured SueBee, who had never had an unfranchised restaurant meal in her life until Zaki bought her a turkey club in the Bull & Bear, draped in ivory satin being served pâté and crustless toast starters by a personal French-speaking butler in a suite the size of Penn

Station. "I hope you didn't eat the little paper panties on those chops," she said teasingly.

"You know what?" SueBee said. "We were fooling around after dinner and Jack put one on his penis. I nearly died laughing."

On his penis. Hilarious, Sandrine thought. And so predictable. What was amazing was that there were still women left in this decaying world who would laugh at something like that, and the Jack Aylers knew it. "I can imagine," she said dully.

"Sandy, I'm so in love," SueBee said with a moan. She rolled over on her stomach and pressed her face into a pillow.

"Hold on, hon. Don't get totally carried away here," Sandrine said cautiously. "Do you really, really want to marry Jack Ayler?"

There was a long silence from inside the pillow. Finally, SueBee answered. "So bad," she said softly. SueBee rolled over and looked across at Sandrine. "There's something I just have to do now, and I need you to help me."

"Sure," Sandrine said, curious. "What is it?"

"Promise not to laugh?"

"Promise."

"Teach me to read. I'm not going to be able to live in Jack's world if I can't," SueBee said, speaking so softly Sandrine could barely hear her. "It won't be easy. I have dyslexia."

So, she had been right after all. She knew something was wrong with SueBee but she never could figure it out. Whenever she left a grocery list SueBee came back with yams instead of jam, candy when she had written candles. Sandrine would leave messages for her on the living-room desk and SueBee would pretend she hadn't seen them. Frustrated, Sandrine once asked her if she shouldn't have her eyes checked. Sandrine was sorry she had asked. SueBee looked at her as though she had been slapped. Now it all made sense.

That's why SueBee never ordered from a menu but cleverly had what someone else was having.

"I never knew," Sandrine said. "Oh, SueBee, of course I'll help you. There must be classes all over, like the Y or NYU. I'll look it up for you," Sandrine said, uneasily watching SueBee's face redden.

"Couldn't you teach me?" SueBee asked frantically. "I couldn't walk into a class."

"Of course you could! Everyone else in the room would be in the same boat."

"No. No," SueBee protested. "I couldn't. Not right away."

"Okay," Sandrine said, patting SueBee's ankle on the couch next to her. "I'll work with you here in the beginning. When you feel better about it maybe we can find a class. Now, I'm going to get out of your hair so you can get some sleep."

"That's okay. Jack said he might stop by after he does an interview. You have a date?"

Sandrine stood up and began to collect the coffee mugs. "Not really. Just dinner with one of my regulars. I better be nice to all of them now. If Angel's out of business I'll be needing every one of them."

"Do you think she's really out of business?"

"I don't know. When I see her lawyer I'll find out."

"Her lawyer?" SueBee asked with a frown. "What do you need a lawyer for?"

"I asked Angel for a recommendation a while ago. My birthday is next month."

"I don't get it."

"That's when I'm supposed to get my father's money," Sandrine said. "And I don't think I'll get it without a fight."

Jack Ayler crossed his legs and shot his cuffs. On the other side of his desk sat a young journalist from *Money* magazine who seemed more intent on impressing Ayler than interviewing him. At the moment the kid was droning on about his interest in no-load bonds. Jack didn't interrupt him. He needed the time to think. He was beginning to feel the jet lag from his European fling with SueBee. It had probably been a mistake to take the girl along on a business trip and perhaps an even bigger one to take her to Lord Benton's country home. The upper-crust Brits didn't take too kindly to a guest arriving with a current squeeze, particularly if she was young enough to be everyone's granddaughter. He would have to do something about the relationship sooner rather than later. At the moment he had to get through the tedious interview.

The little gold chiming clock on the edge of his desk gave him an excuse to cut the reporter short. He stood and offered his hand. "I'm sorry, I have a pressing appointment. Perhaps we could continue this another time."

The surprised reporter stood, took Jack's hand, and apologized profusely, saying he would phone Jack and set up an appointment for later in the week. As soon as the office door closed, Jack reached into a lower drawer of his desk and lifted out one of the small navy-blue leather boxes stacked there. He flipped open the top and studied the bracelet of cornflower blue sapphires, thinking how very close to the shade of SueBee's eyes the stones were. *Yes, this will do the job,* he thought, as he dollied his mental camera back to take in the curve of her cheek and jawline, the way she arched her neck and tilted her head when she listened to him, her lips slightly parted, those eyes wide and staring into his as though each word was something precious and meaningful to be memorized and treasured. His mind moved from her chin to her throat with its tiny crease along the base and just a hint of residual baby fat. Below that, where her high, firm breasts began, was the spot he loved to bury his face in and feel the warm, soft flesh enfolding the sides of his head. She was so soft. Every inch of her was softer than anything he could have ever imagined. Soft and warm. When he nestled there between her breasts he was suffused, engulfed, nearly smothered in the aroma of sun-warmed honey. Licking like a kitten, he could taste her skin, there between her breasts.

He snapped the lid of the jewel case shut and sighed. Damn. They were all so sweet, so delicious, and so exciting. At first. Why did it always happen the same way? The hunt, the targeting, the chase, the conquest. It was all exhilarating. Then . . . then—it was almost too delicious to fantasize about—the kill. The actual bedding was pure luxury. But, oh my, would he miss running his tongue over her breasts and then down between her legs. He loved going down on her as much as she loved it. It was like drowning in lemon mousse.

He cleared his throat and recrossed his legs to discourage the erection that was pulsing inside the trousers of his Savile Row suit. Would there ever be a woman, he wondered, who held his interest for longer than a week? A month? At the most a year?

He leaned across the desk and flicked on the speaker phone. He punched in the number of the limo and slipped the leather case into his jacket pocket.

For the price he could have bought her a BMW but he couldn't put a BMW around her wrist as he pressed his body into hers. One of his theories was to give women gifts they could accept while naked.

He listened to the car phone buzz a half ring before his driver picked up.

"Jerry. I'm on my way. I'll need to make a quick stop on East Fifty-fifth," he barked. "You can swing around and pick up Denton MacGuire and his wife on Park. Then we're going to the Metropolitan Club."

"Right, Mr. Ayler," the driver responded with a snap.

A biting gust of wind whipped his face as he pushed through the revolving lobby door and stepped into the waiting car. The evening traffic didn't look half bad. If they hit the FDR just right they could make good time getting uptown.

He wondered how SueBee would like the bracelet. Hell, he knew she would love it, just like she loved everything he did. He smiled to himself, marveling, not for the first time, at the energy being adored gave him. In Paris he had amazed himself with the nonstop lovemaking that carried them into the blue morning dawn. SueBee had squealed and cried, literally called out for him to stop, then begged him not to. He lost count of his own orgasms. SueBee told him the first time they were together that he had given her her first orgasm. He'd been surprised and delighted to find she was a virgin. Now, that was something special. Something he treasured. A man never forgets it when he gives a girl the first one she's ever had and then repeats the performance over and over. The memory of the look on her face the first time she came was worth a truckload of sable coats and bracelets.

It also made him a bit sad. It was a pity they couldn't go on that way forever, but he knew this was the only way. The minute she turned to him on the plane home and started a sentence with "When we're married . . . ," he knew it was over. He was so busy planning how he would end it, he had not heard the rest of her sentence.

He leaned forward and depressed the stereo button in the polished wood panel above the bar. The lush strains of a Mozart string quartet swirled into the car.

"I don't understand," SueBee said, gazing up at Jack as he paced the worn rug of the little apartment with its Salvation Army furniture and faded travel posters of places the occupants had never seen. "How come you have to go to L.A. all of a sudden?"

To his great relief she stopped speaking. He didn't like lying to her. But from long experience he knew that being "out of town" when he broke off a relationship saved him the middle-of-the-night phone calls and the suicide threats. Not that SueBee would do that, she was a pretty solid kid. But he couldn't take the chance.

Jack's back was to her as he squinted at a poster of a Grecian beach. On closer study the two nude girls in the right-hand corner were actually wearing string bikinis.

"Come here," he said, turning. He pushed out his lower lip in a little pout. "Come to Daddy." He extended both arms, keeping the face of his watch upward. Denton MacGuire's approval of the funding he was looking for on the Remington deal was crucial. He couldn't keep the man and his wife waiting.

SueBee didn't move. She was sitting in the corner of the dreadful orange couch, her knees tight together and her hands in the lap of a terry-cloth robe that belonged to her society-brat roommate. SueBee never said, but he was sure the girl was a high-priced hooker. She had that look, all gloss and gleam. She reminded him of a panther, the way she moved, with all that barely concealed anger. They had hated each other from the moment they met, as do most people who have each other's number.

He studied the Hotel Carlyle crest embroidered on the pocket over SueBee's right breast. It was such a rich-kid thing to do, to swipe a hotel bathrobe. Some poor bastard must have had a couple hundred extra on his bill when he checked out.

He left his arms outstretched until she relented. With a little hopping motion, SueBee stood and jumped into his arms.

God.

She smelled so damn good.

He pulled her into his groin, grasping her firm little butt with both hands, moving against her from side to side. "I'll call, I promise. We can do it over the phone."

"Do what?"

"Screw on the telephone," he said matter-of-factly. "You never did that?"

"No, I can't say I have," she said, shaking her head. "You mean you talk dirty or something?"

"Yup. It's great. The next best thing to being there."

"I don't think so, Jack," SueBee said, speaking against his shoulder. "Not like being with you."

She had just stepped out of the shower when he arrived. He wouldn't have to worry about makeup on his new suit. He held her, thinking that it wouldn't take half a second to pull open the bathrobe and get one last feel of all those goodies. He wondered if there was time for a quick boff. It would mean shedding his clothes, showering, and dressing again. Then again, maybe not.

"Darling girl," he said, openly glancing at his watch. "I truly have to run. I have a dinner meeting at the club and I can't be late."

"I could go with you," she said meekly. "I'm not doing anything tonight."

He bit his lip and tried to smile. She was starting. Why did they all start? Why didn't women understand their place in the scheme of things? He pictured the expression on Lydia MacGuire's face if he showed up for dinner with SueBee on his arm.

"Baby, baby, baby," he crooned into her hair. It smelled like Ivory soap. "You'd be bored to tears. Just remember, you're my honey. Okay?" He knew he was wimping out, but he just couldn't come right out and say it's over, *fini,* thanks for the great piece of tail but the party is over. Jack Ayler travels alone.

SueBee looked down at the sapphires that encircled her wrist and nodded.

"Do you like your bracelet?" he asked.

"Yes, it's beautiful," SueBee said softly. "Thank you, Jack."

"Give us a kiss," Jack said, lifting her chin with one knuckle.

SueBee kissed him, her mouth wide and yielding. The robe fell open of its own accord as she reached up to put her arms around his neck. He could feel her naked breasts through his silk shirt. Once again he felt the stirring between his legs. He *could* do it real fast. Just fling her on the couch and shove it right up there. Maybe he could save the press of his suit, if he was careful.

He pictured Denton MacGuire drumming his deal-signing fingers and his wife carping about Jack's rudeness while she picked at her nails.

He shuddered and removed his tongue from SueBee's mouth so he could talk. "I'll call, doll," he said. "Gotta run. Dream about me, baby."

He reached the elevator and jammed his fist hard against the rubber bumper of the closing door. SueBee had walked him down the hall in her bare feet, the sleeves of the huge bathrobe covering her hands like one of the seven dwarfs.

As the elevator doors closed she pushed back the sleeve of her robe and twisted the sapphire bracelet. She was looking straight at him with those cornflower blue eyes like she knew something.

Jack's last words skittered around in her brain like bright-winged butterflies as she walked slowly back to the open door of the apartment. *Dream about me, baby.*

She would dream of nothing else. There had not been a moment spent with him that she hadn't tried to extend, to hold on to and savor as if it would never come again. She thought of how, when she looked up to see him walk into a room or a restaurant, her heart would race wildly.

She adored him, but no matter how completely bedazzled she was, loving him didn't make her stupid. She knew what he had just done to her. A man didn't take her on the kind of trip they had just had and the very night they were home run off to dinner without her. She didn't believe he was going to L.A. He hadn't mentioned a word on the whole trip back about any such plans. Further, she knew when it started, she felt it the second she mentioned their being married. It was like an ice-cold cloud descending. She had tried to ignore it and deny it later, but he barely spoke to her the rest of the trip home. She knew, but she had been too proud to ask if she had offended him in some way. She *did* want to marry him. Why should she be ashamed of it?

When SueBee worked for Zaki he kept a locked suede-covered chest on a shelf in the bedroom closet. Whenever SueBee came to his bedroom in the morning and found him with a lady, she noticed that before the lady left, Zaki would tell Mr. Hakim to go get the chest. One morning SueBee had played Mr. Python with him for so long that she had him rolling around grunting and squealing, all tangled up in the sheets. She gave him his heart medicine and after he calmed down, he asked her to bring him the chest from the closet shelf. When she handed it to him, he put it on his lap and lifted the cover.

When SueBee saw what was in it, she gasped. It was full of the most beautiful things: great star-shaped pins full of diamonds, ropes of pearls, long coils of gold chains, scarlet- and blue- and emerald-colored stones. It looked like a pirate's treasure in the comic books.

He lifted up a big fistful of the stuff like it was from the dime store. "Whatever you fancy, my lovely one," Zaki had said, beaming at her. "Take."

SueBee stood beside the bed watching how the light caught in the mass in his hand. She reached forward and shut the lid with a final little pop. "No," she said. "Thank you, but no. These are for your ladies. I'm not one of your ladies. I'm me."

Zaki's eyes had widened at what she said. She was terrified that she had hurt his feelings. Without a word he got up out of the bed and carried the chest back to the closet. As he walked back to bed he was smiling one of his little one-cornered smiles. He didn't say a word but she could tell she hadn't hurt his feelings at all.

She wished she had had the presence of mind to say the same thing to Jack when he handed her the long leather box. In her heart she knew why she hadn't. With Jack, she had believed that someone loved her with the same kind of honesty with which she herself loved. Until now she thought love was only denied people who didn't deserve it.

The hurting was going to last for a long, long time.

Through the fog of pain she heard someone calling her name. She tried to sit up but her arms and legs felt as though they were tied to the bed. When she raised her head the ringing in her ears blotted out the sound. She collapsed onto the pillow. It was soaking wet and smelled.

"SueBee?" There was the voice again. Someone was standing by the bed screaming. "SueBee! What have you done to yourself? Oh my God!"

SueBee turned her head and opened her eyes. Sandrine was kneeling by the side of the bed, crying.

When she saw SueBee open her eyes Sandrine grabbed her arm. "Oh thank God. You scared me to death!" Sandrine said, pulling on the twisted sheet. "Oh, honey, look at you. You've thrown up all over your lovely coat. What in the world are you doing in bed in your fur coat? What happened?"

SueBee tried to speak. Her tongue felt like a tube of bologna. She couldn't bend it to speak clearly. "Valium," she slurred. "Took a whole bunch of Valium. Found it in the bathroom cabinet."

"SueBee, why?" Sandrine sobbed.

"Jack broke up with me," SueBee said through her stupor.

"SueBee! No. What did he say?"

"He came by and gave me this," she said, holding out her arm to show Sandrine the bracelet. "Then he scooted out to a business dinner and didn't ask me to go."

"But honey. Maybe it wasn't appropriate. That's understandable."

"He lied and said he was going to California," SueBee said, ignoring Sandrine's attempt to placate her distress. "He's not going to California. I just knew it. He's kissed me off. And after we made love like . . . oh, Sandrine, you can't believe how we made love." SueBee buried her face in the bedclothes and began to sob.

"Oh, honey . . . no, don't," Sandrine said, smoothing her matted hair away from her forehead. "I'm so sorry."

"I know I'll never see him again, Sandy," she said between gasps. "It's over. Why would he do it this way?"

"Because he's a rat, that's why. He never deserved you in the first place. He's an old man who uses young girls instead of goat-gland injections."

"I hurt all over, Sandy. Help me."

Sandrine stood up. "What do you want me to do, SueBee? I'll do anything."

"Don't let me die. Sit me up. Just pull on my arms. If you can, get me on my feet and make me walk. Don't let me sit down."

"I'll try," Sandrine said. "Oh God. This is terrible."

"See if you can get some coffee. Lots of it. Make me drink it even if I try not to."

"Oh, shit!" Sandrine snapped. "I think we're out of coffee."

"Then make up something really nasty. Eggs, ketchup, sour cream, Coke. Anything you can find and make me drink it. I've got to throw up some more to get rid of this stuff."

Sandrine blanched. "SueBee, I can't do this by myself. I'll get Juan. I saw him on the door when I came in just now. Promise not to move."

"I'm not going anywhere," she said, closing her eyes. "Thank you, Sandy. I didn't really want to die, Sandy. It was just the pain I wanted to get rid of. I just want to be in some high, soft place away from the pain." Her words were beginning to slur like those of a drunk who had reached the saturation point.

"SueBee!" Sandrine begged from the lighted doorway. "Please don't. Please don't die! I'm going to get Juan. I'll be right back. Hang on, please, SueBee."

Out in the hall, Sandrine smashed the down button as though force would speed the elevator to her. Then she decided the stairs would be faster. As she tumbled down the cold cement stairway, tears streaming down her face, she swore under her breath. "Bastard. God damn son-of-a-bitch rat-fang bastard. I'm going to kill him," she gasped. She knew just how she wanted to do it. First she would snip his prick into little bite-size pieces. She wouldn't even have to ask SueBee how it's done. Then she would kill him. Any jury with a woman on it would find her not guilty.

CHAPTER
❧ 10 ❧

Peter's Journal Entry—Paris, July 3, 1990

Well, well, well—the world gets smaller still!

I've just hung up from a long conversation with Fiddle. Both of us are wildly excited by Black Jack Ayler surfacing in this story. God, life is wonderful. If you live long enough and pay attention, the whole world comes down to only two hundred people and one half has either slept with or cheated the other half.

We talked for over an hour. I found myself missing her. One thing about Fiddle that I haven't found in anyone else in my sheltered life is that we are on an identical wavelength, right down to agreeing that Hemingway is an overrated writer and that Madonna can't sing. It's rather like talking to myself, talking to Fiddle.

We agreed I have to do an article on him someday. We plotted out the whole piece, opening with him playing suck-face on the plane with the hooker and flashing back to use the information Cleo has provided. Please God, could it be true? Could I find out that Jack Ayler, trying to protect his own interests, tried to off the old lady? Mr. Pulitzer, call your office; Peter Shea has won your prize.

I have a call in to Wendy to bring her up to speed on all this and find my spirits lifting 100 percent.

Our next session will concern how this girl Angel Weinstein figures in all of this. (I've come to the conclusion that my Madeleine is not going to surface. Sad, I'd like to know what became of her.)

I'm going to take tomorrow off. I'm still an American, for Christ's sake,

*and should celebrate my country's birthday. I'll spend the day looking for
a fax machine. When I spoke to Fiddle she was appalled that I didn't have
one yet.*

Giselle brought me a week-old New Republic, *my Con Ed bill from
the New York apartment, and tiny* petit pois *so sweet I ate them raw.*

Angel Weinstein curled her nearly six-foot frame into the back of a
cramped yellow cab. As she slumped back against the sticky seat, she
felt a piece of soiled duct tape, used to mend a tear in the vinyl,
catching the back of her hair. She yanked it free and looked toward the
driver, ready to say something. She caught a glimpse of his leering face
in the rearview mirror and changed her mind. She knew that look. She
had seen it in men's eyes since she was the only ten-year-old girl in her
Brooklyn neighborhood with breasts. Not just little prepubescent buds
pressing against her T-shirt, but formidably rounded orbs as solid as
volleyballs.

By the time she was thirteen she was five foot ten, with a tiny waist
and very long legs. As she grew older her color darkened, giving her an
exotic Mediterranean look. She could have been Italian, Jewish, or
Greek to the casual observer, and they were legion, for she was often
verbally and sometimes physically accosted—in crowded subways, on
elevators, and more than once in street-side phone booths.

These early experiences served to toughen Angel. By the time she
was fifteen her wide-set dark eyes held a sinister warning: "Touch me
and you're dead meat," they signaled. If the eyes didn't protect her, her
mouth and vocabulary served as heavy artillery. Those men foolish
enough to offend Angel Weinstein soon wished they had passed her
by. What they saw and heard was a beautiful Amazon with a killer
instinct. Only Angel knew how close to the surface of her fearsome
demeanor lurked a scared little girl.

The look she saw in the rearview mirror meant that any communica-
tion longer than reciting her destination would be taken as encourage-
ment. She had no patience for the implied hassle.

She deliberately lowered her voice and gave the driver her lawyer's
address, then slumped back into the seat to ponder the mess she was
in. As the cab immediately became snarled in the morning gridlock at
Fifty-seventh and Fifth, she gave in and listened to the sound in her
head. The noise of her world collapsing reverberated in her ears.

It had begun the night before with the crash of a vice-squad
battering ram forcing open the front door of the apartment where she
ran her escort service on East 59th Street.

The bastards! They were actually laughing as they tumbled into the room, stumbling over the splintered wood and plaster. Sons of bitches! When they arrested a Colombian drug dealer or a serial murderer, they bowed and scraped and said, "Excuse me, sir," reading him his fucking rights set to Montovani strings. But when the NYPD busted madams it was one big party. Whoremasters were trash. Forget that a lot of cops used her service and didn't hesitate to ask for freebies. When it came time to bust her or any of the other madams who worked the East Side, they were like something out of *A Clockwork Orange*.

She rubbed her wrists, remembering how tight the handcuffs had been. At least they had let her call Barry before they took her downtown. Barry Rizzo had been her lawyer, as well as a client, for as long as she had been in business. He wasn't perfect but he was on her side. She was faint with relief when he arrived within minutes, but her gratitude diminished considerably when she saw him pushing a detective out of the way so he could get in front of the "Live at Five" cameras.

She didn't know who had called the media, Barry Rizzo or the cops. It didn't matter. What mattered was that the publicity was a disaster and the bust was going to put out her lights. Before, she had just enough money to fix things. There were going to be criminal charges this time, and before they got through with her, she would be penniless.

She had started the business with her inheritance. It was not inconsiderable. Her father, Av, may he rest in peace, had been an IRS agent. For thirty years he had carefully stashed the bribes the garmentos paid him to audit their carefully cooked books instead of the real ledgers. When Av died, Angel and her mother inherited the key to a safe-deposit box at the Bowery Savings Bank and stacks and stacks of yellowing one-hundred-dollar bills.

Within the year her mother's share had gone to put her and her irregular heartbeat in a nursing home in New Jersey. Angel's share went into her first entrepreneurial venture, the Countess de Marco Escort Service. "Let our beautiful actresses and models escort you through the glitter of Manhattan," read the ad in the yellow pages. She'd had five good years, with only a few rough spots. She was all set to buy out a prominent but aging madam in London and take Countess de Marco international when the goddamned cops came busting through her door, throwing her files around and shutting her down.

Angel had begun working at seventeen, fresh out of high school. Her first job was with a computer dating service on Lexington Avenue. There she learned just how many lonely people there were in the world. She also learned the secret of what divided the sexes. It was encouragingly simple. Women wanted to get married and men wanted to get laid. You didn't have to be a Milton Friedman to figure out that there was a way to tap into the two conflicting desires. A business that supplied a product that was in constant demand never wore out, and one that satisfied the customer close to 100 percent of the time couldn't miss. Angel would open a call-girl service. If she could solve two problems.

The first was that there was no place to learn how to run such a business. The second was money. Angel realized that there was no faster way to learn the business than to be in it. She got her hair and nails done, bought a new suit at Alexander's and a pair of the highest heels to be had, and presented herself at an escort service she found in the back of *The Village Voice*. That night she went to work at the Hilton, where the Fire Fighters' Equipment Convention was in full cry.

She wasn't crazy about having sex with drunken strangers, but it wasn't any more boring than having to laugh at their jokes. What made it endurable was knowing it was temporary and a means to an end.

The women who ran the service in an East Side high rise didn't mind her hanging around the office all the time. Angel was good company in a wisecracking, up-yours kind of way, and when she offered to pitch in answering phones when someone was off or sick, she really endeared herself.

No one thought it odd when she volunteered to take the 7 A.M. to 12 P.M. shift, the slowest, dullest time at the office. It was also the time when no one else was around and Angel could go through the files and see how things worked.

Within a month she had it down pat. She knew the entire rather uncomplicated system. She knew who had to be paid off in that particular precinct, which landlords would permit a service to be run out of their buildings, and best of all, who were the dissatisfied girls who worked for the service.

That spring her father died. By that time Angel was very sophisticated about cash. Cash was volatile stuff. You couldn't deposit it without leaving a trail and having to pay taxes on it. It was bulky and inconvenient to use to pay bills. One of the girls she worked with sent her to Barry Rizzo, who had recently been profiled in the media as a "Mafia mouthpiece." For a dime on the dollar, Barry Rizzo "washed" Angel's inheritance by putting it on his office books as an investment in a new escort service. The Countess de Marco Escort Service was born. Thanks in large part to a steady stream of customers provided by Barry Rizzo, it was a howling success. Within six months it showed a profit. Within a year Angel ran an impressive book that provided the services of more than two hundred "model/actresses."

She had thought she was doing everything right, but clearly, despite the payoffs and influential contacts she had accumulated, someone hadn't stayed bought. The first time she was raided, Barry fixed it and she was back on the phones within twenty-four hours. Each successive bust took a little longer to recover from. After the last one he had warned her.

The gridlock at the intersection of Fifty-seventh street and Fifth Avenue finally broke its hold on her cab. It lurched forward, spilling the stack of morning tabloids off her lap and onto the floor. She retrieved them, glancing one more time at her picture on both front pages. There she was trying to pull an Hermès scarf over her sunglasses, her arm looped around the sleeve of Barry Rizzo's raincoat. The reporters, showing their usual flair for completely fucking things up, wrote that she was an Italian countess even though they knew better. It made a more colorful, sexier story.

She thanked the driver and pushed a ten-dollar bill through the slot to pay for a five-dollar ride, reminding herself that that kind of gesture toward the working class was going to have to stop. As she stepped to the curb she knew his eyes were boring into her behind. She snapped her head around and held up one middle finger. It only took a second for the driver's smile to collapse.

"*Puta,*" he hissed in Spanish as he slammed the cab into drive.

Angel stood on the pavement looking up at Barry's building, remembering the first time she had come to his office. She'd had such high hopes for success then. Owning her own operation meant everything to Angel. It made up for not having anything else.

Barry Rizzo looked up from his wide partner's desk to see Angel Weinstein swinging through the door. As usual, her hair was flying and her ample breasts bobbed in unison with each hit of her boot heels.

She stormed to his desk, towering over him. "So?" she asked in a booming, what-have-you-done-for-me-lately tone.

"How are you feeling this morning, *Countess*?" Barry said, lifting a copy of the *New York Post* and letting it fall to the desktop.

Angel threw herself into the chair opposite him with a groan. "Do you believe that crap?" she asked. "Those lousy reporters take one look around my apartment and overnight I'm an Italian countess!" She splayed her fingers into a makeshift comb and raked them through her dark red tangled, hair.

The charges against Angel ranged from procuring and promoting prostitution to resisting arrest for having used her extensive vocabulary in an abusive way on the officer who handcuffed her.

"I've made a few calls this morning, sweetheart," Barry said, consulting a legal pad on the desk. "I think we can get you off with a fine. But I'm afraid you'd better consider another line of work for now. Maybe in a year or two, when the heat's off, you could think about starting up again."

She plunged her index finger into a freshly empty pack of unfiltered Camels, crumpled it into a ball, and threw it in the general direction of the leather wastebasket. "Shit and corruption," she snarled. "I don't deserve this."

Rizzo took in the long legs, the broad shoulders, and the firm breasts straining at the fabric of her red silk blouse. The cosmic engineer who put Angel Weinstein together had given her Lainie Kazan's body and, to protect it, Billy Martin's mouth.

"Goddamn it, Barry. What am I going to do?" she asked. "If I stay out of business too long I'll lose my girls. And they're the best."

Angel sat staring out the window for a long moment. She looked like she was going to cry. Finally she turned to Barry and moaned, "Oh, Barry, what am I going to do?"

Barry took a deep, defeated breath. "Did you know they've had a tap on your phone for weeks?"

"Taps aren't admissible and you know it," she snapped.

"They don't want to see you in court, doll. They want the names and numbers."

"They can have 'em. They'll never figure it out. We speak in code on the phone," she retorted. "I'm the only one who knows who everybody is. It's all in my book locked up at Marine Midland Bank. Fuck 'em."

"Sure, sweetheart, fuck 'em. What good's a book with no place to use it?"

Angel fixed him with her smoky eyes. Two huge tears formed in each corner and rolled down her perfectly made-up face. "Barry, this is the only thing I know how to do. Where am I going to go?"

Rizzo leaned back in his chair and folded his arms across his barrel chest, waiting for her to get herself under control. He liked Angel, always had; she was tough and resourceful and built like a brick shithouse. None of that would be of any help to her now. The NYPD had her number, and they were going to see that she stayed out of business for good. The whole damn thing was so hypocritical. The Angel Weinsteins of the world provided a clean, reliable, even classy service. But when local politicians needed some crime-busting headlines, they always went after the easiest targets: deli owners who didn't sweep the pavement and madams.

He unfolded his arms and rested them on the desk. "You okay now?" he asked in a fatherly tone.

She nodded and pitched her wadded-up tissue into the wastebasket.

"Let's look at your assets for a minute, Angel," he said slowly. "What have you got that's yours?"

She threw up her hands, "I dunno. The car, furniture. My furs and some jewelry. That's it."

"Ummm. No stocks? No accounts receivable?"

"Accounts receivable, Barry? Get real. An escort service is not a retail operation. It's strictly cash. You know that. The girls bring me money. I take my cut. I pay my bills in cash just like the girls do."

"What about the book you mentioned?"

"My book?"

"Yeah. All the names and numbers of your girls and clients. That's worth something."

"Come on, Barry. That's like my jewelry. It's only worth what someone will pay for it," she said, pawing through her bag for a fresh pack of cigarettes.

Barry leaned back and put his arms behind his head.

"I might be able to find an interested party. You'd make enough to tide you over, pay the fine, back taxes, whatever. It might even lead to an interesting job."

"Job? What kind of job?" Angel asked, eyeing him suspiciously. "If you mean going back to hooking you can blow it out your ear, Barry."

"What I'm talking about is about as far from the kind of hooking you're talking about as a Polish suit is to high fashion. This is the big time. You could make more money than you've ever dreamed of."

"And your fee?" Angel said, arching an eyebrow over the end of a lighted match.

"Well," he said with a slow grin, "I can always bill you."

Angel dropped her mouth open. She propelled a solid block of smoke off the top of her tongue. It rolled lazily over the gloss of her lower lip, lifted and disappeared up her rifle-barrel nostrils. She stood up and crushed out her cigarette.

As Angel moved around the desk, Barry pushed his chair back and unzipped his fly. She stepped between his legs. "I'll save you the stamp," she said with a smile, as she slowly sank to her knees.

By the end of January, Sandrine knew she was in deep trouble. She lifted the metal lockbox from its hiding place in the hall closet and carried it to the couch. She opened it and looked forlornly at the dwindling stack of cash. In the month since Angel had been busted, Sandrine had lost the services of Pepé, the messenger who ran around town paying her bills. Now she would have to do it herself. The phone bill was due and Con Ed was leaving threatening messages on the answering machine.

The only money coming in was from the few regulars that Sandrine kept when Angel shut down. She could make her own schedule working free-lance, but if she lost a regular there was no way to replace him. The Greek middleman went back to Athens to cash in on some deal he had made with the government to export olives. The Connecticut lawyer who paid to watch Sandrine masturbate while he sat on the couch chewing the ear of a teddy bear was running for Congress and had gone back to his home district to campaign. Another married his nineteen-year-old secretary. She knew he'd be back, but until then she was out the money. She became more and more dispirited, worrying about SueBee, who for more than a month had remained in the bedroom in a state of deep depression. All she did was sleep and mindlessly watch television. The reading program she had so eagerly asked Sandrine to help her with was never mentioned.

Sandrine tried everything to get her out of the apartment. She suggested that they go visit the horses and go for a ride. She was sorry she had brought it up. The horses reminded her of Jack. The mere mention of riding sent her under the covers to weep. So did Sandrine's suggestion that they check the lunchtime action at '21.'

Now, desperate and scared, she realized that the advice Barry Rizzo had given her might not be so unthinkable.

He had told her, in no uncertain terms, that there was nothing he could do without seeing the papers that spelled out her trust fund. Without the documents there was no way to tell if he could get around her mother's legal right to deny her the money.

When he told her she had to confront her mother in person, she had felt the skin of her arms grow cold. Just the thought of facing her mother and explaining herself made her physically ill. She had run from Barry's office without so much as saying good-bye.

Since then, the thought of what she would have to do had never been out of her mind.

She had closed the lockbox and was carrying it back to the hall closet when she heard SueBee's voice behind her. Sandrine turned to see her friend was standing in the bedroom doorway. She was wearing a pair of her fresh baby-doll pajamas. Her thin legs looked veined and white. She was holding a bouquet of Mylar balloons festooned with a streamer of pink ribbon that dangled to the floor.

"Happy birthday, Sandy," she said in a weak voice.

Sandrine put the box down on the hall table and stood staring at SueBee. "SueBee, my God. Where did you get those?"

"I asked Juan to get them on his break," SueBee said, walking unsteadily toward her. "He brought them this morning while you were down in the laundry room."

"Oh, SueBee," Sandrine said, fighting the lump in her throat. She reached out and took the balloons. "I wasn't even going to think about it being my birthday."

"I'm sorry. Is it okay that I remembered? I didn't mean to make you feel bad."

Sandrine sat down on the edge of the couch holding the balloons. "You don't make me feel bad, SueBee," she said softly. "You're the only person in the world who makes me feel good. If I didn't have you I . . ." Sandrine couldn't go on. Hot tears sprang to her eyes. She looked up at SueBee and shook her head.

"Sandrine," SueBee said, sitting down on the coffee table opposite her friend, "I've never seen you cry. I'm sorry."

"Stop saying you're sorry," Sandrine said angrily. "It's not your fault I'm such a fuckup."

"Come on, Sandy. Don't say that. What have you done to say that?"

Sandrine reached for the tissue box next to the lamp and loudly blew her nose. "I'm a fuckup and a gutless wonder. Here I am, nearly broke, going noplace. I've got a best friend who hasn't been out of her room for a month or even washed her hair. At twenty-five I can't even say I'm a call girl. I'm a call woman with damn few callers and one hundred and sixty-seven dollars to my name while my mother is sitting on a fortune up on Park Avenue that rightfully belongs to me." Sandrine balled up the tissue and threw it across the room. "No. To us. That money belongs to us. Here you are sick and I'm too damn proud to go get the money to get you a good doctor."

"Don't say I'm sick," SueBee said, sounding hurt.

"Well, you *are*, damn it! You need a shrink to get you out of this thing about Jack." Sandrine pounded the arm of the couch with her first. "Every time I think about that bastard I taste blood."

"Don't blame it on Jack, Sandrine," SueBee said calmly. "What's happening to us is our fault. We need to take charge of our lives."

Sandrine's jaw dropped. "Huh?" she said. "I don't believe this. You've been rolling around in self-pity for over a month and now you're telling me we've got to take charge! What's happened to you?"

SueBee looked down at her bare knees and said something Sandrine couldn't hear. "What?" she said, squinting at her.

SueBee kept her head down. "Oprah," she said a little louder.

"Oprah Winfrey?" Sandrine nearly shouted.

"Don't laugh," SueBee said very seriously. "I've spent a lot of time watching her in there." She gestured toward the bedroom. "Most of her shows, one way or the other, have to do with self-esteem. Taking charge of your own life. She had this poor woman on, whose husband was beating her up, and Oprah goes, 'Sister woman. You gotta take charge.' "

SueBee's imitation of Oprah Winfrey was so on target that Sandrine collapsed onto the couch cushions and roared with laughter. SueBee sat looking at her with a wicked little grin. Finally, when she could compose herself, Sandrine sat up. "And what did that do for you, SueBee girl?" she asked.

"I'll tell you what it did," SueBee said, her eyes widening. "It got me out of bed. It got me into the shower. So no more cracks about my dirty hair. It got me to thinking what I could do for the only person who's stuck by me through this mess. That's when I remembered your birthday and worked out a plan with Juan. Who, incidentally, had thought I was dead."

"Well, I'll be damned," Sandrine said in a low voice.

"Sandrine. What will it take to get you your trust fund? It's yours as of today. I know it kills you just thinking about it."

Sandrine studied her hands. "That lawyer said I had to get the papers."

"So?"

"That means I'd have to see my mother."

There was a long pause while SueBee absorbed what that must mean to Sandrine. Finally, SueBee leaned right into Sandrine's face and put her hands on her hips. "Well, what are you gonna do, girl?"

Sandrine threw up her hands in mock defense. "Okay. Okay. Okay. Don't start."

"Do you want me to go with you? You know I will."

Sandrine slowly shook her head. "No, SueBee. This I've got to do myself."

"Then you'll go?" SueBee said, clapping her hands.

Sandrine stared into space before she answered. If crushed little SueBee had found the strength to get out of bed, she'd find the strength to take a cab up Park Avenue and face her mother.

"Yes," Sandrine said firmly. "It will be the hardest thing I've ever done. But I'll go."

"When?" said SueBee, pushing.

"Tonight. I know she's home. She's giving one of her sick-making parties. I read it in Suzy's column when I was waiting for the dryer."

SueBee reached over and grabbed Sandrine's face with both hands and kissed her on the forehead with a loud smack.

Sandrine wished she had taken SueBee up on her offer when she saw the crowd pushing its way into Tita Mandraki's penthouse. She could have used the moral support.

There was live music coming from somewhere, and white-coated waiters milling around carrying silver trays loaded with canapés and glasses of champagne.

She stood in the foyer with her coat over her arm and looked around. There were plenty of faces that she recognized, but no one that she knew.

The apartment had been redecorated in varying shades of lavender and filled with bucolic landscapes that heavily featured flocks of sheep.

She knew her mother would be in front of the library fireplace where she always received guests. Sandrine wasn't ready to see her yet. She needed time to collect herself. She dropped her coat on a chair and tentatively pushed open the swinging kitchen door. The familiar smell of Martha's cooking filled her with nostalgia.

Martha was standing at the stove, sliding biscuits from a hot cookie sheet.

"Marthy," Sandrine whispered around the edge of the swinging door.

The cookie sheet fell with a clatter to the top of the stove. Martha turned around and gasped, throwing her arms up in the air. "My Dreenie!" she cried. She stepped around the butcher-block table with her arms extended toward Sandrine. "Thank you, Jesus! My baby's alive!"

Sandrine fell into her former nanny's arms and let herself be engulfed in the unconditional love. She had never felt anything so wonderful. As she rested her head on Martha's ample, flour-dusted bosom, she felt all the pent-up anger drain out of her soul.

Suddenly, Martha released her. She held her at arm's length and looked into Sandrine's eyes.

"You couldn't call a body?" Martha asked sternly. "You couldn't send a note to let me know you were okay? Your fight is with your mother, not with me."

Sandrine looked down at the floor, "I know, Marthy. I've been terrible. Don't be mad at me. I just couldn't. I was afraid to. I was so hurt, so angry."

"Me, too."

"I did miss you. Terribly. Please try to understand."

Martha reached for the teakettle on the back of the stove and began filling it with water from the tap. "Somehow I knew you'd come today," she said, a little more cheerfully.

Sandrine was stunned. "How did you know that?"

"It's your birthday."

"Oh, Marthy. You remembered."

"Of course I remembered. Why wouldn't I remember? But that's not why you're here, is it?" Martha said, placing two tea mugs on the kitchen table. "Sit."

Sandrine sat down. "I'm here to talk to mother about my trust fund."

"I know," Martha said, dropping a tea bag into each mug. "I'll sit for a minute. There's only one more batch of biscuits to go."

Sandrine studied the lovely, aging face of the woman who had been more of a mother to her than her real one. "Think I've got a prayer, Marthy?"

Martha shook her head. "I don't think so, darlin'," she said sadly.

Sandrine felt a flush of anger climbing up her neck and onto her cheeks. "It's my money, Martha. My father left it to me. He must have meant me to have it. Besides, I need it. I'm broke."

"It's my understanding that your mother can refuse. Mr. Mandraki was wild in love with your mother, honey, and that's the way he wanted it."

"Maybe I shouldn't ask for it. Maybe I shouldn't give her the satisfaction of saying no," Sandrine said, trying to keep from shouting.

"You could get a lawyer."

"I've got a lawyer, damn it! He says he has to see the actual papers to help me. I can't get the goddamn papers unless I ask her for them."

"Watch your mouth, Sandrine," Martha said with a frown.

Sandrine leaned her chin on her hand and smiled across at Martha. "You never change, do you?" she asked lovingly.

The teakettle began to whistle. Martha picked it up and filled both mugs. "What kind of a life are you living, Dreenie? What are you doing for money? How do you get on?"

"Don't make me lie to you, Martha."

"Then don't tell me. At least if you need money you can't be doing anything real bad."

"I'm not hurting anyone, if that's what you mean by bad."

"What I mean by bad is, are you doing anything to hurt yourself?"

"I'm okay," Sandrine said, knowing she didn't sound convincing. Martha deserved to know what she was doing. But Sandrine knew she wouldn't press. Martha had probably guessed and didn't want to hear.

"Are you happy here, Marthy?" Sandrine asked as the older woman stood to turn off the oven and take out the new batch of biscuits.

"There are a lot of fights," she said with her back turned. "This is not a happy house, Dreenie."

"Fights? You mean Mother and Jamey?"

"Ummm," Martha nodded. "Even though they're getting this divorce, he's always around. He yells, she yells, he leaves. He comes back. She throws things. She leaves, she comes back. Then there's all the drinking and his young friends. I know they're doing drugs when she's not around. I see but I don't say. They probably think I'm a stupid old woman but I know the smell of dope when the air's so thick you could cut it with your shoe."

"How do you stand it?" Sandrine said angrily.

Martha turned, wiping her hands on her apron, and sat down again. "I've been here since the day they brought you home from the hospital. That's twenty-five years. There's no place I can go now. If I leave, she'll keep the money she says she set aside for a little pension for me. Lord knows she's threatened. Then where will I be? Out on the street like that poor devil crazy woman over on Third Avenue."

"Martha, I swear to you, I would never let that happen. One day, as soon as I can, I'll send for you. You can live out your days in peace just keeping me company. I'll get you your own cook and maid, even a little house. Anything you want."

Martha offered Sandrine a tired, sad smile. "You have big dreams, my girl."

"That's no dream. I swear to you."

"Are you going in there now?" Martha asked, nodding in the direction of the library.

"I thought I would. I just want to get it over with."

"She's drunk."

"Now?"

"Uh-huh. She started drinking in the middle of the afternoon. She was three sheets to the wind by the time the first guest arrived."

Sandrine buried her face in her hands. "Oh God. I can't face her if she's drunk. There's bound to be a terrible scene."

Martha got up. She leaned her back against the stove and folded her arms. "She keeps her papers in the bedroom wall safe," she said flatly.

"I know. She always did."

"I could get them after she passes out. She always does. You couldn't wake her with a baseball bat."

Sandrine looked up in awed surprise. "You would do that?"

"I would do that," Martha said without inflection.

There was not a doubt in Sandrine's mind that Martha would be true to her word. Hadn't Martha always covered for her? Hadn't she tried to protect her during the necklace business? Her mother had figured out that Martha knew Sandrine had lost it and nearly fired her. Sandrine couldn't put such a friend in jeopardy again. She would never forgive herself.

"I can't let you do that, Marthy," Sandrine said, shaking her head. "I just can't. I'm going in there. I don't care if she's drunk or not. I've got to grow up sometime."

Sandrine got up from the kitchen table, turned, and slammed out through the swinging door, banging into a waiter's back. She pushed by the waiter, weaving through the crowd clustered in the foyer. As she made it to the double doors of the library she could hear her mother's voice braying over the others. She was telling some long-winded story, punctuated by gales of her own laughter. She was wearing a dark-blue velvet gown with a high ruff of darker blue feathers, which matched the feather fan that dangled from one wrist. Her heavy black eye makeup made her look like a raccoon.

Sandrine walked to a clearing in the center of the room, lifted her chin, and looked straight at her mother. It took a moment for her mother to see her. Tita Mandraki stopped speaking and blinked, once, twice, and then lifted her fan and began to shake it in front of her face. "Well . . . well . . . well," she said with an exaggerated drawl. "The prodigal daughter returns."

"Hello, Mother," Sandrine said evenly, although her knees were trembling.

Her mother moved toward Sandrine, wearing a wide smile. She extended the fan as though to clear a path. When she got as close as she could to Sandrine's expressionless face, she hissed behind her teeth. "What are you doing here? As though I can't guess."

"May I speak to you for a moment, Mother? Alone."

Sandrine could smell the odor of liquor and lemon breath mints as her mother spoke.

Tita Mandraki took Sandrine by the upper arm and without another word guided her out through the double doors of the library and into the large powder room off the foyer.

Sandrine sat down on the foot of a quilted chaise.

Her mother locked the door and turned to face her. She still had the big fake smile on her face, all teeth and thinly disguised fury. She didn't seem to be as drunk as Martha had described her, but maybe she'd learned to hold it.

"Well, now," she said after taking a deep breath. "Kiki Boudreau tells me you are quite the lady about town."

"Kiki Boudreau?" Sandrine said, frowning. She didn't know anybody named Kiki Boudreau.

"She saw you at Doubles with a man old enough to be your father."

Sandrine seized the opening. She had no intention of spending any more time on this unpleasantness than was necessary.

"Speaking of fathers," Sandrine said. "Today, not that you'd remember, is my twenty-fifth birthday."

"Yes?" Tita said, raising one eyebrow.

"Don't be coy, Mother. I don't like this any more than you do. I want the money father left me."

"Oh, really," Tita said in a lofty voice Sandrine remembered her using on sloppy waiters and presumptuous salesgirls.

"Really," Sandrine answered calmly. "I know you can stop me from getting it. I'm asking you not to do that. I realize you don't think I have a right to ask you for anything, but that money is mine and I want it."

"We're being very direct, aren't we?"

Sandrine didn't answer. Her knees had stopped trembling and she felt oddly light-headed, as though the worst was actually over.

"Then I'll be direct, Sandrine. I know you expect me to deny you that money. You'd have to be pretty insensitive to think you've pleased me with your behavior. Disappearing. Never calling. Never coming by even to see your old nanny who you loved so."

"Go ahead, Mother. Spread the guilt around. I deserve it."

"I don't have to agree or disagree about whether you have a right to that money. It's not yours either way."

"What are you saying? Of course it's mine. My father left it to me."

A slow, cold smile crept across Tita Mandraki's strangely beautiful face. Her voice dropped to a patronizing drawl as she lowered her black eyelids. "Sandrine, darling, Otto Mandraki was not your father."

Sandrine's head snapped back as though she had been struck. "What are you doing?" she hissed. "Have you gone mad? Of course he was my father."

"Well now, who should know better, you or me?" Tita asked almost too politely. "I'm telling you he was not your father and you can never prove he was. It's that simple."

"I don't believe you," Sandrine said. Her knees began to shake again, as well as her hands.

"I'm thinking of cashing it in and replacing my Bulgari necklace," Tita said, studying her perfect red nails. "The one you stole."

Sandrine stood up and pushed the chain of her handbag higher on her shoulder. "Step aside, Mother," she said sharply. "And unlock the door."

Her mother made no move to do either.

"Step aside, Mother, and unlock the door, or I'll tear your throat out."

"My!" Tita huffed. "Is that how people get things done on the street now?" She turned and unlocked the bathroom door.

Sandrine brushed by her without a glance. She pushed through the crowd of startled guests, grabbed her coat off the chair, and hit the kitchen door with both hands. The door flew back and hit the wall.

Martha, who was arranging little biscuit-and-ham sandwiches on a silver tray, jumped.

"Sandrine? What happened?" she said, alarmed.

"She told me Otto Mandraki was not my real father."

Martha's hands flew to her face. "The woman's gone mad," she whispered. "What a terrible thing to do."

"Well, was he, Marthy? You should know," Sandrine asked, trying to control the tremble in her voice.

Martha slowly wiped her hands on a tea towel and sat down on the kitchen stool. She looked tired and so old. "Honey," she said with a sigh, "there's only one reason she'd bring that up now. Your trust fund represents a lot of money. There's certainly no way we could ever find out for certain. Your mother had a lot of—well—let's just call them 'friends.'"

Sandrine snatched a piece of paper off the notepad beside the kitchen phone and scribbled her phone number on it. "Marthy, I'm going to take you up on the offer we discussed. Even if Otto Mandraki wasn't my father, he left me that money and wanted me to have it," she said, handing Martha the slip of paper. "Call me. My lawyer will be waiting."

Martha slipped Sandrine's number into the pocket of her apron and nodded.

Sandrine turned as she was halfway through the door. "I'll send for you, Martha. No matter what it takes. I promise, from the bottom of my heart," she said, and stormed out of the apartment.

The following night, Martha phoned Sandrine to say she had retrieved the packet of papers from her mother's wall safe. Sandrine called Barry Rizzo, who dispatched a messenger to meet Martha on the corner of Park and Seventy-second Street to pick up the papers.

An entire agonizing week passed as Sandrine and SueBee waited for Rizzo's opinion on her legal right to receive the trust fund. Sandrine had told him of her mother's outrageous claim and, to Sandrine's relief, he told her he agreed that it probably didn't matter whether Mandraki was her real father or not. He had meant her to have the money.

Sandrine was standing in the kitchen painting the refrigerator, more to ease the tension than because it was chipped and dirty, when the phone rang. She called out, "I'll get it," to SueBee, who was watching a how-to-read video in the bedroom.

Sandrine wiped her paint-covered hands on her jeans and rushed to the phone in the living room. Please, let this be Barry with good news, she prayed as she lifted the phone. "Hello?" Sandrine said expectantly.

"Good morning," said a male voice with an English accent.

Sandrine didn't recognize the voice. Immediately she stiffened. Ever since the raid on Angel she was never sure who might have her name and number.

"This is Martin Bourke-Lyon. I'm sorry to disturb you on your weekend. Might I trouble you to speak to Sandrine, please."

Sandrine paused. "Just a moment, please," she said, attempting to pitch her voice a bit higher to disguise it. "Will she know what this concerns?"

"Regretfully, no," he said. "I apologize. Could you tell her I'm an associate of Mr. Barry Rizzo, calling at his suggestion."

Sandrine breathed a sigh of relief. If Barry had given out her number the guy had to be okay. "This is Sandrine," she responded cheerfully.

"Oh my, it *is* you. Hello," he said with a chuckle. "I thought I was speaking to your secretary."

"That was sort of the idea."

"That's very wise," he said, clearing his throat. "Let me put your mind at ease. I am the representative of a very private, very discreet organization. Mr. Rizzo does some legal work here in the States for my employer and suggested I meet with you concerning a position with us."

Sandrine was bewildered. "I don't understand, Mr. . . . ."

"Bourke-Lyon. It's hyphenated."

"Right, well, I don't understand why Barry wouldn't call me himself."

"You mean he hasn't?"

"No, Mr. Bourke-Lyon, he hasn't. And until he does, I don't think I should be speaking with you," she said, smelling a rat.

"I'm afraid I must apologize again. Clearly, we've got our wires crossed. I'll say good-bye for now and wait until you have spoken to him. Perhaps then you might want to contact me. I'm at the Pierre. Suite ten-fourteen."

Completely confused and agitated, Sandrine thanked him crisply and hung up.

"Who was that?" SueBee asked from the bedroom doorway.

"Some guy," Sandrine said with a shrug. "He says he's an associate of Barry's. Not a friend, not an old chum—an associate. Sounds fishy to me."

"Was it about the, you know, the money?" SueBee asked.

"No. And I don't know why I haven't heard from Barry," Sandrine said, punching in Barry's home number. She had never called him at home, but this was important. It took seven rings for him to finally answer. He sounded half asleep.

"Barry? This is Sandrine. Do you know a guy named Bourke-Lyon-it's-hyphenated?"

"Oh Christ," he moaned. "I completely forgot. I'm sorry. I got in real late. I was going to call you this afternoon." He was beginning to wake up. His voice sounded stronger and mildly concerned. "Listen, Sandy. I'm afraid I have some unpleasant news."

"Oh, no." Sandrine breathed, and sat down on the couch.

"About your trust fund. I've studied the papers and it's going to be more work than I figured to break the provision of your mother's approval. It can be done, but it will take time."

"And money," Sandrine said, feeling her heart sinking.

"That, too," Barry said. "Actually, that's why I wanted to put you together with this Bourke-Lyon fellow. This could be a big opportunity for you. How about we meet for drinks with him later. Say the Jockey Club? Six, all right? We can out-Brit the guy."

"The three of us?" she asked, surprised. "You mean he's for real?"

"In spades."

"Could you and I meet a little beforehand? You could tell me what this is all about."

"Sure. Five, then?"

"Should I dress?"

"To your pearly teeth!" he said with a chuckle.

As she hurriedly dressed, Sandrine told SueBee she was going to meet her lawyer. There had been a snag and she would call her later.

Her cab pulled up in front of the Jockey Club entrance of the Ritz Carlton on the dot of five. As Sandrine stepped through the door she felt a bump from behind. She looked around to see Barry smiling at her. He was wearing a menacing-looking broad-brimmed Borsalino hat and a double-breasted raincoat. "Going my way, dollface?" he said, lowering his voice.

"Barry, you idiot," she said, laughing. "I thought I was about to be molested."

"Hey! I can arrange that, no problem," he said with a leer.

There were two men pushing through the door right behind Barry. They were his height but heavier. They each took up positions on either side of the door as though waiting for instructions. Barry made no move to introduce them. He turned and grunted something to one of them. The man nodded but didn't move.

"Gimme your coat, doll," Barry said, unbuckling his raincoat.

As they walked toward the captain's station, Sandrine whispered, "They with you?"

"Yes and no," he said, adjusting the turquoise silk tie that matched a pocket square. "Forget 'em."

The restaurant was nearly empty on a late Saturday afternoon. The captain spoke warmly to Barry and led them to a table beyond the bar. The two men took a small table toward the back of the room. Barry ordered two scotch-and-sodas without asking Sandrine what she wanted.

"You always travel with an entourage?" she asked, smiling across at him.

"Nah, not all the time," he said, brushing imaginary crumbs from the spotless tablecloth. He turned and looked at Sandrine's suit. "That's a great outfit. Chanel, right?"

"Um. This is my proper-lady uniform. Is it okay?"

"More than okay," he said admiringly. "What is it with you girls and Chanel? It's like some kind of uniform."

"Not entirely, *Mister* Rizzo," Sandrine said, tossing her thick dark hair. "Only those of us who can afford them. Those who can't, wear Adolfo."

"How's that? Better nooky?" he asked, wiggling his eyebrows the way men like Rizzo did when they mentioned anything sexual."

"Better men," Sandrine said with a wink.

When the drinks arrived Barry took a long pull at his, exhaled noisily, and leaned toward her. "I hope you're not too upset about this delay of your trust fund," he said, patting the back of her hand. "The language is very clear, but I'm sure we can break it. It all depends on getting the right judge when we take it to court."

"To court?" Sandrine moaned. "That could take forever. What am I supposed to do about eating and rent until then?"

Barry rearranged himself in his chair and leaned closer. "Ah, now that's what I want to talk to you about before this fellow shows up," he said. "This guy Bourke-Lyon is wired. What I mean to say is that he has one of the most important connections—I won't say 'one of,' I'll say *the* most important connection—in the world. For a certain kind of business, you understand."

"Stop waffling, Barry," Sandrine said firmly. "What does he actually do?"

"He's a . . . let's see, ah . . . let me put it this way: he's a kind of high-level talent scout."

"Talent scout?" Sandrine said, frowning. "And he wants to see me? I don't have any kind of tal—" Sandrine hesitated. "Oh, I think I'm getting your point."

"This is the guy who bought Angel's book."

Sandrine stared at him. "Bought Angel's book? What are you talking about?" she said, her voice rising. "Barry?"

He reached over and grabbed her wrist. "Now, don't go flying off the handle, kid. It happens all the time. Wait till I tell you the rest of the deal."

"I don't think I want to hear it, damn it," Sandrine said angrily. "What gives Angel the right to sell my name and number! Who are these white slavers, anyway?"

"Will you just cool it," he growled. "These 'white slavers,' as you call them, run the classiest operation going." He turned and put one arm across the back of the banquette. "Let me ask you something, babe. Does flying around in private jets interest you? Does having dinner with the presidents of countries and some of the richest men in the world turn you on at all?"

"Go on," Sandrine said, sulking.

"How much money you got squirreled away, cupcake?"

She shook her head and stirred her drink. "Next to none," she answered sullenly. "You know that. Why would I be so desperate about my trust fund if I had anything?"

"For you, I'll make a loan, but you gotta think what you're gonna do if you don't get it," he said. "How would you like to sock away a couple of million in hard currency, jewelry, real estate, blue chips, you name it, in, say, the next five years? How would you like to mingle with the most important people—celebrities, world figures, billionaires? And I don't mean in hotel rooms or hideouts. I mean in their homes, at their parties, on their yachts. You would be one of them, not just a pretty bang from a call-girl service. Who knows, a real looker like you, babe, you could end up marrying one of these guys. It wouldn't be the first time. Huh? Huh? I ask you."

"Don't get excited, Barry," Sandrine said, calming down a bit, but not much.

"Yeah . . . well . . ." Barry said, looking hurt.

"I suppose now you're going to tell me I don't have to screw any of these people? They want me for my mind."

Barry's face brightened. "As a matter of fact, Sandrine, sex is only a small part of the deal."

"Oh, come on, Barry," she said, rolling her eyes. "That's right up there with the-check-is-in-the-mail and I'll-only-put-it-in-an-inch. This is me you're talking to."

"Look, Sandrine," he said, exasperated, "you got nothing to lose talking to this guy. It's just an interview. I'm only trying to take care of you, babe."

Sandrine took a sip of her drink. "You mean I have to audition?" she asked sharply. "That's outrageous."

"They don't take just anybody, kid, and you can check this out. Just the phone number for this operation goes for ten grand out on the coast. More here. Ask Angel. From the three dozen or so names she sold them, Bourke-Lyon is only interested in meeting a few girls. You're one of them." Barry threw up his hands in disgust. "Here I thought I was doing you a favor."

"Why me?" she asked suspiciously.

Barry mumbled something into his drink.

"What?"

He turned to face her. "Because I recommended you."
You mentioned who my mother was, didn't you?" she said, glaring at him. "Barry Rizzo, you are such a shark."

He held up one finger. "Yeah, but a smart shark, a caring shark, a shark who also told them you were beautiful and classy and could speak French. So, sue me for my sharkness," he said, faking a pout. "I'm your pal, kid. Trust me."

Sandrine sat silently for a while staring out into the room. She knew he was trying to help her. He was also trying to get her into bed, but his ego wouldn't let him pay for it. She probably wouldn't have done it, even for money. Barry was the kind of guy who fell in love with you and came nerding around, stealing your underthings from the basement laundry room to take home and sniff.

In her panic about money, she had told him more than she should have, the anxious life she was leading, her paralyzing hatred of her mother made even more intense by the attempt to plant doubt in Sandrine's mind about her father. She even told him about SueBee and Jack Ayler and how she wanted to do something to help her friend.

One element of Barry's hard sell stuck in her mind. Whatever the drawbacks of his current scheme, it offered a future and the chance to find a wealthy man who would solve her problems. How ironic, she thought, that her mother had done the same thing. All her life she had heard her mother's "talent" and ingenuity praised and fussed over when, in reality, her mother involved herself in a high-profile, frothy career to snare men who would support her financially or, in Jamey's case, stroke her raging ego. At least with Barry's plan there was a chance of a better life, for herself, for Marthy, and, somehow, for SueBee.

"Who are the other girls he's meeting?" Sandrine said finally.

"I don't know if he's picked everyone yet, but hey," Barry said, as though he'd just had a brainstorm. "How about your roommate?"

Sandrine reeled back in shock. "Barry Rizzo! Have you lost your tiny gangster mind? SueBee isn't a call girl. She's a sweet, innocent girl from Texas."

"Sure. You told me yourself she lived with Omar Zaki."

"Barry," Sandrine protested, "she was his nurse."

"Bullshit. I know Zaki. He wouldn't have a cute little girl living with him unless he was playing hide-the-sausage with her."

"God, Barry. You have such a dirty mind."

"We'll see," he said, signaling the waiter for a refill. "But let's not discuss her now. This guy's going to be here any minute. Are you game or not?"

"What happens if he likes me?"

"You get a Concorde ride to Paris, France, to meet the big boss. I fixed it. You can take your roommate. Whether she's in or not. How 'bout it?"

"I guess," she said with little enthusiasm. "So what's this guy's role in all this? He sounds like some kind of Euro-trash pimp."

"No-no-no-no-no," Barry said, machine-gun style. "He just interviews new girls and recommends the best to his boss. Then she interviews those."

"She? Who is she?"

"They call her Madame Cleo."

Sandrine made little circles on the tablecloth with her swizzle stick. She didn't want to let Barry know how the name excited her. Every working girl with a shred of ambition knew who Madame Cleo was. So did every high-rolling, free-spending player in the world. "Okay,

Barry," she said. "I'll go, if only to see what it's like to ride the Concorde. Oh, and Barry. . . "

"Yeah, babe?"

"Do yourself a favor. It's just Paris. Leave off the France. Everyone knows where it is."

Sandrine opened the door to the apartment and found it dark. From the bedroom door she could see the blue light of the television set. "SueBee?" she called. "You here?"

She switched on the lamp beside the couch and walked into the bedroom. SueBee was sitting up in bed wearing her baby-dolls. Her knees were pulled up as a resting place for a yellow-lined pad. SueBee's nose was only inches from the pad, her tongue in the corner of her mouth as she pressed hard on the paper with a stump of a pencil.

Sandrine smiled at the sight. "I think that's how Emily Dickinson did it."

"Who?" SueBee said, not looking up.

"It doesn't matter," Sandrine said, laughing. "All things in time."

"Ummm," SueBee responded.

Sandrine pushed SueBee's legs to one side and sat down on the side of the bed. "How'd you like to go to Paris this Friday?" Sandrine asked smoothly.

SueBee blinked and finally looked at her. "What?"

"Paris. You and me. Fly away on big silver bird."

"Crikey," SueBee whispered. "Are you serious?"

Sandrine reached into her handbag and pulled out an envelope. "The Concorde. The plane that all the movie stars and millionaires use because it only takes three hours. We've got reservations at the Ritz for the whole weekend."

"Oh my Lord. I've died and gone to heaven! What's this all about? What did you do?"

"I've got a job interview there and they're paying for it. Barry thought I might like to take you along."

"I don't have anything to wear," SueBee said.

Sandrine hooted with laughter. "Now I know you're well, Sooz. That's the healthiest thing I've heard you say in weeks."

"Seriously, I've lost so much weight. Nothing I have will fit."

"Don't worry about it. I have more clothes than Cher has," Sandrine said. She walked to her closet and flung open the door. "Help yourself."

"Can I wear my fur coat?" SueBee asked in a childlike voice.

"Yes, sweetheart," Sandrine said, smiling. "You can wear your fur coat. I'll go call them now and tell them we'll be there."

Madame Cleo had been interviewing new girls throughout the winter—1986 was shaping up as a busy year. Her regular clients usually informed her of their needs months in advance and there was little doubt that she would need at least two to three new, above-average girls, if any of her girls could be called average. What she wanted was three *extraordinary* girls.

For years she had done her interviewing during the morning hours in the second-floor drawing room of the mansion. The high windows facing the Seine had the best light even in winter—brilliant and unflattering to any but the most beautiful. The relentless glare picked up the tiniest flaw: a slight puffiness around the jaw, the imperfect thigh, or a dipping breast.

The room was large enough to permit a girl to walk several feet while Cleo assessed her posture, the lift of her breasts, the way she held her head. The acoustics provided by the unadorned walls and undraped windows allowed her to judge the timbre of the voice, the slightest nuances of speech.

The morning had been a tiring one. She had seen and dismissed a Spanish girl, a former model, recommended by Madame Lili—too dark for the Arab clients, too old for the Americans, and too unsophisticated for the rest.

She had then seen a Swedish girl whose drooping breasts would have required surgery, which Cleo would have financed if the girl also hadn't had a personality in need of intense psychiatric assistance.

"Martin," she said, speaking into the intercom on the little Louis Quatorze desk between the high windows, "who's left?"

"The American girls are here," said the disembodied voice of her aide.

"Girls?" she asked. "I thought you said there was only one American today."

"May I step in for a moment, ma'am?"

"*Oui, bien entendu.*" She turned off the intercom.

Once he joined her, Martin stood with his back to the door and pushed a long hank of pineapple-yellow hair away from his forehead. "Madame, the girl I interviewed in New York is here. She wouldn't travel without her friend."

Cleo shuffled the folders on her desk around, lifted one, and squinted at it. "Would that be Sandrine?"

"Quite," he nodded.

Cleo read the notes in the file. "Recommended by Barry Rizzo. Worked for Angel. Attended Hammelburg College. Mother, designer Tita Mandraki. Excellent dancer. No drugs. Speaks French." She put down the file and nodded, tapping the end of her closed Mont Blanc pen on the folder. "Mandraki," she said thoughtfully. "Why do I know that name, Martin?"

"Probably because you have three Tita Mandraki gowns. The beige chiffon, the pink—"

"No, no, that's not it," she said, waving her hand. "Oh well, I'll think of it later. Now, what's the girl's medical?"

"I'm sure that's not a concern," Martin said, leaning against the door.

"That's always a concern, Martin," Cleo said with a reprimanding snap. "Let's never forget the lovely Rhodes scholar, Diana, who infected half of the NATO high command before we caught up with her."

"Yes, Madame," Martin said sheepishly. He hadn't forgotten. Diana had cost them a bloody fortune.

"You say she has a friend with her? I don't see anyone else on the schedule."

"Oh, I don't think her friend is here for an interview, Madame."

Cleo nodded. "Ah, I see. But what does she look like? I'm always curious."

"Blond, very sweet-looking with a face you could eat a meal off of. Seems well to do, or at least she has on a very good fur."

"Hummm, too bad. We never have enough American blondes," Madame Cleo said. "You don't suppose the girlfriend would like to interview, do you?" Cleo asked, only half kidding. She was short a blonde and an important client, a wealthy Italian who demanded American blondes, was growing impatient.

"No go, I'm afraid," Martin said, shaking his head. "She's not a working girl. . . . Still, maybe something could be worked out."

"What are you up to, Martin?" Cleo said suspiciously.

"Never mind," he replied lightly. "I'll take care of it."

"All right. If she's going to wait for her friend, ask if she'd like some tea and see that she's comfortable."

"Should I bring Sandrine in now?" Martin asked.

"Please," she said. "I'm running late."

Cleo watched carefully as Sandrine entered the room, walked the few paces to the straight-backed chair in the middle of the rug, and sat down. Martin was right, she moved like a dancer. Very nice, Cleo thought, but let's see if she has a mind. *"Bonjour,* Sandrine. Do you speak French?" she said, smiling.

"Oui, Madame."

"Would you prefer to be interviewed in French or English?"

"Either, Madame, but you will understand my replies if I speak English," she said prettily.

She liked the response. The girl was poised and self-confident. "Now, Sandrine," she said lightly in English, "Martin has given me a fairly detailed file on you. He recommends you highly, as did Mr. Rizzo. You will be interviewed in greater detail later. However, there are a few basic things I'm particularly interested in."

"What would you like to know?"

"You've been doing this kind of work for some time. Why do you want to continue?"

"I like the life. I like beautiful things," she said, her voice as even as her gaze. "This kind of work provides me with them. I like adventure. I like new experiences. And, I suppose more important, I like men."

"Just so," Madame Cleo said, tenting her fingers. "You realize that many of my girls have made brilliant marriages while in my employ."

"I've heard that."

"Would that possibility also be one of your interests?"

"Which would please you more, to say 'yes' or to say 'no'?" Sandrine asked with a mischievous smile.

Cleo laughed out loud. No wonder they all recommended this girl. She tapped the top of Sandrine's file. "You've had no trouble with the police?"

"No, never."

"And your health? Any problems there?"

"No. I'm pretty particular about that."

"Yes, well . . . so are we," Cleo said sternly. "What sort of men do you prefer?"

Sandrine thought for a moment, pursing her lips. "Sophisticated. A bit older, perhaps. A man with normal sexual proclivities."

"What do you consider abnormal?"

"Any act that causes pain. To me or to my partner."

Cleo nodded slowly. "That's fine," she said. "We have other women who provide those services. What would you say your *spécialité* would be?"

"Accommodation," Sandrine answered, without missing a beat.

"Would you care to elaborate?" Cleo asked. She was liking the girl more and more.

Sandrine had not moved from the position she had taken when she first sat down, ankles and pumps side by side, hands resting lightly in the lap of her expensive suit. Every glossy dark hair was in place. When asked to explain herself she shifted slightly and crossed her legs. "I feel I am being paid to please."

"And do you?" Cleo asked.

"No one has ever complained," she said. "Oh, I do have one little trick. I've kind of perfected it, and it seems to be very effective."

Madame Cleo tilted her head with interest. "What would that be?"

"I can give myself an orgasm on cue."

"That's nice, but I don't see that as terribly effective."

"It is if I'm fully clothed in public, and a man thinks he caused it."

"Ahhh, I see," Madame Cleo said, nodding. "Take your clothes off, please?"

Madame Cleo made the request abruptly for very specific reasons. It was one of her favorite interview ploys. A girl's reaction told her as much as seeing her nude. If a girl balked or showed reluctance to comply, she was not engaged. Further, a girl could do clever things with clothing. As nudity was the ultimate uniform of her work, Cleo felt it good business to ask. The process permitted her to inspect a girl's true posture. If a girl had a tendency to slump, she did it while naked. Cleo needed to see the size of the waist, how the breasts fell and whether the nipples were brown or pink. Brown nipples were a dead giveaway that a girl had given birth at some time in her past, something Cleo needed to be aware of. The pubic hair pattern was important. Some men disliked bikini waxing, which left only a tiny dark line of hair. Some men specifically requested a full bush. Cleo also needed to check for unsightly birthmarks, scars, dimpled flesh, body hair, and any sign of needle use that some girls were clever about hiding. She would tolerate no imperfection that plastic surgery could not correct.

Sandrine did not disappoint.

She stood, put her small quilted bag on the floor, and took off her suit jacket. In seconds she was nude, except for her high heels, which she had slipped back on after peeling off her stockings and garter belt. The underwear was another giveaway. Cleo had never met a truly professional working girl who wore panty hose.

Cleo rested her chin on her hand and studied Sandrine's body the way a curator might judge a work of art. "Walk for me, please," she requested. "To the fireplace and back."

Walking in the nude in heels in broad daylight with any measure of confidence is difficult for anyone except a confirmed exhibitionist. As Sandrine reached the fireplace she turned, smiled charmingly, and paused for effect. She raised her arms slightly as though showing a frock on a runway and crossed the room again. Sandrine could have been modeling at the spring showings. She wore her nakedness like a couture gown. Her skin was smooth, without any imperfections in color or texture. Her hips were slightly flared. Her bush was a wide triangle that spread, as dark and glossy as mink, between her thighs. Her performance was both erotic and sedate.

"Your résumé says you dance, Sandrine," Cleo said. She reached behind the desk and clicked on a tape recorder. Sam Cooke's "Everybody Loves to Cha Cha Cha" swirled into the room. "Do it," Cleo commanded, extending her hand palm up as though serving up the suggestion on a plate.

Sandrine threw back her head and swiveled in a descending motion that coiled down her body. For a moment or two she stepped around the room, oblivious to anything but her own beauty and the music. From the expression on the girl's face it was clear to Cleo's experienced eye that she loved being observed. Even more refreshing was her utter delight in her own perfection.

Many of the girls she interviewed and worked with hated their own bodies, considered them somehow defiled, as many of them had been early in life. Cleo was not unaware that many girls chose the profession in order to masochistically continue that process. It was one of the sad facts of her trade, but she didn't dwell on it. She didn't exploit her girls. Indeed, she offered them ample monetary rewards and a glamorous life-style. The choice was theirs.

The sight of Sandrine made her heart sing.

The girl was the quintessential Cleo girl: intelligent, freshly youthful, and blatantly sexual.

Already her mind was searching her list of clients for those who would be clamoring for Sandrine, the newest Cleo girl.

Madame leaned across the desk and pushed Martin's button twice, their signal for him to step into the room. She watched Sandrine's reaction closely as the door opened and he joined them. Often, a girl would involuntarily cover her pubic area when she saw Martin. Sometimes she would scurry back to where she had left her clothes and grab a blouse or skirt to cover herself.

When Sandrine heard the door open, she pivoted a half turn and faced Martin, her right hand cupping one of her breasts, one foot in front of the other with the knee relaxed, fashion-model-style. She lowered her eyes in an expression of provocation.

"*Merveilleuse!*" Martin sighed in a half swoon.

Madame Cleo stood. "Please dress, my dear," she said to Sandrine before turning to Martin. "You do good work, Martin. I like her."

"Didn't I tell you?" Martin asked excitedly.

"Yes, well, we have a bit more business," she said. "Martin, would you see that Sandrine has a copy of our information packet?"

As Martin slipped soundlessly out of the room, Sandrine picked up her lingerie and proceeded to dress.

"My dear. Are you possibly free this evening?"

Sandrine's answer was slightly muffled as she pulled her skirt over her head. "Yes, of course, but I have my friend with me. Why do you ask?"

"We like to start our new girls with friends of the house, so to speak," Madame Cleo said as she stepped around the desk. "Perhaps your friend would like to be Martin's companion for dinner. He could pick you both up at your hotel at eight."

"That would be nice," Sandrine said, now fully dressed. She slipped the chain of her bag over one shoulder and extended her hand. "Thank you for seeing me."

"It's my pleasure, Sandrine. I think we're going to get along just fine," Madame Cleo said, holding her hand a second or two longer than necessary.

Cleo watched from the second-floor window as the two women left the house and walked in the direction of the Petit-Pont. The girl she had just hired was lovely. Her little blond friend was even lovelier.

She checked her appointment book for her lunch date, then walked into the little foyer outside the drawing room where Martin worked. "Martin, darling," she said, pausing in front of his desk, "would you call the restaurant and say I'm running late?"

"Sure."

"Then call Mr. Ayler at the Meurice and tell him we have a beautiful new girl for him this evening. You take the blond friend along. I want a full report."

"I'm way ahead of you," Martin said with a knowing smile. "I already asked the blonde to come along."

"Martin, you sly fox. I know what you're up to."

"Do you approve?"

Madame Cleo shrugged. "It's worth a try."

"This new girl is going to be terrific, don't you think?"

"I think Mr. Ayler will approve."

"Ohhh, I'm sure he will," Martin said with delight. "I know how he likes to break in the new ones."

That evening, Jack Ayler strode purposefully through the lobby of the Hotel Meurice feeling very, very good about himself. Just being in Paris energized his libido, suffusing him with memories of those early, heady days during the war when he first discovered Madame Cleo's little house of love. In those days she ran a far smaller business in a hotel on the rue St.-Denis. She had been very young, younger than some of her girls. She saw to it that the scared and lonely American military-police lieutenant learned the lessons of love that would set his preference in women for the rest of his life.

One of the most consistent threads of his life had been the relationship he had maintained with Madame Cleo. Over the years he had spent hundreds of thousands of dollars with her girls and never regretted a penny of it.

He reveled in the special treatment his long friendship with Madame Cleo entitled him to. Better than Lakers' season tickets, more exciting than a box above the fifty-yard line at the Super Bowl or dropping from a chopper onto the packed powder of the Bugaboos was the privilege of "checking out" a new Cleo girl.

As he neared the entrance to the small bar in the corner of the ornate lobby he slowed his pace and nodded to junketeering Senator Kent Mendenhall and an exquisite redhead. They were standing just inside the door waiting for a table. Sure of himself and his place of privilege in the superb hotel, he sailed by the senator and his companion and surveyed the room, one hand stroking his silver tie. The instant the headwaiter saw him he rushed forward.

"*Bonsoir*, Monsieur Ayler," he said. "Your table is ready, sir."

Jack nodded and let himself be shown to the only empty table in the room. His table.

The Hotel Meurice, a three-star bastion of quiet elegance and superior service, was Ayler's home away from home. For sentimental reasons, he always reserved suite 1108, which faced the Tuileries. It was in those magnificent rooms that General Cholitz had his office during the Nazi occupation of France. Staying in the suite never failed to remind Jack Ayler of how far he had come.

He always started his evenings on the town at his personal outpost in the corner of the Meurice bar. He liked the understated refinement of the room. The walls were lacquered aubergine and the lighting was less subdued than in most smart drinking spots in Paris, an ambience more conducive to deals than dalliance. A cocktail there at the end of a busy day permitted him to relax and regroup before venturing into the seductions that Paris offered even his somewhat jaded appetite.

Whenever he was expecting a new Cleo girl, he arranged himself strategically on the banquette facing the room. From his position he could observe how the girl carried herself as she crossed the vast lobby.

Without having to be asked, the waiter fluttered a napkin onto the low table at Jack's knees and placed a tall Black Label and soda on it.

"What brings you to Paris this time, Mr. Ayler?" asked the waiter.

"Another one of those conferences, Georges," Jack answered, adjusting the perfectly placed knot of his tie. "One needs one of your city's nights after a day of boredom."

The waiter smiled and took two small steps backward before turning to his other chores.

Jack took a long pull on his scotch and blissfully closed his eyes. Evenings such as these were the ultimate power perk of being who he was. He could have done without the presence of Martin, Cleo's fey British factotum-secretary and talent scout, but Madame Cleo insisted on the arrangement. With the new ones, Martin judged the part above the table. Jack's expertise involved the part below.

"Jack?"

Ayler opened his eyes to see Martin standing over him. His hair was pulled back in its usual ponytail, a style that emphasized his angular face and high cheekbones. He wore a beige Armani suit and a beige Armani shirt buttoned to the throat and no tie. His beige patent-leather shoes had brass tips on the toes and heel risers.

"Ah, Martin!" Jack said with a start. "Forgive me. I was just relaxing a bit." He stood and gave Martin his two-handed power greeting, grasping the younger man's right hand and elbow.

As Jack executed his he-man body language he peered over Martin's shoulder. "Isn't something missing?" he inquired with a wide grin.

Martin bent, pinched the knees of his trousers, lifted his cuffs, and sat down next to Jack. "Ah! The girls are in the loo for a moment. You know how they are," he said with a wink.

Jack snapped his fingers for the waiter and turned toward Martin. "Girls?" he asked, his eyes widening with anticipation. "How extraordinary. Your message said . . ."

"Champagne, please," Martin said with a nod to the eager waiter who had done a ligament-stripping pivot in the middle of the room when he'd heard Jack's signal for service. Martin turned to Jack and lowered his voice. "Now then," he said, "your lady will be the dark one. The blonde is just *une amie de la maison*. Madame Cleo thought it would be pleasant if the four of us had dinner. Might make the new girl more comfortable."

"Delighted, I'm sure," Jack said, not feeling quite that delighted. He much preferred being the center of attention and found foursomes somewhat limiting. "Tell me about the new girl." He shifted his weight and leaned closer to Martin, giving him his full attention.

"She's quite extraordinary. Let me put it this way: this afternoon I had the advantage of viewing the entire package, don't cha know."

Jack beamed across at Martin. "Is she French? Not that it makes one whit of difference," he said.

"No. As a matter of fact, she's American. Extremely elegant. Dark hair. Excellent background. Lovely, truly. You won't be disappointed."

The waiter placed a glass of champagne in front of Martin along with a plate of canapés.

Jack raised his drink. "To you, Martin, my good man," he said effusively.

If Jack's glass hadn't hit the edge of the plate of canapés when he dropped it, the mess wouldn't have been quite so bad, nor would Martin's pale trousers have been so extensively splashed. As it was, the impact fanned liquor and ice cubes in an exaggerated arc studded with flying anchovies, truffle-studded pâté timbales, and smoked salmon on buttered-toast fingers.

For a heartbeat all was silent. Then there seemed to be far too many people around the little table as two waiters and the bartender leaped from their stations to help. Someone hissed, *"Merde!"*

What made Jack drop his drink was the sight of two fashionably dressed, slender young women poised in the doorway of the bar. He had seen Sandrine first, but it was the sight of SueBee that caused his drinking hand to go limp.

The girls stared across the bar at the frantic scene. One of the waiters was pouring club soda onto a clean bar cloth to attend to the damage to Martin's trousers. The bartender was working on Jack's stained tie.

For a frozen, surreal moment, Jack, Sandrine, and SueBee stared at each other in disbelief. It was SueBee who made the first, almost imperceptible move. She was standing a few paces in back of Sandrine, her eyes riveted on Jack's. Slowly, she shook her head and mouthed the words, "Don't . . . say . . . anything."

Completely flustered, Jack looked down to see that the bartender's efforts were only expanding the dark stain on his gray silk tie. The waiter working on Martin's trousers was having even less success.

Impatiently, Jack pushed the bartender's hand away and turned to Martin. "Come on, let's go up to my suite," he said. "The hall valet can take care of this more efficiently." He grabbed Martin's arm and propelled him toward the door.

"Excuse me, ladies. We'll be right back," Martin called over his shoulder. "Order something. Terribly sorry."

Sandrine and SueBee watched the men leave in stunned silence. The distraught waiters hovered a few feet away, unsure of what to do. Finally, the one who had been working on Martin's pants gestured toward the banquette. "Please, may I bring you a drink? I'm sure Mr. Ayler will only be a few moments."

By then, SueBee had regained her composure. "Yes, thank you," she said, turning to Sandrine. "Champagne?"

Sandrine nodded mutely and sat down hard on the banquette. She reached for SueBee's hand and pulled her down beside her. "This is awful, SueBee," she whispered.

SueBee stared into space. "What should we do?"

"Do you want to leave?"

"No," SueBee said firmly. "Do you?"

"I don't know what to do," Sandrine said, shaking her head. "I loathe the man. How am I supposed to have sex with Ayler after what he did to you? He makes my flesh crawl."

SueBee turned and stared at her friend. "He's not *that* bad," she said defensively.

They both looked up as the waiter served their drinks, then waited until he was out of earshot before speaking.

"SueBee, I'm sorry," Sandrine apologized. "I didn't mean it that way. It's just . . . oh, I don't know. I just don't want to do it."

SueBee's mouth opened slightly. She shut it quickly and made a face.

"What's the matter?"

SueBee sat silently for a moment, thinking. "You have to do it, Sandy," she finally said.

"Why do I *have* to?" Sandrine asked, taking a sip of her champagne, then swallowing hard. "If I explained the situation to Madame Cleo, I'm sure she'd—"

"Now look," SueBee interrupted, her voice stern and sharp. "All I heard from you before we left New York was what a swell opportunity working for Madame Cleo was going to be. How this was the perfect way to make a ton of money, move in the highest circles, and meet the richest men. Now the first one you meet you're ready to turn down."

"But SueBee," Sandrine protested. "Never in my wildest dreams did I think Jack Ayler would be one of the men," she said with a shudder of revulsion.

"Don't do like that, Sandy," SueBee said, angered at Sandrine's gesture. "Jack is lovely in bed. Trust me. I don't love him anymore, anyway. That's over. I know I just fell off the last turnip truck from Abilene, but I didn't fall on my head, and good sense tells me you signed away your flesh-crawling rights when you took this job. If you were a surgeon and they brought in your worst enemy, would you go all fancy and say you weren't up to the job?"

Sandrine stared, speechless, at SueBee. She blinked once, then again, as though absorbing what, for SueBee, had been a very long lecture. Then she started to laugh. "Well, I have to admit that's an interesting way to look at it."

"It's the only way to look at it," SueBee said with finality.

"SueBee girl, you are truly too much."

"Thank you," SueBee said, with a little bob of the head. "I think."

"And it truly doesn't make any difference for you. I mean about Jack?"

"Not a spit of difference, Sandrine, so don't go using that as an excuse."

Sandrine threw up her hands. "You're right, you're right. I know you're right. Still, it's going to be hard to act like I like it."

"No, it isn't. Just remind yourself why you went into this business in the first place."

"What do you mean?" Sandrine asked, puzzled.

SueBee positioned herself closer to the edge of the banquette and folded her arms on the table. "There was this shrink on Oprah once who said that no one really does anything they don't want to do."

"SueBee," Sandrine groaned. "Couldn't you have at least watched Donahue?"

"I did, but this particular shrink was on Oprah. Now just think about it. When you have sex it has to do something for you or you wouldn't do it, let alone make it a career. You are doing, for whatever reason, what you want to do." SueBee leaned back, warming to her subject. "How do you feel when you have sex for money? Do you feel like you're doing something you don't want to do?"

"Not really," Sandrine said after some consideration. "Actually, I feel good. It makes me feel, oh, I don't know, powerful. In control. It makes me feel like I do when I'm dancing, out on the floor, the lights on me, everyone thinking how beautiful I look, wanting me. It's exciting. I'm turned on because I'm turning them on. It's like a performance."

"Do you think about the guy at all, I mean, when you're doing it?"

"Truthfully? No," Sandrine said. "All I care about is what he's thinking about me. Like he was someone watching me dance."

"Great!" SueBee cried, clapping her hands. "That's all you need to focus on. It's a form of narcissism. You're loving yourself, and how bad can that be?"

"Narcissism!" Sandrine said with a whoop. "My God, Sister woman. I'm not even going to ask where you learned *that* word."

"Wait a sec," SueBee said, reaching into her quilted Chanel bag and grinning slyly. "I didn't learn everything I know on Oprah." She burrowed around for a moment and extracted a roll of wintergreen Life Savers. She handed them to Sandrine. "Here, take these."

Sandrine stared down at the roll of mints. "Life Savers and champagne?" she said, wrinkling her nose.

"They're for later. Put one on your tongue for a few minutes, then take it out just before you go down on him. It'll drive him wild."

Sandrine's jaw dropped. "Why, SueBee Slyde, you naughty girl! Here I've been doing this for years. How come I don't know that trick? Better still, how come you do?"

"Zaki taught me," SueBee said, lowering her eyes.

For an evening that began as a virtually assured disaster, Jack couldn't believe it had turned out so well. When the two men (Martin's trousers adequately repaired by a hair dryer) arrived back in the bar, they found the girls already giddy on champagne.

Jack was mildly surprised when SueBee and Martin left after a third round of drinks, but by that time he was so enamored of Sandrine he was glad to have her to himself. She was nothing like the society brat he had met in SueBee's New York apartment. Quite the contrary, he found her utterly charming. It wasn't just the contrast between a girl with no makeup in a terry-cloth bathrobe and a stunning woman in a Chanel suit. There was something about her, her poise, a delicacy of hand movement, and the way she looked at him when she listened to him. She was truly interested in what he had to say all evening long. Her attention intoxicated him as much as the scotch, the excellent Bordeaux with their meal, and the brandy later. He talked too much but he couldn't stop. Sandrine hung on every word.

The looks of approval he received from the maître d' and waiters at dinner and the smiles of appreciation from the members of the private club at the Ritz where they went for a nightcap after dinner confirmed his opinion of her. Even the doorman and elevator operator smiled knowingly when they returned to the Meurice arm in arm.

As they rode to his suite holding hands the glowing report he would give Madame Cleo in the morning began to form in his besotted mind.

At some point during the evening he had asked about SueBee as nonchalantly as possible, only to have Sandrine sweetly refuse to discuss her friend. He liked that. He would include that in his report as well. The girl was not only beautiful but loyal and discreet.

It wasn't until he felt the transcendent tingle at the tip of his penis as he lay on the king-size bed that he thought, for a brief instant, of SueBee again.

Sandrine nearly made it into bed without waking SueBee, but as soon as she punched her pillow she heard her stirring in the other bed.

"Sandrine?" SueBee said in a perky, wide-awake voice. "Hey, sugar."

"Ummm," Sandrine mumbled, gripping the covers.

"Please don't go to sleep. We gotta talk."

Sandrine had been expecting this. Poor SueBee, she thought, with a guilty twinge. She'd probably been back in the room for hours, bored out of her mind and lonely, but she was exhausted. "Later, Sooz," she groaned. "I'm beat."

"Sandy, I really have to talk to you, right now. I've been thinking about it for hours."

Sandrine gave up and turned on the bedside lamp. "Okay," she moaned, squinting across to the other bed in the brightness of the lamp. "Real short sentences, all right?"

SueBee swung her bare legs over the side of the bed and hooked her heels onto the ledge below the mattress. She wrapped her arms around her knees. A strap of her thin blue nightie slipped down one arm.

Sandrine propped herself up on one elbow and smiled across at her friend. SueBee's sweet round face was scrubbed clean of makeup and her tangled blond hair was a mass of fat Shirley Temple curls. There was a glint of excitement in her eyes that Sandrine had never seen there before.

"How did it go?" SueBee asked.

"Huh?" Sandrine said, being deliberately vague.

"You know."

"Actually, it was okay," Sandrine said, knowing the subject couldn't be avoided. "We went to a spectacular restaurant. I think I saw Alain Delon at a back table. Jack was really very pleasant and—"

"Come on, come on," SueBee said, cutting her off. "How was the sex part?"

"Well," Sandrine said, "having sex with him was a breeze. It's the hours of listening that's hard work with guys, pretending they hang the moon, that every damn breath they take is fabulous and interesting and unique. Like, this restaurant we were in, La Seine or something, if you ever go there you can wow your date with the fact that there are exactly four hundred and forty-three little blue tiles around the street-side ceiling of the dining room."

"How would you know that?" SueBee said, laughing.

"Because I counted every fucking one of them over his shoulder while he told me in so many words how cool, how smart, how sharp he was. He was wearing a Countess Mara tie! God help him, Countess Mara! It has little swirls that you can make go counterclockwise if you lower your eyes and stare at them long enough."

"You were bored," SueBee stated flatly.

"You got it."

"But it was okay. Not yuck-making?"

Sandrine smiled. "Flesh-crawling rights, yuck-making rights. Those are all gone, like you said. It was no different than back in New York, only the pay is much better. I'm sorry you waited up all night to hear such tiresome news."

SueBee lay back and got under the sheet. "But that's just what I wanted to hear," she said. "Because, I've been thinking. Could you . . . would you . . . do something for me?"

"Sure. What?"

"Now don't laugh, I'm serious."

"Okay."

"Would you tell Madame Cleo something for me?"

Sandrine frowned. "Madame Cleo? Yeah, I guess," she said, wondering what in the world SueBee had dreamed up all alone in a Paris hotel room with nothing else to think about. "What do you want me to tell her?"

"I'd like to come and work for her," SueBee said, smiling.

Sandrine jerked herself upright in the bed. "You what?" she shouted.

"I want to be a Cleo girl."

"Hold on. Hold on," Sandrine said, shaking her head. "I don't believe this."

SueBee turned her head on the pillow and faced Sandrine. "You don't have to act so shocked. If you can do it, why can't I?"

"Oh, Jesus," Sandrine said with a heavy sigh. "Not you, Sooz. You deserve a different kind of life."

"Different?" SueBee said angrily. "Like what? Vanna White already has the only job I could do standing up. I've got to earn a fucking living, too, you know."

"SueBee, don't swear."

"Why the hell not?"

"Because . . . because . . ." Sandrine searched for a reason, not really sure why the idea of SueBee as a working girl offended her so. "Swearing isn't ladylike. Neither is hooking, that's why."

SueBee jumped to her feet and stormed to the foot of Sandrine's bed. "How'd you get so fancy, Miss Park Avenue?" she screamed, red-faced. "You don't own me. You've been a great friend and I love you but don't pull that 'lady' stuff on me. Just because that's what was expected of you doesn't mean anybody ever expected anything from me. Nobody ever told me I had to do anything but make a living. You're going to keep doing this till you meet somebody rich who'll take care of you. Who's going to take care of me? What's gonna happen to me when I get back to New York? I got no job. I got no money and no apartment."

"SueBee, your language is atrocious. Now just calm down and speak properly. If you have any ideas about working for Madame Cleo, you have to know that her girls are supposed to be . . . well, you know."

"Well, what?" SueBee snapped. "Say it. Go on. Say it."

Sandrine paused. She didn't want to answer. Anything she said would only hurt SueBee's feelings.

"Classy. Right?" SueBee continued. "High style. Smooth as a baby's butt. Like you. Right? You don't have the nerve to say I'm too common."

"SueBee, don't . . ."

SueBee held up her hand. "Look, I know what I am. I'm a hick, a redneck. Up until I met you I couldn't even read. I don't even know how to eat out right. I couldn't get meat out of a lobster with a machine gun and, heaven help me, I still don't know whether the entrée is the stuff that comes first or the big meal later, but Sandy"—she broke off and knelt at the foot of Sandrine's bed—"I sure know how to please a man. I know how to listen, I know how to laugh at unfunny jokes, and I sure as hell know how to fuck."

Sandrine drew a deep breath. "It's not just about . . . *that*, SueBee. I'm not saying you *couldn't* work for Madame Cleo. I'm saying you wouldn't be happy doing it."

"Wrong!" SueBee shot back. "You wouldn't be happy with my doing it. You're jealous. Besides, what's not to like? Good restaurants, lovely trips, beautiful clothes. Men who take you to fine hotels and do you on clean sheets. Madame Cleo doesn't service men who screw you standing up in hallways or beat you up. It was you who told me they're gentlemen who practically fall in love with you just because you're a Cleo girl."

"SueBee, don't shout. You'll wake up the whole hotel," Sandrine said, trying to calm her down.

"Well, I'm sorry," SueBee shouted even louder. "It's easy for you to make rules for me. You had footmen behind your chair and a nanny to lay out your clothes. The first time you had sex I bet it was your choice, too. Not me, boy. I had the town mouth-breather break into my room and try to stick his thing in my mouth."

Sandrine was now sitting on the edge of the bed reassessing her gentle friend. The friend who could sit patiently for hours waiting for an aging sheikh to shit. The friend who had never uttered an unkind word about anybody in all the time she'd known her. Sandrine smiled across at SueBee, seeing her in an entirely new light. She had grossly underestimated her. "You really want to work for Madame Cleo, SueBee?" she asked.

"More than anything," SueBee said sincerely. "Martin told me at dinner that she likes each girl to have a specialty. I haven't figured out what yours is other than the fact that you have a body that makes cars run up over the curb and you speak all fruity-tootie and right, but I sure know what mine is."

Sandrine was wide awake now and intrigued. As far as she was concerned, SueBee's specialty was being the sweetest, most genuine girl alive. Not something anyone other than Loni Anderson or Mary Tyler Moore made a living at.

"What's your specialty, SueBee?" Sandrine asked.

"I know how to give an enema," SueBee said in dead earnest.

Sandrine collapsed, shrieking with laughter, into the pillows.

"I'm serious, Sandrine," SueBee said, undeterred. "I know how to give CPR and intravenous injections. I can pop boils and set broken legs and, let me tell you, if someone has a bad heart, I can see cardiac arrest coming five minutes before it hits. You don't have to be a lady to save somebody with mouth-to-mouth."

Sandrine listened, fascinated by SueBee's determination. She was certainly making her case.

"And you know what else Martin told me? He said Madame Cleo has some kind of school somewhere in England where they train girls she likes who need a little, you know, extra." SueBee looked away, embarrassed.

"SueBee, I don't know what to say."

"Say yes," SueBee said eagerly. "Say you'll ask Madame Cleo if she can use me. Tell her there must be some rich quadraplegic somewhere who needs a little tenderness."

"Or a wintergreen blowjob?"

"Yeah," SueBee said with a wide grin. "*Lifesaving* blow job. You can't tell me a guy in traction somewhere wouldn't pay big money for one of them there lifesaving blowjobs."

Sandrine threw her head back against the headboard and howled. "Oh, SueBee," she said, shaking her head. "Who knew you were so ambitious?"

"It's not ambition to know what you want, Sandy," SueBee said, her smile fading. "I always felt that life wasn't supposed to be dull and flat. It was supposed to be exciting and full of surprises. But I can see you have to position yourself to be surprised. You have to take a risk."

"And that's the way you feel about working for Madame Cleo," Sandrine said.

"Exactly. She's my ticket to something better. The something better I knew was out there when I jumped on that helicopter. I wasn't running away from something. I was running toward it."

"But, honey. When you got on the helicopter you pretty much knew that you'd only have to deal with one man. This would mean a lot of men."

"A lot of men means a lot of opportunities. Look," SueBee said, pushing Sandrine's knees aside to make room for her to sit closer. "My daddy was a big cardplayer. He always used to tell me you can't be in the game unless you're at the table, and you gotta be in the game to win. I just want a seat at the table. Just deal me a hand and let me figure out a way to play it."

Sandrine thought for a moment. "And what will you say someday when you fall in love and he finds out you were a hooker?"

"The same thing they say on Oprah when they bring on a sex slave or a former hooker," SueBee answered, pressing an index finger into each cheek and bobbing her head. " 'I was young and I needed the money.' It works every time."

Why not? Sandrine thought, smiling. SueBee might not be the most polished individual around, but she was awfully cute and could take care of herself. If she didn't go falling in love she'd be all right. "Okay, Sooz," Sandrine said. "Okay. I'll talk to her today. I have to go over for my long 'biographical' interview this afternoon. I'll speak to her then."

SueBee squealed, then clapped her hands and jumped off the bed. "Oh, hot damn," she said. "I'll never be able to thank you for this, Sandy."

"One thing, SueBee."

"What?"

"You realize who sometimes checks out the new girls for Madame Cleo?" Sandrine said, with a slightly twisted grin.

SueBee thought for a moment. When the realization hit she collapsed onto her bed and rolled over. "Good!" she squealed with glee. "Maybe Jack Ayler can be my first heart attack."

Sandrine awoke and checked the clock. She had been asleep for only three hours and yet she felt wide awake. She attributed it to a combination of jet lag, the excitement of being in Paris, and her first night of working for the infamous Madame Cleo.

She looked over at SueBee, still fast asleep. She looked like a little girl with gold curls falling over her closed eyes. If Sandrine had had any misgivings about SueBee coming into the life, they had disappeared with the dawn. Now she was enthusiastic about it and couldn't wait for the afternoon to talk to Madame about setting up an interview.

She padded to the bathroom to phone Martin and ask if she could come over. When she told him about SueBee, he sounded overjoyed but not surprised.

It was past noon when she slipped out of the hotel. A fawning doorman leaped to the curb upon seeing her push through the revolving door and whistled loudly for a cab that was two feet away.

She rang the doorbell of the mansion and waited. Soon she could make out Martin coming toward her through the oval-etched glass in the front door. The Indian maid who had let her in on her last visit was nowhere in sight.

Martin reached for the knob and unceremoniously yanked it open. "Hello, darling," he said breathlessly, having run down the staircase from the upper floor. "Come in. You got here sooner than I expected."

"Did I? Sorry," Sandrine said hesitantly as she stepped inside shaking her thick hair loose from the bright silk scarf she had tied on against the damp winter air. "Did you get a chance to ask Madame about my friend?"

"I certainly did," he said, closing the door. "She said to have her come around this afternoon. For now, we have a surprise visitor who is also a friend of yours. Madame's with her now."

"A friend of mine? Here in Paris? I don't know anyone here."

"She just flew in, courtesy of our pal Barry Rizzo."

Sandrine stared at him wondering who in the world it could be.

"It's Angel," Martin whispered, closing the door and turning back toward the stairs.

"Angel?" Sandrine whispered.

"None other," he said, climbing back up the stairs, two at a time. "Come on up. You can wait in my alcove. They should be finished soon."

Sandrine followed him up the stairs. She knew Cleo had bought Angel's book, but she was surprised by the coincidence of actually running into her at the mansion.

Martin stepped onto the second-floor landing and spoke over his shoulder. "I don't think Madame likes her," he whispered conspiratorially.

That really surprised Sandrine. "Why? Angel is a knockout, and she certainly knows the business."

Martin settled back behind his desk and glanced nervously at the closed door. "Please, sit," he said, gesturing toward the bergère chair in front of his little desk. "Perhaps I'm speaking out of school. It's not that she doesn't *like* her exactly. I mean she didn't *say* anything directly when Angel arrived. But I could tell. I've worked for her for a long time now. All I have to do is look at her expression. It may have been the silver fox chubby," he said with a shrug. "Or it could have been her reference to the—and please excuse the language—'fucking frog cab driver.'"

Sandrine moaned and covered her eyes. "Oh God. That's Angel, all right."

"Well," Martin said, tossing a runaway strand of yellow hair out of his eyes. "If Madame takes her on, she'll have to go to our training school, Wellington Close. That's for sure."

Sandrine didn't comment. She still found Martin a bit grand. But obviously SueBee was right; she'd be going to this Wellington Close, too.

Martin ruffled through the papers on his desk for a moment. "How did your evening with Jack Ayler go?" he asked nonchalantly.

Sandrine had just opened her mouth to answer when the door behind her flew open and Angel stormed into the alcove. She was wearing a waist-length very fat silver fox jacket, a too-tight, too-short black jersey skirt, and five-inch heels. Her dark red hair was piled haphazardly on top of her head. The heels made her almost grotesquely tall. "Call me a fucking cab," she barked at Martin, her back to Sandrine.

Martin didn't move. "There isn't a cab in Paris that fucks, darling, but I'll get you one that moves a little."

"Hello, Angel," Sandrine said quietly from her chair.

Angel spun around. When she recognized Sandrine her eyes widened like a horse seeing fire in its stall. "Holy shit! Sandrine," she squealed. "God, am I glad to see you."

Sandrine glanced toward the door Angel had just burst through. It was being quietly closed by an unseen hand. "Is everything okay? I mean . . ." She gestured toward the other room.

"No, everything is definitely not okay," Angel said, casting a savage look at Martin. "I'm being royally fucked over." She stepped closer to the edge of Martin's desk and addressed the top of his head. "Doesn't she know who I am, for Christ's sake? I ran an operation bigger than this in New York, and she thinks she can talk to me like I had a mattress on my back waiting for curb service."

Before Martin could respond the intercom jumped to life. "Martin, would you step in, please," Madame's disembodied voice said in French.

"What'd she say?" Angel asked, narrowing her eyes at Sandrine.

"She wants him to come in."

"Oh, really," Angel said, affecting a broad English accent.

Martin stood and pulled the papers on his desk into a ragged pile. He turned to Sandrine. "Darling, why don't you show Angel downstairs for me and help her find a cab. Nanti's at the market. I don't know how long this will take. Perhaps you could come back in an hour or so for your chat with Madame. All right, darling? Excuse me, ladies." He straightened his tie and hurried into Madame Cleo's office.

"Come on," Angel said sharply as she headed toward the stairs. "Let's go for a walk."

"But I thought you wanted a cab," Sandrine said, following her.

"I saw a stand over by the bridge on the way over," she called from halfway down the stairs. "I don't need that twit. He's the one that got me into this in the first place."

The two women walked along the quayside for a few moments. The only sounds were the click of Angel's high heels and the cry of an occasional gull swooping over the river.

Angel stared at the ground, her hands jammed into the pockets of her fur jacket. "Fuck 'em all," she finally said. It was more of a defeated murmur than an angry oath.

"What happened, Angel?" Sandrine asked gently.

"Oh, nothing. My fucking world collapsed, that's all."

"In there? With Madame?"

"No, back home. That's the only reason I'm here. Sandy, I'm scared."

"You mean because of the raid?"

Angel nodded, took a deep breath, and began to tell Sandrine why she had made the decision to come to Paris and reluctantly go back into the life.

Barry Rizzo had been able to get the D.A. to drop the charges against her if she promised to stay out of business and paid an assortment of fines and back taxes. Coming up with the money all but wiped her out. A week after the arrest, she got word from the nursing home that her mother needed an operation, the cost of which forced her to go to Barry for a loan, the final humiliation. She spent a week in a motel in New Jersey to be near her mother during the operation, but her mother's heart was too weak and she died a day after the surgery. When Angel returned to her apartment she found all of her belongings stacked on the pavement, being watched over by a haughty doorman who informed her that the landlord "didn't want nobody selling whores in the building" and had obtained a court order to evict her.

"There on the sidewalk was everything I owned," Angel said. "Even my Countess de Marco coat-of-arms wall decoration. It was leaning up against an old Vuitton trunk I found in a thrift shop. All my clothes, my shoes, underwear, everything was piled in a soggy heap because it had rained. No one gave a shit if it all got ruined, which my couch and mattress did. A lot of stuff was missing. I figured whoever moved it down helped themselves. There was only one phone from the fancy phone system I put in six months ago. It wasn't even paid for."

"Oh Angel," Sandrine said, "how awful. All of it. Your mother, then your apartment. You poor dear."

"Yeah, well. My mother had been a vegetable for the last five years. She wasn't the mother I remembered. Even when I was a kid we weren't—like friends. She was my mother and I was her bad-girl daughter. But I did love her. It hurt, but to be honest with you, Sandy, seeing my stuff lying there wet and spotted with dog droppings was worse. George Carlin once said, 'Happiness is a place to put your stuff.' He was right. When someone touches your *stuff*, it makes you crazy."

They were passing an iron bench that faced the river. The sun had come out and the cold mist had dissipated. "Shall we sit for a minute?" Sandrine asked.

They both sat down and crossed their legs. Angel opened the front of her fur jacket. She was wearing a gold lamé blouse underneath.

"So what did you do?" Sandrine asked.

"Like I said, went crazy. I started to scream bloody murder and hammer on the doorman's chest because he was the only one around to blame. Then I ran to the phone and called Barry. He came and got me and took me and what was left of my stuff over to his place. I stayed there for a while. All the time I was there he worked on me to work for Madame Cleo. I'd already spent the money she paid me for my book and I was flat broke. Finally, I agreed. One of the things that convinced me to do it was having to blow Barry three times a day. Then, when Barry told me you were coming over and I figured if it's good enough for a class act like you, Sandy, how bad could it be? Maybe I'll make some really good contacts and I can start my own business again on a really big scale. It kills me that that old crone has everything I ever wanted."

"Is that why you were so angry back there at the house?"

Angel squinted out over the river. A long glass sight-seeing barge was gliding by. Faceless tourists waved at them from the deck. Sandrine waved back.

"What I was angry about is that the bitch says I can work for her if I go to some school. I mean, give me a fucking break. It's insulting. She doesn't like the way I talk. She doesn't like the way I dress. Who the hell does she think she is?"

Sandrine tried to keep her voice nonjudgmental. "Well, your outfit is probably a little too . . . American . . . for her. What you have to understand about this operation is how demanding she is about the way we look and sound. Gold lamé and a liberal use of the word 'fuck' is not Madame Cleo style. Unless, I suppose, you're with a man who likes to hear it."

"What are you talking about, Sandy? I hardly ever say fuck."

Sandrine didn't want to argue. "Did she make you take your clothes off?" Sandrine asked, smiling.

"Yeah, yeah, yeah," Angel said impatiently. "I never asked a girl to take off her clothes, never. I think that's a dyke number, don't you?"

"Not really. It seemed like good business to me. I mean, our bodies are the merchandise."

Angel shrugged. "Well, my merchandise is what turned her around," she said with a satisfied smile. "She wasn't cutting me any slack until she saw the bazongas. She looked like she could see dollar signs on both nipples."

"Angel, you are outrageous," Sandrine said, laughing. "So are you going to do it?"

"Would you?"

"I already have. I did my first job last night."

"No, I mean about the school."

Sandrine thought for a moment, "Well, yeah, sure. Why not?" she asked cheerfully.

"How much did you make last night?"

"Five thousand," Sandrine said, looking away.

"Francs or dollars?"

"Dollars. Thirty-five hundred is mine."

Angel emitted a long low whistle as she slowly shook her head. "Holy shit . . . I mean, goodness gracious, for pity's sake, hug-a-bunny."

"That's better," Sandrine said.

"When is your next job?"

"Well, this morning when I phoned Martin he asked if I could leave for Rome this evening. Private plane, some film award dinner, an hour or so at the Ritz, then back to Paris."

"Who's the john?"

"The *client* is the American producer who is getting the award."

Angel sat silently staring out over the river, a slight smile lingering at the corners of her mouth.

Finally, Sandrine stood up and clasped Angel's wrist. "Come on, hon. I've got an hour or so. Let's go buy you some clothes. My treat."

"Oh, Sandrine, I couldn't do that."

"Yes, you can," Sandrine said, pushing up off the bench and offering Angel her hand. "And every time you say fuck I'm going to pinch you very hard. If you aren't black and blue within the hour I'll take back everything I said."

CHAPTER
∾ 11 ∾

Peter's Journal Entry—Paris, July 6, 1990

I celebrated the glorious Fourth by myself. I spent the day walking and thinking about the spin this Angel woman puts on the whole story. She sounds like an ambitious little whiner. She's got a mob lawyer (I've known Rizzo by reputation for years, ever since he defended Vinnie "the Thumb" Mancuso), and God only knows what entangling alliances his clients may have had with Madame. I couldn't get either of them out of my mind.

I had lunch at a café I had never been to before. Strolled the Seine like a tourist, stopping at the pet shops and bouquinistes to browse. It's like I've never seen this city. Then I realized that when I was here for WorldWide, I only saw it from the back seat of a hired car or through the bottom of a glass of scotch.

I found a fax machine in an electronics store on the Boul Mich, brought it home, plugged it in, and faxed Fiddle and Wendy the number. I went out to see the new Louis Malle film. When I got back and opened the door there was a frantic fax from Fiddle on my living/work-room floor. It reads "Peter, dear: Wendy is half crazed. She just got your last package of transcription notes and she's hysterical that Madame still isn't talking about herself. She says all the stuff you're sending about the girls is fine but you should get rid of your preoccupation with who wants Madame dead and start earning the big bucks SHE got you to write Madame's story. Keep the faith, Fiddle."

That really pissed me off.

I then sent a fax to Wendy explaining that I've just about had it with Madame myself and suggesting that because she represents Madame as well as me, it might be a good idea for her to put some pressure on HER client. Her response was too angry for her to fax—you can't shriek on a fax machine—so she called me.

Suffice it to say she thinks I should mind my own business. We hissed and scratched for a bit longer, then she slammed down the phone. Great, now she's pissed at me, I'm pissed at her, and nothing is getting done.

Before I left Madame Cleo today, she announced that the subject of our next session will be her unique finishing school in England. I hope this means she's ready to start talking more about herself.

When Martin's mother, Lady Jellica Bourke-Lyon, executed her last will and testament, there was no question that her eldest son, Martin, would be left with nothing more than a small trust fund. He had proved to his mother with his profligate ways, his drug use during the late sixties, his attachment to an Indian guru and a failed rock band in the seventies, and, at the time of his mother's death in the eighties, his mystifying relationship with an infamous French procuress that he was deserving of neither funds nor property. Lady Bourke-Lyon left her money to the African Violet Society of Great Britain. Wellington Close, the lovely seventeenth-century brick manor surrounded by sixty-five acres of parkland, was passed down to Cyril, Martin's younger brother.

After a year of trying to heat the enormous old house and keep the grounds in some sort of repair, Cyril pleaded with his brother for financial help. Martin went Cyril one better. He offered cash. Madame Cleo's cash.

Martin and Cleo then set about turning the estate into a unique finishing school.

A faculty was hired to offer courses of Madame Cleo's choosing in a variety of subjects. The student body consisted of girls who, while they physically met her high standards, still needed certain refinements to qualify them as proper companions to her demanding clientele.

The stables were refurbished not only for equestrian instruction but for lectures on the intricacies of the buying, selling, and breeding of racing stock and seminars on betting. A casino was installed in what had once been the greenhouse. Many a top croupier and chemin de fer and blackjack dealer vacationed at Wellington Close in return for instructing the girls. A small forest near the house had been leveled and replaced by an auto raceway where the girls were taught how to drive expensive sports cars and use evasive tactics just in case they found themselves with a political figure in threatening circumstances.

The atmosphere and routine at Wellington Close reflected a life-style of understated elegance. Everyone—students, staff, and instructors—was expected to dress for the dinner that was served in the paneled dining hall. After dinner, groups would separate for lectures on fine art, music, ballet, and opera, choosing fine wines, cigars, and menswear from Savile Row tailors. There was instruction in the rules of such spectator sports as football, baseball, and soccer, as well as in the games of bridge, backgammon, cribbage, and Madame Cleo's mandatory course on chess.

The girls were taught the use of firearms, both defensive and sport. It was assumed that each girl who attended Wellington Close already knew about proper makeup and clothes, but a course on the Paris couture houses was offered.

Many of the girls had never danced anywhere other than in a discotheque and didn't know how to touch a partner. On Saturday nights male professors served as partners for classes in the samba, the mambo, and the waltz, all dances a Madame Cleo client was likely to know.

The west wing of the manor house was divided into small class-rooms devoted to the daylight hours. There the girls were given a working knowledge of art, history, geopolitics, and world economics.

They were expected to have a basic understanding of the law, as multilitigation was often a depressing factor in her clients' lives. Often a client hired a Cleo girl to simply listen to him complain about his lawsuits.

In the arts, the girls were expected to be able to recognize a Rubens or Degas on a client's office or library wall, whether the gold leaf on a bedroom ceiling was real or paint, and if the sheets they were slipping into were from a department store or Porthault.

Each student was required to read the London and New York *Times* every morning and at least glance at the *Financial Times* if possible before joining in the general discussion of current world affairs over breakfast led by John Robert Conroy, a retired professor of political science at Oxford University. Professor Conroy was a permanent member of the staff at Wellington Close as well as the resident wine expert.

At 9 A.M. sharp, classes began and continued until five, except for a lunch break, during which the girls were lectured on various national cuisines. From five to seven they were free to study and dress for dinner and the activities of the evening.

It was a long and grueling day. Some girls, unaccustomed to a life of discipline, were unhappy, and they were free to leave. Others, like SueBee Slyde, thrived.

"Angel! Come quick! Look!" SueBee cried to her roommate. She was kneeling on the window seat under the leaded-glass bay window in the room they were sharing at Wellington Close.

"What for?" Angel growled from one of the twin beds.

"It's snowing!"

"Go figure," Angel replied dully, plumping the pillows supporting her back. She was propped on her bed watching one of the instructional cassettes assigned to each "student" in a class. This one was called "VIP ID."

"I've never seen anything so beautiful," SueBee said. "I can see all the way to the lake. It looks like a picture in a book of fairy tales."

"SueBee, please. We have to be downstairs in an hour and I gotta get through this stupid film."

"Sorry," SueBee said, stepping down from her perch and returning to her work desk.

Angel and SueBee had arrived at Wellington Close just a day after SueBee's successful interview with Madame Cleo. As they were the only two American girls there at the time, it had been Martin's decision to have them be roommates. Living together took some adjustment on both their parts, but now, after a month, they had gotten used to their differences.

Angel had watched SueBee take to the environment with a remarkable cheerfulness. Sandrine had told her about SueBee's reading problems, and yet SueBee became a voracious reader, forever writing in her daily journal in a tense, concentrated longhand. She recopied most of her journal entries into long letters to Sandrine, to which she signed both her own and Angel's names. Sandrine answered SueBee's letters by phone once or twice a week, each time from some other exotic city as she moved around Europe on her assignments for Madame Cleo.

The happier SueBee became with her stay at Wellington Close, the more depressed and bored Angel felt. To her, being there was like serving a prison term.

SueBee adjusted the gooseneck lamp on her desk. "Do you want me to quiz you on that cassette?" she offered without looking up.

Angel pressed the button of the remote control that lowered the sound. Lee Iaccoca's unsmiling mouth moved soundlessly on the screen. "This is such bullshit," she snapped. "Anyone who watches the evening news knows who these men are. It's like everything else we do here, childish crap. I can't wait to get out of here."

SueBee put down the pink highlighter she used to mark words she didn't understand in anything she was reading. Her current project was understanding Mortimer J. Adler's *Aristotle for Everybody—Difficult Thought Made Easy*. "Angel, you know you can leave anytime you want to. Nobody's making you stay."

"Sure. Then what would I do?" Angel asked, swinging her legs over the side of the bed and pulling on a pair of heavy socks. "God, it's freezing in here."

She walked to the window and looked out at the snow. She had to admit it was pretty outside. Lonely looking but pretty. "I wish I were looking at Central Park," she said wistfully.

"Come on, Angel," SueBee said cheerfully. "Think of all the fabulous places we're going to see, all the parties and balls. Just look at the life Sandrine is living."

"Get real. We'll be doing the great ceiling tour of the world screwing rich old men."

"That's okay," SueBee said with a sweet smile. "I like old men."

Angel flopped back onto the bed. She was wearing the long granny gown she always wore in the room that was never warm enough. "You know what, SueBee?" she said, leaning on one elbow. "When Madame said I had to come here I was insulted. That's when I thought this was a real school. Now I feel even worse because it's nothing but a rat-fuck. One big bullshit power trip for Madame Cleo and that fagola flunky, Martin."

"Whoa!" SueBee said with a smile. "And they sent you here to class up your language? If you had said that downstairs it would have cost you ten dollars for the F word and three for the B word. I think it's a dollar for calling someone a 'fagola.' I can't remember."

"That's exactly the kind of thing I mean. Paying money for using slang. Tea dances, cigar sniffing, little string orchestras while we identify wines. Don't they know it's nineteen eighty-six, not thirty-six?"

"What did you expect, Angel?"

Angel rolled over and stared at the ceiling. "I thought somehow I would get some insight about how the old broad built such a successful operation. Something I could use later, when I start up again."

"It's right in front of you," SueBee said matter-of-factly.

Angel turned to look across at SueBee. "Huh?" she said.

"The two of us. That's how she does it. Couldn't be simpler. She's spent a lifetime recognizing girls like us who have potential. Girls like you who want the money and the power guaranteed in this kind of work and girls like me who want the adventure. She recruits us, buffs off the rough spots, and raises her price because she provides the best product. Forgive me, but if you'd spend more time observing instead of complaining, you'd learn a lot."

Angel sat up. "Well, excuse me," she huffed. She stood and padded across the room. She opened the small refrigerator, found a diet soda, and popped open the tab.

"You know, SueBee," Angel said, taking a swig of soda, "when I was running my own call service, I'll bet I never had a john who gave a rat's ass whether any of my girls knew the time of day, let alone the GNP of Portugal or how to samba." She picked up the remote control and aimed it at the cassette that was soundlessly playing. "Take this damn film, for instance."

SueBee turned to watch King Hussein of Jordan reviewing his troops on an airstrip as the voice-over droned on about the king's vital statistics.

Angel pushed fast-forward and stopped the picture for the spoken résumé of the president of the New York Stock Exchange. "Why do we have to watch this thing? Are these guys some of Madame Cleo's johns or what?"

"No," SueBee said. "It's just to help us recognize these men in case we meet them at some dinner or on someone's yacht."

"Oh, sure. I'm going to be stuck between the fish course and the palate-clearing sorbet and not know I'm next to the King of Jordan," Angel said. Then, in a more theatrical voice, she added, "And that big fuzzy white guy across the table is Harvey the Rabbit but I wouldn't know that if I hadn't been to Wellington Close, the whore's finishing school. Don't you see, SueBee? This whole thing is a con. Madame Cleo has some kind of delusional psychosis, a messianic complex to control not just our bodies but our minds."

SueBee mouthed the word "messianic," picked up her notebook, and laboriously wrote out "m-e-s-s-y-a-n-n-i-c-k." She would look it up later.

"And this!" Angel continued, reaching for the little leather-bound French-English dictionary issued to all the girls when they arrived. "Did you know this dictionary was published in nineteen thirty-nine! Nineteen thirty-nine! It's the only one Madame Cleo permits and we're supposed to memorize it like Chairman Mao's Little Red Book."

SueBee turned back to the pile of books on her desk. "Who's Chairman Mao?" she asked pleasantly. "Is he on the tape?"

Angel rolled her eyes and hit the rewind button. "Mind if I shower

Lucianne Goldberg

first?" she asked, walking toward the bathroom. She was tired of talking about it all. SueBee was too hopelessly in love with the stupid scene. She would just muddle through and count the days until she could leave. "Remember," she said in her imitation English accent, "cocktails and Vivaldi in the Orangerie at seven sharp, followed by tonight's lecture."

"Oooh," SueBee said excitedly, "I forgot to check the schedule. What is it?"

"Determining His Needs," Angel said from under lowered lids.

"Is that the one where they tell you the man is always right, no matter what? The girls were talking about that at breakfast."

"That's the one. Couldn't you barf?"

"Angel, we're not in training to be flight attendants," SueBee said.

Angel loaded bottles of shampoo and skin cream into the crook of her arm as she passed the dresser. "I'll be out in a minute. Determining His Needs. God help us. *He* wants to fuck. That's all I've ever needed to know."

SueBee smiled and closed her notebook. "Should I wear my black with the spaghetti straps?" she called toward the bathroom. "Or my black with the spaghetti straps?"

"Why don't you wear the black with the spaghetti straps?" Angel called back, laughing. She let the hot water pound on the back of her neck, resting her chin on her chest. She squeezed a puffy blob of shampoo onto her wet hair and began to massage it into her scalp. *One of these days,* she vowed, *one of these days. I'm gonna be back on top again. It's only a matter of time.*

Sandrine awoke alone in the darkened bedroom of a three-room suite. She lay for a long while with her eyes closed, listening. There was no shower running, no television or radio chattering the morning news. Just the dim rush of traffic beyond the drawn drapes and a faint sour smell of old cigars and room-temperature whiskey.

She groped for something on the nightstand to remind her of where she was. Her hand brushed against a matchbook, knocking it to the carpet. As she leaned over the side of the bed to retrieve it, the top of her head felt as though it were going to explode. She snatched the matchbook and rolled back onto the pillows. She opened one eye and looked at the address on the cover. Claridge's was scrolled in gold. London. She was in London. Maybe.

She flopped back onto the pillows and tried to remember what day it was, what month it was. From the color of the trees outside the window it had to be fall already. In the months that she had been a

Cleo girl she had been in every major city in Europe and had gone once to Istanbul. She was in and out of Paris with more regularity than the trains. Her life was a timeless swirl of airplanes, cars, hotel lobbies, beds, and three-star restaurants, of faces and hands and penises erect and occasionally flaccid, no matter how cleverly she manipulated them. Men with lovely manners and a few so rough and gross she had turned around and walked to the nearest phone to call Madame Cleo. Actually, it had happened only twice, but the rules were very specific. She did not have to be with anyone she found unpleasant in any way. The basic and oddly democratic rule of working for Madame Cleo was a constant: although Madame and Martin did the booking, the girls got to choose. She had learned, however, that Madame Cleo could be subtle in her assignments for girls who were cooperative. Sandrine was convinced that she had received so many and varied assignments because she had turned few of them down.

Still, there was too much drinking, too much having to look perfect, and God! the smiling. She was always smiling, perpetually leaning forward to hear each golden word of snore-inducing wisdom, every unfunny, raunchy, stupid punch line. Having sex was a stroll in the park compared to the relentless drudgery of paying attention. At least when she was having sex she felt as though she was staying in shape. During sex, she was in control. On a banquette, in the back of a limo, on the fantail of a yacht she was just a prop, an arm piece, as insignificant and flickable as a piece of lint. The phrase she coined for being in that condition was "playing the fucklet." There were starlets who aspired to dazzling careers, and wifelets who aspired to brilliant marriages. And then there were the fucklets. At the moment she was a fucklet trying to make it to wifelet. The hangovers from booze and soft drugs, the psychological and physical wear and tear, all seemed to be cobbled together into a seamless blob. At least she had learned to listen creatively.

When she was with a man, the harder she listened the more he gave himself away, dropping clues. She found the clues in the little conversational digressions that men made; they told her how rich he was, how unhappy he was with his current emotional life, what his sexual preferences were, and whether or not she might make the effort to run him to ground.

Sandrine knew that should she ever find herself sitting across the table from a man she truly wanted, he would be hers. It mattered not if he was married. Any man could get unmarried. She thought of the women she had known who whined because they were in love with a married man and feared he would never leave his wife. One truth she had discovered was that the really rich and powerful ones *always* left their wives for a truly professional wifelet.

The hardest work, outside of listening to the men, was personal maintenance. Despite the couture clothes, the first-class accommodations, and never having to carry anything heavier than her makeup case, work was work. There was no time in which she did not have to look spectacular. That meant that nails, hair, teeth, skin, figure, clothes, and accessories all had to be kept at the highest level of perfection and allure. She hadn't worn a pair of jeans or opened a can of tuna or plugged in a vacuum cleaner in so long that she doubted she would now know how. At the moment, as she lay in a thousand-dollar designer nightgown in a two-thousand-dollar-a-day hotel suite, she had fantasies about a day spent in a knee-length dirty T-shirt, flip-flops on her unpedicured feet, and a fridge full of chocolate Yoo-Hoo and buckets of fried chicken.

Other than dreaming of a day off wallowing in total slobhood, she did not hunger for a simpler life. She was doing what she had to do to position herself for that quantum leap into wifelet nirvana—marriage to an incredibly rich and powerful man, preferably one who traveled incessantly and was old. Really old. Madame Cleo could get her only so far. It was up to her to do the rest.

Her biggest disappointment was that she saw SueBee and Angel so little. Their paths seldom crossed. Occasionally she would get a phone call through to one of them, like the time in May when SueBee had the flu and was holed up in the apartment Madame Cleo provided in Paris. SueBee was being lovingly attended to by the loaned valet of one of her regular clients who paid her not to have sex but to listen to him read the poetry he wrote while traveling around Europe buying up companies. The two women had talked for hours. SueBee had clearly found a life she loved. She was needed; she was making people comfortable and happy. Her only complaint was that she'd prefer to be doing all that for just one man instead of dozens.

Sandrine had seen Angel in the Frankfurt airport in August. Despite the warm weather, Angel was swaddled head to toe in red fox. Her enormous coat had linebacker shoulders and a hem that brushed the toes of her alligator boots. Her fur hat was so huge and fluffy Sandrine would not have recognized her if Angel hadn't screamed her name so loud that every head in the Lufthansa First Class lounge swiveled around to see who was being attacked. As Angel threw her arms around Sandrine, she was enveloped in fur and Calvin Klein Obsession. When Angel finally released her and stopped squealing, Sandrine was able to get a good look at her.

"Have you had something done?" she whispered after Angel introduced her to a very small man in a military uniform who she said was a general in the Turkish army. The little general, seeing that the women wanted to talk, excused himself and disappeared.

Angel raised her chin and dropped her eyes. "How do you like it? I had it done in Rio last month, a freebie from a doctor who wanted to marry me."

"You look fabulous," Sandrine said truthfully. "But you know Madame would have paid for it. She's always offering."

"I know, I know. But I don't want to take anything from her but assignments." She turned and smiled at the bartender. "Two Bloody Marys on the rocks, please. Hold the spice, hold the juice."

"What's that?" Sandrine asked puzzled.

"Vodka on ice. He knows. He's used to me by now."

"You've been here that much?" Sandrine said, glancing around the lounge.

Angel leaned closer and lowered her voice. "Twice this week," she whispered. "I'm working on a deal."

"What kind of a deal? A man?"

"No, no, no," Angel said impatiently. "Nothing like that." She leaned even closer and rested her hand against her cheek to cover her mouth. "You can't breathe a word, okay?"

"Sure," Sandrine nodded, thinking, *Oh God, here we go.*

"I've just met with two of the biggest madams in Germany. One controls territory as far south as Budapest. They're both pretty old. I want to get to know them. If all goes well, I'm hoping to buy them out."

"Good Lord, Angel. There'll be hell to pay if Madame Cleo finds out."

"She's not going to find out," Angel said, taking a sip of her vodka. "All I need is another year or two and I'll have the money. Maybe less if I can stop buying clothes. That's why I'm with the little Turk over there."

Sandrine looked around. Angel's companion was on the phone in the far corner of the lounge. "What's a general got to do with clothes?" she asked.

"Oh, he's not a general," Angel scoffed. "He just likes to dress up. It gets him better service. He's an exporter, raw fur, fine leather, good stuff. I get it wholesale and my seamstress runs it up in Paris. You like the coat?" Angel stood and swirled around.

Sandrine laughed. Angel seemed to be having the time of her life while she plotted. "I like the whole put-together, love," she said, standing to give Angel a kiss on the cheek. "But I gotta go." Sandrine's plane was being called.

Sandrine left Angel standing in the door of the lounge, looking like a movie star. As she walked down the long corridor toward the boarding gate, she couldn't help wondering if Angel wasn't risking the life she had. Madame Cleo had long and powerful tentacles. There was every chance her friend would get caught and end up back where she had been that cold, unhappy morning they had walked along the Seine together.

Sandrine rolled over and buried her face in the pillow that smelled of the perfume she had worn to bed. She thought of little SueBee sitting on the edge of some boring tycoon's bed listening to his boring poetry. She thought of great big Angel bouncing the little Turkish exporter off some hotel ceiling, planning the cut and style of her next fur outfit.

They were getting closer to what they wanted than she was.

It would be the middle of the night New York time. She wondered if, even in her sleep, her beloved Martha was waiting for the phone to ring and to hear the joyful news that Sandrine had a rich husband and a villa in Spain or an enormous flat on the Avenue Foch for them to make a life together. For months she had played the scenario out in her mind. Once she had her billionaire, the beautiful home, and Martha in place, she would have Barry Rizzo or, preferably, one of his hairy-fingered thugs, notify her mother that she could take her trust fund and, as Barry had so delicately suggested, "shove it where the moon don't shine."

Sandrine pushed herself up onto her elbows and shook her head hard to clear it of the residue of smoke and booze. She remembered she was here with the judge, and thanked God he had left for whatever he did all day. The last thing she wanted to do at the moment was listen to him.

The judge was becoming a regular. He was pleasant enough, easy to arouse and quick to satisfy, but a dead end as far as her wifelet career was concerned.

She squinted across at the phone on the other side of the king-size bed. She had not checked in with Martin since she arrived and knew he would be annoyed with her. Now that she was alone she might as well get it over with.

When Martin's plummy voice came on the line she rolled over on her stomach, cradling the phone.

"*Bonjour*, Martin, daaaaah-ling," she drawled in her smokiest voice.

"Well! High time," he huffed. "You really shouldn't go off the map like this, Sandrine."

"Don't scold, Martin," she groaned. "My head won't take it. You knew this was a three-day gig. Look at the log if you don't believe me."

"I don't have time to argue with you. If you're free now I have another job this evening."

"Listen, Martin, I've been thinking. These three-day jobs . . . would I earn more if I took, like, a different guy each day?"

"Sure," he said flatly. "Why would you want to?"

"Money," she said.

"Money, of course, darling. But you make a bundle now."

"I need more than a bundle, Martin. I want you to start booking me by the day. Right through the fall, okay? I'll need a week or so at Christmas to go back to New York. You can start scheduling me again for the first week in January."

"I'll have to speak to Madame, Sandrine," Martin said in the clipped way he had when he didn't want to accept responsibility.

"You do that, darling. Tell her I'm dead serious about it."

She hung up and sat on the edge of the bed thinking. It took money to get money. She knew she could never earn enough on her own to afford the life she wanted, but in the meantime she was determined to look and live as though she were that rich.

That Christmas she stayed at the Plaza. She slept and shopped and tried not to drink or smoke too much. She invited Martha to a wonderful lunch in the Edwardian Room. Over coffee and dessert she handed Martha a velvet box that held a strand of pearls, real and lustrous and the size of marbles. She had bought them in Geneva one afternoon while killing time between assignments.

She didn't know whether it was the pearls or her promise to send for Martha within the coming year, but suddenly her former nanny's lovely, weathered face crumbled into tears. Embarrassed, Martha placed her hands over her face until she could get herself under control.

"Oh, Marthy," Sandrine said, patting her hand. "Don't. The waiter will think you don't like the crème brûlée."

Martha slowly lowered her hands. "I know what you had to do to buy these beautiful pearls," Martha said.

Sandrine picked at her dessert. She wasn't going to lie or apologize to Martha. She knew Martha wasn't criticizing her, simply stating a fact. What she was doing for a living wouldn't change their unconditional love. Yet, seeing the sadness in Martha's eyes, Sandrine felt she owed her some kind of explanation. "It's not a terrible life, Martha. I travel, I go to beautiful places and meet fascinating people."

"Your mother did the same thing before you were born," Martha said evenly.

If Martha had picked up her fork and stabbed it deep between Sandrine's eyes she would have suffered less of a shock. "What did you say?" she asked, knowing exactly what she had heard but needing time to absorb it.

"Your mother worked for a woman named Cleo, in Paris, in the late fifties," Martha said evenly.

"How do you know that?"

"I've been around her for a long time. I hear things. I know things."

"Why didn't you ever tell me?" Sandrine said around the lump in her throat.

"Because I didn't want to hurt you."

"It might have helped."

Martha shrugged. "Is that who you work for, Dreenie?"

Sandrine nodded helplessly.

"Are you upset with me?" Martha said, her eyes wide and pleading.

"Of course not," Sandrine said, patting Martha's hand again. "I probably would have guessed about Mother eventually. I'm just sorry I didn't know before. Knowing would have given me a little more ammunition to fight her with over the years."

Sandrine helped Martha into a cab waiting in front of the hotel. She bent and kissed her on the forehead. "I'll call you when I get back to Paris, darling. Please don't worry about me. I'll send for you as soon as I can."

She watched Martha waving out the back window of the taxi as it pulled onto West 59th Street and headed toward the East Side.

Saudine needed some air to clear her head. She turned and walked toward the park. The trees around the beautiful old hotel were covered with thousands of Christmas lights. Across the street even the horse-drawn carriages waiting for holiday tourists were decorated. A horse with lights wound around his harness nodded at her. It made her feel a little less lonely.

The cold crisp air helped to clear her head as she walked. She found herself, for the first time in her life, feeling sorry for her mother. Tita Mandraki had hidden her secret for so many years. How many times had her mother walked into a room and wondered if a former john would spot her? How many times had she gone to a meeting or a presentation involving her work or to a banker for backing, afraid that a background check might reveal her past?

For the first time she realized that her mother's ghosts were no different than the ones she was putting away for herself. Would the day come when she would have to do her own hiding and lying, living in terror that whatever world she built for herself would disappear if she were found out? Would there be a man someday that she wanted more than life itself who had to be lied to?

She knew she would have to insulate herself from discovery the same way her mother had, with money. The rich didn't have to answer questions. The rich could buy off any threat, silence any critic. Perhaps that explained why her mother had refused to give her the trust fund she was owed. That money was sure protection if talent or love failed. Well, her mother could have the damn trust fund. She had probably earned it in her own way. Sandrine would start building something of her own. Something no one could get their hands on.

Surely, Madame Cleo had to know. It must have given her some kind of perverse pleasure to hire the daughter of a former Cleo girl. The thought made her like Madame Cleo less.

Of all the lies, those of commission and those of omission, omitting the truth seemed the most dishonest. To know something about someone and not tell was a form of control. It made the one with the knowledge feel that she was superior. Figuring that out made her like Madame Cleo not at all. One day she would confront her.

Sandrine turned and walked back toward the hotel, knowing that what she was looking for, the power that would protect her against everything and everyone, was somewhere in Europe. Nineteen eighty-seven was going to be her year. The year she found the man who would solve everything.

In the spring and early summer of 1987 the mansion on the Ile de la Cité buzzed with activity. A new group had finished up at Wellington Close and there were not enough apartments available in the buildings around Paris that Madame used for housing. Four girls had to be temporarily placed in bedrooms on the upper floors of the mansion. Their demands and chatter and constant coming and going drove Martin berserk. He begged Madame to let him get someone to help him with the books, saying he couldn't be a houseboy and a manager at the same time.

He had done a preliminary accounting and the operation's three top-grossing girls were the Americans, Sandrine Mandraki, SueBee Slyde, and Angel Weinstein. Sandrine had been taking double and triple jobs to such a degree that it was hard to tell what city she was in without looking it up. SueBee had become the darling of the English gentry for some reason, and had acquitted herself so beautifully in the royal enclosure at Ascot last week that Martin had her booked well into the fall. But as hard as Angel was working, her behavior was becoming more than troubling. She was sloppy about keeping her schedule. Several clients reported back to Cleo that she had approached them to become exclusive, private customers. She had been sighted in places she was not supposed to be. It was all adding up to a dangerous pattern. Martin knew Madame didn't like what Angel was doing, but was too busy to put a stop to it. He knew a day of reckoning would come. In the meantime they both had La Fantastique to plan. The baron had already phoned with his special instructions. Three girls would be selected for special assignments there, and because of her high earnings, Angel would certainly demand to be one of them. Those Madame had chosen would be announced at the formal dinner she always gave for all the girls in late June. Something would have to be done about Angel soon.

On a warm June morning, Martin sat behind his desk. Piles of ledgers, logs, and monthly medical reports on the girls were each weighted with whatever he could find to anchor them against the breeze wafting in through the high windows behind his desk.

For a change, everything in the house was still. The girls upstairs were out or asleep. Nanti was puttering uselessly around, pretending to dust downstairs. For once Martin had a few moments to speak to Madame alone.

He stepped to her office door and tapped twice.

"*Oui.* Come."

He pushed opened the door and stuck his head in. She was reading something at her desk and did not look up.

"Do you have a moment?" he asked tentatively. "I'd like to go over the dinner with you. We need to call the caterers with the menu before Friday."

"Come," she said briskly, still not looking up.

Martin settled into his usual seat in front of the desk. He much preferred seeing her in this room. It was airy and cool, not like her little hideaway on the ground floor, which gave him claustrophobia.

Recently, the little room had been turned over to two men her lawyer had retained to go over her books. That was another bit of business that added to the tension around the mansion. Madame had always kept her tax situation her little secret, discussing it only with Jack Ayler and her attorney. The government was claiming she was delinquent in her payments, but Martin felt they were being generous. In the years he had been with her he had never known her to pay one franc in taxes. Jack Ayler paid frequent visits to the little room downstairs, and often, when Martin passed by it on his way home at night, he could hear shouting coming from behind the closed door. Whatever was going on would not be good news, he knew. Something else to deal with down the line, he mused, as he waited for her to finish reading.

Madame finally closed the manila file on her desk and pulled the little gold-rimmed reading glasses off the tip of her nose. Her face was tight, her mouth a tense, narrow line.

"We have a problem," she said, drumming her long nails on the top of the file.

Martin hoped whatever was wrong didn't have to do with the men downstairs. "What seems to be the matter?" he asked.

"Have you looked at Angel's itinerary lately?" she asked.

"Why, yes, as a matter of fact. I just got through doing the books. She's done exceedingly well. Better than last year. Why do you ask?"

"Are you tracking her free-lance work?"

"Yes. From what I can tell she's paid us commission on everything. Of course, there's no way to know what she's not telling us about."

Madame sighed deeply. "I can't stop my girls from making a little on the side. That's gone on for ages. But from what I've just read here"—she held up the file, then tossed it down in disgust—"Angel is getting completely out of line."

"What are you reading?"

"This is a report from a close friend in Munich. A man I've done business with for years. It seems Angel has recruited him as a personal client. She told him she was going to buy out Madame Lili and would welcome his patronage."

Martin was stunned. In the past, other girls had attempted such things. When Madame discovered it (and she always did; her network could serve as a model for Scotland Yard), the guilty girl was dismissed before she could get the hot rollers out of her hair. Further, Madame would see that she was blackballed in the business. No respectable madame would touch her once Cleo put out the word.

"I did notice that she was making an inordinate number of trips in and out of Frankfurt. I'm shocked, truly shocked," Martin said. "Do you want me to find her and call her in?"

Madame Cleo said nothing for a long time. She seemed to be plotting something. Finally she spoke. "Not just yet," she said pensively. "If I let her go now she could do me a lot of harm. If she's recruiting clients God knows what mischief she can cause with our girls."

"What can we do?" Martin asked.

"I'm going to make a few calls. I need to catch her red-handed. That way I can control her when I send her to the worst place I can think of."

Martin pushed back myriad images of hooker hells around the world that sprang to mind—Moroccan souks, Pakistani brothels, and Chinese opium dens. "Where's that?" he asked, wide-eyed.

Madame Cleo lifted the phone and began to punch in a number. "Las Vegas," she said. Her tone was the same as she might use when referring to the Paris sewer.

In his years with Madame he had seen girls fined, fired, called on the carpet, and tongue-lashed for various transgressions such as stealing or drugs. Some had even been shipped out of the country, never to be heard from again. Those cases were as rare as they were swiftly handled. Never had he known a girl to remain indentured in some way unless she owed Madame a great deal of money. Usually Madame was angry enough to forgive the debt and write off thousands in cosmetic surgery and haute-couture clothes just to get rid of a girl who betrayed her. The idea of Angel Weinstein, so grand, so haughty, so full of pride, working a lounge in Las Vegas intrigued him no end.

Madame smiled across the desk at him. He knew that smile. It had no mirth in it whatsoever. "Find Sandrine. I'm going to send her with Angel on a special assignment."

"And?"

"Just get me Sandrine. I'll tell you the rest later."

"She left for London early this morning—our man there has her scheduled for a party this evening. But I'll try to reach her. What then?"

"Tell her to be on a plane to Zurich in the morning. I have a client there who is going to get a free evening with two exquisite girls."

Martin rang Sandrine's hotel only to be told that she had gone out shopping. He left a message for her to call as soon as she came in. Then he called Jeremy Wilks, who was Madame's contact man in London. His answering machine picked up.

"Damn." Martin cursed under his breath and hung up. He called Angel at her apartment and told her to stand by for a special assignment. At least he had her nailed down. All afternoon he continued to call London. By six he gave up for the day, having left a half-dozen urgent messages at Sandrine's hotel and on Jeremy's machine.

Martin hung around the office until nearly midnight, hoping one of them would call. When the phone finally rang he leaped at it, yanking up the receiver before it had completed the first ring.

"Where have you been?" he demanded without even saying hello.

"At the airport, Martin," said a familiar voice. "Here. I just arrived and thought I should check in."

Martin slumped back in his chair. "SueBee," he sighed. No one else he knew made his name sound like "Mutton."

"What's up? Do you need me for anything?"

Martin slapped his forehead. "Hold on, love. I'll check."

He quickly buzzed Madame's boudoir on the next floor.

Madame, who was always awake until the wee hours of the morning, said yes, it would be all right to send SueBee if he couldn't find Sandrine, even though it might be a bit awkward.

The client in Switzerland waiting for two Cleo girls was Sheikh Omar Zaki.

In London, Sandrine knew Martin was trying to find her, and she avoided him. She spent the afternoon having her hair washed and set. She had a bikini wax, a sauna, an herbal scrub, an hour-long massage, a manicure, a pedicure, and a skin vacuum and mint facial. As a final touch she had her makeup professionally done.

She emerged from Ma Eglantine in Oxford Street glowing and radiant. From there she cabbed to the Chanel boutique in Chelsea and bought a seven-thousand-dollar dress that fit like a second skin. During the afternoon she periodically excused herself from ministering hands to call her hotel for messages. They were all from Martin, each more frantic than the last. She called Jeremy Wilks and told him not to speak to Martin if he called. She knew Martin could only be calling with a pressing assignment for her. After each message was delivered she thanked the desk clerk and went back to making herself the best she could be. No way was she going to be distracted from the night's mission.

Jeremy had been waiting at the airport that morning when she arrived from Paris.

Rushing up to take her bags, he'd nearly squeaked with excitement. "Darling girl, I can't wait to tell you about the party tonight."

"Oh, Jeremy," she had moaned. "What's so wonderful about a dumb cocktail party for an Andrew Lloyd Webber show? You know it will be a bore."

The only reason she had taken the quick London assignment was that someone was overpaying to have a few beautiful girls mingle around the Savoy ballroom and be nice to whomever. Jeremy was a girl short and asked Martin to help out. It was a no-hassle arrangement that meant she would probably end up having dinner with some dull old man and could make the early morning flight back to Paris, a few thousand dollars richer.

Jeremy interrupted her thoughts as they walked through the airport lobby. "I've booked an afternoon of pampering for you at Ma Eglantine," he said. "Do you prefer sauna or steam?"

"Why all the fuss?"

Jeremy paused for dramatic effect. "Jourdan Garn is the host."

That did it. She stopped walking and stared at him. "Yikes," she said.

"He's arriving from New York with a private planeload of guests. He'll be staying at his house here. If you play your cards right you might get to see the most exquisite house in Belgravia. Not to mention making the close acquaintance of the third-richest man in the world."

Sandrine said nothing as Jeremy tossed her bag into the trunk of his Rolls parked at curbside in front of Air France.

My God, she thought, feeling the tips of her fingers begin to tingle. *This could be it! Jourdan Garn!* She had seen his picture a hundred times; she had read about him in *Fortune* and *Forbes*.

As she settled into the back seat of Jeremy's car, she glanced up to make sure the partition between the seats was closed and turned to Jeremy. "You could have given this to one of the other girls," she said.

"I know," Jeremy said with a half-smile. "I felt you deserved it. I knew you'd know how to handle someone like Garn."

Sandrine smiled. "Thanks, Jeremy. And you're right. I'll know just what to do with him."

At seven sharp that night Jeremy called for her at her hotel. She noticed him swallow hard when he saw her. Wordlessly, he helped her into the waiting Rolls. It wasn't until they moved away from the curb that he spoke.

"Jourdan Garn won't know what hit him," he said.

There seemed to be a Jeremy clone in every city Sandrine went to. Madame Cleo's men were all young and thin and tall. They were either photographers or artists or just hangers-on who looked good in a tux. Madame used them as errand boys. If they were straight, which Jeremy wasn't, they were allowed to occasionally take a new girl to bed to check her out, in much the same way as she favored Jack Ayler in Paris.

As they neared the Savoy, the Strand became clogged with traffic and their car had to inch its way forward.

"You think there's going to be anyone there I'd like to meet?" Jeremy asked as the Rolls came to a dead standstill.

"Um. Are you up for actors?" Sandrine asked, staring out the window.

"Not really," he said, making a face.

"Well, you're on your own, Jeremy. I've already got my target for the night."

"Indeed," he said, smiling. "Is there anything you want me to do?"

"Yes. I want you to find someone to introduce us. He doesn't have to know I'm a working girl, not right away. It makes men feel better if they think they got you with their charm."

Jeremy threw back his head of long silky hair and laughed. "All right, Sandrine," he said, "let's go for it."

Suddenly, Jeremy grabbed her hand and opened the door of the car, which hadn't moved an inch for over five minutes. "We'll walk, ducks," he said, pulling her across the seat. "We'll never get there in this traffic."

Sandrine stepped to the curb and adjusted the top of her gown. It was a long black satin sheath, high at the neck in front. In the back a soft cowl fell, exposing a breathtaking sweep of alabaster skin that plunged to several inches below her waist. Anyone who danced with her would not be able to avoid touching cool, silken skin. She wore a high Victorian choker consisting of alternating strands of seed pearls, garnets, and onyx that Jeremy had retrieved from the collection of jewels Madame Cleo kept in a safety-deposit box at the Coutts bank on Sloane Square. Over her shoulder she had looped a long black fox throw, again from Madame Cleo's lending collection of furs in a vault at Harrod's. Her makeup was perfection.

As they stepped onto the red carpet leading from the curb to the revolving door of the Savoy, the lights on the television cameras swiveled around, flooding them both with an eye-popping glare. Someone in the crowd began to applaud, and was quickly joined by other onlookers pressed against the police barricades.

"It's Raquel Welch, for sure," Sandrine heard someone say in a thick cockney accent.

"Naaahh, the bird's too young. It's Cybill Shepherd."

"Gooo on," the cockney voice answered. "Cybill Shepherd is a blonde."

"Well, that girl has to be *somebody!*"

Sandrine looked down at her tiny black-strapped sandals and smiled. She loved it when people thought she was someone famous. The reality of what she really was seemed a delicious, secret joke on the world.

As they moved slowly through the high open doors, Jeremy put a protective arm around her. Once inside the lobby they could hear a string ensemble playing show tunes somewhere in the distance.

The party was under way in an enormous room just off the lobby.

They stood in the doorway for a moment taking in the scene. Lavish buffet tables stretched the length of both sides of the room. At either end were bars with frantic bartenders filling waiters' trays with drinks and flutes of champagne. There appeared to be about two hundred people in the beautifully dressed crowd. The men wore black tie or fully decorated uniforms. The few women in the room looked like models or actresses. Sandrine wondered how many of them were professionals as well.

Jeremy guided her through the crowd toward the bar at the far end of the room. On a small bandstand a string quartet was softly playing. As a waiter whizzed by, Jeremy snagged them both glasses of champagne. They eased back to a clearing in the crowd, glasses in hand. Not a head went unturned in Sandrine's wake.

She stood very close to Jeremy's tuxedo sleeve and scanned the room.

"See him yet?" Jeremy asked with a knowing grin.

"Not yet," she answered coolly. "From his pictures, I don't think he's very tall. In this sea of penguins he's going to be hard to spot."

"What color hair are we looking for?"

"Ummm, dark. A real dark brown with silver temples. He always has a tan."

"That makes it a snap. Most of these men are either bald or have skin the color of oatmeal," Jeremy said disdainfully before he took a sip of champagne.

"Must be the English air," Sandrine said, as she continued to scan the room. Suddenly she stiffened. "I've spotted him!"

"Where?"

"Over there. Just to the right of that high fern. See?"

"Hold on!" Jeremy said excitedly. "We *are* in luck. He's with Sir Peter Knight. I did some work with him when he was on the *Express*. We'd better hop. They're shaking hands. It looks like Sir Peter is moving on."

Jeremy cupped her elbow and propelled Sandrine along the edge of the dance floor toward her prey.

Sandrine fixed her eyes on Garn, sizing him up. He was handsome enough and wore a tux with a European cut, tailored high under the arms and nipped at the waist. As he spoke his full mouth curved slightly at the corners. In profile he looked not unlike a young Brando but without the brooding scowl. This, she thought, straightening her spine with the model's trick of pretending someone was tugging on a wire attached to the top of her head, is going to be a piece of *gâteau*. She felt the familiar power rush building, the feeling she used to get when she moved toward the dance floor in the discos back in New York. She felt suspended in a bubble of energy in which she knew that within seconds she would be the center of attention and could do no wrong. Before, her goal had been to capture and hold the undivided attention of a crowd. This time the energy was directed at only one man. He didn't stand a chance.

When they were less than fifteen paces away Sandrine suddenly grabbed Jeremy's sleeve. "Wait," she said urgently.

"Wha—" Jeremy said, one leg suspended in front of him.

"You go up and say hello. Let me hold back. He'll notice you're with me and ask to be introduced. It's better that way."

Jeremy stared down at her skeptically. "You better be sure. We've only got one shot at him. We can't go chasing the man all round the room."

"Trust me," Sandrine said with a slow smile. She took two small steps backward and let Jeremy approach the two men. She watched as Jeremy, speaking in a terribly correct voice, bowed slightly and greeted Sir Peter. Sir Peter, in turn, introduced Jeremy to Garn. She had to admit, Jeremy was smooth as silk. He lightly flattered Garn with a brief reference to an article in the *Times* mentioning his involvement with the show.

As they chattered on, Sandrine maneuvered herself into Garn's line of sight, fixed her eyes on him, and waited for him to notice her staring. It only took a moment. As soon as his pale blue eyes focused on her face, they took a short, appreciative trip down her body and very slowly back up again. When his gaze returned to her face she bore in, holding his gaze in an eye-lock that sent as many erogenous signals as she could flash through her mind's eye. She let her lips part ever so slightly and lowered her eyelids no more than a centimeter.

She felt the heat run up her spine and nestle under her breasts. It was working! He continued speaking to Jeremy but the words were losing force. Finally, he simply stopped talking and gave her a practiced, sexy smile. Slowly, she bit the corner of her lower lip, then just as slowly released it. His reaction told her he was a player. Here was a man with utter confidence in his own sexuality, a take-charge, hands-on, just-tell-me-what-you-want lover. That lack of self-doubt in one's own appeal was sexy in and of itself. She had known far less attractive men who had that attitude. It was a turn-on no matter what the man's station in life was. If only the nerds of the world could get that message, she thought, there would be fewer serial murders and rapes.

Finally, Garn blinked. He broke their eye-lock.

Sandrine had won.

For a flustered moment he tried to politely extricate himself from the others. She knew it was only a matter of seconds before he would be moving toward her. As Garn shook hands with Jeremy, she turned and slipped through the double door to her left into a smaller, darkened room where she stepped behind a column. Over her shoulder she could see Garn standing in the lighted doorway looking for her.

She waited until he left, walked slowly back into the main room, and circled away from where the men had been standing. Suddenly, she felt a hand on her shoulder and turned to see Jeremy frowning at her.

"What's all this?" he asked disapprovingly. "You playing pussy-in-the-corner?"

"So to speak," she said, laughing as she pulled him onto the dance floor. The string quartet had been replaced by a band that had just swung into a pounding rock number. Sandrine pressed against Jeremy's starched shirt and let the beat vibrate up her legs. She was back at Wings again, letting the music lift her out into the center of the floor. As she threw her head back and began an undulating, loose-jointed dance, she knew somewhere in the room Jourdan Garn had to be watching her.

"Jesus," Jeremy breathed, bug-eyed, as she moved around him, her high heels prancing as she arched her back and raised her arms high above her head.

Teasingly, she raised one eyebrow at Jeremy. "You like?" she asked, knowing the answer.

"Incredible," he said, then glanced over her shoulder. "Ooops. Someone else appreciates you too, darling. Mr. Garn is right behind you, staring."

"That's the idea."

Jeremy made a fast turn, thrusting his hips at her playfully. "I think he's getting ready to drool. Heeeere he comes!"

Sandrine did not turn around. She kept dancing until she felt what had to be Garn's body brushing against her back. With one smooth turn, in perfect sync with the music, she spun around into his arms.

A perfect fit, they moved as one entity as the music drifted into a slower number, as if the bandleader sensed the sexual drama taking place and wanted to assist them. Neither of them spoke for the next two numbers. There was only the sound of the music and his breathing in her ear. She was determined that he speak first.

Finally, he placed his lips in her hair and said, "Who *are* you?" drawing the words out as though he found them difficult to speak.

She pulled back her head and locked eyes with him again. "My name is Sandrine," she said softly.

"That's it?"

"Ummm." She smiled.

"Lose the pansy," he said roughly.

"I'm sorry?"

"That photographer. You came with him, right?"

"Don't call him a pansy," she said sharply. "And I wouldn't walk out on him even if he were."

"Why not?" Garn asked, moving his hand farther down her back until his fingertips gently traced the curve of her spine.

"Because I always go home from the dance with the guy who brought me," she said. She did nothing to stop his caressing hand.

"God, you feel wonderful," he said, pulling her closer.

"So do you," she said, moving her hips so that her right thigh was between his legs. "Too wonderful." As she spoke she tensed the muscles of her thighs until they began to tremble. She knew he could feel the gentle vibration of her taut flesh.

Sandrine was rewarded with a soft moan and a hard bulge in his trousers, confirming that her strategy was working. She lowered her forehead onto his shoulder and murmured, "I'm so embarrassed."

His lips were back in her hair. "What's the matter?"

"Can't you tell?"

"What?" he asked breathlessly. "What's going on?"

She stopped dancing and put her arms around his waist, then ground her hips against his groin, hard. With a gasp, she convulsed in one long shiver.

Garn held her in stunned silence until she made a little animal sound and went limp in his arms. "I don't believe this," he whispered, laughing softly in dazed delight. "Did what I think just happen, happen?"

Sandrine kept her head in place on his shoulder. "Please forgive me. I'm mortified," she said with a tiny sob.

"Mortified? You darling girl! You had an orgasm, didn't you?"

Slowly, Sandrine lifted her head and pushed the dark curtain of hair away from her face. "Please, I . . ."

"Shhhh, baby, don't say a thing," he said, brushing her lower lip with his thumb. "Don't be embarrassed. It's beautiful. Does that happen a lot?"

"Never!" Sandrine said, wide-eyed. "That's never happened to me. Ever."

"I really turned you on that much?"

Sandrine took a deep breath and nodded as she scanned the room for Jeremy. She saw him laughing in a circle of people by the door. "I've got to go," she said quickly. "This frightens me."

She pushed away from him and hurried toward Jeremy, not feeling the least bit scared. Indeed, quite the opposite, she felt as though she had just wrapped the world up with a big red ribbon.

As she reached Jeremy, she did not slow her pace but grabbed his sleeve, spun him around, and pulled him toward the door.

"What the hell is going on?" he said as she pulled him through the lobby and out onto the street. "What the hell did you do in there?"

"I came," she said, scanning the street for their car.

"You *what*?"

"Let's go," she said. "There's the car. Quick."

"I don't get it," Jeremy said, short of breath.

"He did. Just you wait and see."

Their driver snapped to attention when he saw them hurrying toward the car and opened the back door.

They slid quickly into the back seat. As the big car moved out into the street, Sandrine turned to Jeremy. "Okay, here's what I want you to do. I'm going back to my hotel. You go straight home. When he calls you, really make him work to find out where I am but make sure you tell him."

"Jourdan Garn is going to call me? You must be joking. He doesn't know me from Adam."

"He knows Sir Peter. He'll find you. Trust me. He'll call. Don't you move from your phone until he does."

Less than an hour later Sandrine picked up the ringing phone in her suite and heard the desk clerk announce that a Mr. Garn was on his way up.

She stood by the open door and watched him step off the elevator. He moved down the corridor toward her, his tanned face slack with lust.

"Get your things," he said as he stepped into the room. "And don't run away from me again."

The next morning, exhilarated with sexual exhaustion, he left Sandrine asleep amid the crumpled satin sheets in the bedroom of his house in Belgravia. When, at noon, he returned from his appointment, hungrier for her than he had ever been for any woman, she was gone.

It took Angel and SueBee a good half hour to get to the Frequent Flyer lounge at Heathrow airport. Before they were even through the terminal lobby, Angel stopped to talk animatedly to two Egyptians wearing enormous Rolexes and wraparound dark glasses.

While they waited for the porter to check their bags, a very tall German with white hair stepped out of line and clutched at Angel's elbow. That conversation took another five minutes.

She made no attempt to introduce SueBee to anyone, hoping to keep the encounters brief. Finally, she freed herself and the two women walked toward the First Class lounge.

"Good heavens, Angel," SueBee said, laughing. "Do you know every soul alive?"

Angel tossed her hair and adjusted the strap of the Gucci carryon that was sliding down the arm of her fur jacket. "Not really," she said airily. "But they know me."

The noon flight to Zurich was delayed and there was nothing to do but make themselves comfortable. Angel spread herself out, her coat taking up half of a couch near the receptionist's desk. The two of them must have made quite a sight for the other travelers. Two beautiful young women, expensively dressed, wearing fur coats in June and carrying hand luggage that cost more than a thousand dollars apiece.

Angel tried to pretend she was oblivious to the attention, direct or indirect, but she loved it. It was that way everywhere she traveled and was the most enjoyable part of her life as a Cleo girl. She had only to find a way to translate the adulation into something bigger for herself. But that was a thought she did not share with SueBee.

She had not been displeased when Martin called with the assignment. She liked SueBee and had seen very little of her since their days at Wellington Close. It would be fun traveling with her. Martin had been vague about who the men were that they would be meeting. It didn't matter. They were all beginning to seem the same. The only reason she remembered any of them was that they were potential clients for her future plans.

The assignment wasn't exactly in Zurich, she found to her displeasure. It was typical of Martin, whose grasp of geography was limited to the nearest airport. A car had been rented for them once they arrived. From there they would drive to the jet-set ski resort of Klosters. Reservations had been made at the Chesa Grischuna, where they were to check in and wait for a call.

The car, a sleek black Porsche, was waiting at the curb in front of the SwissAir terminal. Angel automatically took the wheel as SueBee settled into the passenger seat.

As the two women drove through the cool, failing light of the winding mountain road that led to Klosters, neither spoke. It was as though they were two road-weary salesmen moving toward another buyer.

Angel was not in the best of moods. She was tired. Her last job had been at a dreary Third World legation in Brussels, where glowering men in ill-fitting suits sat around watching *Godfather* one and two on a VCR and drinking scotch.

"If I don't see someplace to pee along this damn road soon, my snatch is going to start to yodel," she snarled to SueBee, who was looking out the window in awe at the scenery.

SueBee turned toward her. "Lordy, your vocabulary hasn't changed a bit."

"Yes, it has. I don't talk that way except when I'm with friends."

"Well, you sure have got a load of friends, hon," SueBee said, smiling at her. "Just getting through the airport with you is a piece of work."

"Oh, them." Angel sighed and eased the rented Porsche into first gear to take another hairpin curve. The winding Alpine road was far more treacherous than the car-rental agent in Zurich had predicted, and though she was a skillful driver, it required more than casual attention. "They aren't friends, cookie. They're money in the bank."

SueBee pulled the collar of her silver fox jacket up under her chin. Even though it was early summer, there was still snow caught in the craggy landscape. " 'Snatch' is such a vulgar word, don't you think?" SueBee persisted.

"Ease up, SueBee," Angel said, squinting through the tinted windshield into the tiny swirling flakes of snow blowing down the mountain. "You've been hanging around with too many Brits."

"It's such a man's word," SueBee said, refusing to let the subject drop.

"Well," Angel huffed. "Let's find a word for our working equipment that won't offend your delicate sensibilities. How about 'vagina'?"

SueBee sighed deeply and stared out the side window at the gray mist that hovered halfway up the mountains. The snow on the peaks was navy blue. In the valley beneath them lay a sprinkling of lights from a ski resort. The ancient farmhouses and ski chalets all had hand-carved balconies and primitive paintings on their whitewashed walls. Wisps of smoke curled upward into the night sky.

" 'Cunt'?" Angel snapped. "Okay with you, Mrs. Onassis?"

"What's the matter, Angel?" SueBee asked. "Are you in a bad mood?"

Angel turned to look at her friend. SueBee's pale face seemed to be floating in the glow of the dashboard lights. The fur of the fox coat borrowed from Madame Cleo's collection mingled with her pale hair. The rest of her body seemed to have vanished into the darkness of the speeding car.

"I'm getting weary of the life, SueBee," Angel said, breaking the silence. "I'm beginning to feel like a piece of lost luggage. All I see is airports and hotels. Remember all the crap they promised at Wellington Close? Well, what I want to know is, when does it start?"

SueBee turned. "Pardon?"

"The glamour, you know, the glitz, the high life, Khashoggi's fantail, the king's Gulf Stream, the first table at Côte Basque. Huh? All the good shit that we're supposed to get when we work for the infamous Madame Cleo? Has it started yet for you? Because I'm still waiting."

"For pity's sake, Angel. You're so bitter. Here we're riding in a Porsche. We're wearing furs. We've got a thousand dollars cash spending money and more to come. We're in Switzerland and in a while we'll be meeting some very rich, powerful men. I don't know about you but there are several firsts there for me. It's not like we're slapping our handbags against a lamppost on Times Square."

"What if these guys turn out to be creeps?"

"They won't be. Martin said they were special friends of Madame's. She doesn't tolerate creeps. If we don't like them we just find the nearest phone, call Martin, and say, 'Martin, darling. These guys are creeps.' I've had to do it once or twice. I know Sandrine's done it. No problem."

Angel sighed and shook her head, weary of dealing with SueBee's relentless good nature.

"Boy, has she ever gotten lucky," SueBee continued.

Angel's head snapped around. "Who's lucky? What's happened?"

SueBee thought for a moment. "I guess I can tell," she said tentatively. "She called me this morning as I was leaving. She was absolutely giddy. She went to some fancy thing in London last night and met Jourdan Garn. She was calling from his house in Belgravia. After Garn left for a meeting a butler walks into the bedroom with a breakfast tray. Instead of an egg in the egg cup there was a string of Sri Lankan opals with a diamond-and-sapphire clasp. She was so whacked out about it she had to tell someone."

"Sandrine has Jourdan Garn as a client?" Angel nearly shouted. "Jourdan 'Fortune Five Hundred' Garn? Mr. Takeover King? Mr. 'Private-Jet-Bucks-Up-the-Butt' Garn?"

"I think that's the one," SueBee said flatly. "But he wasn't a client. She met him at this party."

"Sure," Angel said.

"True, Angel," SueBee insisted. "She hasn't told him she's a professional yet. She told the butler she'd prefer a four-minute egg and had him take the opals back to the kitchen."

"Is she crazy?"

"Nope. She's holding out," SueBee said.

"Holding out? Holding out? For what?"

"Marriage, of course."

"Give me one long, fucking break." Angel was nearly shouting. "She's a call girl. Jourdan Garn is going to marry a call girl? In her dreams!"

"Well," SueBee drawled with a small smile. "Don't underestimate Sandrine. As a matter of fact, Angel, don't underestimate call girls. Let alone Cleo girls."

"Oh, please," Angel said, tossing her head.

"Look out!"

Angel's head snapped back to the road. She gripped the wheel and yanked it sharply to the right, narrowly missing a large dark object in the middle of the road. "What the fuck was that?" she gasped, quickly righting the wheel.

SueBee turned in the bucket seat and looked out the back window. "Awww," she said. "It was some kind of animal. A goat or something. Someone must have hit the poor thing."

"God," Angel growled. "Its guts were all over the road. Yuck. I'm gonna be sick."

"The only thing to be sick about is that the poor animal is dead."

"And we're not," Angel snapped. SueBee was getting on Angel's nerves with her goody-two-shoes attitude, her perkiness, and, worst of all, her eternal optimism. She had been like that at Wellington Close, and nothing had changed. In her heart, Angel knew her real problem with SueBee was that she was jealous. She envied SueBee. She envied her self-esteem and her relentless curiosity about life. To learn that Sandrine had phoned SueBee with such personal information and not herself hurt. Angel had known Sandrine longer than SueBee had back in New York. God. Whatever was going to happen to her due to her affiliation with Madame Cleo—her main chance, her golden opportunity—couldn't come soon enough. She hadn't been so depressed since she left New York.

SueBee's head had practically disappeared into the neck of her coat as she closed her eyes and went to sleep to the soft-rock station broadcasting from somewhere in Germany.

So Sandrine has found her billionaire, Angel thought. She would just have to speed up her own schedule for success.

The short, pink-cheeked night desk clerk at the Chesa Grischuna glanced up to see the two striking women walking toward him in similar black wet-look ski suits and pale fur jackets. Behind them the bellman was struggling with a pushcart piled six feet high with black alligator luggage with gold bindings, locks, corners, and handles.

Amid the Alpine decor, the cuckoo clocks, the red-and-white-checked curtains and beamed ceilings of the cozy lobby, the women looked extraordinarily out of place. The people who came to Klosters came for the skiing, and, whatever these women were, they weren't athletes.

The two women stepped up to the counter, and the clerk found himself enveloped in a cloud of expensive perfume. He stepped forward with his usual smile of greeting.

"Reservation for Countess de Marco," the red-haired one said in a smoky voice.

His smile froze. "Let me check, Madame," he said grandly. He pushed through the swinging door behind the counter and disappeared.

"Oh, shit," Angel muttered.

"What's the matter?" SueBee asked.

"He's going to check us out."

"How do you know that?" SueBee asked with irritation.

"Because the damn book is right there," she said, nodding at the open registry on the desk.

The clerk walked to the phone on the office desk farthest from the door and rang the managing director's cottage just up the hill in back of the hotel. "Sir, I'm sorry to disturb your dinner but you asked me to call if a Countess de Marco checked in. Well, she's here." He exaggerated the way he said "Countess de Marco" to leave no doubt that, as a sophisticated man, he knew a dubious name when he heard one. He listened for a moment, his mood decidedly changing at the response he was getting from his superior. "Yes, sir . . . yes, sir. Immediately, sir. But you asked that I . . ." He paused for further instructions. "I'll have room service send a drinks tray to the room. Right away, sir. Thank you, thank you."

He hung up the phone, red-faced. "Sheikh Zaki's guests," he said to himself, mimicking his superior's voice. "Show them every courtesy." *Goddamn towel heads and their fancy hookers,* he thought, as he walked back to the front desk. They had discovered the quiet little village two seasons ago, and while their oil money was welcome, their presence offended the people who did not approve of their behavior or share in their free spending.

Without another word, the desk clerk escorted the girls to their room. After he left them, Angel stood in the middle of the hotel room on the top floor and examined the scene. Swiss lithographs, embroidered pillows, and vases of meadow flowers nestled next to table lamps with ruffled shades. The floral linen wallpaper matched the curtains at the leaded windows. The two beds were buried in eiderdown duvets that looked like three feet of snow. "Jesus, it looks like the Trapp Family Singers threw up," she said with disgust.

SueBee let out a whoop and flopped flat on her back into the deep fluff of one of the beds, nearly disappearing from sight. "*The hills are alive with the sound of mucus,*" she sang at the top of her lungs.

"God!" Angel said. "Can you believe this!"

"I think it's kind of sweet," SueBee said from deep inside the cloud of eiderdown.

"All this place lacks is a goose in a bonnet," Angel said, throwing herself into the feathery softness of the other bed as she began to laugh. They were both laughing so loud that they didn't hear the phone until the fourth ring.

Angel frantically waved her hand at SueBee. "Quiet!" she commanded, reaching for the bedside phone, knocking over a beribboned basket of infinitesimally tiny pink roses. She dropped her voice and said, "Yeeeesss," drawing out the word until it fairly dripped with promise. Quickly, her voice tightened. "Yes, yes, she is. Just a moment, please." Without a word she handed the receiver to SueBee.

With a look of bewilderment, SueBee reached for it, soundlessly mouthing, "For me?"

"Hello?" SueBee said. There was a long pause as she listened. She jumped to her feet. "I don't believe this! Oh, my goodness."

"Who is it?" Angel hissed.

"Zaki!" She put her hand over the phone and said excitedly to Angel, "It's Zaki!" She turned back to the phone. "Zaki. Why are you laughing? You silly," she said, giggling and close to happy tears. "Where are you? I think I'm going to faint. I'm so excited. Oh . . . wonderful," SueBee finally said. "We'll see you at eight, then. I can't wait." SueBee replaced the phone. Her hands flew to her face as she made a little squealing sound.

"I'm impressed," Angel said with flat sarcasm. "In town five minutes and already she knows someone."

"I'm flabbergasted," SueBee said as she sat down with a sigh.

"That was your old boss, Sheikh Omar Zaki! The constipated Arab from the Waldorf Towers? How the hell did he know you were here?"

"I guess the desk phoned him. He's our client this evening, Angel," SueBee said blithely as she walked toward the bathroom with her makeup case in hand.

"I see them," Angel said under her breath as they entered the hotel restaurant. "The two guys at the back with the shades. I'll bet you anything."

"That's Zaki all right," SueBee said, peering over Angel's shoulder. "I wonder who his friend is."

"Oh, great. Greaseball City," Angel groaned, rolling her eyes.

"Now be nice, Angel. Zaki was very kind to me."

"Then you can screw them both," Angel snapped.

"Suit yourself," SueBee said airily. She lifted her chin and sailed past Angel straight toward the two men in Armani suits seated at a banquette against the far wall.

The two men stood as the women approached their table. Sheikh Zaki held his linen napkin against his ample stomach with both hands. He wore a huge gold crest ring on his right pinkie and the beatific expression one might have when greeting an angel.

"My darling girl," he said as SueBee approached the table with an outstretched hand. He lifted it and brushed his lips across the back of her hand.

"Sheikh Zaki," she said, being deferential to the stranger with him. "May I present my friend, Angel de Marco."

Zaki released SueBee's hand and shook Angel's. "Countess," he said, exhaling in a low, respectful voice. "May I present Prince Ali Ben Dadi." He gestured toward the man standing beside him. The prince was at least two decades younger and three shades darker than Zaki, with skin the color of the sugared walnuts Angel remembered her mother making for the sweet on the seder plate. His eyes were completely invisible behind his opaque glasses. His smile revealed very straight, blazing white teeth. Angel liked that. She had a thing about a guy's teeth; even if she never kissed him, the teeth were important. Princey's kinda cute, she thought, straightening her back to her bust's advantage.

As the group went about taking seats and arranging themselves, Angel glanced at SueBee's sheikh, taking in the broken capillaries in his not inconsiderable nose, the slight tremor in his hands. She tried to picture SueBee in her little nurse's uniform spooning soup into his mouth with one hand and jerking him off with the other, until she had to swallow the laughter welling up in her throat.

"You have a beautiful smile, Countess," the prince said, moving his arm across the back of the banquette. She could almost feel the weight of it against her shoulders. Across the table, Zaki was leaning forward, holding SueBee's hands, whispering something into her hair.

"Why, *thank* you, Prince," she said sweetly.

"You don't have to call me 'Prince,'" he said with a sheepish chuckle. "Zaki does that to be clever. Call me Al."

Angel turned to face him and lowered her eyelids. "Al," she said slowly. "Oh . . . kay, Al. What do you do, Al?"

"I'm Sheikh Zaki's driver."

Angel did little to hide the insincerity of her smile. "Driver," she repeated drily.

"Yes," he said with a smile, looking up as a waiter appeared, unbidden, with a silver champagne bucket. He placed it on the table and set about distributing fresh glasses.

After the waiter had poured the wine, Sheikh Zaki snapped his napkin back into his lap and raised his glass. "To beautiful girls," he said, grinning first at SueBee, then turning toward Angel.

Angel smiled down into her champagne and fumed as she planned how she was going to maneuver the evening. Zaki had millions. Zaki had given SueBee two matching Arabian horses he still paid to keep stabled in New York. SueBee's Zaki stories had relieved many a boring night at Wellington Close.

The chauffeur wouldn't do. She wanted Zaki. She smiled sweetly and began to plot just how she was going to get him. She only needed to get her hands on him for an hour and give him the ring-ding-do of his life. By the time she was through with him he would knee-walk to the moon to get some more from her. If Zaki could take care of SueBee all that time for a few hand jobs and spoonfeeding, the least she would get out of him would be enough to set herself up in business with some of his fancy friends as clients. She pushed away the distracting thought of how delicious it would be to steal one of Madame Cleo's longtime clients. There would be time enough to gloat.

The waiter returned with menus the size and heft of a bed tray and fanned them out around the table. Angel peered over the top of hers and, in disgust, watched the gooey, lick-face reunion going on across the table between SueBee and the smitten old Saudi.

It wasn't until she glanced down the columns of offerings on the vast menu and her eyes came to rest on the listing for stuffed figs that a tiny portion of SueBee's revealed history sprang to mind and made her smile.

Throughout dinner the conversation consisted primarily of SueBee and Zaki's reminiscences of their days in New York. In elementary Cleo-girl fashion, SueBee let Zaki do most of the talking. Angel had to give her credit. Never having seen her friend in action, she had to admire the skill SueBee had acquired. She asked only questions that would elicit sparkling, self-serving answers. She pretended to have forgotten some event in which Zaki was the star and asked him to recount the incident in detail to refresh her memory of their golden days at the Waldorf. Angel knew all too well that SueBee forgot *nothing*.

From time to time Zaki's hand disappeared beneath the table. SueBee would giggle prettily and offer no resistance.

When coffee and brandy were served, Angel turned and concentrated all her charms—which, driven by her private scheme, were considerable—on a delighted if not bewildered Al the Driver. She leveled her dark, perfectly made-up eyes at him and said softly, "Tell me about yourself."

As it neared midnight, both men became openly anxious to leave. Zaki suggested stopping at a disco to check out who was in town. Al, having no choice, agreed with his employer.

The two women excused themselves to go to the ladies' room. As soon as she shut the door behind them, Angel plopped down on a little tufted chair in front of the vanity and buried her head in her hands. "Oh, SueBee. I could just die," she said with a convincing catch in her throat. "What am I going to do?"

SueBee stopped back-combing her hair in front of the mirror. She turned with alarm and stared at Angel. "Honey, whatever is the matter?"

"This Prince Ali . . . he . . . he . . . oh God." She broke off, unable to go on.

SueBee knelt on the tile in front of Angel and pulled her hands away from her face. "Angel?"

"He's got a problem and I just can't do it. I just can't," Angel said, shaking her head, her hair tumbling forward into her eyes.

"For heaven's sake. What can't you do? Is he some kind of sicko?"

Angel paused for effect. "No, not a sicko," she said. "Just sick. Oh, SueBee, it's so sad. That's what we were talking about all evening while you were schmoozing up Zaki."

"I was wondering what that was all about," SueBee said. "I thought you two were getting along famously."

"We were, until he told me what happened to him. See, he was in some kind of Arab-Israeli conflict and was wounded. God. He described it in detail. It took him months and months to get better. In the meantime his wife was killed in a wreck with his children. I don't know, just terrible things. His mother died before he could get out of the hospital to bury her." Angel could tell her tale was having the desired effect on SueBee, as she watched her face grow longer and longer. She took a deep breath and went for it. "Anyway, he has this kind of stomach wound where he can't get an erection unless someone . . ."

"Yeah? Unless someone what?"

"SueBee, I know you can do it," Angel pleaded. She made a face, then shivered with disgust. "You told me you could do it. You told me you did it for Zaki."

"Angel . . . I . . . Oh, for goodness sake. Are you talking about an enema? Is that what all this is about?" SueBee asked calmly, as though Angel was telling her the guy wanted his balls tickled with a feather duster or his back scratched.

"SueBee, I'll die. I just can't. Help me, please. I'll give you every penny I'd make from this job. Please."

SueBee reached out and smoothed Angel's hair out of her face. "Don't you worry, sugar. This is nothing to get hysterical about. I'll explain things to Zaki. You'll like him. He's cute—and quick," she said with a wink.

"Oh, please don't tell Zaki what I told you," Angel said, alarmed. "Tell him I'm hot for him or something."

"Okay," SueBee said with a little nod. "That would be better. He'll like that. Now, let's get going. I've got to get to know the prince a little bit to make him feel comfortable."

Martin was poring over the caterer's suggestions for Madame's dinner party when he heard the clatter of a dropped tea cup and heard Madame shriek, "She what?" through the closed office door.

At his desk in the foyer just outside her office, Martin threw down his pen and muttered, "*Merde* on a stick. What is it now?" He listened for a moment longer to determine whether or not he should go in. Madame had been on the phone for the last half hour getting the report from Zaki, who had returned from his mission in Klosters. Clearly, Madame didn't like what she was hearing.

Life at the mansion had been unusually tense in the last few days. Sandrine had disappeared with a man she met at a function in London who Jeremy Wilks *said* was American billionaire Jourdan Garn. From the beginning, Sandrine had been one of Madame's best girls. In the past year she had worked harder, taken more assignments, and made more money than any of the others. This recent behavior was not like her, and worrisome. Madame most definitely planned on sending Sandrine to La Fantastique and the thought that she might leave before then had made her irritable and out of sorts. Now, it seemed, there was to be a showdown with Angel.

"Martin! Come in here!" Madame called without benefit of the intercom, something she did only when highly agitated. He rushed around his desk and opened her door.

She was still on the phone, moving one arm at Martin in a circular motion, beckoning him to come in and sit down.

"I see. I see," she said, making furious notes on a lined pad. Crumpled tea-soaked tissues were strewn around her desk. Martin stepped forward and began to pick up the mess, but she waved him away. "Unconscionable," she snapped. "I will take care of this immediately. Thank you, Zaki. Thank you very, very much. I can't tell you how important this is for me to know. Now, can I have Martin put Justine on the next plane to Zurich? She's yours for as long as you like. No fee. May I send someone for your driver? I have an exquisite Vietnamese girl. Simply exquisite."

She paused for a moment listening, then nodded and slammed down the phone so hard Martin jumped for the second time.

"Outrageous!" she said, raking her hair away from her face with both hands.

"As outrageous as the time that former Bunny we hired shot up the Fellini gazebo at Cannes?" Martin asked. In attempting to make light of the situation, he was underestimating both the seriousness of the situation and the level of Madame's fury.

"I was right," she said between clenched teeth. "She's trying to stab me in the back. I knew I should never have taken that Angel on."

Martin realized something more serious had happened, and was secretly glad Angel was in trouble. He had never trusted her. There had been a few girls like Angel in the past. Girls who signed on just to learn the ropes and then tried to steal Madame's business. It had never worked before. He was sure it wouldn't work for Angel either.

"She made a run at Zaki, right?" he asked.

Madame threw up her hands. "A run?" she wailed. "How do the Americans say, 'a body tackle'? She asked him for money to set up her business. She told him she could get my best girls to come with her, including SueBee and Sandrine. Everything would be free for him. She was smart enough to know that any mention of SueBee would get him interested."

"Good Lord," Martin breathed, amazed at the sheer chutzpah of Angel's move. "Zaki must have been torn," he said, only half kidding.

Madame was in no mood for jokes. She suddenly looked very sad and old. "She could do it, Martin. She could take me over with someone like Zaki behind her. She could buy out Lili or someone else on the Continent. After all, she did run one of the best out-call services in the States."

"No one could ever compete with you, Madame."

"Don't be so sure," she said, sounding more weary than angry now.

"What are you going to do?" Martin asked, lifting a cigarette out of an exquisite Fabergé case, tapping it, lighting it, and blowing out a long stream of smoke.

"Give me one of those," she said.

When he did, she studied it for a moment. "What *are* these?" she asked with a frown.

"Scarborough Ovals. They're English. Custom-made."

She wrinkled her nose and lit it. "I think we should wait until after the dinner at the end of the month. We're going to have to let her think she's going to La Fantastique. That way we can stall her from making a run at the others." She mashed out Martin's cigarette in the large crystal ashtray on the desk. "*Mon Dieu*, this tastes like horse manure."

Martin shrugged and stared at the floor, pouting. As much as he distrusted Angel, he thought it was mean to let her think she had been chosen for La Fantastique. There was an enormous fee involved for the girls who went, and knowing Angel, she would spend it before she found out she wasn't going.

"Did you have something you wanted to say, Martin?" Madame Cleo asked.

"No, not really," he said, still staring at the floor.

"Martin?" she said menacingly.

"Well, it's just that this weekend thing of the baron's always makes me nervous."

"Nervous? Why, for pity's sake? Do you realize the size of our commission?"

"That's not it. It's just that he always uses one or two of the girls for some scheme he's hatching. I'm particularly fond of SueBee and Sandrine. They don't deserve it. They should be able to go and have fun and be with anyone they like."

Madame waved her hand, "Don't worry about it, darling. It's not like the old days when he interviewed the girls afterward and picked their brains. He's gotten far more subtle in his advancing years."

Subtle, sure, Martin thought. Just last year the baron set up a member of the British parliament he was trying to get for some reason or another. Later, during the guy's divorce case, the poor girl was subpoenaed. Her picture was in all the tabloids. "You've forgotten Cynthia already," he said. "The last thing I heard she was a hostess at a House of Pancakes in the States."

"Yes, well, that was unfortunate," Madame said briskly. "Particularly for us. She was one of our top girls."

"Well? So are Sandrine and SueBee. Maybe he's got some bit of business for them, too."

"Not to worry, darling," she said, lighting a cigarillo. "SueBee's already assigned to be with my friend Billy Mosby. He's done a lot of favors for the baron."

"And Sandrine?"

Madame flipped open her ledger and ran her finger down the page. "Not a problem there either," she said, reading some notes. "The baron has invited some American journalist he's going to ask to do a favorable interview sometime soon. Probably when he's in trouble again. A fellow named Shea, let's see, yes, Peter Shea of WorldWide." She closed the ledger and sat back in her chair, a smile of contentment on her face.

"What are you smiling at?" Martin asked, pushing out of his chair.

"I was just thinking what a waste. A beautiful girl like Sandrine with an ordinary journalist who could never in his life afford her, poor devil."

"Poor? Why?"

"Because he'll never forget her."

CHAPTER
❧ 12 ❧

Peter's Journal Entry—Paris, July 13, 1990

So there it was. My fantasy, the woman I could never forget, was a girl who could have an orgasm on cue. Madeleine was, of course, Sandrine Mandraki Garn. I was numb at first. Sitting in Madame's back garden, listening to the next installment of "Who Tried to Kill Madame Cleo" turn into "The Rise and Fall of Peter Shea." I felt an odd, smothering sensation. It was as though the noose that had been lightly looped around my neck since this project began had been given a sharp, painful jerk.

Madame relayed the story of Sandrine's mission to La Fantastique as though she were talking only to a tape recorder and there was not a flesh-and-blood person involved. I was so stunned—frozen in my seat—that she stopped speaking and raised her eyebrows as if to ask if we were through for the day.

She had been mimicking Martin's English accent during his part of the story and was so absorbed she asked, "Is there something wrong?" in the same accent.

"Did you know I lost my job because of that weekend?" I asked when I finally got my breath. I could feel the anger welling up in my chest and fought it desperately.

"I didn't know that," she said as though I had asked her if she knew there was a housefly on her sleeve.

"You've known I was the one with Madeleine—excuse me, Sandrine—all along."

"Yes," she answered evenly.

I waited for her to say more, frantic for her to explain why she had been misleading me all this time.

She said nothing. Just stared at me with those wolf's eyes as if to say, "So who's the fool, you dumb ox? This is my party, not yours. Read your contract."

I stood up. I guess I was rude but I knew if I stayed another moment I would reach over and strangle her. It would not have been hard. I would only have to yank the long strand of pearls she was wearing upward, twist it, and pull. She would have been dead in seconds and I would have been in jail for life.

I walked out without another word for no other reason than to save my life.

Now that I'm back here in these tiny rooms (thank God there's a breeze tonight) I'm thinking a little more clearly and I'm going to confess to you, my green-screened friend, and this is harder for me to admit than the fact that I sold myself for a million bucks: I see now that the woman has been deliberately stalling me since the beginning of this rat-fuck. The "why" of it will drive me mad.

Fiddle, Fiddle, where are you when I need you? I need you here so I can tell you how right you were when you told me not to trust anyone. I was ready not to trust this whoremonger. And I didn't for—okay—a day or two. But she was so open, so honest—oh, shit.

In all my years as a journalist, I have taken pride in keeping myself out of a story, observing the iron rule: Never get involved.

Well, I'm involved. Right up to the butt Wendy says the whole world isn't wired to.

I quit in the middle of the paragraph above last night because I couldn't go on. I had to get out and walk. If I had stayed here I would not have been able to keep myself from calling Wendy, Fiddle, Billy Mosby, Dawson Segura and the putz lawyers, anybody and everybody concerned with this project. By then I would have been drunk and would have called a buddy at the New York Times and dictated a story that would have blown this thing sky-high. Wendy isn't the only person who can leak in this nest of thieves. But on my walk something happened—nothing dramatic or soul shattering. It wasn't like I was Saul on the road to Damascus. Still, it was an epiphany. And like most epiphanies among the cynical and world-weary, it came from a simple source—my shoes.

My walk took me, of course, to territory I knew. I found myself in front of the little hotel where I did my serious drinking in my other life. The one where Ava Gardner supposedly dallied with Sinatra.

The place was empty and the bartender wasn't Ronnie. Otherwise it hadn't changed. As I sat at the end of the bar sipping my scotch and wondering what to do, I looked down at my shoes. They were Italian loafers, as soft as butter and so beautifully made they can be folded in half and slipped into a suede envelope. I had purchased them the first week I returned to Paris. I have never owned shoes like that, probably because they cost six hundred dollars. The shirt I was wearing was linen, as weightless as a handkerchief and so light I could barely feel it on my skin. The monogram was so small and unobtrusive that for the first three times I wore it I kept brushing the front thinking the little PS was a piece of lint. My slacks and jacket were from Armani, of a cut and fabric so fine they never have to be pressed.

But it was the shoes that did it. I wanted to live the rest of my life wearing shoes like those loafers.

I came to the conclusion that Madame Cleo had brought me up to this part of the story because she figured I wouldn't be able to resist hearing the rest of it and in order to do that I would have to continue with the interviews.

Well, she may have a plan. But now, thanks to the fear of losing my shoes, so do I.

I'm going back there Monday and I'll act as though absolutely nothing has happened. I'll tell her I left so abruptly because I had a headache. Women do that, so can I. At least now I know what I'm dealing with, and I'm determined to win.

To everyone's relief, Sandrine reappeared, explaining that she had met a man, not a Cleo client, with whom she'd wanted to spend some time. Cleo accepted her explanation without comment. Sandrine took her compliant attitude to mean that Cleo considered her too valuable to scold or punish. Why else would she have been asked to go to La Fantastique?

Something about Sandrine had changed since she had been out of touch. If possible, she was even more beautiful. There was a serenity about her, a calmness that Madame and Martin remarked on and read as the dreamy distraction of a woman in love. Only Sandrine knew the truth. And SueBee.

Sandrine wasn't in love. She was winning.

For seven days and nights she had played a cat-and-mouse game with Jourdan Garn, running to see him, pulling away. Making herself unavailable, then reappearing more erotic and absorbed in his every word than ever. She knew, even if Jourdan had not told her several times, that he had never in his life met anyone like her. She told him little about herself, preferring to remain mysterious. Then, the last night they were together in London, she told him about Madame Cleo, that she had been a call girl both in New York and now in Europe, and that it was time for her to go back to work. She had jobs in Rome and Spain for the upcoming week and had to get back.

Stunned, he tried to pay her. She refused the money as firmly and sweetly as she had refused his expensive gifts, saying that she was with him because she wanted to be, not because she was being paid.

His mood seemed to change then, and he seemed his former self. That night she took him to bed one more time in the glistening white mansion in Belgravia, making love to him time and time again until he lay spent and euphoric.

The next morning he watched her dress, too weak and bewildered to protest her leaving. Gazing up at her with pleading eyes from the rumpled sheets, he asked how he would find her.

"I'll find you, darling," she had said. Those had been her last words. She knew the effect they would have. In every relationship she had ever had with a man, she knew who was in control. That is what produced the look she carried back to Paris, the eyes that glowed with confidence, the skin and hair that shone as though polished with some secret elixir. Sandrine had manufactured the elixir of control. She knew that sooner or later Jourdan Garn would be hers.

She then returned to her apartment in the little building where Sandrine, SueBee, and Angel lived on the same floor. It had once been a hotel. The small suites had been converted to apartments with a whisper of a kitchen tucked into a corner, big enough to chill champagne or boil tea water. There was a working fireplace and enough closets to accommodate extensive wardrobes.

The girls were looked after by an ancient concierge named Madame Solange, who fussed over them like a mother hen.

As usual, when one of the girls returned from a trip, Madame Solange came to the room to help unpack. She was with Sandrine when SueBee phoned to tell her she would be one of the girls going to La Fantastique.

Sandrine shrieked with delight. "Me, too! I just heard this morning. Come on over, we'll celebrate.

"I'm in the kitchen," Sandrine called, as she heard Madame Solange let SueBee in on her way out.

"Hi, precious," SueBee called.

Sandrine poked her head around the kitchen door. "Hi, yourself. Wanna drink?"

SueBee plopped down on the love seat next to the fireplace. "No thanks," she answered. "I missed you."

Sandrine stepped out of the kitchen carrying a very dark drink. She was wearing a bathrobe and her hair was still damp from her bath.

Sandrine sat down next to SueBee and took a long pull on her drink. "I'm so excited we're both going to the baron's."

"Me, too. But I'm a little surprised you're going," SueBee said.

"Why shouldn't I?" Sandrine asked, baffled.

"I thought you might want to be with him."

"Which him?" Sandrine said, playing dumb as she leaned her chin on her shoulder and fluttered her eyelashes.

"Come on, Sandy. There are some really important men at that thing. What if someone Jourdan Garn knows tells him you were there? Aren't you scared he's gonna find out?"

"That's okay," she said calmly. "He already knows about me."

"He does?" SueBee said breathlessly. "You told him?"

"Yup," she said, smiling mischievously.

"What did he say?"

"At first he was floored, then, I think, it turned him on. The night I told him he was puffed up like he'd just won the lottery."

"Wow," SueBee breathed. "You know, I've been out with men like that. It's like, 'I've got her and you don't.' But you better be careful, hon. Remember Anna Lisa? The one who married that rich Swede? Well, he loved it at first, then he started to get jealous and threw her out."

"Ummm," Sandrine said, sipping her drink. "That isn't going to happen here."

"How can you be sure?"

"Jourdan Garn is no dumb Swede. He's a rich, powerful man. You should never try to please the rich. Everyone does that. You've got to be a bit of trouble, a bit of a problem. My life excites him. He knows I'll never bore him and he wants that more than anything his money could buy him." Sandrine rattled the ice in her empty glass and walked toward the kitchen. "Come, I'll fix you a cup of tea. You going out?"

"Later," SueBee said. "Diana has the flu so I told Martin I'd do it. Dinner, that's all. Some corporate type."

While Sandrine waited for the pot to boil she took a swig of scotch directly from the bottle before pouring herself another tall, dark drink.

"Lordy, this is nice," SueBee said, curling her knees up into the cushions. "It's almost like being back on East Fifty-fifth Street, isn't it?"

"Ah, the bad old days."

"Not so bad. We had some giggles. Only Jack Ayler and being broke were the bad parts."

"SueBee," Sandrine said pensively, returning to her spot on the couch with SueBee's tea and her drink on a tray, "things are about to get better than we ever imagined."

"I know. I've heard such stories about La Fantastique. Martin says the most important men in the world show up."

"Sweetheart, I'm not talking about La Fantastique. I'm talking about a permanent job as Mrs. Jourdan Garn."

SueBee stared at Sandrine, her mouth hanging open. "He asked?" she gulped.

Sandrine held up her hand. "Not yet . . . not yet. Soon."

Sandrine settled back and began to tell SueBee what had happened in the last few days to convince her that Jourdan Garn was about to give in.

As Sandrine had moved from client to client in Italy and Spain that week, everywhere she went, at every hotel, at each airport, there was a message, flowers, small, expensive gifts from Jourdan Garn. She ignored the messages and sent the jewelry back.

One afternoon, as she was stepping out of a dress shop in Málaga, she saw a dark man in a leather windbreaker and Porsche sunglasses leaning against the wall of a shop across the street. She recognized him as the man she had glimpsed in her lobby in Rome the day before. Before that she had seen him at the Barcelona airport, and earlier on the night she was with Garn at Simpson's in London. He had been sitting a few tables away, pretending not to see them.

Only partially angry, she decided she had had enough. She shifted the handles of her shopping bags to her shoulder in case she had to chase him, and marched directy toward him. He made no attempt to run. She stopped only inches from his nose and said, "Tell Jourdan thank you for the goodies but if he wants to know what I'm doing he should come see for himself." She lowered her eyes toward the man's crotch. "And tell him to stop sending a boy to do a man's work."

The man, whose face until then had been utterly impassive, broke into a smile. "Okay, I'll tell him," he said, then turned and walked down the street.

The next night, her jobs completed, she boarded a flight back to Paris. As she emerged from the walkway into the terminal at Charles de Gaulle, she saw Jourdan Garn wearing a camel's-hair coat and a gray homburg. His hands were shoved into the pockets of his coat. His face was very pale.

SueBee's hand flew to her mouth. "Oh . . . my . . . God," she whispered. "Could you just have died?"

"Wait, wait," Sandrine said excitedly. "So he grabbed my wrist. I thought he was going to make a scene right there. He asked me why I kept returning his stuff, and I told him I don't take jewelry from men I don't belong to. Then he started in about how my seeing other men was driving him crazy. I very sweetly told him that was my job. Then I acted real hurt that he would have me followed. I must say I was very good."

"How did he know exactly where you were going to be?"

"I'm sure he called Madame Cleo."

"She would tell him where you were?"

"Of course. He's rich, isn't he? She loves having rich men go crazy after one of her girls."

"Sandrine, you devil. The poor man."

"Poor man, my eye! He's married, you know."

"So? Men get unmarried all the time, at least in that league. It never makes any difference to a real fortune hunter."

"I know," Sandrine said, frowning.

"So go on, go on," SueBee urged.

"He said his divorce was about to be final. Believe that and I'll sell you a bridge. Anyway, I didn't bat an eye. I think that really steamed him. Jourdan Garn is not a man one puts on hold."

SueBee put down her tea cup. "Golly, Sandy. What did you want the poor man to do? You want him, don't you?"

"Of course I want him, but I want him to ask me to marry him. I want things definite and public. *Saying* he's getting a divorce, *saying* he can't stand to see me with other men is software. I want hardware. All I need is one good violent shove to get him to come around."

"But Sandy," SueBee said, pleading Garn's case. "The man's had you followed. He came to Paris to meet you. Obviously, he's mad for you."

"'Mad' doesn't cut it."

"What about a stick of dynamite?" SueBee said, giggling.

Sandrine stood and headed for the kitchen again. "And that I've got," she said over her shoulder.

"What?" SueBee asked.

"La Fantastique."

Martin, resplendent in white tie, wing collar, and a red ceremonial sash that signified nothing except that it looked elegant, watched them from his perch at the top of the wide staircase.

Below him, Madame Cleo's satin army was assembling. The central hall of the mansion on the Ile de la Cité was aswirl with women more beautifully, and competitively, dressed than at any event to which men would have been invited. The old house, usually shrouded and still, now blazed with light and echoed with laughter and the squeal of happy reunions.

Martin could not help but dwell for a moment on the tiny crisis that must have existed when hundreds of anxious men, wherever they might be that night, learned that a Madame Cleo girl would not be available—at least until after midnight.

The annual event was a sight that never ceased to amaze him. Once a year, the girls of Madame Cleo gathered to preen, gossip, check each other out, compare notes, and participate in the politics of their profession at its highest level.

The dinner was a command performance for the girls currently working, and a sentimental reunion for those in a position, in their new lives, to attend.

Martin often fantasized about what it would be like if all former call girls could convene like doctors or lawyers or farm-equipment salesmen. If so, the scene below him would include famous faces from film and television, society women, and the wives of power brokers the world over. There was a recognizable face or two in the room, however. A nightclub singer from the fifties always came. Tonight she was wearing red sequins and a feathered hat. Felicity, the owner of a string of discos from L.A. to Marrakech, was also back. She was one of the few who used her former affiliation with Madame Cleo as publicity for her business.

Martin smiled down at them as they made their way up the broad staircase toward the ballroom, amused at the irony of who wasn't there as much as who was.

On this particular evening, Martin was considered hired help, of no more significance than the waiters or bartenders. Few were aware that it was he who supervised the decoration of the second-floor ballroom.

He had filled it with a forest of trees sprayed silver, and hung with thousands of tiny twinkling lights. The pillars that circled the room and the high windows were draped and swagged with miles of transparent tulle and gold satin streamers. Tables set amidst the silver forest were lit by silver candelabras and set with vermeil bowls of heavy white roses.

He had dressed the waiters as Nubian slaves. They wore white-and-gold harem pants and were naked from the waist up, their chests gleaming with oil and their turbaned heads adorned with jewels and feathers.

Martin had selected the buffet as well. A horseshoe-shaped table between the gauze-draped windows was laden with crystal bowls of cracked crab, giant shrimp, and eight-pound tins of pearl-gray beluga. Chilled champagne and iced Russian vodka stood in tall silver buckets on each of the bars. Later, after Madame's brief greeting, pasta with truffles and cold lobster would be served. By far the most popular feature of these dinners was a separate buffet table set a little off to one side for those girls who spent more time in three-star restaurants than in bed. With the help of an American chef who worked in a tourist trap near the Pompidou Center, it offered Texas chili, double cheeseburgers, potato salad, macaroni and Velveeta, and—ambrosia of the gods for those who subsisted on braised endive and unborn carrots—an enormous tuna-noodle casserole with canned fried-onion topping. Not a few paper-thin beauties would gorge themselves into oblivion before the night was over.

A second table on the opposite wall held frosted pastries, petits four, tureens of chocolate sauce—hot and cold—for the cakes, ices, and mousses, plus wild strawberries in champagne.

Trays and trays of sweets were to be passed around with coffee after dinner. He had long known that women in groups had no compunction about gorging themselves on desserts. It was only when they were with men that they pretended not to indulge.

As the women passed him at the top of the stairs, most of them nodded a greeting or blew a kiss. There were some who ignored him or averted their eyes, still remembering some dispute or slight of scheduling he had long forgotten.

Each was more beautifully dressed than the next. Most wore long dinner dresses, some haute-couture cocktail dresses or suits. A majority wore hats, fanciful little arrangements with veils or adorned with jewels. He assumed they wore them out of respect for Madame's somewhat old-fashioned insistence that it was something ladies just did.

Two hundred and four women had been invited. Two hundred and two were in attendance. Carlotta's drug problem prevented her from leaving the sanatorium in Berlin, and a botched face-lift kept Yvette in Palm Springs.

The glitter of jewelry—some owned, some borrowed, all decidedly real—caught in the light of the wall sconces that rose along the curve of the staircase wall. To appear at Madame Cleo's, where every eye became a jeweler's loupe, in anything faux would have been unthinkable.

By seven the ballroom had filled. Martin stepped to the nearest bar and helped himself to a flute of champagne. The decibel level in the room was rising steadily. There was something about women in large groups that animated them to produce a unique sound not particularly pleasant to the ear. The high-pitched chatter of voices speaking in German, French, English, Italian, and Spanish soon nearly overwhelmed him, reaching a spot in his middle ear that caused physical pain. The essences of thousands of dollars of perfume that wafted about his head compounded his discomfort, and he stepped to an open window to gulp the cool evening air and survey what he had produced.

Madame was scheduled to appear at eight to speak to her guests. She liked to stand on a slightly raised platform in front of the fireplace, say a few words of greeting, and have the waiters distribute a bauble to each of her guests.

This year Martin had purchased a jeweler's lot of vermeil brooches in the shape of a cat with a jeweled eye. After dinner, the special-assignment women who had been selected to attend La Fantastique would receive the additional lagniappe custom-made by the baron. This year they were gold Cartier lighters adorned with the baron's crest.

Madame was particularly fond of the baron's annual gesture, as it provided a guessing game for her guests as to who had been chosen not only to attend but to carry out some specific intrigue.

"Amazing," said a voice behind him. "There isn't a fishnet stocking in the room."

He turned to see Angel surveying the scene. She was wearing a long black silk de la Renta with an exaggerated ruffled collar that displayed her spectacular cleavage. "This is far grander than last year, Martin, old bean," she said, obviously in a fine mood. "You've outdone yourself."

"Thank you, Angel," he said, perhaps a bit too enthusiastically, trying to cover his nervousness. He had hoped to avoid her for as long as possible. Madame had scheduled the unpleasantness concerning Angel for after dinner.

"Have you seen Sandrine and SueBee?" Angel asked, scanning the room.

"Over there." Martin nodded toward the bar on the far side of the room.

The two were standing together chatting and laughing with Delia and Dalia, German twins in strapless black velvet Scaasis. The twins talked, laughed, ate, slept, and worked together.

"Argh," Angel groaned. "They're listening to the stereo Germans. I'll wait. I want to talk to them about what we should take to La Fantastique, and the Germans aren't going. Right?"

"Right," Martin said tightly. He didn't want to be pulled into a conversation about La Fantastique, knowing that Angel was not aware that she wouldn't be going either.

He looked back over to where the two girls were standing. SueBee was wearing black satin; Sandrine, vanilla chiffon. Once again he marveled at how fabulous Sandrine was looking since she returned from her "leave" with Jourdan Garn.

For the time being, Madame was encouraging his interest in Sandrine. If, in the unlikely event that a man like Jourdan Garn actually wanted to take Sandrine out of the business, there was always either a direct cash buyout or the purchase of Sandrine's records. Not a few Cleo girls had been able to erase their pasts at a price.

Suddenly, the chattering subsided. All heads turned toward the door as Madame made her entrance. Only at that moment did Martin realize that a majority of women in the room seldom saw her on a day-to-day basis. She was an invisible power in their lives, as their dealings were mainly with him and by phone. If a girl was working well and behaving herself, there was no reason to meet with Madame face to face. To most she was an enigma; to many, an idol. To some, a mortal enemy. There was not a life in the room that had not been irrevocably altered by the tiny woman making her way through the applauding crowd.

She had outdone herself for the evening, wearing color for once, a nice departure from her constant beiges and grays. Her long velvet Yves Saint Laurent dinner suit was a cobalt blue, with black fox at the neck and cuffs of the jacket. She wore, of course, her signature long double strand of pearls around a diamond choker. She was followed by one of the most attractive Nubians, who carried a jeweled minaudière that, most assuredly, held her smoking accoutrements and, perhaps, for later, her jeweled worry beads.

As she stepped onto the little platform before the fireplace, the hush in the room fell to total silence. Even the bartenders and waiters were still.

"Good evening, my pretties," she said sweetly in English. "Everyone looks extraordinary tonight. No?"

A ripple of laughter, then applause filled the room as each woman turned to look at those standing nearby with smiles of approval.

"This evening," Madame continued, "for those of you who count, and I do—I count money, days, blessings—this evening marks the thirty-fifth year I have been in business. Twenty of those years right here in this beautiful house. I have each and every one of you to thank for my good fortune and I hope I have been able to repay all of you in kind. Please enjoy yourselves, and after dinner, if you can tear yourselves away from what will surely be the most delicious gossip in any room in Paris, I'd like to greet each of you personally at my table. Now, please, relax, have some more of our marvelous champagne, and one of our charming 'slaves' will distribute a token of my esteem and gratitude." She turned and smiled coquettishly as another Nubian stepped to the side of the platform holding a silver tray heaped with small blue velvet boxes.

A collective sigh floated up from the crowd. As she nodded and smiled to another round of applause, Madame caught Martin's eye and made an infinitesimal gesture with her head, leaning it to one side.

He pushed his way through the crowd and made his way to her side. As he approached, the Nubian with the handbag fell back a pace.

"Bring Angel downstairs, would you please?" Madame whispered.

"Now? Before dinner?" he asked, surprised that she had changed her plans.

"This is too pleasant an evening to have it hanging over me. I want to get it over with."

Martin nodded and turned to scan the room for Angel. He found her at the far side of the ballroom standing in a circle that included SueBee and Sandrine. The German twins had disappeared. Someone in the circle had just said something hilarious and the group was convulsed with laughter.

As Martin approached they all turned, still laughing. He made straight for Angel and leaned close to her ear.

"Madame wants to see you downstairs," he said softly.

"Now?" Angel said, frowning. "What for?"

"Something about La Fantastique, I think."

That seemed to relax her. She excused herself and took Martin's arm.

As they made their way down the stairs to Madame's office, Angel said nothing that would indicate that she was troubled at being summoned.

Martin pushed open the office door without knocking. Madame was seated at her desk. The only light in the room came from the crimson-shaded lamp by her elbow. In the background gloom Martin could see stacks of ledgers piled about every flat surface, the detritus left by the little gray auditors who were still poring over the books.

He held the door for Angel, who swanned past him, her chin

high, the silk of the designer gown making a slight crunching sound as she walked.

"Ah, Angel," Madame said pleasantly, and stood. "Thank you for coming down. I hope this won't take long."

"Me too," Angel said, taking the chair in front of the desk without ceremony. "What's up?" she said, crossing her legs and leaning one elbow on the front of Madame's desk.

Martin cleared his throat as a vague hint that perhaps her posture wasn't appropriate, but to no avail.

"I'll come right to the point, Angel," Madame said, sitting down. "Your services here are no longer needed."

Angel blinked and looked at Martin. "What?"

"You have betrayed my confidence in you. I appreciate that you may feel you took a step down, so to speak, when you came to work for me. I'm not unimpressed with your success as a madam in the States. Nor am I ungrateful for the girls you brought to us. However, your recent activities leave me—"

Angel's face had colored noticeably in the dim light. "Hold the fucking phone here," she snapped angrily. "You can't do this." She swiveled around to face Martin, who was perched on the arm of the tufted couch. "You little turd," she said through clenched teeth. "You said this was about La Fantastique."

Martin lifted his hands and let them fall to his sides in a gesture of helplessness.

"This *is* about La Fantastique, Angel," Madame Cleo interrupted. "You won't be going."

Angel's eyes widened in disbelief. Her mouth hung open and she ran her hand through her artfully tousled hair. "What did I do, huh?" she asked. "What did I do that a hundred other girls haven't? I ask you."

"I'm sorry, Angel," Madame said. "A hundred other girls have never betrayed my confidence as you have. Frankly, in all my years, no girl has ever approached other madams and clients to deliberately undercut me. Sheikh Zaki, for instance, tells me you asked him for a substantial loan to put yourself back in business. Further, you implied you could obtain the services of my two best girls, SueBee and Sandrine. Surely you had to know Zaki has been a friend for over thirty years."

"That greasy little shit," Angel said hotly. "I get it. You set me up so he could rat on me!"

Madame sighed and looked soulfully at Martin. "Angel here is living proof that we must rethink the syllabus at Wellington Close."

Angel shot out of her chair. "Why, you sanctimonious old whoremonger," she said, her eyes wide with rage. "Of all the pompous, phony bullcrap—"

Martin stood up and cut her off. "Hold on, Angel. There's no call for—"

"Did SueBee know about this? Was she part of your trap with Zaki?" Angel demanded at the top of her lungs.

"She did not," Madame said, steely-eyed.

"She didn't." Martin shook his head emphatically.

"And what about Sandrine? Did she fink on me?"

Martin straightened his ceremonial sash. "Neither of them had anything to do with this, Angel. Not that we owe you any explanation, but Madame doesn't need to rely on information from her girls. And for your information, Sandrine and SueBee are your best friends."

"Well, this is the biggest crock I've ever been through," Angel said, her voice beginning to soften in the realization of defeat. "I worked very hard. And, by the way, you thieves, I'm owed a bonus."

"Now look here—" Martin said, coloring.

Madame held up her hand to silence him. "That's all right, Martin. Sit down. Angel has a right to her bonus." She turned to Angel and softened her voice. "Angel, you have worked hard. Maybe a little too hard. Perhaps you didn't mean to damage me personally, but I can't permit anyone to undermine something I've worked to protect all my life."

"I didn't do a tenth of the harm the government's going to do," Angel mumbled.

"I beg your pardon," Martin said, outraged.

Angel looked across at the piles of ledgers behind Madame's desk. "I know what's been going on in here for months," she said, pointing at the ledgers with her chin. "I made it my business to find out. It looks like you're in big trouble yourself, Madame." Angel sat back and smiled.

Martin held his breath and waited for Madame to explode. To his stunned surprise she said nothing. She reached for a cigarillo, tapped it on the top of the desk, then waved a gold lighter in front of it. "I have to admire your enterprise, Angel," she said calmly. She snapped shut the lighter and leaned forward. "Here, I want you to take this as a token. You are an artful adversary, but threatening me is not worthy of you. I have survived far more threatening forces than the French government."

Martin knew it was an act. Madame was extremely concerned about what was going on in the little room by day. But she was wise to downplay it to Angel.

Angel took the lighter, studied it for a moment, then closed her hand around it. "So this is as close to La Fantastique as I'm going to get."

"Well," Madame Cleo said contemplatively, "the Baron's place is southwest of Paris. Your plane will probably fly directly over it."

"My plane? Where am I going?"

"Martin?" Madame Cleo turned and handed Martin a manila envelope. He unwound the string closing it and checked the contents, then handed it to Angel.

"Here is a one-way First-Class ticket to New York on the late flight," Martin said. "Someone will meet you and see that you make the connecting flight. We've packed your things. Your luggage is waiting in the car. There are also traveler's checks there in the sum of ten thousand dollars, the amount in your account here."

Martin continued, "A colleague of Mr. Rizzo's will meet you at your destination. You have a job. You have a reservation at a top hotel. You have our best wishes." He handed the envelope to Angel, who took it and laid it, uninspected, on her lap.

"Where am I going? If you don't mind telling me," she said defiantly.

Martin looked at Madame. Madame nodded back at him. "Las Vegas."

Angel stared straight ahead. "Shit," she said, and stood up. "So. Not only am I getting the heave-ho, you snakes are turning me over to the mob. What sweethearts you both are." She stood up, grasping the envelope. "If you don't mind I'd like to go up and say good-bye to my friends."

Madame Cleo stood. "I mind."

Angel turned. "What?"

"You're to leave now. You are not to speak to anyone. Particularly not any of the other girls," said Madame Cleo, pressing a buzzer on her desk.

"What's the matter? Afraid I'll steal them?"

"Afraid you'd try," Martin said. He walked to the door and opened it. Standing in the doorway were two of the larger oiled Nubians from upstairs sans serving trays. "Please show this lady to the car outside," he said to the men.

Angel raised her chin and turned. Without a word, she pushed by the two half-naked men and stormed toward the front door.

"Don't bother," Martin said to the two men who looked at him for instructions as to whether to follow her or not. "She'll do as she's told," he said, then added under his breath, "for a while."

Madame Solange opened the front door as SueBee was halfway up the steps. She had been shopping all day for the weekend at the baron's château and was dog-tired. Madame Cleo had given any girl going down for the weekend time to prepare. It would have been a giddy few days were it not overshadowed by the fact that Angel would not be going with them.

They had learned about it at their briefing meeting at the mansion the day after the dinner and were heartsick. They didn't truly believe Martin's assurances that Angel was only being punished and that, eventually, Madame would call her back.

SueBee shifted her packages and stepped sideways through the door.

"Mademoiselle SueBee," Madame Solange said in an urgent whisper, "there is a gentlemen in your apartment. I had orders to let him in."

SueBee frowned. She wasn't expecting anyone. "Orders?" she asked. "Whose orders? He can't be a client. They wouldn't dare send him here."

"Madame's orders," came the sheepish reply. SueBee knew that as much as she pampered and catered to the girls in the house, the concierge's first loyalty was to Madame Cleo.

"Okay, I'll go right up," SueBee said, starting toward the stairs. If for some crazy reason the man really was a client she would make short work of him. All she wanted now was to take a hot shower and get some sleep.

SueBee tried to push open the door to her rooms but it wouldn't budge. Something was in the way. Assuming Madame Solange had hung her dry cleaning on the doorknob again, she put her shoulder against it and shoved. The door opened with a scraping sound.

As she squeezed herself and her packages through the opening, something brushed against her face. She reached to push it away and saw that her living room was completely full of flowers. Potted flowers, flowers in vases, a flowering bush that was blocking the door, flowers lying around in boxes, everything tied with yards and yards of pink ribbon.

"What in the world is this?" she said aloud.

"Paris was fresh out of yellow roses," said a voice coming from the kitchen.

SueBee spun around to see a man standing with his back to the overhead light. "Jack Ayler," she gasped. "As I live and breathe." It was the only thing she could think of to say. It had been a long time since she had been alone with the man. All the memories of their times together and the pain flashed through her mind. She felt oddly numb.

"Hello, gorgeous," he said, grinning.

The sound of his voice, the look on his face, made her slightly queasy. She wondered if other women felt the way she was feeling when they were confronted by a former lover. She wondered if, like her, they asked themselves, "Whatever did I see in him?"

SueBee put her packages down on the table by the door.

"I'm a professional now, Jack," she said in as businesslike a tone as she could muster. "If you plan to stay awhile I'll have to charge you."

"SueBee, SueBee, SueBee," he said, reaching for an open bottle of scotch on the kitchen counter. "I'm here as your friend. I've been over on the Ile helping Madame with a little tax situation and I saw your name in a ledger. She was kind enough to tell the concierge to let me in. I hope you don't mind. I wanted to see you."

"Why didn't you make an appointment, Jack?" SueBee asked coolly, pushing back her damp hair. "I'm a working girl now."

"SueBee, honey, don't," Jack said. She knew that he thought the way he said it, all slowlike, was sexy. It only sounded dirty to her. "Come, have a drink with old Jack. He's missed you."

She sighed and slipped out of her heels. She hated it when men referred to themselves in the third person. The ones that did that invariably named their penises. The names they chose were always things like *Monster* or *the Snake* or *Killer*. "Jack," she said with exaggerated patience, "I have a long trip tomorrow. I have a hundred things to do. If you aren't here for business may I suggest you finish your drink and toddle along."

"Ah, yes, the baron's famous weekend," he said.

"You know about that," she said flatly, not pleased that he knew anything at all about her business.

"Why yes, Madame leaves all kinds of little notes and things around her office."

"Does she know what a snoop you are?" SueBee asked curtly.

Jack smiled. "Madame tells me you went to that ridiculous school of hers. You're really taking this business seriously, SueBee girl." He opened the fridge, retrieved a few more ice cubes, and plopped them into his drink.

While his back was turned, SueBee eyed the bottle of scotch. It was almost half empty. Apparently he had been waiting in the apartment for some time. She carefully stepped between two large terra-cotta pots of giant mums and picked a few pieces of mail off the coffee table. They were all bills and she tossed them back, wondering how rude she would have to be to get him to leave. It had been a long time since she had been able to be deliberately rude to a man, and it felt not all bad.

She folded her arms and planted her feet firmly in the center of the rug, not wanting to sit down for fear he would take it as an invitation to stay. "Is there something I can do for you, Jack?" she asked in a no-nonsense manner that she hoped would get through the scotch haze she saw developing around his eyes. "You want to use the bathroom? The phone?"

"What I want is you," he said, not moving from the kitchen doorway.

"Now you want me," SueBee said, nodding slowly. She knew they would be the last calm words she had to say to the man. She could feel the anger flooding her brain already.

"Remember how it used to be?" he said with a crooked smile. "We had a lot of fun, didn't we, SueBee?"

SueBee cleared her throat. "Sit down, Jack," she said, pointing toward the couch.

The lustful gleam in Jack's eyes flickered just a touch; he was clearly misreading her words as an invitation. He walked to the couch carrying his glass, sat down, and held out his hand. "Come, sit by me," he said.

"I'll stand, thanks," she said. "What I have to say won't take long."

"Uh-oh, the sugar bear is mad."

Now the flush of anger had reached the back of her throat. *Sugar bear,* she thought, *how adorable. He never called me sugar bear. That must be left over from the last girl he jerked around.*

"I don't know who sugar bear is, Jack. I'm SueBee Slyde from Wayleen, Texas."

"Come on, babycakes," he said, pushing out his lower lip and patting the cushion of the seat next to him. "Come over here and talk to Daddy."

"Jack, let me ask you something. How come you're coming around? Is it because I get paid for it now? That must turn you on. You figured I'd be a little free piece of tail. Isn't that how Madame's paid you for your advice all these years?"

"No, honey. I missed you. And when Madame Cleo told me—"

"Don't lie," SueBee said, trying to keep her voice down. "Working girls excite you, right, Jack?"

"Yeah, sure, babe," Jack shrugged. "Whazza matter with that?"

"Nothing, as long as I'm not involved," she said, and began to pace. "Look, Jack, I was once terribly in love with you. You hurt me. Now I want no part of you."

Jack's face looked as though she had hit him with a dead fish. His mouth opened slightly as though to speak. She held up one finger. "I haven't finished. I can just imagine how exciting it was for you to find out little SueBee Slyde had taken all the stuff you taught her and was out selling it. You thought you could just walk in here and I'd roll over, didn't you? Well, I'm not interested in you *or* your twisted libido."

Jack slapped his knee with the flat of his hand and laughed. "Dr. Freud, call your office," he whooped. "Did you learn about libidos at that school Madame sent you to?"

"Probably," SueBee said calmly. "I also learned about Kant and Hegel and Shelley and Keats. I learned about Disraeli and the Crimean War. I'm not in the mood for a discussion of world events, but trust me, if you wanted my opinions on anything from Iran-Contra to earthquake probabilities in Peru, you'd get 'em."

"SueBee, come on," he said, starting again. "Can't we just have a little party, just the two of us, for old times' sake? We could go back to where we left off in New York."

"Go back?" SueBee said, directly opposite him now, leaning into his face. "Go back to being treated like a bimbo? Go back to being lied to? Stop it, Jack, you have me trembling with excitement."

His face suddenly turned red with anger. "Look who's talking," he yelled. "You're a hooker, for Christ's sake! You fuck for money!"

"That's right. Money, not flowers," she said, giving one of the pots a little kick. "Money, not promises. Money, not lies. Now, I have things to do."

"Which one of those big shots are you fucking this weekend? I hear you have a special assignment."

Damn, she thought, dragging her suitcase into the center of the room and throwing the latch. *The bastard must have pawed through every file in Madame's office.* No way was she telling him her "date" was Billy Mosby. "I don't know," she said. "But I hope it's someone who knows who you are so I can tell him you have a pecker smaller than your thumb."

Jack stood up unsteadily and reached for his zipper. "Now you *know* that's not true," he said, fumbling with his fly. "Here, let me refresh your memory."

Suddenly, she was transported back to the little trailer in Wayleen. Big Boy's face swam in front of her.

SueBee stood up and reached for the letter opener lying beside her mail. Grasping it tightly, she pointed it at Jack's fly. "Do it and lose it," she said evenly. "It wouldn't be the first time I cut off one of those old wrinkly things."

She braced her lower legs against the edge of the coffee table and leaned closer. "I could scare you to death, Jack. How would you like your very own heart attack? I'll give you one. You try to fuck me and you'll leave this apartment in a body bag. Have you ever seen a person having a heart attack? The tongue turns black if you wait long enough without help. And trust me, I'll wait. I'll file my nails and watch. The pain is supposed to be incredible. Worse than any other sudden illness. Sometimes the pain is so bad that if you have the strength, you'd grab this here letter opener and try to kill yourself before your heart did it for you."

SueBee stepped back to make room for Jack, who had slammed his drink down on the coffee table and was pushing his way between the couch and the coffee table. He stormed toward the door, where his jacket hung over a chair. He yanked it off and opened the door. "You're crazy," he said. "You are stark raving nuts."

Within seconds she found herself staring at the closed door. He was gone.

"Damn," she said aloud. "The least the bastard could have done was stick around so I could tell him about the part where you get so scared you lose control of your bowels and shit yourself. I was just getting started."

The black Bentley with the opaque windows moved slowly up the rue St.-Denis. Puddles of light from the street lamps did little to illuminate the driver's task. His window had been lowered a few inches so he could check the building numbers. In front of No. 42, the big car nosed to the curb.

The uniformed driver got out, climbed the steps, and pressed the button under apartment number seven. He waited. Then he buzzed again. He returned to the car where his passenger waited with growing impatience.

"Sorry, Mr. Garn," he said, tipping his hat. "There's no answer at number seven."

"Ring the concierge," a voice boomed from within, angrily.

The driver nodded and trotted back to the foyer to the buzzer that read: *Dexia Solange, Concierge.* After several pushes of the bell a very old woman with bright red hair peeped out the crack of a door at the back of the hall.

"*Oui?*" she croaked.

"Ah, Mademoiselle Sandrine?" the driver said, tentatively. "Is she here?"

"They left," she said in English.

"Who is 'they'?" a voice demanded. The driver turned and saw Jourdan Garn standing behind him.

"Mademoiselle SueBee and Mademoiselle Sandrine," the old woman said. "They go. Country. Big car." She waved her hands to imply a great commotion had attended the women's departure.

Garn pushed by the driver and spoke directly to the woman. "When did they leave? Where did they go?" he shouted in the manner non-French-speaking people use to make themselves understood to the French.

The door closed further until only one eye, smudged with black mascara, was visible. "The country. I don't know anything else. Go away. Go away," she said, and slammed the door.

The driver helped Garn into the back seat. "Where to now, sir?" he asked.

Damn Felix, that bastard. Damn him and his damnable house party. Garn had himself been invited this year, as usual, but had declined. He hadn't really believed Sandrine would go. She had almost promised him she wouldn't—and yet, had she? Now that his anger was clearing his head, he had to admit to himself that she had promised him nothing the last time they were together. She had only smiled up at him, her chin resting just below his navel, before she made tiny circles in his pubic hair with the tip of her tongue.

He passed his hand over his eyes to try and erase his thoughts, then stared out the window at the dark streets of Paris. He knew he could stand it without her only a few hours longer.

"To the Loire Valley," he told the driver. "The château of Baron Felix d'Anjou. To La Fantastique."

Since the day Sandrine had walked up to him on the dance floor at the Savoy, his life had been a shambles. He could not concentrate, he could not think, he had lost three very important business opportunities and fifteen pounds.

She didn't fool him for a goddamn minute. She was holding out for the big time. That crap with returning the jewelry, the way she would disappear after they had been together, her insistence on continuing to work for Madame Cleo—all were part of her game. And a hardball game it was. In a world of disposable, fawning women, he had never met anyone like Sandrine. When she was with him she made him believe he was the only man alive, the only man who could satisfy her insatiable sexual desires. There hadn't been a woman in his life he could bring to orgasm two, three, four times a night until Sandrine. And when she entered a room his heart felt as though it would leave his body and slam against the wall. He had to have her. He'd be damned if he'd spend the rest of his life being bored and catered to. What was all the money he had amassed for, anyway, if someone didn't want to spend it? Well, Sandrine could spend it. She could spread it all out on the ground and roll around in it for all he cared, as long as she was his.

He knew the men who went to the baron's house party all too well. The thought of Sandrine copulating with any of them made a large vein pound in the side of his head.

He had to stop thinking about her. He would drive himself mad. He was determined to find her and give her whatever she wanted. In the pocket of his coat was the one piece of jewelry he knew she would not return once she saw it.

His divorce from Edytha was imminent, and damn it, if it was the only way he could have her to himself, he would marry Sandrine. He could, quite simply, not live another day without her.

SueBee couldn't sleep. She had watched the sun come up over the sloping vineyards in the distance from the seat under the high leaded-glass windows of Billy Mosby's room in the château. If possible, the baron's house in the rolling French countryside was more beautiful than Wellington Close.

She heard Mosby stir and returned to the bed, slipping under the sheets and leaning on the pillows. She looked down at Billy Mosby's sleeping face. His breathing was shallow and labored. She had noticed the bright color in his face the night before when she applied his makeup and knew it meant high blood pressure. When he awoke she would order breakfast for him herself. Clearly, he was eating all the wrong things.

Not wanting to wake him and knowing she couldn't go back to sleep, she got out of bed again. She dressed quickly, feeling a little silly to be in a black, very dressy Chanel at such an early hour, and padded down the long dark corridor in her stocking feet. She was anxious to check on Sandrine and hoped she would be back in her room.

She tapped once, twice, and then pushed open the unlocked door. Sandrine was standing at the bathroom sink brushing her hair. She was still wearing the gown she had worn in the library the night before.

"Hey, you're here," SueBee chirped, setting her shoes down on a chair. "How come? I thought you and the journalist would still be at it."

At the sound of SueBee's voice, Sandrine turned with a shout and threw her arms around her. "SueBee! I did it! I did it! I did it!"

SueBee hugged her back, bewildered. "Of course you did it, that's what we're here for." She slipped her arm around Sandrine's waist and swirled her around in an impromptu little dance. *"Girl, you gotta do it or ya' don't get paid,"* she sang. *"A john won't give you money if he don't get laid."*

Sandrine pushed away and plunked down on the edge of the bed. "I'm not talking sex, Sooz," she said excitedly. "I'm talking marriage. Sadie, Sadie, married lady!"

"Wait, wait," SueBee said, still laughing at Sandrine's infectious giddiness. "Marriage, who, what . . ."

"Jourdan Garn," Sandrine said breathlessly. "He's downstairs waiting for me. It worked, Sister woman. It worked."

"Oh my God," SueBee said as Sandrine thrust her left hand in front of SueBee's face. On the third finger was the largest stone SueBee had ever seen. "What *is* that?"

Sandrine held up her hand and smiled at the ring. "I don't know. A diamond, I guess. Who knows? Who cares? All I know is that this baby's a keeper."

"But how did this happen? The last time I saw you, you were leaving the library with that journalist."

"This morning at dawn the hall porter came running up to say there was someone who wanted to see me right away. Down in the courtyard. I ran down to see what was up, and there, sitting in the back seat of his big car with the door open and one foot on the ground, was Jourdan Garn!" Sandrine whooped his name and twirled around the Oriental rug.

"You mean he drove all the way down here just to . . ."

"Just to propose, SueBee," Sandrine shouted, jumping up and down. "He didn't even say hello, or how are you, or why the hell did I stand him up for dinner. He just grabbed me and tongue-kissed me like he wants my tonsils, and when I came up for air he said—and get this—he said, 'I can't stand it anymore. I have to have you. Will you marry me?'"

"Holy cow," SueBee whispered, stunned. She wanted to be happy for Sandrine but somehow it all seemed so—so—artificial. She'd never heard Sandrine say she loved Jourdan Garn. All she had ever said was, "I'm going to nail him and I know how to do it."

"So what's going to happen now, Sandy? Are you going to go back with him?"

"Absolutely," Sandrine said, pulling her gown over her head. "As soon as I can dress and pack. His plane is waiting for him at the private terminal at Orly. We'll be in New York by tonight."

Sandrine tossed her dress into her open bag, unhooked her bra, and walked back to the bathroom wearing just her garter belt and stockings. At the door she turned to look at SueBee.

"Come with me," she said softly. "Come back with me, SueBee. All the way to New York. I don't want to get married alone."

"Sandy, I can't," SueBee said.

"Why not?" Sandrine asked, looking hurt. "You're the best friend I have in the world. Aren't you happy for me?"

"Of course, I'm happy," SueBee said, still not sure how she felt. "But I promised Mosby I'd go riding with him today."

"Oh, excuse me," Sandrine said sarcastically as she pulled off her stockings and unhooked her garter belt. "Then of course you shouldn't accompany your best friend back to New York so she can plan her wedding to one of the richest men in America."

"Don't, Sandy. It's not like that. I feel I should see this weekend through with Billy."

"Why? All you had to do was go to bed with him. Don't you think Madame Cleo would forgive you this once?" Sandrine said, folding her arms and leaning stark naked and guileless against the bathroom doorway.

"I don't know how to explain it. But I like him. He talks to me. He's got a little thing about dressing up. But so what? I've had weirder guys." SueBee stared down at the bedspread and picked at it absentmindedly. "Besides, he doesn't know how to take care of himself."

"He's kinda old, isn't he?"

SueBee shrugged. "Ummm, I guess. But I can sense he needs me, and I like that. He wants me to spend a week in Paris with him. He says he hasn't had a vacation in fifteen years and that he'll have to turn the world upside down to get away for that long. I can't disappoint him."

"Okay, sweetie, I understand," Sandrine said, not sounding like she really did. "But promise you'll be there for me when it happens."

"When is that?"

"As soon as his divorce is final," Sandrine said, wiggling her eyebrows. "Maybe in as little as a month."

"I'll be there," SueBee said, getting up off the bed.

Sandrine wrapped a bath sheet under her arms and walked toward SueBee. She took both of her hands and looked into her eyes. "This is what I've always wanted, Sister woman," she said softly.

"I know, sugar," SueBee said. "I know. You've done it and I'm thrilled for you. What's the first thing you're going to do when you get back?"

A look of sheer determination crossed Sandrine's face. She didn't look like a girl making wedding plans. "I'm going to find a way to tell my mother to stuff it."

"You really mean that, don't you, Sandy?"

Sandrine kissed her on the cheek and walked back toward the bathroom. Over her shoulder she said, "With all my heart," and closed the door.

As SueBee picked up her shoes she could hear the shower running. She slipped back down the hall. When she reached Lord Mosby's room it was empty. On the pillow was a note reading: "I've gone down to breakfast, darling. I had the porter locate some riding gear for you. It's in the closet. See you at the stables at noon." It was signed, "Your Bedazzled Billy."

SueBee got out of her clothes and crawled into bed wearing Billy's tuxedo shirt, which he had left hanging on the bedpost. She drifted off to sleep disapprovingly picturing the sausages and eggs and buttered toast that were inevitably on Lord Mosby's breakfast plate.

On the twenty-ninth of July, Sandrine Mandraki, wearing a long, beaded Givenchy gown, with two white orchids in her hair and three overlapping tiers of diamonds falling from each ear, stood before a Supreme Court judge in the Gold and White Suite of the Plaza Hotel and married Jourdan Garn. A string quartet played discreetly in one corner. The music was a medley of the songs that were played the night Sandrine and Garn met in London. Jourdan had remembered every song.

When, at the judge's signal, Sandrine turned and handed her bouquet to SueBee, Sandrine leaned closer and whispered, "Did you make the call?"

SueBee nodded, cradling the trailing bouquet on her arm. "Everything's ready," she whispered back.

Then it was over. The dozen or so people in the room, all friends or colleagues of Jourdan's, gathered around them saying the appropriate things.

Waiters materialized on cue and poured champagne. A seated dinner at Doubles, the club in the Sherry Netherland, was planned, and after one toast, people began to make their way toward the club, which was but a short diagonal walk across from the Plaza.

As Sandrine and Jourdan moved out through the Fifth Avenue entrance of the Plaza, bystanders vied with the assembled paparazzi for a better view. Waiting at curbside was an all-white carriage pulled by two Arabian horses, complete with high white plumes mounted on their bobbing heads.

The driver, wearing a white tux and high white hat, hopped off his perch and extended his hand to the bride. "Great Scot," said a surprised Jourdan Garn. "What's all this?"

Sandrine turned and smiled at her new husband. "It was SueBee's idea," she said, "Those are her horses. Aren't they magnificent?"

"Absolutely," Jourdan said, clearly delighted. "But we're just across the street, darling. They won't have much to do."

"Come on," she said, taking his arm. "We're making a little detour."

Jourdan could only grin and follow her. He didn't seem to care what she was up to. She was his now.

As the bride and groom arranged themselves on the carriage seat, Sandrine nodded to the driver, whom she knew SueBee had instructed. To the applause of the crowd that had followed them out of the hotel, the carriage pulled out onto West 59th Street and headed east.

"Where are we going?" Jourdan asked, bemused.

"You'll see," Sandrine said smugly.

The carriage trotted to the corner of Park and turned north. As they waited at the light on East 79th Street, Sandrine saw them: two women, one beautifully dressed in a red silk suit and a huge red hat; the other in a simple, dark blue polyester dress with white collar and cuffs, a small blue straw hat trimmed with large white buttons perched on her head.

The carriage moved through the light and pulled to the curb in front of the two women. The driver reached down and helped the woman in the blue dress up into the seat opposite Sandrine and Jourdan. As the woman in the red dress reached up for his hand he withdrew it, turned in his seat, and snapped the reins against the horses' flanks.

As the carriage pulled out into the traffic on Park Avenue and picked up speed, Sandrine did not look back to see her mother standing slack-jawed at the curb. She fixed her eyes on her beloved Marthy and said, "Welcome home, Marthy. Please don't cry."

SueBee, Sandrine, Jourdan, Martha, and two of Jourdan's aides flew to London in his private plane immediately after the wedding supper.

At Doubles, SueBee had been called off the dance floor to take a call from Lord Mosby. When Jourdan and Sandrine walked back to the bedroom at the back of the plane, giggling and tipsy, SueBee asked the steward if she could make a call.

Seconds later a white phone was placed on the table in front of her club chair in the lounge. SueBee checked to see that Martha was still asleep in her chair farther down the aisle before she dialed the number Mosby had given her.

When he picked up, the line was clear and crisp. "Hello, Billy," she said softly. "I'm up in the air."

"Me too, but in a different way," he said with a chuckle. "Have you had a chance to think about things?"

"Not really."

"What worries you, darling?" he asked. "I promise, as soon as the decree is final. It should only be a couple of months at the most. You do want to be with me, don't you, SueBee?"

"More than anything. That's the problem. If I did anything to hurt you I couldn't bear it."

"What could hurt me?"

"Billy," she pleaded. "What will people say?"

"I don't care."

"What if it gets out? I mean about Madame Cleo?"

"I don't care."

"I do, Billy. I care terribly . . . someone in your position."

"I can do the same thing for you with Madame Cleo that Garn did for your friend, but it won't be necessary. All I have to do is make one phone call and it's done."

"Then do it, sweetheart. If anything ever came out I'd die. Not for myself but for you. I won't have anyone thinking bad things about you."

"Done is done," he said with finality. "I'll be at the airport to get you. What did you do with the horses?"

"I found someone at the stables to sell them for me. It's not right to let Zaki keep paying for their board. I had Martin find out where Zaki was and called him to find out where I should send the money. He told me to keep it as a dowry. He was very sweet."

"Where are the newlyweds going after they drop you here?"

"Jourdan has a villa on Corfu. Marthy is going with them."

"And you're staying here with me, forever."

"Yes, Billy, forever."

"I love you, SueBee," he said. "You are my heart."

"I love you, too, darling," she whispered, noticing the steward moving down the aisle toward her. She hung up, handed him the phone, and thanked him.

She couldn't wait to tell Sandrine. If she weren't back there on that circular bed doing wifey things she could tell her now.

She pulled the monogrammed cashmere lap robe over her shoulders and went to sleep. When she woke up she would be with the only man since her daddy who really loved her.

Two days before Christmas 1987, a friend of Cleo's who was highly placed in the French ministry called to tell her that a variety of formal charges were being prepared, all having to do with nonpayment of taxes and moneys earned from procuring going back to the early 1950s. These, he cautioned her, could soon lead to her arrest.

The next morning, she began a series of phone calls. First she contacted André Guibbaud, her longtime attorney who had drawn up the papers whereby Madame would receive "certain sums" for never disclosing that Sandrine Garn had worked for her.

Next, she called Billy Mosby to ask him if he still took those golfing holidays in Scotland with his friend in the French tax department. She wanted more information.

It was no use. Mosby and SueBee had married in a simple London ceremony the week before. He was still on his honeymoon in Amsterdam. Later she learned that Mosby and SueBee spent their honeymoon in Amsterdam's notoriously raunchy red-light district, seeing porno shows, indulging in theater of the flesh, and generally wallowing in all the forbidden pleasures Mosby had only dreamed of in the past.

Cleo then called Sheikh Zaki to see if he had any influence with the French president. Zaki told her that the failure of some real-estate deals on the Côte d'Azur might cause the president to refuse his call, but he would do his best.

She then called Barry Rizzo in New York and Jeremy in London and asked them to start actively recruiting girls. They were going to need a lot of money and were going to add on as many new girls as they could handle.

For two more agonizing years, clever and expensive legal maneuvering combined with the glacierlike speed of the French legal system kept the hounds of justice, if not in hand, at least at bay.

By the spring of 1990, Madame Cleo and her legal team had exhausted every other recourse. The French authorities came to the house on the Ile de la Cité to arrest her just before dinner.

Martin bailed her out the next morning, expecting to find a terrified and broken woman. Instead he found her furiously determined to do something, anything, to never see a jail again. The next day, an emergency summit meeting was called in André Guibbaud's office. It was there that the unthinkable was proposed, and Madame heard the name Wendy Klarwine for the first time.

The only thing she had left to sell that she truly and legally owned was the story of her own life.

Peter's Journal Entry—Paris, August 2, 1990

Well, now I've done it! But let me back up a bit.

My meetings with Madame have been less frequent, as she claims to be especially busy now that it's August and everybody's on holiday. I had been getting more and more anxious by the day, so by the time we settled down for our session yesterday afternoon I was not in the best of moods.

We gave up around six last evening (we are still meeting in her garden). Martin joined us, bringing a particularly nice Graves, poured us all a glass, and nattered on for a while. I said nothing. I was waiting to pounce as soon as I saw the mood was relaxed enough. I knew she had reached the point where she had told me everything she knew about the girls. She knew so much, in fact, that increasingly, these last sessions, it's as though she has recently had her memory refreshed by all of them.

After Martin poured the third glass, I struck. "So," I began nonchalantly. "Do you still think one of the girls tried to kill you?"

"Yes," she said.

At that moment I realized how profoundly my decision to see this project to its end had affected me. Taking control of my destiny, even though I had had to wait to execute it, now made me giddy with abandon. I took a deep breath and plunged.

"Madame Cleo," I said, glancing at Martin, always so sensitive to any unusual nuance in anyone's voice, "I don't give a flying fuck who tried to kill you." Saying the F word in front of her for the first time only heightened my determination and I plunged ahead. "I am ready to entertain the very real possibility that you never intend to tell me about yourself. Therefore, I am now going to demand that you be totally forthcoming or I am going to walk away from this project and let the French government send you to jail. I don't like being jerked around."

I heard a tiny yelp from Martin. His hand flew to his mouth, a reaction I fully expected. It was hers that stunned me.

She got up from her big peacock chair, turned, and walked into the house without another word. A moment later, Nanti, the spooky Indian maid, came out, and announced that "Madame est tres fatiguée," and couldn't talk to me anymore.

I was being dismissed. Shooed out of the place like a houseboy who barfed on the Aubusson rug.

With no recourse, I put down my glass, gathered my things, and headed into the house. Martin danced around me all the way to the door like a big, love-deprived dog, apologizing for her, apologizing for any misunderstanding, apologizing for being alive, jabbering on about how someone should have told me that Madame never talked about her origins or distant past. As far as she was concerned she was born the day she became Madame Cleo. How could the publishers not have known that? How could her lawyers not have known? Blah, blah, whimper, whimper.

By that time we were at the front door; I turned to Martin and bellowed "Bullshit!" at the top of my lungs. Martin, who surely has heard the phrase, looked as though I had hit him in the face with a handful of the stuff rather than having just said the word.

Then, he did the most remarkable thing. He threw his arms around me and began to sob. I don't think I've ever been so uncomfortable in my life. I turned him around and walked him over to a little settee by the door. When he regained his composure he went on about how Madame had never wanted to do the book in the first place, that she had panicked at the thought of going to jail. Her lawyers had talked her into it. Then he began to plead with me not to walk away from the book. Madame Cleo was his whole life, and if she went to jail he would be destroyed.

Then, and I suppose this was mean (the poor guy seemed truly undone), I told him I didn't give a shit. Not about him, not about her, not about the project. I'd done enough to have earned my money, or at least enough of it to buy a few more pairs of shoes made out of Italian babies' butts.

He didn't understand about the shoes, but he clearly knew I meant what I was saying. That's when he got hysterical. He started screaming. "She'll never talk to you about herself. Don't you understand? It's too painful!"

I did not have the strength to give him a lecture on pain—my own.

I turned to go, and out of the corner of my eye I saw her standing in the shadows at the top of the stairs, listening, so I turned back and raised my voice. I told him I thought she was stalling, buying time until she could find somebody who would rescue her, that she thought she could string me along indefinitely and that I would stick with her because I wanted the money. People have waited years for books to be written. It made sense; she'd operated in a world where anybody and everybody could be bought, including writers from New York. Then I told him that just because she had been dealing with whores all her life didn't mean I was one too.

It sounded okay as an exit line, particularly because I could see she hadn't moved.

I slammed out and went and did the one thing I'm truly good at in moments of personal crisis. I went back to my old Left Bank bar and got anesthetized on Pernod with brandy shooters, a combination that put me on the Planet Zork in less time than it took to say, "How does a person get control of his life?" It was my opening line to a woman drinking by herself at the other end of the bar. She had bad teeth and tiny mends in her fishnet hose.

She sipped on the double vodka the bartender slipped in front of her (which I soon realized I had purchased) and listened. I went on to tell her how I had resigned myself to the fact that I had achieved my own personal Peter Principle, rising to the level of my own incompetence, thinking I was a talented charmer when I really was a Boston–Irish smartass who thought he should control everything. I didn't really believe what I was saying, but I wanted someone to feel sorry for me. Then the bartender came over and told me, out of the side of his mouth, that the woman did not speak a word of English. That's when I went home.

Somehow, the grace that protects babies and drunks got me back to my rooms without anyone stepping on my fingers.

I think I called Fiddle before I passed out. I'm not real sure.

When I woke up it was late afternoon.

PART
III

CHAPTER
⚤ 13 ⚤

Peter turned off his laptop and slowly closed the cover. He was starving. With his food-bearing mailperson on vacation, there wasn't a thing to eat in the tiny kitchen. He'd have to get something to eat soon or risk getting sick.

A light drizzle had started sometime during the afternoon and was persisting. He grabbed his raincoat from the hook by the door, slipped his bare feet into a pair of scuffed Top-Siders, and trotted down the stairs to the street.

He pulled open the ancient front door, heavy with years of paint, and stepped into the dampness of the early evening.

As he reached the foot of the steps he saw a heavyset woman in a neon green raincoat getting out of a cab. She had a zebra-striped scarf tied over her head. The collar of her raincoat, which looked like purple vinyl, was turned up.

"Excuse me," she said in halting American-accented French. "I'm looking for number forty-two?"

He stopped short. "Fiddle?"

"Hi, Peter," Fiddle said with a familiar throaty trill.

"What the hell . . . I just talked to you."

"Almost twenty-four hours ago, ducks."

"But what the hell are you doing here?"

"Oh, dear," she said solemnly. "The memory cells are the first to go. You don't remember? I thought you sounded a bit squiffed. The last thing I said to you was to hold tight, I was on my way."

Peter stepped toward her. He stretched out his arms and pulled her into an embrace. "Fiddle, I *don't* remember. God, am I glad to see you."

She returned his hug, slipping her arms around his waist. She felt warm and soft and smelled of some kind of lemony perfume. Gently, he pushed her away and looked at her.

"You feel different," he said, puzzled.

Fiddle smiled at him with a crooked smile. "How would you know how I feel, Peter? I don't think we've ever touched."

"My loss," he said. He felt a great warm rush of affection for her. He knew why she had come all the way from New York. It wasn't to save a deal that she had no real vested interest in. She was there because she gave a damn about him in his hour of need. He tried to remember the last time anyone had given a damn, let alone flown across an ocean, for him. He couldn't. It had never happened.

He turned her around and put one arm around her shoulders. "Come on, boss lady," he said, grinning at her. "I know a place that has the most spectacular cassoulet in Paris."

"If you say so."

"Have you ever been here, Fiddle?"

"I'd never been to Queens until I cabbed out to catch the plane."

"Never been to Paris," he sighed, moving his arm down to her waist to guide her over the puddles in the sidewalk. "Lady, am I going to show you Paris. You're going to think you've died and gone to heaven."

She smiled up at him, and he was reminded what a lovely face she had. "You mean I haven't?" she asked.

All the elements were there, the right city, the rainy night, two unattached people in a hidden café down a cobbled Left Bank alley, a café complete with lace curtains, a working fireplace, and the smell of slowly roasting food.

All the elements were there for two healthy people who shared a common bond to follow their natural instincts and fall in love.

If life were a movie. But, of course, it wasn't. They were not exactly two healthy people. Fiddle had her own emotional skeletons, and Lord only knew, Peter told himself, so did he. Work was their bond. As inviting as Fiddle looked sitting across from him—and he really was only now realizing, seeing her again, how much he'd missed her—he was too fragile to take it any further.

The last time Peter had been in this restaurant he had been with a French girl, a model, as sexually neurotic as he was. He remembered dating that girl, impossible as she was, only because he liked the way they looked together.

He had never had a sexual thought about Fedalia Null. He had never seen himself with Fiddle in any circumstances other than a working life filled with respect and humor, comfortable understanding, and, perhaps, because he knew how far she had come, not a little awe.

No, he thought, in his experience, being able to talk and laugh with an intelligent woman, let alone holding her in awe, was not the stuff of romance.

The waiter ceremoniously presented and poured their wine. Over the rims of their glasses their eyes met and held for a silent, telling instant. She smiled, and he knew she was experiencing the same sense of cliché in the atmosphere and circumstances.

Fiddle dropped her eyes. "So," she said, studying the menu. "My guide recommends the cassoulet so I won't have to translate this. I'm your willing pawn," she said, closing the menu and reaching for her wine.

He ordered for them both, adding two orders of pâté *en croûte* to start, feeling better by the minute. "Fiddle, I can't tell you how impressed I am that you're actually here," he said. "I can't wait to show you around. Other than seeing Paris, I'm afraid I've put you to a lot of trouble for nothing.

"Not if I succeed," she said briskly.

"Succeed?"

"In what I came for."

"Oh? I thought you came to comfort a fuckup."

She leveled her gaze at him. "In no way did I come to bring you comfort, Peter. I came," she said, lowering her voice to the register of a threat, "to kick your Irish butt."

"You're serious," he said flatly, seeing the rising anger in her eyes.

"Serious as cancer, pal," she said. "Do you remember anything you said to me on the phone?"

"No," Peter said, sheepishly. "Sorry. I assume I told you about my blowup with Martin."

"Yes, in vivid detail. I can assume you don't remember my reply."

Peter shook his head.

"Good," Fiddle said, smugly. "Then I was right to make this trip."

"I'm embarrassed to ask this. What was your reaction?"

"What I said was that you had made a terrible mistake. Women like Madame Cleo can't be pushed, nor should they be yelled at, nor should they be issued ultimatums."

"Fiddle," he pleaded, "I've been over here all summer. I've spent hours taping and transcribing this woman. I'm not saying it was dull or that I didn't learn a lot, but she's hidden her life so thoroughly I can't find it. My whole reason for blowing up was part of a master plan. I figured she would never let me walk."

"So you said," Fiddle said in a bored voice as the waiter arrived with their pâté. Fiddle jabbed her fork into hers and popped a large hunk into her mouth, chewed and swallowed. "Blowing up was a lousy plan if you didn't have a fallback position, Peter."

"It never occurred to me she wouldn't cave in," Peter said defensively.

"Oh, Peter, Peter, Peter," Fiddle moaned, slowly shaking her head.

"I should never have taken the money," he said, ignoring his food although his stomach was growling. He was determined to defend himself. "I should never have agreed to be this woman's patsy. The whole thing has been very demeaning."

"That's called work, Peter. Hard work for a brilliant writer for extremely good pay."

"I'll give the money back," he said, hating that he sounded petulant.

"Go ahead. Give it back. You're still going to do the story—book, article, series, whatever. I'm not letting you weasel out of this, because I get the feeling that all your life, when your back is to the wall, you quit. You weasel and wimp and put your tail between your legs and run home to some figurative mommy and say 'it's the other kid's fault.'" She finished her pâté and nodded as the waiter offered more wine. "Eat that," she ordered, pointing to his plate with her fork. "Or I will."

Peter dutifully picked up his fork and began to eat. The pâté, which he knew from many visits was the best in Paris, tasted like sawdust.

"What do you want me to do, Fiddle?" he said between bites. "I'm tapped out. I guess I just don't understand women. How you people think, what you react to."

"Then I'll share a secret with you, Peter," she said leaning forward. "We confuse you because we don't play by guy rules. You expect us to react like men. Now, if you bullied a guy like you bullied Madame, albeit through Martin, a guy would have to come out and fight. Madame would have had to march down those stairs and put up her dukes. The whole place would have been awash in testosterone and you'd still have lost. But she's a woman who has been hiding a painful past for years. You're not going to get at it by causing more pain. She'll just curl up in a little, inaccessible ball and let you swing in the wind."

"Then what am I supposed to do, oh Mighty Wizard, oh Master of the Game?"

"Play by girl rules."

"How the hell do I do that?" Peter asked, completely frustrated.

"All you need to know is that the first rule in girl games is that there aren't any. If you want something badly enough, go get it." She looked up as the waiter approached with two steaming plates. "Ah, food," she said, her face lighting up.

They both ate in silence. Peter didn't know what to say. He felt stupid for thinking Fiddle's trip had been to cheer him up. Her attitude was doing anything but.

"Let's skip dessert," she said abruptly. "I'll get the check. *Garçon, l'addition, s'il vous plaît.*"

Fiddle fished a credit card from her bag and slapped it onto the table. "I'm a tad jet-lagged. I really have to get some sleep."

He grabbed his coat and followed her out of the restaurant.

As they stepped out onto the street, he said, "That's it? You fly all the way over here just to bawl me out? What about Paris by night? What about me showing you around?"

Fiddle turned to him, looking down at the cobblestone street. "Peter, I've never interfered in a writer's work, ever. But after your drunken call, I felt I had to step in."

"What are you talking about?" he said, shaking himself into his raincoat.

"You'll see, Peter. Go home, we'll talk more in the morning," she said, scanning the little alley. "Paris by night can wait."

"What are you looking for?"

"A cab," she said.

"They never come down this alley. We'll walk up to the Boul Mich."

Fiddle put two fingers up to her lips. An ear-piercing whistle rent the night air. At the end of the street a taxi moving north suddenly snapped a hard left turn and headed straight toward them.

Peter walked back to the rue St.-Denis alone. He took a long, deep gulp of the night air and told himself that whatever Fiddle was up to it wouldn't work. Nothing was going to work. The old lady was a fraud. The project was a fraud, and for having played along with it for so long—so was he.

He closed the front door and glanced down the long dark hall. There was light showing under Madame Solange's door, which was rare. Usually, the muffled racket from her television set was stilled well before midnight.

He was halfway up the stairs to his landing when he sensed rather than saw a figure standing in front of his door. Puzzled, he climbed the rest of the steps.

"Yes, can I help you?" he asked.

"I think it's the other way around, Peter," a woman's voice said with a lilt of amusement.

Peter blinked and then gasped. "Oh, my God. It's you."

Madeleine—Sandrine Garn—stepped toward him, smiling. "It's nice to see you again," she said evenly.

Peter tried to be as cool as his shock and surprise would let him be. Fiddle! he thought. Fiddle did this. That was what she meant when she mentioned interfering. Jesus H. Christ. She's gone out and found Sandrine Garn. He didn't know whether he felt mortified or thrilled. "Yes . . . well, ah," he managed to say as his mind Ping-Ponged with what to call her. "Here," he said, fumbling with his keys. "Let me get the door."

"It's open," Sandrine said, lightly. "Madame Solange let me in. We're old friends."

"How . . . ah, how nice of you to come out to greet me," he said feebly.

"I didn't think finding me on your couch would be a good idea."

"Right, right," Peter said, pushing open the door. When he reached around her to find the light switch, the smell of her perfume made his knees threaten to buckle. "Come in, come in, ah . . ."

"You can call me Sandrine," she said, still smiling as she crossed to the couch and sat down. "You wouldn't have a bit of brandy?"

"Of course," he said. "Please sit down. Oh, you're sitting down. Just a minute. I'll be with you in just a minute. It'll just take me a sec . . ." His voice trailed off helplessly.

"Relax, Peter," she said, calmly. As she crossed her legs he could hear the tiny swish of her stockings. "I should have called, but Fiddle told me not to."

Peter turned, grateful for something else to focus on other than the utter surprise and shock he was trying hard not to show. "How do you know Fiddle?"

"I don't, really," Sandrine said. "Well, I do now. You can't cross the ocean sitting next to someone and not get to know them."

Peter cleared his closing throat. Girl rules, he thought. That's what Fiddle meant. Of all the devious, underhanded, sneaky deals. He felt surrounded. "You flew over with Fiddle?" Peter asked.

"Weren't you on your way to get some brandy?"

"Oh, yeah, sorry," Peter said, turning toward the kitchen. Shit, he thought, fighting hard against the encroaching fear that he would make a complete fool of himself.

He found an unopened bottle of duty-free Remy Martin and two nearly clean glasses on a high shelf. He blew into them, wiped them haphazardly on his sleeve, and carried everything into the living room.

Only after the second gulp did he feel his heart slowing down. If it killed him, he wasn't going to refer to their one and only meeting, no cute references to wine cellars or country châteaux, nothing. He wasn't even going to admit he knew anything about her—although he knew virtually everything—until she showed her hand.

He dared to look down at her as she took a sip of her brandy. Good Lord, he thought, she's more incredibly beautiful than I remembered. She was wearing a simple beige Chanel suit without all the chains and pearls and crap the rich ladies around Paris wore. Her hair was pulled back like a ballerina's, and her skin looked like you could see through it.

"So?" he said lamely, sitting down at the opposite end of the couch wishing his hard-backed working chair were within reach. "How did you get together with Fiddle Null?"

"Martin Bourke-Lyon called your agent in New York yesterday. He was terribly distraught. He told her you had walked out on Madame so Wendy told him to call Fiddle."

Peter moved forward on the couch. "I didn't walk out on her, damn it. She walked out on me!"

Sandrine held up her hand. On one finger was a yellow diamond the size of a matchbox. "Just let me finish. Then you can tell me your version," she said.

Peter took a deep breath and nodded. "Go on," he said.

"Anyway, Martin and Fiddle seemed to have had quite a long discussion about what to do. Then Fiddle got on the phone and found me and explained the problem."

Peter had witnessed Fiddle on the hunt many times. There was no one quite like her when she wanted to find someone.

"So you just hopped on a plane, just like that," he asked, a bit more sarcastically than he intended.

"Well, yes, more or less," she said, holding out her empty glass. Peter refilled it wordlessly. "You see, Peter, Madame Cleo is very important to me. I don't want to see her go to jail. This whole thing can work, but there is a way to go about getting to her, and I'm afraid the way you're going about it simply won't do."

Peter suddenly stood up. Now he was finally feeling something other than complete bewilderment. He was angry. "Will you please tell me, damn it, what is going on? Everyone seems to know everything but me. I'm the one doing this fucking book, or at least I was. Sorry about the language."

Sandrine flashed the big diamond again. "That's okay, I've heard the word," she said, calmly. "Don't get angry. Just sit down and listen."

Peter marched over to his work desk, yanked out his typing chair, and spun it around. He sat down opposite her before he realized his brandy was now out of reach over on the coffee table.

"Look, Peter," she said, getting up and handing him his glass. "I feel partly responsible for the fix you're in."

Peter didn't want to ask why. If she referred to La Fantastique he would have to make some comment on their having been together. Something he dreaded. He just accepted her statement and said, "So?"

"So, Fiddle and I had a long talk and we came up with an idea."

Peter blew out a long stream of air. It fluffed the cowlick that had drooped onto his forehead. He smoothed it back and waited.

"There is one person who knows everything about Madame. I can get you to that person but, you're going to have to be very sweet, very gentle. You can't scare her."

"What the fuck is this?" he said, getting even angrier. "When have I not been sweet? I don't go around scaring people for Christ's sake. You broads. Sometimes I . . ."

"Broads?" Sandrine said, cocking her head as though she hadn't quite heard him. "Broads?" she repeated. "I was a whore once, Peter Shea. But trust me, no one ever called me a broad. I'm not sure I even know what a broad is."

Peter waved his hand as though to erase the word from the air. "I'm sorry," he said. "It's just that I feel like I'm being dicked around. I have a very big problem on my hands and you women don't seem to be taking me or it seriously."

Sandrine leaned back into the cushions, a slow smile playing on her exquisite face. "On the contrary, Peter," she said. "I know exactly how you feel. Not being taken seriously is a very painful experience. One we 'broads,'" she said, hooking the air with her index fingers, "know a great deal about. Now, if you'll just come with me, I'll show you how serious we are."

Peter felt his face flush as she uncrossed her legs. Her skirt was fashionably short and he cursed himself for his inability not to stare at the flash of alabaster skin between her thighs. With horror, he realized how much he wanted Sandrine Garn and how unthinkable it would be to do anything about it.

He rose from his chair in a daze when he realized she was actually walking toward the door. "Where are we going? he asked, alarmed.

"Not far," she said. "Just downstairs." She pointed to the open brandy bottle on the coffee table. "You'd better bring that. You may need it. And your tape recorder."

Madame Solange's apartment was larger than he expected.

The old woman was clearly expecting him. As he and Sandrine stepped into the little foyer that led to the heavily draped and overcrowded living room, she bowed slightly and smiled.

"Come in, please. Make yourself comfortable, Mr. Shea," Madame Solange said in a low, well-modulated voice.

Peter stood in the half light cast by the lamps with dark silk shades that were dotted around the room. He felt foolish at having an open bottle of brandy in one hand.

"Here, let me take that," Madame Solange said, gently taking the bottle from him. "How thoughtful of you. I have only a spot of scotch in the house."

As she walked toward the kitchen, presumably to fetch glasses, he looked around. The walls of the living room were covered with hundreds of faded photographs of what appeared to be scenes from long-ago plays.

"Dexia was a very famous actress before the war," Sandrine commented from her position near the door. "I'm sure she'll tell you all about it."

"Dexia? Is that her first name? Should I call her that?" Peter asked.

"Better not," Sandrine said in a half whisper. "She's quite a grand lady. She's also had a very rough life, so be sweet."

"Look, Sandrine," Peter said, saying her name for the first time in the excitement of what was apparently about to transpire. "I don't eat babies for breakfast, for Christ's sake. I'm really a very nice guy."

"I know," Sandrine said, raising one eyebrow.

Peter felt his face flush again, but before he could respond Madame Solange returned with two glasses and a little porcelain bowl of mixed nuts that she placed on the table next to the couch. Peter stared at the glasses for a moment, then looked back at Sandrine. "Aren't you having a drink?" he asked lamely.

"I'm not staying, Peter. You and Madame Solange have a lot of work to do."

"But . . ." Peter started to protest.

"Don't worry," Sandrine said, soothingly. "She knows exactly why you're here. There shouldn't be any problem." She quickly crossed the room to where Madame Solange had settled herself in the corner of the couch. She bent down and kissed the old lady gently on the cheek, whispered something in French, then turned and brushed past Peter on her way to the door.

"Will I see you again?" Peter asked with a gulp as her perfume reached his nostrils again.

"Maybe," Sandrine said over her shoulder with another slow smile. "One never knows."

Before he could say anything more, she wiggled her fingers at him and closed the door.

Feeling strangely ill at ease in the fussy, overstuffed apartment with a virtual stranger, Peter stood facing Madame Solange, waiting for instructions.

"Such a lovely girl," the old lady said. "She lived right here in this house, you know. When she worked for my friend."

Peter took the chair opposite the couch without being asked. "You mean Madame Cleo?" he said. "Was she a very good friend?"

"Yes," she said, leaning forward and pouring brandy for them both. "For many years. She has been very good to me. As have the girls. I love the American girls. Some of them, well, they live other lives now and cannot know me. But not Mademoiselle Sandrine. Every Christmas, every birthday, she always remembers me." She sighed deeply and took a long drink of brandy. "But," she said, continuing somewhat more energetically after she swallowed, "you have not come to hear about Sandrine. You are here to talk about Madame Cleo. No?"

"Yes," Peter nodded with rising excitement. He pulled his tape recorder out of his jacket pocket and held it above the coffee table. "May I?"

"Of course. No problem."

"Does she know you are speaking to me?"

She puffed out her lower lip, very much the way Madame Cleo did when she wanted to dismiss a remark. "It does not matter. I'm doing this for Mademoiselle Sandrine. I'm an old woman and have little to give anyone. If talking to you is something that my American friend wants, then turn on your little machine and we shall start."

Peter checked to see that he had extra blank tapes in the case. There were plenty. He placed the recorder in front of Madame Solange and adjusted the microphone, remembering a thousand interviews where the subject would not permit its use, remembering the sweaty nervousness with which he had secretly wired himself to record important sources. Now, not only had the most important story of his life been handed to him by the women who seemed to be in control of his life, but the subject was insisting on a public record.

By dawn, he had used up six one-hour tapes.

On a cool spring morning in June of 1940 as Bronna Charnov walked to her morning classes at the *académie*, she smelled smoke. Her eyes stung in the cool morning air, which was now the color of lead.

All night long the French army had been frantically destroying the fuel depots outside the beleaguered city lest they fell into the Germans' hands. All night long her parents had huddled beside the radio in the back office of the small hotel they owned on the rue St.-Denis. Upstairs, Bronna and her sister lay side by side unable to sleep, wondering what would happen to them all. By morning everyone knew it was only a matter of hours before the hated enemy army would march into the city.

As she moved through the clogged streets she glanced furtively at those passing to see if anyone she knew was leaving. For days, every street, avenue, and road leading out of the city had been choked with cars, trucks, wagons, and carts. Anything with wheels had been pressed into service as people fled south. Others jammed the train stations, pushing, shoving, clamoring for space aboard anything that moved.

Doctors, lawyers, tradesmen, and teachers, anyone with money, connections, or a place to flee to with their loved ones and belongings, were running for their lives. She glanced over her shoulder to see a cart groaning under the weight of a grand piano and an antique clock. It was followed by honking cars, beds tied to their roofs, paintings lashed to the fenders. As many as ten people were stuffed inside. Some hung from running boards while others walked. Fear and smoke and panic were everywhere.

In the last forty-eight hours more than two million had fled the City of Light.

Not everyone left. Those who were duty bound to keep the city running—police, electrical and telephone workers, some doctors and hospital aides—and many students stayed to face a terrifying and uncertain future.

Bronna's father, Yasha, a big fifty-year-old man with tired eyes and an informal manner, loved his adopted city, steadfastly refusing to abandon her in a time of need. He had run from death before as a young man in the Ukraine, fleeing the purges and persecutions that followed the Bolshevik Revolution. Like so many others, he had made his way to Paris and a new life. He drove a cab, waited tables, moved furniture, took any work he could find to support his young family. Finally, he put aside enough to buy the little hotel in the rue St.-Denis.

The hotel was his dream, everything he had in the world. The hotel and his family. He vowed to stay, to offend no one and wait the Germans out. Surely the rest of the world would not abandon France. He was not a political man. He minded his own business. He assumed he would be left alone no matter who governed the city or the country. The girls would go to school as always; he and his wife would continue to run the hotel. If it meant letting rooms to Germans, so be it. As long as they were gentlemen and paid their bills he could live with it. Yasha Charnov, despite the warnings of friends less trusting than he, and the pleadings of his wife, would not be moved.

On the morning of June 14, 1940, the Germans entered Paris.

Bronna, pale-eyed and fragile, her long brown pigtails making her look younger than seventeen, stood huddled against her father's side among the silent crowd that lined the Trocadero and watched. Some watched with tear-stained faces, crying openly in shame and anger. Others simply stared, mute and motionless, unbelieving, furious at their weak leaders who had capitulated to the enemy. Paris was taken by an occupying force without a shot having been fired.

The men goose-stepping by Bronna looked identical. Their jackboots glistened in the high spring sunlight. Their heels hit the cobblestones with the same force and rhythm as her pounding heart; their black uniforms were pressed and properly creased and looked as though they had never before been worn. Their helmets with their odd, menacing scoop-shovel backs moved up and down together, creating a wavelike effect that made her stomach roll.

Suddenly, with a roar, a V-shaped wedge of motorcycle troops moved past the spot where she stood. Each had a sidecar carrying another soldier holding a machine gun at the ready.

In the deafening roar, a motorcycle passed close enough to blow the hem of her pleated skirt above her knees. The soldier in the sidecar, a blond god with pale blue eyes, looked straight into her face, raised his black gloved hand, and waved at her. Instinctively, for she had been raised to be a polite and friendly child, she raised her hand and waved back.

Instantly, she felt a hand grip her shoulder. Her father, who had never done anything more violent than open the stuck lid on a jar of cold *shchav*, slapped her across the cheek with a force that ripped the air out of her lungs. The look on his face and the throbbing sting of his rebuke told her, more than any words he had uttered, his feelings about the invading force.

During the summer that followed, Paris was declared an Open City, and for a time the occupying forces behaved correctly. There was no looting, no arrests, no confiscation of property. Soldiers offered their seats on the *metro* and buses to the elderly and smiled at the young girls without attempting to fraternize. They behaved like tourists, snapping pictures of one another in front of famous landmarks and comporting themselves properly in the bars and cafés.

For Bronna, the world did not change that much. There were rumors, always rumors, of terrible things that were happening somewhere else in the city to people she didn't know. People were beaten and arrested for various infractions, but that was something the adults talked about. Bronna and her sister, Alyssia, went back to school, Bronna to prepare for her dreaded baccalaureate. Life seemed almost normal again except for the air of tension in the tiny apartment in the back of the Charnovs' hotel lobby.

Her father complained constantly about the unavailability of meat and fresh vegetables for the hotel dining room. Not that there were many guests to feed. Commercial travelers and tourists no longer came to Paris. By the end of that summer he closed the dining room altogether.

There were constant blackouts and power failures. Toilet paper, soap, and new bedding were nearly impossible to find. Added to that was the endless paperwork and permits required of everyone trying to stay in business under the hated occupying regime. Bronna suspended belief and tried to ignore her parents' frightened whispers long after she had gone to bed. Her free days were spent with her sister doing chores in the hotel. The maids had fled to relatives in free France, and the handyman had disappeared.

Early one evening in July, a visitor in a German officer's uniform appeared at the front desk. He was tall, with a high forehead and piercing eyes. He arrived so silently that Bronna, who was behind the front desk, jumped when he spoke. In a deep, accented voice he asked to see the proprietor and announced himself as Major Josef von Kessel of the German General Staff.

Gestapo.

To Bronna, the word sounded like the thrust of a knife. Frightened, she hurriedly left the front desk and ran to summon her father. She found him at his desk in the back office where the now-forbidden radio was hidden under piles of old blankets in a storage chest.

When she told him there was a German officer waiting to see him in the lobby, Yasha Charnov began to tremble.

"What does he want?" he asked.

"I don't know, Papa."

"Did he ask for me by name?"

Bronna thought for a moment trying to remember. "No, Papa. He asked to see the proprietor."

"Does he have anyone with him?"

"No, Papa. He's alone."

Her father slowly pushed back his chair. "You stay here. If I am not back in five minutes you must go and tell your mother I am at the police station."

"Papa! Why?" she cried. The thought of her father being arrested filled her with terror.

"Do as I say," he said harshly. He shrugged into the black jacket he always wore outside the office and hurriedly left the room.

The officer was idly poking through a rack of old brochures beside the front desk when Yasha stepped up behind the counter. "May I be of help?" he asked pleasantly.

The major started and turned. "Ah, yes. I certainly hope so," he answered. "May I ask you, sir, if you have a suite in the hotel? Something larger than an ordinary room?"

There was one on the top floor. It was seldom used and was not in the best repair. But Yasha knew better than to refuse. "Yes, we do," he said. "A very nice one, as a matter of fact, and only just now available. Two rooms, nicely furnished, with a sitting room and a small kitchen facility."

The major beamed. "Perfect!" he said, pulling a roll of bills from his pocket. "I would like to pay you for the first month."

Yasha stared at him. A German? Paying for something? He couldn't believe his eyes and ears. He had only to "requisition" the whole hotel if he wanted to. "For one month, sir?" Yasha asked, incredulous.

The major began to count out new franc notes, placing them on the counter with a black-gloved hand. "Perhaps longer. We shall see." He picked up the stack of bills and handed them to the startled owner. "Will this be sufficient?"

Yasha could only nod as he picked up the money and carefully folded it. "Will that be for one, Major?"

"Ah, well . . . yes, for one, but I shall be visiting."

"And what name should I use?" Yasha asked, opening the register.

"I would prefer you not to use a name if you'd be so kind," he said, lowering his voice. "But you can be expecting a Madame Solange sometime later this evening."

The major thanked the astonished hotel owner, touched the visor of his cap, and walked out through the lobby and into the night.

Bronna, who had been waiting by the door straining to hear, nearly fainted with relief as her father returned to the office and dropped into his chair.

"Is it all right, Papa?" she asked breathlessly. "Is he gone?"

"Yes, yes," he sighed, wiping his forehead with the back of his hand. "He's gone."

"What did he want?"

"We have a new guest arriving for the rooms on the top floor. Go tell your mother, quickly. Get your sister. The two of you can give your mother a hand."

"The suite? Someone is renting the suite?"

"Yes, a lady. A friend of the major's. Now, go, there is much to do."

Later that evening, as the women were finishing their frantic efforts to make the accommodations presentable with the few supplies available, an enormous Vuitton trunk banded in brass arrived. A note attached gave instructions that the contents were to be removed and placed in the suite.

As her mother knelt on the worn carpet of the lobby and opened the lid, Bronna and her sister ran to look inside. The aroma that greeted their astonished nostrils made them squeal with delight.

Inside lay treasures that were the stuff of dreams. Creamy, thick bath sheets, lace-encrusted bed linens, and silk nightgowns and beribboned robes thin enough to pull through a wedding ring. Separating each gossamer layer was row upon row of fragrant pastel soaps, lacquered boxes of perfumed talcum, and creams of every sort. At the bottom of the trunk they found brushes and combs and vanity mirrors set in tortoiseshell and backed with silver.

There were tears in Lily Charnov's eyes as she lifted a powder puff the size of a rabbit in hands worn raw from cleaning with kerosene and yellow soap. "Look, girls," she whispered. "Smell."

Bronna buried her face in the soft ostrich feathers and let the bouquet of scented talc fill her senses.

"Oh, Mama," she sighed, her eyes closed as she handed the puff to her sister. "Whoever this Madame Solange is, she must be someone very special."

Every Friday night for as long as Bronna could remember, the Charnov family had taken the evening meal in the hotel dining room. It was always a festive night. Often, friends joined them for the lighting of the candles and prayers. On the High Holy Days even more people came, and there was music and singing and many bottles of sweet wine. Her father told stories of the old days in Russia before the terrible things happened.

After Madame Solange arrived to occupy the suite at the top of the hotel, Shabbas dinners were no longer observed in the dining room but in silence in the family apartment, doors bolted and window curtains tightly drawn. No one had to tell Bronna that Madame Solange's frequent visitor was the reason why.

After dinner they would gather around the hidden shortwave radio, as usual, to listen to the Free French broadcasts from England.

It was on the radio that Bronna heard the word *resistance* for the first time. Throughout France people of every walk of life were beginning to shake off what had until then seemed like stunned indifference to their oppression. They were fighting back.

When she mentioned what she had heard to the small circle of students who were her friends, they greeted her with silence and tight, knowing smiles.

One crisp fall afternoon as she was leaving the *académie* after class, Maxim Boisolette, a boy she had known since grammar school, caught up with her.

"Bronna, wait," he said. "You're coming to the Armistice Day demonstration, aren't you? Everyone will be there."

"Who's everyone?" she asked, eyeing him suspiciously.

"The whole school. We're all going to meet at the Tomb of the Unknown Soldier. Students from all over Paris will be there."

"I really couldn't," she said, demurring. Her father would be furious if she involved herself in something so dangerous. Demonstrations were strictly forbidden by the regime, and those who disobeyed had been shot.

Maxim's face reddened. "What do you mean?" he said angrily. "You are a Jew, like me. Don't you know they are arresting Jews in the night? There are concentration camps already in Le Vernet, in Argelès, in Rivesaltes, and Gurs. How can you not raise a hand to these murderers?"

"My father is a Jew. My mother is not," she said, knowing she was making a flimsy, shameful defense.

"Ha! You live in a dreamworld, Bronna," he scoffed, shortening his pace to accommodate hers. "Don't you know the new definition of a Jew? The Commissariat of Jewish Affairs says if you have three grandparents who are Jews you qualify. If you have two Jewish grandparents and are married to a Jew you qualify."

She thought for a moment then said, "That leaves me out. I have only two Jewish grandparents and I'm not married to anyone. I don't qualify."

Maxim stared at her. "Your father does, Bronna. Not only is he a Jew but he's foreign-born. Those are the ones they are taking first. Thousands of them are already in the camps. One night they will come for him."

A shiver of fear knifed down her spine. "That's not true," she screamed at him. "My father runs a little hotel. He does nothing wrong. He isn't even political; he's a loyal Frenchman. He has been for years. My sister and I are French, as is my mother!" She stopped only because she had begun to cry and realized how foolish she sounded.

"Bronna, we have to stick together," Maxim said sharply. "We have to show them we are willing to die even though they won't dare shoot at thousands of kids."

"I can't, Maxim. My father—" she broke off, realizing her protests were falling on deaf ears.

"Suit yourself," he said curtly, brushing by her as he walked quickly away.

All day she felt guilty. When she tried to bring up the subject of the student demonstration at dinner that night she was met with her father's stony silence. Under the table her mother kicked her briskly on the ankle.

That night she lay awake next to her sleeping sister. She was filled with rage. Rage at the way she and her family had to live their lives, rage at being treated as less than human by the outside world and like a child at home. Her single voice meant nothing, but many voices, hundreds and hundreds of voices raised in righteous anger, could mean something. If Maxim and the others weren't afraid, why should she be?

The next morning she sought out Maxim after class and told him she would march with the others.

On November 10th, the day before the demonstration, the teachers at school informed the students that there would be no holiday the following day but classes as usual. No one would be excused.

The announcement was greeted by angry muttering from the students, who then whispered among themselves and passed notes.

Maxim and some of the other student leaders met after class in the courtyard of the school, where word was passed that they would come to school as told, wait until attendance was taken, and then leave, defying the order, and join up for the march.

The plan was for the students to meet at the Arc de Triomphe *metro* station, join the others, and march to the tomb en masse.

The next morning when Bronna saw the others sliding away, she gathered up her things and joined them. As they moved up the avenue toward the Place de l'Etoile, more students stepped in among them. By the time they reached the Tomb of the Unknown Soldier their ranks had grown to well over a thousand young people. The group moved in an orderly fashion. No slogans were shouted, no banners or flags of protest were flown. The point was to make a silent protest, letting their numbers show their outrage. They were to walk ten abreast down the avenue to the tomb and stand, heads bowed for a few moments, as the orderly conscience of the youth of France mourning their war dead.

As they moved down the avenue, Bronna was halfway back in the group. She had linked arms with Maxim and Jean Copeau, a round, pink boy in her medieval history class. They both had trouble keeping up with Maxim's long stride. They were about a block from the plaza in front of the tomb when they heard shouting. Up ahead they could see a few German soldiers who must have been on guard duty at the tomb. From her place in the line of march Bronna was unable to tell who might have started an argument, the students in the lead or the soldiers.

The line slowed as people ahead of them realized a fight had broken out.

The students around her began to pack in closer, shoving and pushing to see what was going on up ahead.

Suddenly Bronna panicked. She grabbed at the back of Maxim's leather jacket and tried to pull him out of the line of march. "Let's get out of here!" she screamed. Pulling and dragging him, she made for the curb. Her head was down as she pushed through the crowd. When she looked up she was staring into the face of a German soldier.

"Go back!" he snarled. "Go back!"

She looked over her shoulder. There was nowhere to go. Down the sidewalk she could see more soldiers moving into position to block the streets leading away from the plaza.

"Here, put these in your bag," Maxim yelled, handing her the schoolbooks he had slung over his shoulder by a leather strap. "Grab the bottom of my jacket and hold on. I'm going to try and push through."

She threw his books into her schoolbag, looped the strap around her neck, and held on to his jacket for dear life.

Suddenly, the sound of gunfire exploded around them. The soldiers were shooting. She could not tell if they were shooting into the air or directly at people. In her terror she let go of Maxim's jacket. She found an opening in the now hysterical crowd. The pushing that had started became complete panic at the sound of the guns. People were knocking others to the ground, running hopelessly in all directions, screaming. She put her head down, hunched forward, and hurled herself between the people in front of her. She realized she had made some space for herself and began to run. Out of nowhere something smashed against her chest, and her head flew up as she felt herself falling backward. Something had hit her hard. It was a soldier with a rifle. He had slammed the butt of it against her chest. She reeled in pain and collapsed to the ground in a dead faint.

When she opened her eyes she was seated in something that was moving. The fetid air reeked of vomit and fresh blood. She tried to straighten up from her slumped position and realized her arms were tied behind her with a rope attached to something. She turned and saw Maxim and Jean seated on either side of her. They were all lashed together. Seated opposite them on a wooden bench was a line of grim-faced German soldiers not much older than they were. Each had a rifle between his knees.

This is insanity, Bronna thought. Her head throbbed and the pain in her chest was excruciating. Surely they were just trying to make an example of them to other students to stay off the streets and behave. They would probably put their names on a list, scold them, and send them home. Her only real fear was what her father would say when he learned that she had gotten mixed up in something so futile.

When the lorry came to a halt they were herded into a building she recognized as the police station. Inside, they found themselves in a large gray room. The walls were hung with red flags bearing big black swastikas. Between the row of flags was a life-size photograph of Adolf Hitler in the uniform of the Third Reich. Only then did she begin to panic. She tried to calm herself. They were only students. They hadn't done anything, really. They were just in the wrong place at the wrong time. Surely they would just be given a lecture. Perhaps the head soldier would make her father come and pick her up.

As the soldiers who had ridden with them in the lorry shoved them against the police-station wall, she noticed poor Jean. He could hardly walk. He stumbled against her, tethered by the communal rope, trying to keep his weight off a leg that hung limp and useless, a dead thing. He tried to hop on one foot as the soldier behind him kept pushing him along with the butt of his rifle.

An officer ordered them to stand against the wall and not to speak. He then approached each of them and demanded their identity papers.

For over an hour, they stood against the wall. Before long, she realized it was painful to move. Perhaps they were notifying their parents. She tried assuring herself that any minute her father would be walking through the door. By now she was beyond caring how angry he would be. She just wanted to go home.

Finally, a soldier came over to them and stood in front of Bronna, close enough for her to smell his garlic-laced breath. He reached behind her with a knife and cut the rope. "Come with me," he said roughly, grabbing her by the elbow.

He dragged her, stumbling, into another room where a *commissaire* sat at a small, scuffed desk. He looked up at her with a sneer and pushed some kind of form across the desktop. "Fill this out," he ordered. "And sign it."

She tried to still her shaking hand as she reached for it. It asked for her name, address, her parents' names, and her religion. It was the first time she had ever been asked, officially, to state such a thing. Other than that, the form looked harmless enough. There was more writing further down the page, which she was too frightened to read. She filled out the form as best she could, signed it, and handed it back to him. He glanced at it, nodded, and informed her she was under arrest. Just like that. No one said what the charge was; no one said what she had done.

Without further explanation, she was taken back to the lorry. By nightfall she was in a cell in the Cherche-Midi prison.

She lay curled in a ball for a long time on a lumpy mattress so slick with dirt it felt cold and wet to the touch, listening to the sounds around her. The only thing she heard was someone sobbing on the other side of the wall.

She tried to analyze the pain in her chest. She didn't think anything was broken. Perhaps she was just badly bruised. Slowly, she pulled herself up and squinted into the darkness. The cell was approximately eight feet wide by ten feet long. Its walls were blackened from years of candle smoke. There was a small high window with bars, a toilet but no washbasin. On a shelf under the tiny window sat a candle, which provided the only light.

The cell was freezing. She looked around for a sheet or blanket, anything to wrap herself up in to stop shivering. There was nothing. Only the thin jacket she had been wearing.

She noticed a dark lump at the end of the mattress and poked at it. It was her bag! By some miracle they had not seen fit to confiscate it. She fell on it as though it were a hot meal, unzipped it, and dumped the contents out on the mattress. There wasn't much—a comb, two pencils, her small notebook, her empty wallet. They had taken her lunch money.

Another miracle! There, still held together by a frayed leather strap, were the books Maxim had asked her to carry. She studied the bindings. One was an English-French dictionary. She supposed the Germans considered a dictionary politically acceptable. The second was a book on how to play chess, a game she neither played nor understood. The third was a world atlas, a boring reference book assigned at school.

She put them aside, incapable of focusing on anything but her immediate situation. She thought of her family and how distraught they must have been when she hadn't returned from school. Perhaps Jean or Maxim had been let go. Surely they would tell her parents where she was. Gradually, she convinced herself that her family's feelings were beyond her control. Next she focused on her hunger, for she had not eaten since early morning. She was also distracted by the unrelenting pain in her chest and the paralyzing cold.

She took the candle from the high shelf and carried it back to the mattress. She carefully shielded its guttering flame lest it go out and leave her in total darkness. She held her numb fingertips to the flame, then her frozen palms, until it nearly burned the skin. When her hands were warm enough she placed them inside her shirt, then to her temples and wrists. A little warmer, she pulled the edge of the thin mattress around her legs and willed herself to sleep. With daylight someone would come and let her out. It had only been a student demonstration; she had done nothing except walk down the street. Surely, the way they had been arresting people, cells were needed to house people guilty of far greater offenses than hers.

There had been little in her life to prepare her for the circumstances in which she found herself except the hunger she had known since the occupation. She had never known real physical pain, and therefore had nothing to compare to what she was feeling now. She convinced herself that her pain was minimal. Curled up and somewhat covered she was almost warm, and the fatigue of her ordeal offered a half sleep that permitted her mind to deal with her fears.

Fear of being beaten was high on her list. She dismissed the possibility of being shot. As brutal as she knew the Nazis were, she didn't think they would shoot her. From what she could tell, they shot people for definite political reasons, people who had done something against the new regime. Surely, the punishment for a seventeen-year-old girl walking in the street wasn't death.

There was something else. Only recently she had heard her mother whispering with the part-time cleaning lady at the hotel, something about a thing the soldiers did to women prisoners. Bronna did not truly understand. It had happened to the wife of the baker in the next street who had worked for the Resistance. He had been arrested, and they came looking for his wife. From what she could tell, what had happened to her was like a beating but worse, something so degrading and barbaric it could only be talked about in secret. Bronna had been studying at the kitchen table when she heard her mother and the cleaning woman. When they realized she was listening, they stopped talking and went back to their work.

Maybe whatever happened to the baker's wife would happen to her. Not knowing exactly what it was made it even more frightening.

The more she picked apart and examined the strands of her fears, the more she turned inward. Even in this terrible place, she could still control her mind. She vowed to live one minute at a time. If she was alive and sane at the end of each minute she would count that a victory and live the next minute.

She dared not cry. It would sap her strength and make her weak. She would not call out or scream. From that moment forward, until somehow she was out of this sewer, this frozen, dark, rank hell, she would live one minute at a time inside herself, in control.

She was sleeping fitfully when she heard the heavy metal door scrape open. The pounding of her heart woke her completely. They were coming to set her free. It had all been some kind of bureaucratic mistake. She rolled over in the darkness and tried to sit up when a fist smashed into her mouth, sending her head crashing back against the wall. She tried to sit up again but was too dazed. Warm, meaty-tasting blood filled her mouth.

There seemed to be two of them. Rough hands were tearing at her clothes. Another pair of hands forced her legs apart. She began to shake violently. She could smell sour whiskey-tainted breath and felt the rough cloth of a uniform. After the sound of ripping zippers she felt flesh against her flesh. Fingers penetrated between her legs. A man with his knees on either side of her forced something that felt both soft and hard at the same time up between her legs. He plunged into her, deeper and deeper. She felt as though she were being ripped in half. The pain made her see little flashes of light behind her eyelids. Finally, he moaned and rolled off of her, and the other took his place.

She focused on her own breathing. If she was breathing she was alive. They were entering her body but they could not enter her mind.

She knew little about men and what they were doing, but what she did know was that what was happening couldn't last forever. Eventually they would finish the wet, painful slapping of flesh upon flesh and go away.

She thought of the warmth of her home, the way the kitchen smelled right before a holiday meal, and the great black stove that filled the room with an all-embracing heat.

The second man was muttering strange words, German words she did not understand. When he was finished, he rolled to his feet and spat on her. She felt the thick wet spot burning into her cheek and kept her eyes tightly closed until she heard their boots scuffing on the grime-covered floor and the door slam closed. For a very long time she lay paralyzed, curled in a fetal position, listening for sounds that warned they might be coming back.

She wrapped her torn clothes around her and tried to sleep. At least when they were on top of her she had been warm.

At dawn she heard the door open again and cringed against the wall. She heard the scrape of metal against the floor and turned to see a female guard place a tin can of dirty lukewarm soup and a small chunk of a stale baguette beside the mattress. She fell upon it like an animal, consuming it before she could even taste it.

All that day and into the next night she lay facing the wall, waiting, dreaming from time to time about her real life. The guard came again with more soup and bread. This time she ate more slowly.

Day passed into night and still she did not move. Her nerve endings would not permit her to concentrate on anything but warning sounds that the men were coming again.

For three straight nights they came. She submitted silently, removing her brain from her body until they left. Afterward, whatever habits of hygiene she had been taught persevered. What little water there was in the toilet bowl after she flushed it she used to wash her face and hands, dipping a corner of her torn skirt. She used the hard crusts of the bread that was brought twice a day to scrub at her teeth. Her comb was useful not only to untangle her hair, which was now matted with grease and soot, but to dig the dirt from under her fingernails.

She was digging at her thumbnail when it occurred to her that if she were dirty, if she were repulsively unclean, perhaps the men would stop coming. She slid the comb under the mattress and stopped making any attempt to clean herself. She did not keep track of how many nights it took. Eventually they stopped coming.

On the morning after the men stopped coming to her cell she awoke to find her mind amazingly clear. The panic and hatred that had gripped her had subsided into a sort of cold resignation fueled by pride. She was alive. She was sane. She had not cried out.

She was in control.

What the men had done to her was not the worst thing that could happen. Being punched she didn't like, but the rest of it, while nasty and painful at first, had broken no bones nor left an open wound. Her body meant nothing to her now. It was only important as long as it supported her head—where her brain was. Her brain inside was pure and whole.

That morning the sun shot a long, slanted funnel of pale gold light through the barred window. It was thin and transmitted no warmth, yet it puddled on the floor beside her mattress and filled her with unspeakable joy.

She returned to her washing routine. Afterward, she moved the filthy mattress next to the pool of sunlight and pulled Maxim's book on chess from under the mattress. Slowly, squinting in the dull light, she began to read.

That first morning, the screams and sounds of gunfire from what could only have been a firing squad in the courtyard below her window began. She listened for a while, waiting for silence so she could continue. When the air grew still again she returned to her book.

As the day passed she found she had entered a fantasy world, a royal court of kings and queens, knights and bishops. A world of strategy and stealth, mathematics and endless intrigue.

She was still reading when the guard came with soup and bread. She made no attempt to hide her book.

The guard waddled across the cell, put down the tin plate and cup, sniffed with disgust at Bronna as she lit the candle for the night, and then left, closing the door behind her.

Bronna smiled. In the time it took the fat Nazi pig to lock the door, Bronna realized something very important had happened. If the guard had tried to take her books, Bronna would have been ready to die for something. As weak as she was, she would have strangled the woman with her bare hands. They would have come and taken Bronna to the courtyard to be shot. She would have died for a reason.

When it grew too dark to read, she brought the candle back to the mattress, went through her ritual of warming her frozen hands, and by candlelight started back on the first page again. Upon the second reading she found she had completely memorized the book.

At night she dreamed of a huge chessboard.

Excitedly, she placed imaginary pieces on it, moving them about in a precise re-creation of the gambits described in the book.

She woke the next morning exhilarated, released from all fear, eager to begin the day. If this was hell, she pondered, it was not inside of her. Hell was being externally imposed upon. She was no longer lonely. Her ability to think and learn peopled her cell.

If she survived this monstrous thing that was happening to her, nothing in her life would be as bad.

She began to save a scrap of her bread from each meal, hiding the crumbs mixed with candle drippings in her skirt. When she had enough bread and wax she began to fashion a crude chess set. First she made the king and queen, carefully fashioning their crowns. Then she worked on the bishops and the towers for the rooks. The pawns were simple triangles with a ball of bread on the top.

On the floor, she outlined a board two feet wide and two feet long. She used the candle soot from the wall to fill in the squares and to stain the black chess pieces. Eventually, she was finished. To hide her handiwork she pulled the mattress over the chessboard. With her comb and pencil she managed to dig a crevice in the crumbling plaster wall large enough to hide the makeshift chess pieces. When all was ready she turned to the first page of exercises in Maxim's book and sat down to play against herself.

The days that passed were no longer endless. So absorbed was she in mastering the complicated game that she would often look up in disbelief when the guard came to light the candle. Again the hateful woman sniffed. This time she studied the board on the floor for a long moment, shook her head as if to indicate that her charge had surely gone mad, and slammed the door.

All day long Bronna's mind left the filthy cell as she maneuvered chess pieces about the makeshift board.

At night, by the light of the candle, she read Maxim's dictionary one word and definition at a time, committing to memory a language she had never heard spoken.

When she felt fluent enough, she turned to the atlas and began to study world geography, forcing herself to use only her new language.

One morning the guard told her it was Christmas. That day she heard the first spoken words other than her own voice attempting English pronunciation and her own muttered prayers.

The guard paused long enough at the door to tell her that because it was Christmas there would be a special meal of roast pig, baked potatoes, and *gâteau au chocolat* for the *Christian* prisoners. As she said it, she handed Bronna her usual tin of soup and crust of bread. Eagerly, she slipped the bread into her pocket. One of the black pawns had crumbled. Now she could replace it.

When the weather began to warm she could sense spring through the tiny window. The walls didn't sweat so much and the light came earlier in the morning. She was finishing her morning wash when she heard the cell door open. A man, a guard she had never seen before, filled the door. "Out!" he commanded.

Bronna rose unsteadily from her kneeling position beside the toilet. She stood blinking at the guard, trying to comprehend.

"Take your things and go, before they change their minds," the guard snarled.

Not quite believing what she was hearing, Bronna snatched the books and her bag from under the mattress, walked around the guard and out the door. Calmly, without a flicker of apprehension or fear, she realized she was going to be shot.

The guard walked her down the long corridor past the other silent cells, out through a double door and down another corridor. The guard opened the front door of the prison and roughly pushed her out onto the steps.

The blaze of sun and smell of fresh spring air so overwhelmed her that she reeled and fell against the side of the building. Behind her the door slammed closed.

She was free.

At first she walked very slowly. She had not walked more than six feet at a time for months. With each step she expected to hear a shout, feel a hand on her shoulder, hear a shot ring out and feel the thud of it striking her in the back. When none of those things happened she began to run down the familiar side streets, across the remembered boulevards, toward home—running until the pain in her chest became unbearable and slowed her to a stagger.

She rounded the corner of her street, tasting blood every time she coughed. Strangers passing, seeing this barefoot filthy creature, her skeletal body hung with the shreds of tattered clothes, hacking blood and gasping, looked away. They had seen too much already in their terror-driven lives to take much note.

As she reached the steps of her father's hotel, she had no strength to continue and gave up, sinking to the stone steps unconscious.

"Shhhhhh!"

Bronna heard the sound and tried to open her eyes. She had no strength to lift her lids.

She heard someone whispering. Behind her closed eyelids she saw the soot-covered walls of her cell in flickering candlelight.

"Don't wake her, she needs her sleep," a gentle voice said very near her head. She could smell something wonderful, like violets. The aroma grew stronger. She could feel soft breath on her face as a cold cloth was pressed to her forehead. Only then did she realize how hot she was, a scalding hot that one feels after a day in the blazing sun, as heat radiates from the skin.

"I think she's waking up," the voice said. It was a woman's voice, bell-like and concerned.

Slowly, painfully, Bronna opened her eyes. She was not in her cell but in a room with wallpaper. Paper that looked somehow familiar, as did the woman leaning over her. She had a pretty, yielding face, gone slightly fleshy around the jaw, and large, dramatic eyes.

"Hello," the woman said sweetly. "How do you feel?"

Bronna could only stare.

"My name is Dexia. How are you feeling?"

She lifted the cloth from Bronna's head and dipped it into a metal basin on the night table.

"Where am I?" she asked, her voice cracking. As she spoke she heard a whistling sound in her chest and she began to cough uncontrollably. It was not until she tried to place her hands over her mouth that she realized they were heavily bandaged. When the spasm passed, she lay back down on the pillow, exhausted. "What's the matter with me?" she said weakly.

"You have a collapsed lung," the woman said. "You've been unconscious for almost five days with a terrible fever from an infection, but we have medicine for that."

"My hands," she cried. "What's the matter with my hands?"

"They were badly burned. They became infected as well."

Bronna studied the woman's beautiful face. "You're Madame Solange," she said. She hadn't recognized the woman at first. She had never seen her with her thick mahogany-colored hair falling down around her shoulders and without makeup. "I'm in your rooms. I remember the wallpaper. You still live here?"

"Yes, my dear. I'm the only one left now," she said sadly. "But do I know you?"

Before Bronna could answer someone spoke from the foot of the bed. "Everyone else is gone."

Bronna looked down at her feet to see a young, dark-skinned woman wearing a long flowing gown she recognized from the section of her prison atlas on India.

"This is Nanti," Madame Solange said, nodding to the young woman. "She takes care of me here and helps me dress at the theater. She's been taking care of you, too."

"Where are my parents?" Bronna asked, afraid of the answer.

The two women exchanged quizzical glances. "Where *is* everybody?" Bronna asked. Something was terribly wrong. "My mother and father. My sister. Where are they?"

"Nanti! *Mon Dieu.*" Madame Solange pressed her hands to her cheeks. "This must be Monsieur Charnov's daughter!" She looked crestfallen. "Dearest girl, I didn't know who you were."

"But Madame!" Nanti said with a shocked expression. "Monsieur Charnov thought his daughter was dead."

"You poor child," Madame Solange cried. "Where have you been?"

"In prison. Since last fall. I was arrested in a student demonstration," she said. "But where are my parents? Do they know I'm all right?"

Madame Solange squeezed Bronna's hand tightly, her eyes filled with tears. "They are gone," she said softly. "Everyone is gone."

"You said that, but where? Did they go to the south? My mother had a sister in Rouen. I can't believe my father would abandon the hotel."

"No, my precious," Madame Solange said quietly. "They were arrested some months ago. From what I know they were taken to the camp in Gurs. I'm afraid we must face the truth, *chérie*. They are surely dead."

Bronna began to cry. Great, choking sobs exploded in her chest. Every time she tried to catch her breath she felt as though she were lifting a cement block with her shoulders. The only way she could ease the pain was to stop crying. She pressed her knuckles against her teeth and swallowed hard, trying to separate her mind from her body as she had done in prison. "My sister, too?" she asked in a tiny voice.

The two women nodded.

"Oh God . . . what happened?" Bronna said through her tears.

"I was not here but I was told about it," Dexia said sadly. "They came one night last November with guns. They found your father's radio and accused him of being with the Resistance. They took everyone away in a truck. When Nanti and I returned from the theater the hotel was empty. There were soldiers guarding the hotel. The only reason they let us back in was because I was with my friend, Major von Kessel."

"The major," Bronna said flatly.

"*Oui,*" Madame Solange said, surprised. "You know the major?"

"I saw him," she said, closing her eyes. "Here . . . before . . ."

Behind her eyes she saw the dark bulk of the men who came to her cell and felt the pressure of the brass buttons on their uniforms against her naked stomach. Buttons like those on the major's uniform. "You're one of them, aren't you?" she said under her breath.

"What do you mean?" Madame Solange said, releasing Bronna's hand.

"A Nazi. You must be a Nazi. They didn't arrest you. They didn't shoot you or send you to a camp because of your friend. That's why you have wonderful creams and soap and hot chocolate and silk things to wear when no one else does. That makes you a Nazi."

"You are quite wrong, my dear," Madame Solange said calmly. "I do what I have to do. Perhaps when you are well you will understand."

Bronna thought she was going to drown in her hatred for what had been done to her, to her family, to her innocent, peaceful life. She took a deep breath in order to scream. It was no use. It was like trying to drink through a straw with a hole in it. Just the attempt produced another violent coughing spasm. Tiny specks of blood splattered across the lace embroidery of the snow-white sheet.

"Madame, should I find the doctor?" Nanti whispered urgently, moving to the other side of the bed and putting her arms around Bronna's shoulders to comfort her.

"No, Nanti," her mistress said sharply. "We can't risk it now that we know who she is. If they realize she's here we're all in terrible trouble. They will take her away as well."

"*Oui*, Madame," Nanti said. She poured a glass of cold water and held it to Bronna's lips. When the coughing stopped, Bronna lay back against the satin pillows exhausted and unable to speak. For the first time she realized how terribly sick she was.

Madame Solange stood beside the bed looking down at her. She was taller than Bronna remembered. Her skin was whiter than milk. Her deep-red hair fell forward against her high cheekbones. The hairline came to a sharp widow's peak in the middle of her forehead. She had an actress's proud posture and presentation. She was the most magnificent-looking woman Bronna had ever seen outside of a film.

Madame Solange turned and walked toward the armoire against the wall. She opened it and began to remove some clothes. "I can dress myself tonight, Nanti. You stay here with the child." She turned back to Bronna, who was staring at her. "Do you have identity papers?"

Bronna slowly shook her head. "No, they took them at the police station after I signed some form."

Madame Solange looked upset. "You signed something?" she gasped.

"Why, yes. I didn't think it meant anything."

Madame Solange glanced at Nanti, who was biting her full, bright-red lips into a thin line. "Well, I guess I know what has to be done now," she said in a resigned voice. "Nanti, we'll have to get her new papers. It's nothing to worry about, dear. I'll take care of everything. You just concentrate on getting well. Soon you will have a new name."

"But my name is Bronna Charnov!"

Madame Solange placed her finger over Bronna's lips. "No, no, no, my darling girl. Never again. You must never speak that name again."

A black Nazi staff car with flags flying from both front fenders glided to the curb in front of the hotel that had once belonged to Yasha Charnov. Dexia Solange, the leading lady of the frothy Molière play at the Odéon, stepped to the curb. Dexia had been appearing before capacity crowds of German officers and elite sympathizers and their ladies at each performance. Afterward, swathed in what they had had in their closets before the fashion industry shut down, they moved on to Maxim's, the Ritz, or the Lido.

The stolid Germans had never lived such a glittering social life. They were, as their sickening saying went, *freulich wie Gott im Frankreich*—as happy as God in France.

For most Parisians, life was decidedly less pleasant. Fuel was in increasingly short supply, as was food, clothing, and peace of mind. As each day passed, the brutal heel of the Nazi boot ground with increasing pressure upon the fragile life in the City of Light.

Dexia Solange had to employ her acting talents more skillfully offstage than on during these dark days. Outwardly, the hard life around her had little or no effect on the beautiful actress. Inwardly, she seethed with hatred and longed for revenge. The little Charnov girl recovering in her rooms at the hotel was not the only one who had lost her family to the Nazis. Dexia's beautiful young brother Laval had died, a soldier at Dunkirk when the French army was overrun.

She permitted herself to be seen publicly with Major von Kessel. His protection was vital, and the privileges he offered were more important than just sweet-smelling soap for her bath and fresh meat for her table.

It was he who persuaded the authorities to turn the little hotel on the rue St.-Denis over to her.

With the workmen Major von Kessel provided her, she was turning the first floor into a cabaret and supper club for the exclusive entertainment of the officers of the Reich.

At the top of the hotel steps, Nanti was waiting. She took her mistress's copper satin evening cloak and fur muff. "Dr. Gautier is waiting in the lounge," she said, leaning close to Dexia's ear.

"Nanti!" Dexia said, distressed. "You know it is dangerous for him to come here now."

"It's all right, you'll see," Nanti said with a sly smile.

Dexia moved through the lobby with some urgency. Before she had learned who the Charnov girl was, she had used a doctor the major had arranged for. She could no longer trust that arrangement.

As she entered the lounge, the room appeared to be deserted. The drop cloths made the covered furniture look like ghosts huddled against the freshly painted dark-red walls. Halfway up a wooden ladder against the far wall, a man in overalls and a workman's cap was carefully polishing a porcelain chandelier.

"Ah, Madame Solange," he said with a smile as Dexia approached the foot of the ladder. "Do you approve of my work?"

"Come down from there, Edmond," she commanded, suppressing a smile. "You'll break your neck."

Dr. Edmond Gautier, director of the Hospital for Special Surgery in Neuilly, put down his dirty rag and slowly climbed down the ladder.

When he reached the floor he doffed his cap and bowed. "I also do windows and woodwork, Madame," he said with an elaborate bow.

"Very clever," Dexia said, giving in to a smile. "Whose bright idea was this?"

"Your maid's, actually," he said, picking at his overalls. He lifted his head and looked at Dexia, his face tight with concern. "You girls are playing a dangerous game, my dear. Not even your fancy major can help you if someone finds out that girl didn't die as you said."

"Shhhh!" Dexia hissed. "I can't think about that now. What news do you have?"

"It's all arranged. We can do the work at the hospital tomorrow night," he said. "My wife is a nurse; she will assist me. I don't trust anyone else."

Dexia looked at him with love and sadness. The gray hairs in his neat goatee were beginning to outnumber the black ones, and his handsome face had fresh, hard lines. Edmond Gautier and Dexia had been lovers once and remained steadfast friends. Dexia knew of the Nazis' suspicions of his work with the Resistance and worried constantly that his invaluable healing skills might be lost to those of their comrades who were being injured with frightening frequency. For those wounded, shot, or maimed, the word that the Dove, Dr. Gautier's code name, was on his way was the answer to a prayer. She had hesitated to involve him in her scheme to transform the Charnov girl into her "cousin from Lyons," but she had no choice. The girl had suffered enough. She was her responsibility now.

"Give me the details quickly, Edmund," she said, closing the door of the lounge. "I'm afraid the people with whom I am forced to dine demand punctuality."

"I understand," he said.

"How are we going to do this?" Dexia asked, leaning against the drop cloth-covered bar.

Dr. Gautier pressed his fingertips to his forehead before speaking. "All right," he said. "I just examined her. She is still dangerously underweight for surgery. However, her lungs are clear. There isn't much we can do about her hands. The burns were greatly compromised. The embedded candle wax aggravated the infection. There is permanent scar tissue that cannot be removed."

"What does that mean in the long run? Will she be able to use her hands?" Dexia asked.

"Oh, yes. But the fingertips may be permanently numb, and she no longer has fingerprints. All things considered, that might be to our advantage."

Dexia nodded. "You're sure she's strong enough to take this kind of operation?"

"Ummm, not physically, perhaps, but mentally she's a tough one. Considering what she's been through, I'd say she's up to it."

Dexia frowned. "She was strong enough to virtually come back from the dead, Edmond. Certainly a little bit of plastic surgery . . ." Dexia voice trailed off. She knew she was being overly optimistic.

"I'd hardly call what you want to do a *little* plastic surgery. You have to understand, this is a highly unrefined procedure. The work you want done will require several hours of anesthesia. The girl still weighs only eighty pounds. Although the injured lung is fully inflated, it's still weak and might not take the prolonged respiratory depression of the anesthetic. I'm prepared to chance it, but it would really be better if you waited."

"We don't have time, Edmond. I've got to get the club opened. I have already told them that my niece is coming from Lyons to help me run it. She has to appear on the scene as scheduled."

"I take it you have new papers for her."

"Yes, yes," Dexia said briskly, "in the name of Cleo AuCoin, a girl the same age who died of typhus. The papers are perfect, thanks to our friends. The only thing I lack now is her picture."

The doctor shifted his weight against the ladder. "I have to tell you, Dexia, that I strongly advise against any breast augmentation. We don't have the necessary tissue. My supplies are monitored down to the last suture. I can do her nose, however, as well as restructure the jaws and cheeks. We've learned a lot from our work with the maimed faces of our soldiers."

"What about her hairline? I want as much altered as possible. Absolutely no one must recognize her. All we need is one person who remembers little Bronna Charnov and . . . well, you know the price."

Dr. Gautier waved dismissively. "You don't need me to alter her hairline, Dexia. That can be done by anyone with patience and a pair of tweezers. Better than that, change the color and the cut."

Dexia glanced nervously at the door of the lounge and then her watch. "Will she look completely different?"

"Absolutely," he said, smiling confidently. "I can't guarantee she will be beautiful enough to qualify as your blood relative, but one can't have everything."

Dexia lowered her eyes. "Thank you, Edmond," she said quietly.

The doctor took her hand, turned it over, and lightly kissed her palm. It was a gesture so simple, so intimate, that she felt an old stirring for him. "I don't know why you are taking such risks, dear lady. I'm sure you have your reasons," he said. He turned and looped his arm through hers as they walked toward the door. "Now, quickly, here is what I want you to do."

In the last act of Molière's *Le Bourgeois Gentilhomme*, Dexia Solange's character was onstage almost throughout. The night after she met with Dr. Gautier, Dexia stood stage right, as usual, perspiring under the tight bodice of her watered-silk gown and high powdered wig. It was a silly play, full of nonsense and running around the stage, but the sea of uniformed officers out front every evening proved it was not too silly for the Reich. She took her cue and stepped to the footlights to deliver the inane curtain speech she had been saying eight times a week for months. As she reached the edge of the stage, she clasped her throat, threw her head back, making sure her eyes rolled dramatically, and lowered herself limply to the floor. The voluminous skirt of her gown cushioned her fall. She closed her eyes and listened to the reaction. The audience gasped in unison. She could hear footsteps running, and heard Raymond, the stage manager, frantically calling in a stage whisper from the wings for someone to bring down the curtain.

Dexia lay with her eyes closed and her arms outstretched on the cold floor of the stage until Nanti reached her as they had arranged and began issuing orders. She felt strong arms lifting her and carrying her backstage. As she was moved down the corridor toward her dressing room, she heard Raymond screaming for someone to call an ambulance.

As soon as the two actors carrying her laid her on the chaise in her dressing room, Nanti ordered everyone from the room. Within moments Dr. Gautier, who had been in the audience, was rapping on the closed door.

Nanti had already removed Dexia's wig and was unzipping the back of her gown. Wordlessly, Dr. Gautier stepped to the closet and helped Bronna out.

As soon as Dexia stepped out of her gown, Nanti dropped it over Bronna's head. It hung off her thin shoulders and flat chest like so much drapery fabric. Next came the wig.

That nothing fit did not matter. By the time she was bundled onto a stretcher and covered with blankets, the only thing that could be seen were the glistening curls on the top of her head as she was carried out from the stage door to the waiting ambulance, accompanied by a disguised Dexia and Nanti.

That night, as Dr. Gautier and his wife worked by candlelight in a windowless operating room in a Paris suburb, Cleo AuCoin was born.

Cleo's face healed quickly, and while she waited to make her debut in the rooms downstairs, Dexia mercilessly put her through her lessons.

"No, no, no, no, not that way!" Dexia said sharply. "Shoulders back, chin up, tuck your derrière under. *Faites attention et comptes de un à cinq.* One. Two. Three. Four. Five. Turn and—"

"Please, Dexia, can I rest?" Cleo asked, slumping against the back of the couch in Dexia's lavishly redone sitting room.

"*May* I rest!" Dexia corrected.

"May I rest?"

"Yes. You're doing beautifully, *chérie.* A few more lessons and you will walk like a model at the house of Vionnet. Just remember to hold the shoulders back. Think of a piece of string attached to the top of your head pulling up . . . up. Then raise your chin, elongate the neck. How you present yourself controls how people react to you."

"I'm trying, Dexia," Cleo sighed. "Truly I am."

"I know, my dear, but carriage is so important. Now I must rush to the dressmaker's. Tonight I'll take you down to see what we have done. You won't believe the changes."

Cleo collapsed into the chair next to the window and let the thin winter sun flow over her face and throat, something she had not been permitted to do until her scars had completely healed.

All day she had been excited about finally leaving the suite and going downstairs for the first time since her operation.

She had come a great distance in the rooms at the top of the hotel. She was an entirely new person from the broken, filthy eighty-pound child who had collapsed on the front steps of the hotel. She had been dehydrated, nearly consumptive with a collapsed lung, and had a venereal infection that had been raging through her reproductive organs unchecked for months, giving her a soaring temperature that produced convulsions.

Gently, tenderly, Nanti, who knew how to do such things for women from her childhood in the streets of Calcutta, fixed everything.

There was little left of what she remembered as her former appearance. Her oval face was more angular now. The doctor had given her high cheekbones like Dexia's and a distinctive jawline. The new chin made her mouth seem fuller, somehow, and porcelain caps covered the damage that months of malnutrition and brushing with bread crusts had done to her teeth. The stress of prison and the meager diet had left her ordinary brown hair dead and colorless, hanging limply at the temples and away from her forehead.

The magic potions and creams Nanti had applied took away the brown and turned her hair to a pale silver. Nanti then cut what had been a tangled, thinning mass into a blunt Joan of Arc cap with straight bangs that just covered her eyebrows and emphasized her pale eyes. They had experimented with Dexia's supply of stage makeup, even though it was becoming very scarce. One could no more buy kohl for the eyes and lip rouge than fresh carrots or *petit pois*. Whatever luxuries they had—soap, stockings, toilet paper, or chocolate—were provided by Dexia's German "friends" and what Nanti could scrounge on the black market.

As Cleo recuperated, she filled her days teaching Nanti to play chess. In turn, Nanti, who had been a nanny to a British family in New Delhi before coming to work for Dexia, helped her learn to pronounce the English she had taught herself to read in prison. English lessons given by a Hindu to a French girl created an interesting accent.

Their studies were often interrupted by their work decorating the old bedrooms in the hotel. Cleo had not understood the intended use for the rooms until the day Nanti returned with an armload of heavy fabric that she had bartered from an abandoned warehouse on the outskirts of town.

Cleo was in bed reading, as usual. "Oh, Nanti," she said, looking up. "What beautiful cloth. Whatever is it for?"

Nanti dropped the bolts of fabric onto a chair and sighed with relief.

"The drapes and canopies are for the beds. They stole this from a warehouse somewhere. I was lucky to get enough," she answered.

Cleo put down her book. "Drapes and canopies? That's very fancy."

"For what the pigs will pay for an hour in those rooms they have to be," Nanti said. Her dark eyes narrowed into mean little slits.

"An hour? I don't understand," Cleo said, bewildered. "People don't stay in hotel rooms for only an hour."

Nanti stood staring at her with a calculating look that made Cleo realize she was wondering if she should explain. She pushed back the thin fabric of the sari that she always looped over her head when she went out and started to laugh.

"What's so funny?" Cleo asked, feeling hurt.

Nanti stepped closer to the side of the bed. "Forgive me, little Cleo," she said. "I am not laughing at you. Merely the situation that you could be here for so long and not understand what is going on downstairs."

Cleo dropped her book onto the coverlet. "Well, I don't!" she said tightly. "Supppose you explain."

"We are a whorehouse, my friend. The finest whorehouse in all Paris. We will serve the best wine the Reich can supply and the best food the Nazis can steal from the starving people who eat garbage from the street. Our girls are the most beautiful available, and the Nazis will pay dearly for one hour with them in our beautiful new bedrooms."

"You are going to do this in my father's house?" Cleo asked in stunned surprise.

Nanti's pretty face grew a shade less dark. "You must never speak of that, ever. This is the house of Madame Solange. You must never forget that."

It dawned on Cleo then, that perhaps her own transformation had been for purposes she had never been told. "Nanti," she said tentatively, "am I supposed to . . . you know. Is that why Dexia has gone to so much trouble for me? To change me? Am I supposed to be with those officers, in one of those canopied beds?"

"Oh, no!" Nanti said, shocked. "Never. There is no shortage of women who want to work for Madame Solange. They have been coming for interviews for weeks now. Madame Solange loves you. You are her family!"

"You're sure, Nanti?"

"I'm sure, Cleo," Nanti said, unrolling the fabric on the rug and bending to measure it.

From then on, until she was completely well, Cleo did not question the goings-on downstairs. She had plenty to eat, new books to read, and, soon, she would have a brand-new life. From what Nanti told her of what was going on beyond the walls of the hotel, she was a very lucky girl.

When Madame Solange walked her "cousin" through the immaculate new kitchen and into the main dining room, Cleo gasped with delight. When her father ran the hotel it had been a rather dingy room with faded flowered wallpaper and dim light bulbs in ordinary metal wall fixtures. What Dexia and Raymond, the stage manager from the theater, had done to it was amazing. The ceiling was tented and draped with heavy red velvet caught at the center by an enormous red Venetian-glass chandelier. The banquettes along the wall were black leather with brass fittings. Each table was covered with pink silk drops to the floor and heavy glass tops. Through the newly created arched doorway, she could see a slightly smaller room that was a cocktail lounge done in black-and-white lacquer. At one end was a bandstand and a tiny dance floor.

In what had been the dark, cramped lobby, the elevator cage had been moved to the second floor and a spiral staircase with a long curved brass banister installed.

"Well? What do you think?" Dexia asked as they finished the tour. They were standing in the middle of what had been the old lobby.

'I think it's truly amazing," Cleo said, meaning it. She would never have imagined that anything like it could be created from the little back-street hotel in which she had grown up.

"Me, too," Dexia said, smiling. Taking Cleo's hand, she led her back to the cocktail lounge. "Sit down for a minute, Cleo. We need to talk."

Cleo sat down, wondering what Dexia was going to say, still dimly thinking about the rooms upstairs. She sat on the edge of a padded banquette. Dexia leaned across the table and depressed a button on the wall as though to summon a waiter.

"Is someone here?" Cleo asked, looking around the empty room.

"Yes, someone very important who I want you to meet."

Cleo looked up to see a powerfully built man push open the kitchen door at the back of the lounge. He was young, probably in his early twenties, but not so young that he hadn't been able to grow a broad mustache, the ends of which curved dramatically across his cheeks. Instead of a waiter's jacket as Cleo expected, he was wearing black pants and a black leather jacket over a common white undershirt.

"Good evening, Dexia," he said in a deep, resonant voice. "Am I finally to meet your cousin?"

Dexia looked up at him and smiled. "Sit down, Jacques," she said before she turned to Cleo. "Cleo, this is our friend, Jacques. He is going to be our headwaiter, captain, whatever he wants to call himself. During the hours that the hotel is in operation, he will answer to you."

"To *me*?" Cleo asked, pressing her open palm against her chest. "What do you mean? I don't know how—"

"Let me finish," Dexia said a little impatiently. "At other times, when you are doing your real work, you will answer to him, as will the girls who will be entertaining the Nazi officers. He is the head of our maquis. His code name is Fox. When you have worked with him for a while you will see why. Right, Jacques?"

Jacques nodded and took a seat next to Dexia, facing Cleo across the table. "Do you want me to explain the rest?"

"Please," Cleo said. "First, what's a maquis?"

"That is a division of the underground," Dexia explained. "The Resistance divides itself into maquis. Jacques commands ours."

Cleo couldn't believe her ears. So that was what all this was about! She was overcome with a surge of love for Dexia. She cared so much about her that she had come to accept Dexia's open collaboration with the Nazi regime as a means of survival. Now she saw what it truly was.

Jacques swung a chair around and straddled it, wrapping his long arms around the back. "Cleo, we need you," he said. "Dexia could not speak until now. We had to be sure you could be trusted. Clearly we now feel you can."

"Thank you," she said.

"Let me explain how we plan to work. Everything we learn here from our—shall we call them guests?—will be communicated to our counterparts in England."

Cleo was fascinated. "How can you communicate with England?" she asked Jacques. "I don't understand."

"Ah," Jacques said, smiling. He turned to Dexia. "May I show her?"

"Of course. You go on up. I want to check on the kitchen. A new supply of Bordeaux was just delivered. I'd better go count the bottles."

Jacques led Cleo to the second floor and climbed into the tiny cage of the elevator. Cleo said nothing as they ascended to the roof. She was thrilled to be included and trusted with something so dangerous and important.

As Jacques pushed open the heavy metal door that led to the roof he put his finger to his mustache. "Try not to make a sound. If we wake them they'll make a terrible racket."

Cleo stepped onto the roof and peered into the darkness. All she could see were dozens of cages silhouetted against the night sky. "What is this?" she asked, completely bewildered.

Jacques stepped to one of the cages and unlatched the door. He reached in and pulled out a small bird. It lay ruffled and cooing in his hand. He held one of the bird's legs between his fingers. "Look at this," he said.

On the bird's leg was a tiny cylinder the size of half a Gauloise. "These are carrier pigeons. There are a dozen of them mixed among the other birds. You should know that Dexia plans to make her restaurant famous for its roast squab. That way no one will suspect these cages on the roof."

Cleo nodded.

"Now. One of these birds," Jacques said, holding up the baffled pigeon, "can make it to Dover in less than six hours. Our people extract the message, replace it with one of their own, and throw it into the air. Within a day we have exchanged vital information that will make France free again."

Cleo stared out over the city. It lay, as usual, in complete darkness except for an occasional flicker of light escaping from a loose blackout curtain or the taped headlights of a German car on patrol. She had last been on the roof with her little sister. It was their favorite secret place on hot summer nights. Then, the city had stretched before them as far as the eye could see, looking like a blanket of diamonds had been thrown over it. On one side they had been able to see the Eiffel Tower flooded with light. On the other, the Seine wound its way to the sea, glistening and dark as a satin ribbon. Now the brightest thing to be seen were dull stars peeking from behind high night clouds. The city was dead. Her entire family was dead. If it hadn't been for an extraordinary act of kindness on the part of Dexia Solange, Cleo, too, would be dead, if not completely mad from grief.

She remembered the day Nanti had come scurrying in from her rounds through the back alleys of the Left Bank, chattering excitedly. That morning, Nanti had heard that the Jews who had been taken to the camps were being gassed and shoved naked into giant ovens. Men, women, children, babies—cooked before they knew what was happening to them.

Cleo had listened in stunned silence. Later, after Nanti had scurried away on yet another errand, Cleo had buried her face in her hands and sobbed. Two days passed before she could speak. Having no vocabulary to articulate her pain, her hatred had rendered her mute.

Here, at last, was her chance to use her impotent rage. To strike back, and in some small way repay Dexia.

She inhaled the night air deeply. It stank—of filth and fear and man's cruelty to man.

When she had turned away from Jacques to look out over the city, she was still, in her heart, little Bronna Charnov, a pigtailed schoolgirl with nothing more important on her mind than passing her "bac." She turned back to face him, a grown woman with few illusions about what people were capable of on either end of the scale of good and evil. "What can I do to help?" she asked.

He smiled for the first time, a great wide smile that flashed white in the dim light. "First," he said, "you will write the nightly communiqué and bring it here. I will show you how to handle the birds. There are others doing this throughout France, so you will sign your messages by your code name. I have chosen the name 'Anya'."

The girls who came to work for Madame Solange were like no women Cleo had ever seen. Each one was more exotic than the next, but not in the way she had expected. She had seen streetwalkers before the Germans came. She and her sister had whispered and giggled as they passed, eyeing the loud, tightly revealing clothes, the exposed flesh and flamboyant hair. The girls who came to work for Madame Solange looked as though they had stepped out of the films she had seen before the war.

They were absolutely beautiful.

They moved among the tables of the club and dining room like stately flowers. Their laughter from the banquettes sounded like wind chimes, never rising above a certain, very discreet level. Each had a way of looking at a man as though he were the only man alive, never speaking when she sensed he wanted to speak, anticipating a need for a cigar to be lighted, a glass to be refilled.

When they moved onto the dance floor, they curled themselves around the men, sometimes touching, sometimes holding themselves a tantalizing inch away from the front of a uniform.

Cleo watched them in awe, knowing Dexia had chosen them from many who applied, for their beauty, their taste, and their style. Dexia named them to suit their personalities.

There was Ivory, with skin and arms like swan's down. Jonquil was golden, with the eyes of a tiger, Violetta had indigo highlights in her long black hair, and Jade's eyes were like emeralds. There was Melisande, Domineaux, Monique, and a fragile blonde named Fleur. Each was unique, speaking at least French and German. A few spoke English and Spanish as well. None were the flotsam and jetsam of the Paris streets. Some had been aspiring actresses at the beginning of the war, some had been dancers. Some of them were already prostitutes "with possibilities," as Dexia put it.

Nanti found many of them by combing the boulevards and cafés, whispering to them that a hot meal and a kind word could be had if they would come with her to *l'hôtel* for an interview with Madame Solange, a name that more and more was being whispered behind hands in the cafés and smart clubs.

Dexia hired only one in ten who appeared at *l'hôtel*. She wanted a particular kind of girl. They had to be tall. Their figures had to be better than good, and they had to be willing to be trained. What they did in the bedrooms above the main floor of the hotel did not concern Dexia. She would teach them nothing there. What she cared about was what she called a girl's "salon presentation." How could a powerful man be expected to reveal himself to a graceless, dull woman, no matter how beautiful she was or what she did for him in bed?

L'hôtel was an immediate success. Cleo's original misgivings about the sexual aspects of her surroundings soon gave way to her fascination with the information being gathered in the club and its perfumed bedrooms. The place was abuzz with information casually revealed about troop movements, hidden submarine bases along the Normandy coast, ammunition dumps deep in the forests, and what the Gestapo knew of the activities of the Resistance. Information—it was as powerful as sex. The more information one had, the more control.

Sex was not, however, a commodity to be demeaned. The money and influence of sex fed everyone at the hotel while the world outside had little to eat. It kept them warm when all of Paris was freezing. There was electricity to heat bathwater, light makeup mirrors, cook the superb food, and press the girls' dresses.

But nothing more graphically illustrated Cleo's belief that information had more power than sex than a BBC broadcast reporting that a German troop train carrying heavily armed soldiers through the Dordogne had been dynamited into oblivion by the Resistance. Only two days before, Cleo had placed the train's schedule (found in the pocket of an officer's storm coat in the checkroom) in the little canister on one of her birds and hurled it skyward.

Cleo awoke and checked her watch. It would be daylight soon. She just had time to wash, brush her hair, and quickly dress. Before she slipped out the door she splashed a touch of cologne on her throat and wrists.

Jacques would be waiting on the roof. She hadn't seen him in days.

Over the months they had worked out an extremely efficient system. If there was a message to be sent, Cleo would leave the nightclub office in back of the kitchen at midnight and move, unnoticed, toward the elevator. In her room next to Dexia's suite, she would encode the night's message, then write it in the invisible ink Jacques had showed her how to use. It was mixed with a chemical that would react only to the urine of their English agent a few hours after he had ingested a reactive pill. If something happened to their operative, the formula was changed to accommodate whoever took his place. Cleo would write the message, coil it into a tube, and slip it into the hem of her dress for placement in the canister.

At dawn, Jacques would close down the restaurant for the night, and before it got light, go to the roof and retrieve the message from the incoming bird.

At first, when she began meeting him at dawn, he had been cross with her, saying it was too dangerous. She finally convinced him that she was as invisible at dawn as she was at midnight.

It wasn't that the men who frequented *l'hôtel* did not admire Madame Solange's young cousin with the pale hair and erect posture, but there was something off-putting about the girl. An air, an attitude that communicated aloof disinterest.

"No one bothers a thistle in a garden full of eager roses," she had said to Jacques when he asked her about the men who came to the hotel.

He had smiled at her remark and gone about his work, handling the cooing bird with remarkable tenderness for such a strong man.

Often, depending on the winds and weather, there were delays, and the two conspirators lingered on the rooftop.

One morning, just before light broke, Jacques took her hand and, as easily as if he were offering to teach her how to play cat's cradle, taught her how to kill.

He taught her how a sudden jab under the heart with four straight fingers could drop a man dead at her feet. He demonstrated how to choke off the air supply by placing a little finger in the corner of someone's mouth, extending a thumb to the ear, and yanking backward. This revealed the victim's throat long enough to deliver a swift, deadly chop with the side of the hand to the Adam's apple. He showed her how, with a forceful twist of the body, a simple handshake could flip a man twice her size and weight over her shoulder and slam him to the ground.

From time to time Jacques would leave the hotel with no notice. Madame Solange would tell her guests that her maître d' had gone to the country to locate wild strawberries or better goose liver or a secret truck convoy carrying wine for their delectation. Cleo knew that whatever he was doing, it was dangerous. More and more she found herself missing him, and growing faint with relief when he reappeared.

As she stepped onto the roof, knowing he was there, waiting, she found herself trembling, although the summer air had cooled little during the night. She felt a strong breeze. Not good for landings, she thought, brushing her blowing bangs out of her eyes.

She could see him, leaning on his elbows on the low wall that encircled the roof. Above his head a spiral of smoke lifted into the sky in the direction of Notre Dame. He was not wearing his tuxedo but a black open-throat shirt and trousers. He saw her and flicked away his cigarette. She walked toward him quietly, trying not to disturb the sleeping birds huddled in their cages on either side.

"Good morning," she whispered, looking up at him, embarrassed at having soaked herself in cologne, the aroma of which seemed to have intensified in the heat.

He looked down at her, his face unsmiling, and said nothing.

"Are you all right?" she asked, noticing the tense little lines that radiated from the corners of his eyes and knowing that he had not slept.

He turned away and looked out over the city. "It's getting bad," he said in a bone-weary voice.

"Is it?"

"Haven't you been listening? Both the BBC and the French Service from Algiers can talk of nothing else."

"Not since Monday," she answered. "It's been so busy. I did notice the mood of the men, however. They are coming earlier and earlier and drinking more and more. They either drink because they think they are winning or because they think they are losing. That colonel—the one the girls call Piggy?—he told Jade that the electric plants are being sabotaged all over the city."

"Yes, the *maquisards* are causing havoc. But there is something they are doing that makes me afraid for you and Dexia and the girls."

"What?" Cleo asked, alarmed.

"In the past week our people have killed dozens of pro-Nazi French. Last night there was an attack on a depot near Chartres. They took three local men who had been selling fuel to the German army trucks as prisoners."

Cleo stared at him, astounded. "But surely we are safe, Jacques," she said. "They must know what we are doing."

Jacques slowly shook his head, "Not necessarily, Cleo," he said sadly. "There are a few, at the top, of course, but what if something happens to them? Who will speak for all of you here?"

"You will speak!" Cleo said in an angry whisper. "You will tell them!"

"And what if something happens to me?"

Cleo stood silently. The trail of smoke over Notre Dame had disappeared. In its place the first jagged streak of dawn split the dark sky. She tried to imagine what her life would be like without Jacques, without his friendship, without these meetings in the dark. She had never loved or needed anyone besides her family, Madame Solange, and Nanti. She had never bothered to examine her feelings toward Jacques. He treated her like a little sister, a useful assistant in his work. Never, even when he was teaching her to kill someone, when she could feel his breath on her neck and his strong arms around her, had he given any indication that she was anything but a student being taught a useful lesson. In turn, she had never shown a reaction to how touching him had made her feel. She would die before admitting to him that the feel of his arms kept her sleepless on many a night.

Suddenly, she was overwhelmed with the thought of losing him. She threw her arms around his neck and buried her face in his chest. The minute she felt the smooth cloth of his shirt against her cheek she was mortified. She tried to pull away only to have him encircle her in his arms.

He pulled back his head and lifted her chin, staring deeply into her eyes. "We should have done this a long time ago," he said. His voice sounded different, tight and excited.

"Done what?" she asked, watching his lips get closer and closer.

She let herself dissolve into his kiss, his arms, his body, giving in to a feeling that she had never known before—one she did not want to end.

"Come," he said, releasing her. "Let's go downstairs."

"Where downstairs?"

"To your room."

It was the answer she wanted to hear.

When he made love to her it was as though she had never been touched. The horrible memories of what had been done to her in prison dissolved into nothingness. His touch was as light as air, and the gentle kisses that showered every inch of her body made her first tingle, then float. When their passion was spent, she wept. The joy of being loved, the bliss of release, was beyond any feeling she had ever known. Through the morning hours, in her darkened room, she lay in his arms and told him, the first person to truly know, what had happened to her in prison. As she told him about the nights of terror he held her and stroked her hair. Finally, she wept as she had never wept. And still he held her.

When she finally stopped, feeling spent and suffused with relief, she propped herself on one elbow and looked down at him. "Is this what they do in the rooms here?" she asked.

"This? Holding each other?" he asked with a smile.

"No, I mean what we did before that?"

"Of course not," he said laughing. "They do not make love in the rooms here, Cleo, my darling girl."

"I don't understand."

"Yes, you do. Sex in the rooms downstairs is buying and selling release. The sex you experienced in prison was a form of killing. Those men were trying to kill your soul." He lifted her up and gently pressed her down into the pillow and bent over her. "What I am doing here," he said into her open mouth, "is giving you mine."

No one had ever said such things to her. During her long months of recovery she had read poetry and marveled at its music, its ability to explain things in beautiful ways, ways that made her heart soar. His words were re-creating that feeling.

Again, they flowed together. She felt as though they were floating as one being, on a long, tranquil river. The only solid things around her were the sound of his words, the sweet weight of his body, and her overpowering need for him.

By the spring of 1944 Paris was starving.

The supplies of food, drugs, any consumable item that extended physical survival, had almost disappeared.

There was no packaged milk, no potatoes, little bread. Eggs and cooking oil were so scarce that people were not strong enough to stand in the long, never-ending lines. The only vegetables available were cattle-feed-grade turnips. Coffee, if one could call it that, was brewed from acorns collected in the streets and parks, a mixture so vile and bitter only the desperate drank it. Electricity was limited in Parisian homes to a precious half hour a day. The only form of transportation was by foot or bicycle.

For the German officers and the collaborationist elite, life in Paris was considerably more bearable. Every table at Maxim's and Scheherazade was booked. Edith Piaf sang to sold-out crowds at the Moulin Rouge, as did her young protégé, Yves Montand. Underfed horses still raced on weekends at Longchamps and Auteuil, where bets were made with cigarettes, the currency of choice.

Madame Solange's hotel was virtually a private club, where rank and influence were necessary even to take a glass of wine at the bar where other German officers stood three deep each and every night. The rooftop cages still supplied succulent squab. The mimeograph machine in the office had been pressed into service. After the evening's printing of menus for the next day had been run off, Cleo turned to printing copies of the underground newspaper written by members of their maquis.

Some of the original girls were no longer at the hotel. Dexia had dismissed Ivory for a drug habit. It had been supported by a Nazi doctor's access to morphine, while people beaten by the Gestapo had broken bones reset without anesthetic.

Domineaux left to marry a Nazi officer and live in Berlin, sending word that she was dancing with the Führer at parties and balls. Jonquil left to join the chorus at the Gaumont Palace, the popular music hall. Star, a girl the Nazis discovered was Jewish, killed herself when they came to arrest her, not knowing that Dexia had faced them down and sent them away.

In June, when the allied forces landed at Normandy, the lounge at *l'hôtel* was uncharacteristically subdued. Upstairs in Dexia's suite there were muffled sounds of celebration. Dexia had been able to use the clandestine shortwave radio after Jacques had produced earphones for silent listening through the static of the Germans' jamming attempts. When they heard the news, Dexia, Nanti, and Cleo hugged one another and cried for joy.

"This calls for a toast," Dexia said excitedly. "Nanti, do we have any of General Volgren's champagne up here?"

"An entire case!" Nanti squealed delightedly, clapping her hands and scurrying to the refrigerator in the kitchen. *L'hôtel*'s electricity was now provided by its own generator on the roof, supplied by Jacques, who had "liberated" it from a truck carelessly left unguarded near the hotel.

Nanti poured them each a flute of the best champagne left in France. *"Vive la France, vive les Américains,"* Dexia whispered, holding out her glass.

Cleo took a long sip and stared into space, wondering how to ask Dexia about something that had been troubling her since the day Jacques had first mentioned it up on the roof.

"What's the matter, Cleo?" Dexia asked from her favorite spot on the sofa laden with tasseled brocade pillows. "Aren't you happy?"

Cleo paused and put down her glass. "What will happen to us when the Americans come?"

"Nothing! We'll replace our big blond Nazis with big blond cowboys," she said nonchalantly as she polished off her glass.

Cleo noticed that Dexia was drinking more since she had stopped going to the theater. She claimed the hotel needed her full time. Cleo thought the theater bored her compared to the nightly intrigue of her now-famous establishment.

She was more afraid for Dexia than she was for herself. She had survived the Nazis once and remembered all too well her prison revelation. *Nothing will ever be this bad again.* Dexia, she felt, had never been tested. She was so beautiful, so unaware of personal suffering. Cleo wanted desperately not to see her suffer.

"What if people who don't know better come after us?" Cleo asked.

"For what?"

"For being collaborators," Cleo said.

"Trust me," Dexia said, extending her empty glass toward Nanti for a refill.

Cleo smiled and dropped the subject. She had always trusted Dexia.

Cleo woke with a start. The sheer curtains at the window of her room billowed silently in the breeze, which seemed to arrive just before dawn. She removed the dead weight of Jacques's arm from her naked chest, careful not to wake him. As she stood by the bedside she looked down at him for an instant. They had made love until well after two in the morning. There was always an urgency to their lovemaking that made it at once exhilarating and yet sad, as though each time would be the last. As she bent to brush his lips she heard the sound and stopped. Terrified, she ran to the window to listen more closely.

The birds! From the roof two stories above she could hear them. It sounded as though they were throwing themselves against their cages, cooing in a way she had never heard. She glanced at the clock beside the bed and raced across the room for her clothes, cursing silently.

Jacques had once warned her that if one of the carriers from England arrived unexpectedly the others in the cages would put up a fuss.

My God, she thought, tying on her cotton wraparound skirt with shaking hands, they'll wake the house.

She jammed her feet into her shoes and grabbed her sweater from the back of the chair by the door. She was down the hall and into the stairwell that led to the roof before she had completely pulled the sweater on. She raced up the stairs and was brushing her hair out of her eyes when she saw the door to the roof open. She froze.

Major von Kessel stepped onto the landing and closed the door behind him. As he turned and stared down at her she pressed her lips together against the panic in her throat.

"Good morning, sir," she said as respectfully as she could. Her eyes moved slowly from his leather bedroom slippers up along his long silk dressing gown and finally to his face. Nanti had told her he sometimes stayed the night with Dexia in her suite on the top floor, but this was the first time she had actually seen him.

He stared wordlessly down at her, his face like a fist. His bushy eyebrows were uncombed and flattened against his rimless glasses. "What's going on here?" he asked in a low, menacing voice.

"Here?" she said, stalling.

"These birds, their racket woke me."

"I'm sorry. I usually feed them before dawn. I overslept."

The major made no move to descend the stairs. He remained on the landing, one hand on the doorknob. "Who do these birds belong to? What are they doing here?" he demanded.

"They are for the kitchen," Cleo said firmly.

The major stared at her. "You're lying," he said.

"Why would I lie, sir?" she asked. "You've eaten the squab here many times. I've seen you." The minute she said it she wished she hadn't. She was being too familiar. To him, she was only a servant around the hotel, even if she was Dexia's cousin. "I'm sorry they bothered you. Please don't tell Madame I was late."

"I see, so Madame Dexia is in charge of the pigeons," he said. "How very interesting."

Cleo stepped toward the door to the roof. "May I pass, please?" she asked pleasantly. "I really should see to them. They'll quiet down when I give them their feed and water."

To her enormous relief he stepped to one side and let her push open the creaking door. To her horror she realized he was following her onto the roof.

As if by some silent signal the birds, one by one, sensed her presence and ceased their flapping about. They paced back and forth in their small cages, cocking their heads at her and cooing softly. Cleo scanned the roof. There, on top of a cage next to the low wall that enclosed the roof, sat a single, newly arrived pigeon, a canister clearly visible around one foot. Somehow there had been a mixup. No messages were expected so early.

She moved smartly to the large sack of seed resting against the near wall, putting herself between the major and the cages. "They're fussy little creatures when they're hungry," she said, digging into the sack for the tin cup she used to carry the seed to containers inside each cage. The major was standing so close she could smell Dexia's perfume on his robe.

She filled the cup and walked to a cage against the opposite wall, as far from the newly arrived pigeon as possible. She unlatched the door, then turned to the major in the hope of distracting him. "They are really quite sweet," she said. "Would you like to hold one?" She quickly reached inside, clasped the closest bird, and extended it toward the major.

He made no move to touch the bird but slowly turned. "I'd like to see that one," he said, pointing toward the pigeon pacing back and forth on top of the far cage, its head bobbing innocently up and down.

Cleo squinted toward the pacing bird as though she had no idea what he was talking about. "Which one?" she asked. Her heart was pounding so hard she wondered if even he could hear it.

His hand gripped her lower arm. "Let me show you," he said, guiding her toward the far wall. The canister on the bird's leg was so painfully visible she had to do something.

The crash of the seed cup when she dropped it startled them all—the major, Cleo, and the pacing bird. *"Mon dieu!"* she cried, pretending to look down at the spilled seeds but catching a glimpse of the bird as it spread its wings and flapped up and out over the roof wall.

The major tightened his grip on her arm. "Idiot girl!" he shouted. "You did that deliberately, didn't you?"

She looked up at him and blinked. "Of course I didn't," she cried, then looked down at her feet. "Look at this mess. Now I'll have to go down and get a broom."

"You'll go no place, young lady," he snarled. "I know what you're up to here. That bird"—he pointed out over the wall—"that was a carrier pigeon. Do you think I'm a fool?"

"What bird?" Cleo asked, feigning a cross between innocence and stupidity.

In an odd way, she expected the slap across the face and was grateful his enormous hand was open instead of closed. Her hand flew to her burning cheek as she stared at the major, tears behind her eyes.

"You little fool!" he screamed. "You're getting messages up here. Who from, bitch? This is a trick of the maquis! All over the city these birds are flying to England, to the south. Even as far as Spain! You! You little bitch! You are a traitor."

Cleo swallowed very hard and waited for his rage to subside. "Sir," she said when he paused to take a breath. "Your French is very good, but a traitor is one who betrays her country. I have not betrayed my country. I am here simply to feed the birds for the cook."

He wasn't listening. He began to strut back and forth, his slippers grating against the birdseed on the tar-paper roof. "Is this Madame Dexia's doing?" he demanded, scowling at Cleo.

"Sir, Madame has many more important things to do than see to kitchen chores," Cleo said evenly.

"God!" he spat in disgust, "you are nothing but a little maid . . . a little functionary in a whorehouse. You are not doing this alone." He stepped closer and slapped her again. "Tell me! Who are you working with?"

Cleo buried her face in her hands to give herself a few precious seconds to think. She would die before she betrayed Dexia, who, as much as her own mother, had given her life.

And Jacques? Never him, never. She thought of him peacefully asleep in her bed two floors below, his long black eyelashes pressed against the face she adored.

"Speak, or I will have you shot in the street below for everyone to see," the major commanded.

Slowly she lowered her hands and wiped her nose with the sleeve of her sweater. "If I tell you the only thing I know, will you let me go?"

The major stepped between her and the door. "You are in no position to bargain."

"I know nothing about carrier pigeons. As you say, I am just a maid in a whorehouse. No one would trust me to do anything but wash out semen-soaked sheets. I know nothing of politics and secret messages. But I am not deaf. I hear things."

She could tell she had gained his attention by the way the little muscle at his right temple stopped jumping. His expression changed imperceptibly in that way a face reacts when the brain behind it begins to listen.

"You know the girl Fleur?" she asked, stalling for time. She knew nothing about Fleur but knew the mention of someone he knew would rivet his attention. He turned and walked to a small bench by the wall where Jacques kept the few broken and pitted tools he used to repair the wire for the cages.

It happened so swiftly it was as if she was watching herself, out of her own body. It was the curve of his back presenting itself as he bent to sit down that drew her. In three swift steps she walked to the bench, picked up a screwdriver, and with one upward motion plunged it with all her strength into the major's rib cage just below the heart. The screwdriver disappeared into his flesh up to the handle with amazing ease. As his head rolled back, his face held the same look of interest he'd displayed at the mention of Fleur. He slumped sideways and fell against the wall, dead. He hadn't even closed his eyes.

She woke Jacques and told him.

The major fit rather snugly into the wooden feed chest on the roof, except for his feet. Jacques told her to go downstairs while he took care of the problem.

As she slipped through the stairway door, Jacques picked up a pair of heavy shears. When he joined her, they were still wet with blood.

Marie Toulet picked her way carefully down the steep back stairs of her house in suburban Neuilly. To steady her fragile seventy-year-old frame, she let the basket of wet laundry she was carrying slide along the banister. She was too old to be doing her own wash by hand. In the days before—before the Germans came, before the world collapsed—she had a laundress as well as a cleaning lady. Then she had enough food to eat and enough fuel to heat the house that her husband had left her. Now everyone was gone. Her husband dead, her sons dead, one in the first horrible days of the war when the Germans overran the exhausted French army, the other when his ship exploded off the Normandy coast. Now she was tired and alone, living in a single room of the large house.

She moved along the path through what had once been her kitchen garden, redolent with herbs that flavored the meals of their peaceful lives. There was no one to tend it now, and, like the grounds around the house, it was tangled with weeds and brown from lack of watering.

At the far end of the back lawn two weeping willows supported a frayed and sagging clothesline. Weary of soul, she sighed aloud as she bent to place the wicker laundry basket on the ground, then rose to pinch the clothespins open and release them from the line.

Then she screamed.

The arms were tied around the tree by their wrists, which were bright red, evenly red, as though they had been painted. Trembling, she stepped around the tree. The man on the left was nude. His head hung obscenely to one side. The skin on his entire body had been peeled away.

Her eyes began to cloud and she could feel what little she had had to eat that day crawling sourly up her throat. She didn't know the man on the left. The man on the right was her lovely neighbor, Dr. Edmond Gautier, who had been so kind during her husband's illness. The only thing left of him that she could recognize were the few pieces of his black-and-white goatee that clung to what was left of his face. Directly between his eyes was a single bullet hole.

"Does *flayed* mean skinned, like you'd skin an animal?" Cleo asked Nanti when she learned what had happened to the Dove and the man she loved. Nanti frowned. The girl's voice was eerie in its morbid, cheerful curiosity. Nanti was sitting at the well-lighted table in their rooms at the top of the hotel trying to patch, as best she could, one of Madame Solange's beautiful gowns.

In the days since they had learned of the double murder in Neuilly, Cleo had asked the same series of questions over and over again. Nanti had begun to despair. If only the Americans would come. It was only a matter of time. They would somehow help. Wouldn't there be a doctor with the soldiers? Medicine? Someone or something to help. She was convinced Cleo had lost her mind.

"Did they do it after he was dead?" she asked, smiling across at Nanti from her perch on the window seat. She did nothing all day but ask questions and stare out the window. The pigeons she had attended on the roof were gone. Four Gestapo soldiers had arrived the morning before the bodies of Jacques and the doctor were discovered and slaughtered them. No amount of protestation from the furious chef could convince them they were destroying the favorite dish of the General Staff.

Then they found the major, his feet crudely hacked off, stuffed in the old chest on the roof.

When they came for Jacques, he was in bed with Cleo. Now, days later, Nanti could still hear her screams in her war-weary mind.

Just thinking about the sound, she heard it again. She put down the length of sequined cloth and listened. It wasn't screaming! It was singing. Singing and shouting voices were rising from the street.

Nanti ran to the window and looked down. The narrow street in front of the hotel was full of joyful, shouting people. Farther down she saw someone waving a makeshift American flag.

She ran to Cleo and threw her arms around the girl's bony shoulders. "They've come! *Mon petit chou*, the Americans! They've come!"

Cleo, lost and mute in her grief, did not respond other than to gently stroke Nanti's bare arm.

For the next two nights the streets around the hotel were filled with people. The girls at the hotel did not want to work but ran out to join the gigantic party that was sweeping over Paris.

Dexia had just dropped into a shallow, exhausted sleep when the pounding on the door in the lobby started. Concerned, she pulled a robe around her naked body and started down the carpeted stairs toward the sound of angry voices.

As she reached the first landing, Eleni, the girl who checked coats for the restaurant, came pounding up the stairs. She was shaking uncontrollably. When she saw Dexia she burst into tears. "They want you, Madame!" she said in a terrified whisper. "They already took away Babette and Eglantine."

"Took them away? Who did?" Dexia demanded. "Surely not the Americans!"

Eleni looked up at her, her eyes as large and black as Greek olives. "Men from the maquis!"

"The maquis? It can't be? Surely they know I—" She caught herself as the petrified girl turned and ran back down the stairs.

Bewildered, Dexia continued down the stairs. In the lobby, half a dozen men in dark clothes with knitted caps pulled close to their eyes lurched toward her bellowing, "Traitor! Collaborator!" almost in unison. They were not from the maquis! Had they been she would have recognized at least one of them. These were just street toughs crazed and thirsty for revenge.

Dexia was dragged into the street. Her flimsy robe was ripped from her body as she was pulled along, her feet barely touching the ground. A straight-backed chair had been placed in the center of a tiny public park across from the hotel. As she was dragged closer, Dexia could see a circle of something soft piled around the legs of the chair. They were shaving the heads of the girls from the house. Stripping them and shaving their heads in a final humiliation for having fraternized with the hated Germans. She was next. Dear God! she thought as she felt someone binding her hands in back of the chair—why hadn't she told Eleni to hide? And Cleo, next they would go for poor, mad Cleo asleep in her room.

As they approached the chair, Dexia managed to wrench her arms free and elbow the men away from her. She stood and threw her head and shoulders back.

"Do what you will," she said in her most dramatic voice, hoping someone in the filthy mob would realize who she was. "I prefer to stand."

The crowd began to mutter. There were a few calls from the back to let her go, but the anger was too fevered, the crowd too drunk. One of the larger men moved toward her.

A high clear voice pierced the air.

"Let her go!" the voice screamed. "She killed the Nazi major! I saw her do it with my own eyes! On the roof! With these!"

The startled crowd turned as one and stared at the tiny figure that had pushed its way through to the clearing where Dexia stood. Cleo was holding aloft a pair of what looked like gardening shears. The man who stepped forward verified that they were crusted with dried blood. Not a soul in the crowd was unaware that the body of Major von Kessel had been found stabbed and mutilated in a chest on the roof of the hotel.

The crowd began to mill about, clearly wondering what to do, when a young American soldier pushed his way through the crowd. He wore a pistol on his hip and a black armband bearing the letters MP. He walked briskly toward Dexia, bent to retrieve what was left of her torn robe, and gently placed the tattered fragments around her bare shoulders. "Are you all right?" he asked softly.

Dexia nodded. "Yes," she said in English. "I'm okay. Thank you, sir."

"All right, all of you!" he shouted to the crowd. "Move on! Move on! Nothing more is going to happen here!" He put one arm around Dexia's shoulders and guided her back toward the hotel.

"I'm Lieutenant Ayler, U.S. Army Military Police," he said, once they were safely inside the house.

"I'm Dexia Solange. Please, Lieutenant, come in. You are our guest. Anything we have is yours."

Three weeks later more military police came to the little hotel on rue St.-Denis, this time to arrest the young lieutenant for being AWOL. Once inside he had not wanted to leave. At nineteen he could think of no better place on earth to be than surrounded by Madame Solange's superb food, entertainment, and women.

Dexia later heard that he had been dishonorably discharged, but had been able, once he was rich and powerful, to have the records changed. He became a lifelong friend of Madame Cleo's and always made it a point to remember Madame Solange at Christmas.

CHAPTER
∞ 14 ∞

Fiddle retrieved her overnight case from the concierge at the Georges V. She had been so anxious to see Peter that she hadn't even checked in.

Once in her room, she ignored the blinking message light on the bedside phone, found some Coke in the minibar, and lay down, too exhausted to sleep, trying to collect her jumbled thoughts. She replayed the brief, tense scene at dinner with Peter over and over in her twanging head.

She glanced at the bedside clock. It was nearly midnight. By now, Peter would be with Sandrine and aware of the lengths to which Fiddle had gone in order to make the project work.

Springing Sandrine on him was probably a dirty trick, but desperate times called for desperate means. If Peter walked away from this project it would haunt them both forever. To challenge Peter to such a degree would not make her so nervous were she not in love with him.

She knew it was irrational to think Peter still felt anything for Sandrine, but the woman was silky and sleek and clever about men. Fiddle had learned, long ago, that there were women in the world one didn't even bother to compete with. They were from another planet, creatures of such devastating seductive powers that mere mortal women were helpless against them. Women like Sandrine could have any man they wanted. Of course, she hadn't thought of any of that when she called Sandrine in New York, but seeing Peter again, practically shoving Sandrine into his arms, now made her crazy with jealousy. She knew the rest of the night would be lost to torturing herself with mental dirty movies of Peter and Sandrine flying into each other's arms. She would not know until morning if her scheme had worked, and until then she was alone with her demons.

Earlier, in New York, she had been stunned by Sandrine's willingness to cooperate with her in a benevolent conspiracy to rescue Peter, but Sandrine said later on the flight to Paris that for reasons she wouldn't explain, she had changed her mind and now wanted Peter to do the book. Sandrine said she would do anything she could to help, that she had "business" to attend to abroad and would be happy to drop everything and go to Paris with Fiddle.

Sandrine had met her in the VIP lounge of the airline with only a handbag, a raincoat, and a copy of *Vogue*. When Fiddle inquired as to her luggage, Sandrine shrugged, saying anything she needed was in Jourdan's apartment in Paris. Fiddle could have suggested a sudden trip to Rome, London, Zurich, or the south of France and Sandrine wouldn't have had to pack more than fresh makeup. When they were halfway through their meal on the plane Sandrine casually mentioned that, despite her easy access to his homes, she was in the process of divorcing Jourdan Garn. Fiddle was taken aback and wished she'd had that particular tidbit before she left New York. She could have traded it to a columnist for a favorable plug for the magazine.

Fiddle had listened to Sandrine for several hours. Before the flight, all Fiddle had known about Sandrine Garn was what the gossip columnists had told her about her glamorous mother and what the business journals had reported about her disgustingly rich husband. Fiddle's initial take on Sandrine was that she was a society airhead. During the flight, she was pleasantly surprised to find a depth to her traveling companion that belied this impression. It was clear from their conversation that the mother had caused a lot of harm and that being so beautiful had done little to ease Sandrine's pain.

Reminding herself of how beautiful Sandrine was made Fiddle moan again and pound the pillow. She ached to call Peter, to know what was happening at that very moment. Was he still with her? Had she taken him to Madame Solange as she had promised, or had they remained in Peter's apartment for the night, all thought of the project washed away in a sea of remembered passion?

She had been too rough on Peter. She had let him think her motive for running to Paris had been all business. He had no way of knowing how she had dreamed of their next meeting. She longed for him to see her with different eyes.

When she had finally looked at him straight on, as they sat in that charming restaurant, everything changed. Their eyes had met and held for a moment over their wineglasses, and in that second she knew that her daydreams of Peter and Paris and the beginning of a new relationship were shamefully girlish. That was right after she told him she'd come to kick butt. Hadn't she learned by now that there wasn't a man alive who would respond well to that? At that moment she was not looking at a love object but at a writer she had coddled and cared for, promoted and made a star. A man she had spoon-fed an important project to, only to have him let himself become intimidated and sidetracked. The confidence she had so carefully restored in him had somehow disappeared when he signed that million-dollar contract. Wasn't it supposed to be just the opposite? Wasn't financial security the thing that gave one strength and validation?

Madame Solange was her last chance. She knew she'd been right not to tell him about her at dinner. If she had, there would have been lengthy discussions about why it wasn't a good idea. She knew, by now, that a man who had worked himself into a failure mode would, if given the chance, make a very strong case to stay there.

"Shit," she said, angrily. It was going to be impossible to sleep. She swung her feet over the side of the bed and punched the message button on the phone.

Fiddle was on and off the phone with Vickie in New York until well after sunup. Between calls, she sometimes drifted off. But the phone would always wake her again.

All hell was breaking loose in the office. The October cover was to have featured a dramatic picture of the four beautiful wives of an oil-rich Kuwaiti. They had been photographed in Kuwait City, leaning against matching monogrammed pink helicopters in front of a three-hundred-room alabaster-and-bronze house. The story inside was one to which she would have assigned Peter, had he been available. It was a hymn to excess and greed that made one miss the eighties.

From Vickie, Fiddle learned that while she had been indulging in her little transatlantic drama, Iraq had invaded Kuwait. The pink helicopters had been blown up and the Republican Guard had set up a command center, complete with goats and cows, in the three-hundred-room mansion.

"Does that mean the wives won't be available to tour?" Fiddle asked Vickie, half kidding, knowing she had to kill the cover and substitute something else. "Let me talk to the art director."

She was too exhausted to come up with a new idea. She turned the problem over to the art department and one of her editors.

With the coming of daylight, her resolve to leave Peter alone began to fade. Unable to resist, she punched in his number. The phone rang three times before the machine picked up with the same boring message he had recorded when he first arrived. She called his name several times after the beep. Surely, he would pick up if he were asleep.

After ordering juice and coffee from room service, she tried again. Still no answer. Mystified, she dialed the number Sandrine had given her.

A man's voice answered in French, then switched to English when Fiddle asked for Sandrine.

"Madame Garn left word that she is not to be disturbed," he said grandly.

That was when Fiddle's fatigue got the best of her. "Tell her it's Ms. Null and it's an emergency."

After an interminable wait, Sandrine sleepily picked up the extension.

"Sandrine, forgive me, but I'm concerned," Fiddle said, nodding to the room-service waiter to put her breakfast tray on the dresser. She cradled the phone receiver and scribbled a tip and her name on the check.

"S'okay," Sandrine moaned. "What's up?"

"It's Peter. He doesn't answer his phone. It's past nine. I can't imagine where he could have gone."

"To London."

"Sorry?" Fiddle said, alarmed.

"He's on his way to London. The butler tells me Dexia left a message with him around seven. Peter left her a note saying not to worry. He'd be back for the things in his room in a few days."

"Dexia?"

"Madame Solange."

"Did he interview her?"

"I guess," Sandrine said, indifferently. "That's where I saw him last."

Fiddle was furious. "What in God's name is he doing?"

"Beats me, Fiddle."

Fiddle thought for a moment, getting the distinct and very creepy feeling that for all their intimate just-us-girls conversation on the plane, Sandrine was keeping something from her. "Sandrine," she said, tentatively. "Do you know something I don't know?"

There was a slight but suspicious pause on the line. "Listen, Fiddle, I'm seeing my lawyer in London later today. Where would he be likely to stay there? I'll give him a ring later and get back to you."

Fiddle felt ice forming in her throat. "Thank you ever so much, Sandrine," she said, hoping her fury was coming through loud and clear. "I'll handle things from here on. You've been terribly kind."

"Suit yourself," Sandrine said with a yawn a Persian cat would envy. "Stay in touch."

Fiddle slammed down the phone. She wanted to hit something. She drained her orange-juice glass and threw it against the wall over the dresser mirror. It made an unsatisfying clunk and dropped to the carpet.

" 'Where is he likely to stay there? I'll give him a ring later and get back to you,' " she snarled. Sure, cookie, she railed inwardly. Find out Peter's hotel so she can run by and sit on his face. Doesn't she think I could call him in London all by myself?

She grabbed her hairbrush from her carryon and began yanking it through her hair. Now her anxiety about what had happened the night before became even more involved and threatening. She had never so much as kissed Peter Shea, yet she could imagine herself as Sandrine as he covered her face with kisses, begging her to come to bed with him. Sandrine must have pulled away saying, "No, no, not yet my darling. Later, we will meet in London."

Peter, in a sexual frenzy, had neglected to tell Sandrine where he would be and now she was not so subtly trying to find out. Fiddle didn't even pause to remind herself that she'd woken Sandrine up with her call.

"And leave me stranded in this fucking hotel," Fiddle screamed to the empty room. Her hairbrush hit only an inch or so from the dent the juice glass had produced.

Earlier that morning, when the only sign of daylight was a thin sliver of sunshine between Dexia Solange's heavy drapes, Peter put down the cup of coffee she had made him before she dozed off. He slipped his tape recorder into the jacket he had hooked over the back of his chair.

He studied Dexia's face in repose. In the half-light of dawn there was more than just a trace of the great beauty she once had been. Her dark lashes were still thick and lustrous as they lay against the translucent skin of her cheeks.

Several times during the telling of her remarkable story, Madame Solange had wept. She did not sob or cry out, but silent tears coursed down the creases in her cheeks. She cried the way once-beautiful brave old ladies do when they remember certain things too painful to forget.

More than once in the course of the night, he had wondered why

Madame Cleo could not, herself, have told him the story. Could it have been that the single-minded determination required to reinvent herself rendered Cleo incapable of revealing her real self? Eventually, after the trust between them had been established, he asked Dexia what she thought Madame Cleo was afraid of.

He attached his earphone to the machine and ran the tape back to hear her answer.

"Exposure," he heard her say. "If the world knows about your pain, you are unprotected from it. In the beginning, that Klarwine woman convinced her that an American publisher would only want the sexy bits about flesh peddling among the jet set. Madame won't admit it, but, trust me, she reads all those tell-all books you Americans love so much. Many of her former girls have had them written. She felt the truth wouldn't matter as long as there was enough sex to fill the pages. What you have to understand is that Madame Cleo's life had very little to do with anything as frivolous as sex.

"When you started to press her to talk about herself she began to realize that you wanted to do a very different kind of book. That working with you meant going back to being that brutalized, half-dead little girl who staggered to my doorstep nearly fifty years ago. She was too proud.

"Pity is a very demeaning thing, Mr. Shea. Have you ever been an object of pity? It is one of life's most humiliating experiences."

At that point in their interview, Peter had had to turn off the machine and redirect the conversation for fear he would begin to talk about himself. He gave a sigh of relief and turned the machine back on as Madame Solange began to tell him what had happened after the war.

She told him how, eventually, she had returned to the stage. She turned over the running of the house to Cleo. Cleo continued to build the business and in the fifties she bought it outright from Dexia. Later, when she had made a great deal of money and made arrangements to have a client purchase the house in his name, Cleo moved to the mansion on the Ile de la Cité with Nanti and hired Martin to handle the administrative details she loathed.

When Madame Solange retired because of her weak heart, Cleo converted the hotel to apartments and provided Dexia with a permanent place to live.

To her knowledge, Madame Cleo was never again interested in a man, unless, of course, he was a prospective client. She devoted herself totally to the perfection of her girls and protecting herself from her painful past.

Peter had leaned forward and quietly asked Dexia what he felt was the most important question of the night.

"Other than Sandrine, have you ever heard from any of the girls who were here in nineteen eighty-seven?" he asked.

"Anyone in particular?" she had asked.

"Wasn't there a girl named SueBee?"

"Ah, SueBee," she had answered with a broad smile. "Such a delight. So sweet, SueBee. She married a proper Englishman, I read, and has a baby."

"Anyone else?"

"Angel was here. As a matter of fact, she was here only a day or so before you arrived. She came to pick up some things that were stored here when she left Paris. The people who cleaned out her room left some things. I put them in the basement and forgot about them."

"Angel? She was here?" Peter asked.

"She said she had just come from a sort of reunion in London with the other girls."

"A reunion? I know about Madame's big summer party, but do Cleo girls hold other reunions?"

"That's what she called it. She told me Sandrine had called her where she was working in Las Vegas. I was somewhat disappointed to hear that, Cleo girls don't usually end up in Las Vegas."

Peter knew he was onto something. He didn't want to sound too anxious so he had asked for another cup of coffee.

As Dexia returned from the kitchen he had asked her if she remembered reading about Madame Cleo's book in the Paris paper.

To his amazement she abruptly rose from the couch and walked to a bookcase between the windows. She retrieved a bulging leather scrapbook, placed it on the coffee table in front of him, and flipped it open. "Is this it?" she said, holding up a clipping. "I don't have my glasses."

Peter squinted; he didn't have his glasses either. "That's it," he said. He looked back at the book. "Do you save a lot of clippings?"

"Only if it's something about the girls. Some of them have gotten quite famous. I like to follow their careers."

"May I?" he asked, lifting the heavy book.

Madame Solange nodded and smiled, obviously pleased at his interest. "Please," she said.

Peter leafed through the pages thinking how, with just what was in the book, he could go into the blackmail business and live like a king.

"I'd love to go through this some more when I have more time and my glasses," Peter said, placing it gently back on the table. "You wouldn't remember if the, ah, reunion Angel went to was before or after this was in the paper?"

"Oh, after," Dexia said with certainty. "Angel and I even talked about it. We were both surprised that Madame would do such a thing."

Peter had pinched the bridge of his nose against the fatigue that was beginning to fuzz his thinking. "Now, if you will, Madame Solange, indulge me a moment longer. It's been a long night."

"One I've enjoyed, Mr. Shea," she said graciously.

"That article appeared in the paper a day or two before the girls met in London. That means the girls were getting together possibly because of the article, not just for old time's sake."

"Maybe," she said with the verbal equivalent of a shrug.

"Are you aware that there was an attempt on Cleo's life later that week?"

"Ah, oui! Horrible. On the Place de la Concorde."

Peter leaned forward, resting his elbows on his knees. "The way I piece it together, the article appeared here on a Monday, the girls met either Tuesday or Wednesday of that week. Angel flew to Paris to pick up her things on, what would you say, Thursday?"

Madame Solange thought for a moment. "Yes, Thursday. The same day Martin brought those two men around."

Peter was standing by then, pacing the worn carpet and wishing he still smoked. It had always helped him to concentrate. "Two men?" he asked simply, keeping his voice soft and remembering Fiddle's warning at dinner about being a bully.

"Friends of Sheikh Zaki. He's an old, old friend of Cleo's."

"How long did they stay here?"

"Just that night. I put them in the double room at the top of the house. Nice men. The shorter one brought me violets when they came back from dinner," she said. "They left the next morning, as soon as their package arrived."

Peter's eyes narrowed. "What kind of package?"

"Oh, a thick brown envelope," she said holding her hands a foot apart to indicate the approximate size. "Martin said to look for it, that it would be addressed to me and that I was to take it up to them as soon as it was delivered."

"Do you remember where it came from?" he asked.

"I'm sorry, I didn't have my glasses on," she said. "Why are you interested?"

Peter forced himself to chuckle. "Oh, no reason, really. I've been working with Madame for so long I guess I'm interested in every little detail that might have to do with her."

After that, Madame Solange had made more coffee as their conversation wound down. When he noticed Dexia was sound asleep he tiptoed out of the apartment.

He took the stairs back to his room two steps at a time, flung open his door, and tossed the handful of tapes onto the coffee table. He thought about waking Fiddle at the Georges V with his progress so far, but there was one more little detail to be attended to.

When Giselle pushed open the downstairs door with her rump and dropped her mailbag onto the hall table, Peter was waiting on the second-floor landing. He tumbled down the stairs to greet her.

She continued to sort mail while he explained what he needed.

"Pas de problème," she assured him. All she had to do was use his phone. Only a bureaucracy like the French postal service would keep records of foreign overnight packages for up to a year, Peter thought. Minutes later, she hung up and turned to Peter with a scrap of paper in her hand. "The return address on the package addressed to Madame Solange on that date was D-5 Albany, Piccadilly W1, London," she said.

Peter threw his arms around her and kissed her.

The lobby of the Ritz, just off Piccadilly Circus, was filled with depressed Kuwaitis, Saudis, and other rich exiles of the Iraqi invasion. Their faces were drawn and worried-looking under their tans and snow-white headgear. They roamed the hotel, as aimless and bored as guppies in a bowl, waiting for the next fruitless meeting.

In the old days, Peter would have been caught up in what was happening in the Gulf, angling to get himself as close to the action as possible. But all that interested him at the moment was whether he had any messages waiting for him at the desk.

The ego bath he received from the half dozen seemingly interchangeable men in morning suits at the reception desk stunned him until he realized someone else had impressed the men. The message he was handed read: "Lady Susanna Mosby will receive you at 7 P.M. at her flat—D-5 Albany."

He read it twice, relieved and excited. He had been afraid she would change her mind since their brief conversation earlier that morning. He hadn't told her that he was calling from Heathrow. Trying to sound as brisk and businesslike as possible, he had asked if she would see him regarding an article he was doing for *Fifteen Minutes.* She had been very pleasant, saying she knew his name and had read an article he did some time ago. But she left it up in the air as to whether she could see him on such short notice. Apparently, the lady had managed to rearrange her schedule. He didn't kid himself that a quick call to her husband to see if it was all right hadn't been placed as soon as they hung up.

Whatever had prompted her positive response, he now had a straight shot at getting to the bottom of a whole lot of conflicting information—not the least of which was what was in the bulky package delivered to the two men who had stayed the night with Madame Solange.

Once in his room, he rang the Georges V, still feeling guilty about not having called Fiddle before he left Paris. With mounting apprehension he listened to the desk clerk at the Georges V inform him that she had checked out. He knew, wherever she was, she was furious with him. He would make it up to her—soon.

As he prepared for his meeting with SueBee, he played a mental jigsaw puzzle with the pieces of the story Madame Solange had so guilelessly provided.

There was no doubt that there had been a conspiracy to derail the project from the start and that it all had something to do with his participation. Everything had been fine until the papers announced that he and Madame Cleo would be writing the book. Then suddenly, as Fiddle used to say, the fecal matter hit the ventilation system.

He reminded himself that all his best interviews came when he played dumb, and that would be his position in his meeting with SueBee Slyde Mosby, a principal coconspirator in this whole damn deal, that was for sure.

He raised his arm in front of the mirror and drew an imaginary marquee in the air. "'A Conspiracy of Swans,'" he said to his reflection.

He dressed carefully in the dark suit that the porter had returned to him freshly pressed. He smoothed the hair at his temples, noting that he was badly in need of a trim, knotted his best silver tie, and left the hotel with great anticipation.

Albany, a grand old building secreted down an alley, was a short walk from the Ritz. He had been entertained there on occasion in the past. Sarah Jane had talked about one particular apartment for months. It was their first trip to London. They were both young and poor and had no idea people actually lived like that.

The flats at Albany were larger than normal houses, vast, intimidating places from which no one lucky or connected enough to gain admittance ever moved. It was common knowledge that the Mosby flat, twenty-four rooms in all, had belonged to Lady Selena Mosby's family. Through clever maneuvering, the place had landed on Billy Mosby's side of the divorce arrangement.

As he stepped off the elevator onto the Mosbys' private landing, a butler, having been alerted by the doorman, was standing just inside the open door to the flat.

"Good evening, Mr. Shea," he said with an infinitesimal bow.

The butler led Peter down a long hall and into a cool, scented room that glowed. Pale peach, yellow, and varying hues of cream formed a lush background for burnished wood, porcelain *objets*, and antique jardinieres crowded with wildflowers.

Over the wide marble mantel hung an outsize oil portrait of Mosby in some sort of military regalia. The artist had been kind.

Peter stood somewhat uneasily in the center of a rug the color and coolness of lemon sherbet, not quite sure what to do with his hands.

"I'll tell Madam you're here," the butler said before he disappeared.

Peter walked to a glass-topped table covered with a long celery-colored silk drop and standing between the high windows. The entire surface was covered with silver-framed pictures of an ethereally beautiful blond child.

"I see you've discovered Hildy," a soft but firm voice said behind him.

He turned to see the fantasy woman of his youth.

The year after he was sick he could not play sports and spent a great deal of time in the comforting darkness of the movie theater a block from his home. It was there that he learned that the most beautiful, untouchable human being on the planet was Grace Kelly. As he looked across the room he saw her again. The resemblance was startling enough to make him catch his breath.

"You're staring, Mr. Shea," she said, laughing lightly as she walked toward him with her hand outstretched.

"Am I?" he said after clearing his throat. "Forgive me."

"I'm Susanna Mosby," she said taking his hand. "Everyone calls me SueBee." She released his hand and walked to the mantel where a long needlepoint bellpull hung beside the fireplace. "We'll have drinks here and chat a bit, all right?"

Peter nodded and smiled. She spoke with an almost British accent. Clearly, she had worked hard to cover what he knew had to have been a Texas twang.

SueBee was wearing a long lime-colored satin lounging arrangement; it wasn't a robe and it wasn't a proper gown. Whatever it was, the way it fit left very little to the imagination.

"Please, sit down," she said, gesturing to one of the floral-chintz-covered couches on either side of the fireplace. "You couldn't have come at a more opportune time."

Peter thought she meant the time of day. Mosby was nowhere about, and obviously the baby was in the hands of her minders. He sat down and looked around. "This is an exquisite room," he said.

"Thank you," she said, smiling. "It's a 'fur piece' from the orange shag carpeting in a trailer in Wayleen, Texas."

She had taken the overstuffed chair set perpendicular to the couch. Her knees were distractingly close to his own. He nervously tugged at his tie, not knowing how he should respond to her reference to her beginnings.

Peter was about to speak when the butler appeared with a tray holding a single crystal glass containing scotch on the rocks. He accepted it and turned to SueBee in surprise. "How did you know I drink scotch?" he asked.

SueBee smiled sweetly. "I've never met a drinking man who didn't."

His knowledge of SueBee's previous métier made a reply unnecessary. After all, he was in the company of an expert.

Peter didn't know whether to take a sip of his drink or not. The butler had not brought anything for her.

SueBee seemed to sense his confusion. "Please, have your drink. I stopped drinking when I was pregnant and just never took it up again. I was never much of a drinker anyway. Please, go ahead."

Peter's scotch had just touched his lips when SueBee shifted in her chair, pulling her knees up and leaning on the armrest. "You're here to talk to me about Madame Cleo, aren't you?" she said. "This whole book business must have been very frustrating for you."

The sip he had just taken caught in his throat. "Why . . . yes, on both scores," he gulped. "Lady Mosby, forgive me for lying to you about doing a magazine piece."

SueBee tossed her head back and laughed. "Oh, now, Mr. Shea," she said with exaggerated sympathy. "You weren't lying, you were fibbing. I think of fibs as merely social lubrication. I understand your need to see me. What would you like to know?"

"Everything and anything," Peter said. "Why don't we start at the beginning?" He was trying to phrase a question about the envelope she had sent to Zaki's men in Paris when she spoke first.

"I haven't the slightest idea whatever happened to Big Boy. But I'm not about to call the Wayleen police to find out."

Peter gulped again. "I hadn't planned to start that far back. Apparently you know Madame has spoken extensively about you."

"From what Madame Cleo tells me, you know everything about me," she said, still smiling.

"Then you've been in touch with her all along."

She cupped her chin in her hand, "Ummm. Sandrine and Angel as well."

"Perhaps you'd like to explain," he said, grateful that he would not have to be coy about his questions.

"Actually, we were all in on this from the beginning."

Peter reached for his drink again. Now he truly needed it. "I'm afraid you have the advantage, Lady Mosby," he said. She had to be referring to the secret London meeting before the attempt on Madame's life, but he wasn't ready to tip his hand.

"That's twice you've called me that, Peter. SueBee, please," she said, lightly brushing his knee.

Suddenly there were voices coming from the hallway, women's voices and peals of laughter.

"Ah, here they are now, and just in time," SueBee said gaily, uncurling her legs and jumping to her feet.

Peter looked over his shoulder to see two stylishly dressed women walking into the room, their faces shadowed by floppy wide-brimmed hats. Both carried themselves as SueBee did, like high-fashion models. Over their arms swung shiny shopping bags from the chic shops around Oxford Street.

SueBee rushed across the lemon carpet and kissed them both. "Where have you two been?" she scolded. "I told you Mr. Shea was coming at seven sharp."

The shorter of the two put down her packages and removed her wide hat. "We went for tea at Brown's and got to giggling. Sorry, darling."

There was that voice. It was Sandrine. But how . . . Peter thought, before feeling foolish as he realized that she could have gotten to London just as quickly and easily as he had. At the sight of her, he felt his heart leap, pause, and then begin to pound again.

"You wouldn't believe who we saw, SueBee," said the redhead with Sandrine. "Do you remember that girl from New York? The one whose breast implants started to shift on her?"

"Wait, wait," SueBee said, placing a hand on the taller one's shoulder and turning her to face Peter. "First, come and say hello to my guest." SueBee turned to Peter and said in a formal tone, "Mr. Shea, I'd like to introduce one of my dearest friends, Angel Rizzo, who, incidentally, is in London on her honeymoon."

Peter extended his hand as Angel's last name reverberated in his head. "Congratulations, Mrs. Rizzo," he said, attempting with great effort to maintain a deadpan expression.

"And, of course," SueBee said, touching Sandrine's arm, "you know our Sandrine. Sandrine is in town seeing her London attorneys about divorce."

Sandrine made a face at SueBee. "Aren't we the little chat bucket, darling. That's a very private matter."

SueBee hunched one shoulder to her chin and dropped her eyes. "Well, not for long."

"Hello, again," Sandrine said, extending her hand. "I hear you and Dexia had a successful talk last night."

Peter shook her hand. Hers was cool and smooth. His felt clammy. "You spoke to Dexia?"

"Ummm," Sandrine hummed noncommittally as she walked toward one of the sofas.

"Well, here we are," Angel said. She plopped down on the couch opposite Peter's seat. "The yin and yang sisters of matrimony."

Peter took a gulp of his drink and stood waiting for Sandrine and SueBee to sit down.

Sandrine was standing in front of the coffee table. The light of a table lamp behind her illuminated the contours of her hips and thighs under her thin summer dress. She looked down at Peter's glass. "Peter has a drink, SueBee," she said pointedly.

"Sandrine," SueBee said reproachfully. "How many drinks did you have at 'tea'?"

"Two," Sandrine said with a pout as she sat down beside Angel.

"Four. I know. I paid," Angel said, fluffing the folds of her skirt. "Christ, it's hot."

"Angel," SueBee said. "Something for you?"

Angel continued to fluff her skirt. "Tell Rover, Grover, whatever your butler's name is, to bring one of those spritzer bottles you Brits use and just shoot it up my skirt."

The butler, who had been standing at a discreet distance in the foyer, stepped into the doorway. "Madam?" he said.

SueBee turned. "Oh, Glover, would you just bring a little of everything for the bar and some more ice, please. We'll serve ourselves."

"And a fizz bottle," Angel said, fanning herself with her clutch bag.

As the butler disappeared SueBee turned back to Angel. "Angel, as your hostess, I'm keenly interested in your comfort, but Billy hired

Glover from service with Prince Ali Khan. He does *not* shoot fizz water up ladies' skirts."

"Pity," Angel said in a bored English accent.

SueBee returned to her chair and turned to face Peter. "I'm afraid we owe you an apology, ganging up on you like this."

"Ah . . . that's okay," he said feeling like a small boy trapped in the ladies' room at the Waldorf on prom night.

"Now, you have some questions, I'm sure."

"About a thousand or so."

"Shoot," SueBee said.

"Yeah, shoot," Angel chimed in.

"Speaking of shooting . . ." Sandrine volunteered.

"Yes, let's start there," Peter said with a nod. "Who tried to shoot Madame Cleo?"

The women all looked at one another as though silently choosing an official spokesperson.

"Hired help," SueBee said, taking command.

"Right, right," Peter said impatiently. "Who hired them?"

"I did," said a familiar voice behind Peter.

He jerked his head around to see Madame Cleo standing in the door. She was wearing gray chiffon and her ever-present rope of pearls. Peter jumped to his feet. "Madame!" Had he expected anything less? The cygnets had gathered together. Summoned, apparently, by the mother swan, now gliding across the room toward him.

Madame Cleo gestured to Peter to sit down. She walked around the end of his couch and sat down at the opposite end. "I owe you a deep apology, Mr. Shea. In order to distract you and to gain sympathy I did a dreadful thing. It was I who hired two of Zaki's men to fake an attempt on my life. I'm just so sorry the gunman turned out to be such a poor marksman, and wounded my dear driver in the arm." Her words came softly, direct and to the point.

"And SueBee paid for them," Angel chirped.

"Shutsky upsky," SueBee said, scowling at Angel.

"What language is that?" Angel asked.

"I think that's what she uses in front of Hildy so the little thing won't use coarse phrases," Sandrine explained. "Now, why doesn't everybody shutsky upsky and let Madame put poor Peter here out of his misery."

"I'm not in any misery," Peter said. "I'm absolutely fascinated. This is the best time I've had in years."

"Well, get ready to be deeply annoyed, then," Angel said, walking to the drinks tray Glover had placed on the bar. "Because you've been royally jerked around and it's all our fault."

Madame Cleo began to methodically disgorge all of her purse contents onto the coffee table in front of her: her case of little cigars, her worry beads, a little bejeweled glass case, and a gold cigarette lighter.

"Remember this?" she asked Peter, holding the lighter up. She turned it so he could see the baron's crest.

"Jeez, wasn't *that* a bright idea," Angel groaned, returning to her seat with a tall, very dark drink. "You guys wouldn't listen to me. Oh, no. Barry Rizzo would have had twelve ideas better than pretending the lighter was a clue."

"Angel," SueBee said menacingly.

"Barry Rizzo? Was he in on this, too?" Peter asked, looking from face to face.

"Not really," Angel said, scrunching up her face. "It's just that he knows how to pull off this kind of con. We were such amateurs."

Madame Cleo lit a cigarillo with the lighter and returned it to the table.

"So, there was no lighter left at the scene of the shooting," Peter said.

Sandrine punched a needlepoint pillow and dropped it behind her back. "Oh, there was a lighter there. Madame gave one to Zaki's men the night before. The idea was to leave it at the scene so the police would find it. Then she could tell you she thought one of us did it. We all gave her permission to tell our stories in great detail. We figured that would take several months. At the time we were in a bit of a panic. We just hoped by the end of the summer we would find another, more permanent solution to her tax problem."

Peter pulled himself forward on the couch. "And all this was planned at your meeting here in May, right after the article appeared in the paper?"

SueBee and Sandrine nodded.

"Lucky for me," Angel said, studying her nails. "If I hadn't flown over to that meeting I wouldn't have run into Barry. I was walking through the lobby at Claridge's when I heard this booming New York voice say, 'Yo! Dollface, the way you walk reminds me I gotta wind my watch.' So I . . ."

"Angel," SueBee snapped, cutting her off. "Hush, for pity's sake. Mr. Shea doesn't give two hoots how you got back together with Barry Rizzo."

Peter laughed. "Actually, I do," he said sincerely. "But at the moment, I'd really like Madame Cleo to tell me what she thought would happen at the end of the summer when I still didn't have her story."

Madame Cleo glanced around the room at each girl as if to assure no further interruptions, then said to Peter, "I thought, crazily, that you'd get fed up and go away."

"Isn't that exactly what happened?" Peter asked.

"Yes, but for the wrong reason," said Madame Cleo. "I had not expected you to press so hard for personal details. I thought I'd be able to manage you. You turned out to be an even better journalist than I had been warned you would be."

There was a long silence. Everyone seemed to be waiting for him to ask another question. Peter looked straight across at Sandrine but addressed Madame Cleo. "Tell me Madame, are you aware that I spoke with Dexia Solange?"

"Yes," Cleo said, softly, looking down at her lap.

Peter spun around to look at her. "You knew?" he asked, astonished.

"Yes. Sandrine called me from New York and asked if she could set it up."

Peter looked back at Sandrine. Sandrine smiled weakly and shrugged as if to say, "What was I supposed to do?"

Stunned, Peter looked back at Madame Cleo. "Why would you permit Dexia Solange to tell me the things you didn't want me to know? It couldn't be that you had forgotten your own life."

Peter saw the flash in Cleo's eyes before she spoke. "I have forgotten nothing," she said sharply. "I remember every moment, every detail of my youth." She held up her hands, palms out, something she had avoided doing during all of their hours together. At the tip of each finger was a smooth, round spot the size of a pearl. "I have ten reminders with me at all times, Mr. Shea."

Peter looked away, embarrassed. "I'm sorry," he said.

"This is hard for me to say to you or anyone else, Mr. Shea," Madame continued. "There came a time, when I was young and in enormous pain, that I decided the only way to protect my sanity was to put my past behind me. I have never talked about myself. It was much easier for me to have Dexia Solange tell you."

"But why now?" Peter asked.

"I'll get to that, Mr. Shea," she said. "First I want to explain something. We have to go back to the moment when Wendy phoned and said she had a writer for me. You see, your coming into the picture greatly complicated matters."

"But you didn't even know me," Peter said, helplessly.

"No, but I knew of you. You were a well-known journalist. If I turned you down it would look very suspicious. When I originally agreed to do the book we had no writer. I didn't know Wendy would find a writer so soon, and one I couldn't refuse. Unfortunately, our association was announced in the paper—I suspect leaked by Wendy to keep me from backing out. That article galvanized all of us. We had to figure out a way to stall you."

"We?" Peter asked. "You mean the four of you here?"

"Plus Martin, he was in on it, too," Cleo said, tracing the outline of a large green leaf on the pillow in her lap. "Sandrine, who, thanks to her fortuitous marriage, had access to a private plane and ready funds, arranged for us all to meet here at SueBee's. A war council, if you will."

"To figure out what to do about the nosy American writer who was helping to keep you out of jail," Peter said, not caring if he sounded slightly offended.

"I don't blame you for feeling put out," Cleo said. "But wait, it gets worse."

"Go ahead," Peter said, nodding as SueBee picked up his glass to freshen his drink.

"At that meeting, Sandrine and SueBee reminded me that you had been a guest at La Fantastique in 1987. We knew that made you vulnerable."

Peter couldn't help himself; he glanced across at Sandrine. She was smiling at him. In a gesture so small and telling that it hit him like a thunderbolt, she raised her hand and wiggled her fingers.

"I don't remember meeting SueBee at the château," he said, still staring at Sandrine.

SueBee took up the next part of the story.

"We didn't meet, exactly," she said. "But the fact that I was there is important. Do you remember the morning you left the château?"

"Vaguely," Peter said. "Why?"

"You were on your way down the hall and you glanced into the room next to yours. You saw me helping Billy get dressed. He was in full makeup and wearing a dress."

"That was Mosby! I never imagined—" Peter was silent for a long moment, honestly shocked. "Good Lord. I never thought about that from that day to this."

"Well, my husband was very concerned that you had seen him like that," SueBee continued. "You were a reporter. He had no way of knowing if you would use what you had seen in some hurtful way. He had to do something, and perhaps unwisely, he turned to the most well-connected person he knew for help." SueBee pointed to Madame Cleo.

"When Billy called me from Paris," Madame Cleo said, picking up the story, "I phoned Warren Bracknell. He had been a client of mine for some years."

"The chairman of WorldWide?" Peter said, appalled, remembering the long-ago phone call from Gordon Jimison telling him how angry Bracknell was.

"Yes. He met his ex-wife at La Fantastique," Madame Cleo said.

That explained Bracknell's fury. Their May-December marriage had exploded in a divorce that produced some of the nastiest headlines in memory.

"Cynthia Bracknell was a Cleo girl?" Peter asked, surprised and yet not surprised. Her dubious background as an "international model" and her stunning good looks made that plausible.

"One of my best," Madame Cleo said proudly.

"Please don't misunderstand, Peter," SueBee chimed in. "You weren't fired because Billy thought you saw him in drag. It never got that far. When Warren Bracknell heard you had been at La Fantastique, he was being dragged through the courts. His name was on the front page of every tabloid from Wapping to South Street. He needed someone to take his fury out on so he fired you, letting you think it was because you had let yourself be compromised. Madame Cleo only meant for Bracknell to have a quiet word with you. She was just trying to protect an old friend and things got out of control. Unfortunately, you were the innocent victim."

"So," Peter said, amazed at what he was hearing. "Knowing that about me, what was your next step?"

"Controlling you," said SueBee.

"Boxing you in," said Sandrine.

"Making you part of the story," Cleo said. "No man who has been with a Cleo girl ever forgets it. I knew I could hold your interest by talking about the girls, at least until you satisfied your curiosity."

"One thing I'm still curious about, SueBee," Peter said. "Why did you go to so much trouble to force me out of the project? Couldn't you have just asked your husband not to publish the damn thing?"

"Someone else just would have published it, you know that," SueBee said. "And Billy didn't want to antagonize you. Remember, he believes you saw us that day at La Fantastique. He was still afraid of you. If he deprived you of a million-dollar deal he would risk having you retaliate. That's when all of us decided to take matters into our own hands."

"And try to get me to quit of my own accord," Peter said.

"That part seemed to work, right, girls?" Angel said, grinning.

"We hadn't counted on Martin freaking out," SueBee said. "He made us all see how foolish it was to run you off. He pointed out that you knew enough to write the book on your own and leave Madame to swing in the wind."

Angel, who had kept out of the conversation except for the occasional smart remark, leaned forward and said in all seriousness, "You have to understand something about us, if you don't already, Peter: our lives have always been motivated by money. It's hard for us to believe that everyone isn't the same way. When we realized you really meant to quit we knew the money no longer mattered to you. That to you, it was doing the job right or not at all. If you went away mad, with your reputation as a ball-busting investigative reporter who wrote magazine pieces that hung people out to dry, we were all in trouble. Billy Mosby isn't the only one who was afraid of you. Why, I knew a guy in Vegas who lost his gaming license because of a piece you did on him. He sells leisure suits with topstitching on the Vegas Strip now."

"Angel, hush," SueBee demanded.

"The night Martin called Fiddle Null, hysterical, she brought me into the picture," Sandrine said. "I phoned the others and we all agreed that the only thing for us to do was to make sure that, if Madame's story was going to be told, it be told right—and not by an angry journalist. We realized we had to save the book. First, we decided we had to get you in touch with Madame Solange. Madame agreed that while she couldn't tell you about herself, Madame Solange could. It was a way to get you the information you wanted and our last hope of saving the book."

"Look, Peter," SueBee said, "what we're trying to say here is that we think we've come up with the answer, the one thing that will work for all of us. Now that you have all the information, you have to do the book, but don't do it as Madame's autobiography."

"Not her autobiography?" Peter asked, looking from SueBee to Cleo. "Then how?"

All the girls turned to Madame Cleo, waiting for her to speak.

"Write it as a novel, my dear," Madame said. "A novel."

SueBee leaned toward Peter excitedly and clasped her hands on his knee. "Isn't that perfect? That way you can use our stories any way you want. Just change the names."

"I think what we're trying to tell you, Peter," Sandrine said, "is that we want you to go ahead. Please."

"Come on, Peter, no hard feelings," Angel chirped.

"Girls, girls, girls," Madame said, waving her cigarillo holder. "Enough. Let's give Mr. Shea a chance to catch his breath. I think it's time to share our new venture with him."

"New venture?" Peter asked. "You mean, you've found your solution to Madame's tax problems?"

"We didn't know how you were going to react, so we've taken care of the problem," SueBee said, jumping up and heading toward the bellpull again. "Let's have some champagne. I haven't given that up. Champagne is food as far as I'm concerned."

"Me, too," Sandrine said with a grin. "Let's eat."

"You know, Sandy," Angel said, "now that you're no longer a prisoner of love, you might try getting off the sauce."

Sandrine ignored Angel as SueBee instructed Glover to bring them some Dom Perignon. When everyone had a glass, SueBee raised hers toward Madame Cleo. "To the final liberation of Madame Cleo."

All the women except Cleo raised their glasses in tribute.

Peter held the stem of his glass and looked puzzled. "Liberation?"

"From France and the dreaded tax man," Sandrine said, smiling over her glass.

"You're leaving France?" Peter asked Madame Cleo.

"It seems appropriate," Madame Cleo said lightly.

"But what about your house? Your . . . ah . . . things?"

"Poof!" Madame Cleo said, throwing up her hands. "It will take years for the government to sort out who really owns it all. Serves them right."

Peter smiled. The fact that Madame hadn't paid a centime in taxes after forty-odd years in business did nothing to make her feel she owed something to her country.

"Madame can replace anything she can't pack," Sandrine said. "That's what we're all doing here. By the end of the month I'll be free of Jourdan. And I've just found a perfectly adorable mews house in Knightsbridge where Madame can set up her new business."

"And I just bought five new killer suits," Angel said. "I needed a new wardrobe to open the New York branch."

"Angel's in on this, too?" Peter asked, then turned to Madame Cleo. "Didn't you tell me you and Angel had had a falling out?"

Madame Cleo smiled sweetly at Angel. "All is forgiven."

SueBee giggled. "We need Angel. Barry can cut through a lot of New York red tape."

"Oh? You wouldn't want me if I weren't married to the mob?" Angel said, laughing.

Sandrine laughed as well. "We love you dearly, Angel, but your marriage to Barry will be very helpful," she said. "Those are girl rules. A new friend of mine explained those to me just recently."

Peter leveled his gaze at Sandrine. "Is your new friend Fiddle Null, by any chance?"

"Right," Sandrine said, delighted. "Then you know about girl rules."

"I didn't," Peter said with an ironic smile. "But I'm sure as hell getting a crash course now." He asked the group in general, "Where is Martin in all this?"

"Oh, he's coming along," Cleo answered. "Martin and Nanti and I will work out of the mews house. He's thrilled to be coming back to England."

Sandrine raised her hand for attention and credit. "And when Jourdan comes through with the settlement we're going to redo Wellington Close, make it more of a spa."

Angel hooted. "Our new girls can sit around in the steam room saying 'hubris,' 'forswear' and 'charlotte russe.'"

Peter leaned forward and asked Sandrine, "Just why have you decided to divorce Garn now?"

"Sandrine," Angel said, "you have to tell Peter who Jourdan's going to marry."

Sandrine moaned.

Angel whispered to Peter behind her hand, "Jourdan's going to marry Sandrine's mother."

"Tita Mandraki," Peter said, his jaw going slack. "How in God's name did that happen?"

Sandrine shrugged. "After seeing the girls in May, I faced the fact that I had to get out of the marriage. It was killing me. But Jourdan was so possessive, I didn't know what to do. It was Madame's brilliant idea that I introduce Jourdan to my mother. I knew it was a challenge Tita couldn't pass up."

SueBee reached across and tapped Sandrine on the shoulder. "Oh, Sandrine, you're shameless."

"Got rid of him, didn't it?" Sandrine said, tapping SueBee back. "I only married him for his money. Now I have it."

Cleo turned again to Peter. "Now we come to the part about you," she said.

"Me? Oh, Lord, I'm out of this, please," Peter said, holding up both hands as if to ward off any more complications from the group of extraordinary women.

"Hear us out," Madame Cleo said. She nodded to the women. "Should I tell him?"

"Sure," they all said in unison.

"If you agree to do this book as a novel, I don't want anything from it. The money's all yours. After what we've done to you, you're entitled to it."

Peter put his drink down and stared at Madame Cleo. "What are you saying?"

"I just said it."

Peter was quiet for a long time. "SueBee," Peter finally asked, "would your husband publish all this as a novel?"

"I've already asked him," SueBee answered firmly. "He said he would. The money would be less—you'll have to work out the details with him. But you won't have to split with Madame so it will be more than you would have made as Madame's ghostwriter. He thinks the novel is a great idea. Everyone knows you were the one who was working with Madame. He said it would make a good sales gimmick."

Peter stood up. "Thank you all but it's simply out of the question." He had never written fiction. He wouldn't know where to begin. He was a reporter and he was too old and set in his ways to go learn another craft, for any price.

He glanced over at Sandrine. She was staring pointedly down at the floor. He looked down to see what she was looking at.

"Nice shoes," she said, looking up at him.

He stared at her, speechless.

"*Expensive* shoes," she persisted. "I bet you've never had a pair like them before."

Peter closed his eyes for an instant. Good Lord, he thought, he must have confessed everything to Fiddle during his desperate, drunken phone call.

He wondered if he should feel betrayed or take the more mature approach. If so many women were turning themselves wrong side out to make life easier for him, why did he feel as though he were drowning? He had never quite bought Wendy Klarwine's belief that there were no secrets, but if this experience had proved one thing to him it was that there were no secrets between women who play by girl rules.

Now he wondered what else Fiddle had told Sandrine about him and what Sandrine had revealed to Fiddle on their long flight to rescue him. He knew full well the extent to which men describe their sexual conquests. Never before had he considered the excruciating possibility that women did the same thing, only in a far more devastating way. They shared secrets of the heart! While men bellowed on to each other about anatomy and frequency, women whispered to each other about a man's weaknesses.

So Fiddle had told Sandrine about his shoes. Had Sandrine told Fiddle the details of their night together at the baron's château? Except to wiggle her fingers at him, she had never alluded to their having been together at La Fantastique. Perhaps his discomfort was unwarranted. Perhaps she had no memory of their having been together. To her, he was just another john.

He had to go, he couldn't think anymore. He needed to be alone. He needed air.

"Madame Cleo," Peter said, getting to his feet a bit unsteadily. "I thank you for your candor, but I truly must be going."

"I understand," she said. "But please think about reconsidering. I mean about doing the novel. It's the only way I can repay your patience with me."

"The operative word is 'think,' Madame," he said, taking his raincoat from Glover. "I'll think about it."

He thanked SueBee for inviting him and said good-bye to the others. Glover showed him to the door and pointed him toward the elevator.

Just as the elevator doors opened Peter heard the click of high heels on the polished hallway floor. He turned to see Sandrine rushing toward him, brushing her hair away from her face.

"I'm leaving, too. May I ride down with you?"

"Ah . . . ah . . . certainly," he said, nonplussed.

"I want to talk to you alone."

Peter's knees went weak. "You do? I mean, sure, sure. Ah, would you like to go for a drink?"

"Thank you, no," she said. "Could we just walk for a bit?"

Neither of them spoke until they reached the street.

The night air smelled green and moist. The sudden shower that had passed as they all sat in SueBee's apartment had cleared away the muggy air, leaving glistening puddles on the sidewalk.

"So?" Sandrine said, finally breaking the silence between them. "Will you be writing a piece on Jack Ayler when you get back to New York?"

Peter spun around and looked at her. "How did you know I was planning an article on Jack Ayler? Did Fiddle tell you?"

"No. That woman Angel and I ran into at tea this afternoon did," she said, chuckling.

"The one with the floating breasts?" he asked, making a mental note to ask someone just how that worked.

"Christine. When I mentioned that we were on our way to meet you she said, 'Watch the guy.' Seems she got caught in an airplane john with Ayler sometime in the spring. She said you were on the same flight."

"Oh, my God . . ." Peter moaned. "I'm still surrounded."

"She said she saw you making notes and figured that you might be doing an article on Jack."

"You women are amazing," Peter said.

Sandrine placed her hand gently on Peter's sleeve. "So why don't you write about us, Peter? It seems to me a big, successful book would change your life."

"I'm not so sure I want it changed," Peter said.

"Of course you do. Why else would you have agreed to write it in the first place?"

Peter stopped walking and jammed his hands into his pockets. "For a lot of reasons—as you should know. But I'll admit the money was a big factor."

"So you could afford nice things?" she asked, pointing to his shoes.

He rolled one foot on its side self-consciously, then rolled it back. "I can always buy shoes."

"At six hundred bucks a pair? I know, Jourdan loves those shoes, and even he balks at the price."

"I could," Peter protested. "I make a living."

"There's a living and there's a windfall. With a windfall we all give ourselves permission to do things we never would do otherwise."

"A windfall," he said. "Is that what Jourdan's settlement is for you?"

Sandrine shook her head. "Nope. As far as I'm concerned that's money earned and freely invested. A windfall would have been my inheritance. If my mother hadn't cheated me out of it, I would have given myself permission to be a dancer, to be somebody."

"You're somebody to me," Peter said.

"Thanks," she said, smiling up at him.

Suddenly, she looked so fragile, so terribly lonely. In the light of the street lamp he saw little crow's-feet at the corners of her eyes that he hadn't noticed before. If only he could bring himself to speak of their night together maybe he could put it behind him.

Sandrine turned and slowly began to walk again. "I'd love it if you'd change your mind and write the novel," she said. "If you do, for old time's sake, why don't you call me Madeleine?"

Peter held his breath. He started to reach out and put his arms around her but something stopped him. Her words reverberated in his head, now cleared by the fresh air and peaceful dark streets.

399

Sandrine Mandraki Garn was pulling out all the stops to get what she wanted, using a direct hit to his emotions.

Two can play that one, he thought. He looked directly into her eyes. "How much did the baron pay you to sleep with me that night, Madeleine?"

Sandrine looked up into the darkness above them and pursed her lips. "Let's see, less Madame's cut, I would say, um, it would cover a dozen pairs of Italian loafers. We all have something that's worth money, Peter. It just depends how willing we are to sell."

"Is that a girl rule?"

"Yup," she said. "I guess it is."

He nodded and turned, slipping his arm around her waist. "Where are you staying?" he asked.

"At my soon-to-be ex-husband's corporate suite at the Berkeley."

"Come on, lady," he said. "I'll walk you to a cab."

They walked in silence toward a cabstand at the corner. He gave the driver the name of her hotel, helped her in, and closed the door.

"You could come with me, you know," she said, smiling through the open window. "For old time's sake?"

He reached through the window and brushed her cheek. "Thank you, Sandrine. But the old times are over."

Finally, he thought, as he watched the taillights of her cab rounding the corner. He felt a sudden light-headedness that came from the clear knowledge of what he was now free to do.

"Fiddle," he said aloud, "give me a couple of days. I'm coming home."

On Christmas Eve 1990, the lights in Fiddle's office glowed on long after everyone else had left to pick up last-minute gifts and hurry home.

Fiddle was waiting, as usual, for an end-of-the-day phone call. As she waited, she sifted through photos of Sheikh Omar Zaki, his newly acquired grand fatness spreading across three seats of a banquette, at the opening of a new downtown club. On either side of him lolled two Rizzo girls wearing a minimum of clothes. Since the fall, Rizzo girls had become the hottest gossip item in town. She scribbled a memo to Vickie to get the names of the women. Heaven only knew where they would turn up in the future.

When her private line rang, she jumped, picking it up after half a ring.

"Fedalia Null here," she said, cradling the receiver against her shoulder as she stuffed contact sheets back into a manila envelope.

"Peter Shea here," Peter said in the same tone of voice.

"Jingle, jingle on all your bells, Peter."

"And merry, merry on all of yours. Want some dinner?"

"Something gross and fattening," she said.

"I have a present for you," Peter teased.

"What? What? What?"

"The finished draft."

"Oh, my God," she breathed. "I can't believe it."

"Under the deadline with a week to spare. I can't wait for you to read it."

"Bring it with you to the Tea Room. My table. Half hour," Fiddle said excitedly.

"You can't possibly read it there," Peter said, laughing.

"I don't want to read it. I want to fondle it. It's our baby."

"I love you, Mrs. Shea."

"And I love you, Mr. Shea," Fiddle said softly.

She hung up and began to stack the papers on her desk, remembering other Christmases. She hadn't realized then how lonely she had been. She'd had her work. It seemed enough.

When Peter had returned from Paris, Fiddle had maintained telephone silence. She had been beyond hurt. She felt Peter owed her something for setting him up with Madame Solange. Clearly, he had rendezvoused with Sandrine in London. How else could he explain his sudden departure from Paris and the three extra days he spent at the Ritz?

She knew. Peter's American Express charges were billable to the magazine. She had phoned the hotel for a fax of the tab that proved that Peter had stayed on there for the rest of the week. But the most telling item had been the room-service bill. It came to nearly seven hundred dollars! No doubt for gallons of champagne for the bathtub and caviar to spread on Sandrine's boobs or whatever kinky things former Cleo hookers dreamed up.

She hadn't taken his calls because she didn't want to hear what he had to say; the truth or a lie, both would hurt equally.

She posted Vickie at the barricades so she wouldn't have to take his calls at the office, and she let her answering machine protect her at home.

A week after he was back she spitefully told Vickie to cancel his next article.

"We don't have a Peter Shea article scheduled," Vickie had said, looking up from the log on her desk.

"What about the Ayler piece?" Fiddle asked hotly.

"You never officially assigned him the Ayler piece, Fiddle. It's not like you to forget. What's the problem?"

Fiddle couldn't hold out any longer. She covered her face with her hands and began to sob, great gulping inhalations over which she had no control. "I miss him," she managed to say, while Vickie stood in silent bewilderment in front of her desk.

"Fiddle," Vickie scolded. "If you miss him so much why don't you take his damn calls? The poor man's been trying to get through night and day since he got back."

Fiddle reached for a handful of tissues and loudly blew her nose. "I can't," she said. "I don't want to be lied to."

"What's he got to lie to you about?"

"About shacking up at the Ritz with Sandrine Garn."

"Huh?" Vickie said, looking confused.

"Look," Fiddle said, opening her desk drawer and handing Vickie the fax of the Ritz bill. "Cute, huh?"

Vickie ran her eyes down the column of charges and emitted a low whistle. "Jeez, look at that room service. He must have had the Queen's guard in for tea."

"Sure," Fiddle snarled. "He had Sandrine Garn in for a marathon lick-face. Apparently that makes you hungry."

"I don't think so," Vickie said in a slow, dubious voice.

Fiddle shoved the bill back into the drawer. "Oh? You're so smart?"

"That whole bill adds up, to the penny, to the check a messenger just dropped off."

"A check? From where? For what?" Fiddle said, checking her streaked mascara using the glass of her desk clock.

"From Peter Shea, reimbursing the magazine."

"Ha," Fiddle scoffed. "That tells me nothing except that he knows he can't charge her off to his expense account."

"Even if that's true, Fiddle," Vickie said, collecting the crumpled tissues in front of Fiddle and tossing them in the wastebasket, "he really doesn't have to answer to you for his personal life."

Fiddle sat silently for a long moment, then took a deep breath that made her shudder. "You're right, Vicksburg. You are right, right, right. But, the least he could do is . . ."

"Is call," Vickie said, finishing Fiddle's sentence. "He's calling, baby-cakes. He's calling! Talk to the man!"

"Don't shout."

"I'll stop shouting if you'll please climb down off the cross. Give the guy a break, he doesn't owe you anything."

"He sure as hell does," Fiddle said, slamming the flat of her hand onto the desktop. "He owes me a complete explanation as to why he ditched the Cleo book. I got it for him. I tried to save it."

Vickie turned and started back toward her desk. "I know you've been too distraught to notice that Wendy Klarwine hasn't called to peddle anything for some time."

"What's that supposed to mean?" Fiddle said, sullenly.

"You didn't read Liz Smith this morning. Let me get it."

Seconds later Vickie returned with the morning paper opened to the gossip page and handed it to Fiddle. An item at the bottom of the page was circled in red.

"'Superagent,'" Fiddle began to read out loud. "Jesus, nobody can type 'agent' anymore. It's always 'superagent.'"

"Read," Vickie commanded.

Fiddle sighed. "'Superagent Wendy Klarwine, seated at her personal table at Aurora this week, couldn't stop talking about the *secret* deal her *secret* client inked at a *secret* meeting at a *secret* location in London several days ago. Klarwine said that after three days of nonstop negotiations she and her client hammered home a record-breaking advance from an English publisher for a first novel. We know who everybody is but promised to keep it a shhhh! *secret*.'"

"You know what I think the real secret is?" Vickie asked.

"What?" Fiddle said, handing back the paper.

"How someone like Wendy Klarwine, who weighs ninety pounds wearing ten pounds of costume jewelry, could eat her share of that room-service bill."

Fiddle's eyes widened. "Get me Liz Smith," she ordered.

Ten minutes later Fiddle sat back in her desk chair and smiled. She knew the next morning the lead item in Liz Smith's column would splash the fact that Sandrine Garn was secretly divorcing Jourdan Garn and a huge settlement was in the works. The information had been more than an even trade.

She buzzed Vickie, triumphant and enormously relieved. "The next time Peter Shea calls, Vickie, my sweet," she had purred into the intercom, "put him right through."

The deal Wendy and Peter had put together was indeed precedent setting for the amount of the advance involved, but most highly unusual for the freedom granted the author.

The day Wendy arrived at the Ritz to meet with Peter, at his request, a package arrived containing signed affidavits from an attorney representing Cleo Charnov, Sandrine Mandraki Garn, Angel Weinstein Rizzo, and Lady Susanna Slyde Mosby granting Peter Shea and his publisher total rights to their life stories to be used in any way the author so deemed.

Within hours of learning the details of Peter's "new" book, Fiddle looked up from her desk to see a different Peter Shea than the one she had left in Paris. He seemed taller. The gray pallor she had noticed during their abbreviated dinner on the Left Bank was replaced by a clear, high color. The tension in his face was gone and his movements seemed quicker, more confident. He was wearing a beautifully cut linen jacket and a new pair of expensive-looking Italian loafers.

"Wow," Fiddle said. "You look great."

"You could have seen that several days ago, pal," Peter said, leaning across her desk and kissing her lightly on the cheek.

Fiddle looked down, sheepishly. "I know," she whispered. "I was feeling sorry for myself."

"It's not a good look," Peter said, taking a seat on one of the chaise longues.

"You left me stranded, Peter," she said meekly.

"I know. But that's not what upset you. You thought I was in London with Sandrine. I'm flattered, but I wasn't."

Fiddle frowned across at him. "What makes you think I . . ."

Peter held up one hand, traffic-cop fashion. "Don't deny it. I'm an expert on women now. I know how they think, I know how they operate. If being stranded was what had you ticked off you would have picked up the phone and bawled me out."

"Oh," Fiddle said, ready to believe him.

"Besides, Vickie told me."

"Vickie told you! Why, that little . . ." Fiddle reached for the intercom, furious at her secretary.

Peter reached over and stayed her hand. "Don't be angry with Vickie, Fiddle. You have to realize we've spent a lot of time on the phone together. In every conversation she was on your side. All she did was casually mention my expense account, and, well, one thing led to another."

"I'm embarrassed."

"Don't be. Taking Sandrine to the Ritz would have been a thoroughly unprofessional thing to do. As my boss, you would have had every right to be very angry."

"Thank you," she said, relieved that he was taking the emotional motive out of her petulance. Or maybe he was just letting her off the hook.

"Will you let me take you to dinner tomorrow night?"

Fiddle smiled, delighted the subject had changed. "Sure. Where?"

"The Inn at Montauk."

"Montauk? That's a four-hour drive, Peter."

"No problem. I made a reservation for the weekend. I figure I'll need that long to fill you in on my extraordinary meeting with Madame's satin army in London."

"Satin army," she said, smiling. "I like that."

"So did I when I heard it. It's not original. So, you'll come?"

Fiddle felt a tingle of activated nerve endings run down her backbone and recognized the feeling as sexual. Good God, she thought, he's asking me to go away with him. To the Inn at Montauk. Cozy room, wine and candles, long walks on the beach. Jesus, what will I wear?

"Are you still with me?" Peter asked with a chuckle.

Fiddle started, "Oh, yeah, sure . . . Montauk, weekend. Why, sure, Peter, that sounds great, let's . . . ah, let's do that."

Peter stood and buttoned his jacket. "Wonderful," he said, grinning. "I'll pick you up at your apartment at five. I've rented a little convertible. We can pretend we're teenagers. See you in a couple of hours."

"Right," Fiddle said, giving him a thumbs-up sign.

"Fiddle?" Peter said from the doorway. "I've missed you . . . a lot."

"Oh?" she said, raising her eyebrows.

"I've had no one to talk to," he said, then walked away.

That night, in a room that opened out onto a damp, blustery beach, soaked with one of the thunderstorms that plague the outer tip of Long Island in August, they ate a room-service meal, drank two entire bottles of red wine, and talked. They talked and talked. And when they weren't talking they laughed. And when the talking and laughing stopped he held her so tightly she began to cry. Her tears were not the angry, choking spasms she had cried in her office in front of Vickie, but tears of letting go. The tears women cry when they have run out of less adequate ways to express the feeling that comes from having found the antidote to the pain of loneliness and from having and holding something they have wanted for too long.

The following day they read and walked on the soggy beach holding hands and talking some more. He told her Madame's story, and Sandrine's. He told her SueBee's and Angel's and Jourdan Garn's and Barry Rizzo's. He told her about Martin and Wellington Close and how Big Boy got his wing-wang sliced off and how Jack Ayler broke SueBee's heart and how Angel got fired for trying to hustle Zaki. He told her all the names he was going to substitute for the real ones.

Peter took her to dinner at the Inn, just as he had promised, and when they fell into bed exhausted, kicking the Sunday *Times* onto the carpet, they indeed, just like in the romance novels, fit together like two spoons.

"You realize I'm going to be able to use a phrase like that in the book?" Peter said afterward, resting his head on her chest.

"Like what?" she asked, groggy with wine and sea air and love.

"'. . . and they fit together like two spoons.'"

"Don't you dare."

He lifted his head and stared into her eyes. "I'll have to," he protested. "I can't write a whole novel about women and love and sex without some help from cornball phrases."

"Who says you'll be writing about women and love and sex? You're going to be writing about women and sex and greed and ambition, mendacity, avarice, and crime. No throbbing members, no feeling the strength of his manhood, no having her wetness rise to find the thrusting center of his being."

Peter rolled over on top of her. "'. . . and when he entered her, she finally stopped speaking',￼" he said, entering her.

Fiddle stopped speaking.

Peter asked her to marry him the day he put the advance check in a special account at Manufacturer's Hanover. They were having lunch at the Tea Room, but not at their usual table.

To Fiddle's surprise, Oona had directed them to the second-floor dining room where all the tourists got stuck. Fiddle said nothing, knowing that Peter must have made the change for some reason, probably to avoid people stopping by their usual table, which was right by the front door. With the publicity for his novel now working its way into print he had begun to hate explaining himself and making polite noises.

He ordered them each a glass of white wine and lifted the menu he knew by heart. "Let's do it," he said from behind the menu.

"What? Blinis?"

"I don't mean food."

"You don't? What do you mean? Do what?"

"I can't say it," he said, lowering the menu and scrunching up his face. "It sounds so corny."

"For heaven's sake, Peter. What is the matter with you?" Fiddle said. As she looked up at the waiter bringing the wine she thought she saw Vickie at the top of the stairs. She swiveled around and stared. It was Vickie! "Peter," she said, "There's Vickie. What's she doing here?"

"Oh God," Peter moaned. "She's too early."

"Peter. I'm going to scream in a second. What is going on?"

Peter reached across the table and took both of her hands in his. "Fiddle, let's get married."

Fiddle gulped and looked around to see if anyone was listening. She turned back to Peter. "Why would we want to do that?" she deadpanned, her heart thundering in her ears.

"Because we're a team. Because we love each other. Because we shouldn't live apart. I don't want a roommate, I want a partner. And, okay . . . I'll say it. Because we fit together like two spoons."

Fiddle bit her lip to keep from trembling. All she could manage was a slow nod of her head.

"Is that a 'yes'?" Peter asked.

"Yes," she said, nodding more vigorously. "That means 'yes' when you make your head go like that."

Peter turned and signaled to Vickie, who was still standing at the top of the stairs.

In a flash, she was standing beside their table. "What did she say?" Vickie asked breathlessly.

"She said she'd do it," Peter said, beaming.

"You gonna eat first?"

"I thought we would."

"Okay, I'll wait."

Fiddle looked from Peter to Vickie and back to Peter again.

Peter was still holding her hands. "I called Judge Lowry. She's waiting in her chambers. I thought you'd like Vickie to stand up for you."

"Sure," Fiddle said, rolling her eyes. "Why not? Sounds good to me. Who's going to stand up for you?"

"My doorman."

"I don't believe any of this."

"I was in a hurry."

"You still are," Fiddle said, laughing. "Are you afraid I'll change my mind?"

"Kinda."

"No way," she said, tugging on his hands. "And no lunch. Let's go."

The service took only five minutes. They all rode back to the office, opened the champagne Vickie had hidden in the office fridge, and invited whatever staff there was around to come in for a toast.

That weekend they went back to the Inn at Montauk. They talked and talked and laughed and made love and read the paper and some draft pages of Peter's novel and planned the cover of the upcoming issue of *Fifteen Minutes* and made love again, fitting together like two spoons.

Now, as she gathered up the Christmas gifts to give Peter at dinner, Fiddle glanced out the office window. It had begun to snow, making it truly Christmas. The first Christmas ever that she had the only things in life that really matter: love and work.